- You can return this item to any Bournemouth library but not all libraries are open every day.
- Items must be returned on or before the due date. Please note that you will be charged for items returned late.
- Items may be renewed unless requested by another customer.
- Renewals can be made in any library, by telephone, email or online via the website. Your membership card number and PIN will be required.
- Please look after this item – you may be charged for any damage.

Bournemouth
BOROUGH COUNCIL

Libraries

bournemouth.gov.uk/libraries

In November 2009 Mills & Boon bring
you two classic collections, each
featuring three favourite romances
by our bestselling authors

PASSION & PLEASURE

Savage Awakening by Anne Mather
For Pleasure…Or Marriage?
by Julia James
Taken for His Pleasure by Carol Marinelli

TEMPORARY MISTRESS

Mistress for a Weekend by Susan Napier
Mistress on Demand by Maggie Cox
Public Wife, Private Mistress
by Sarah Morgan

Temporary Mistress

SUSAN NAPIER
MAGGIE COX
SARAH MORGAN

MILLS & BOON

First published in Great Britain 2009
Harlequin Mills & Boon Limited,
Eton House, 18-24 Paradise Road, Richmond, Surrey TW9 1SR

TEMPORARY MISTRESS © by Harlequin Enterprises II B.V./S.à.r.l 2009

Mistress for a Weekend, Mistress on Demand and *Public Wife, Private
Mistress* were first published in Great Britain by Harlequin Mills & Boon
Limited in separate, single volumes.

Mistress for a Weekend © Susan Napier 2006
Mistress on Demand © Maggie Cox 2005
Public Wife, Private Mistress © Sarah Morgan 2005

ISBN: 978 0 263 87143 2

05-1109

Printed and bound in Spain
by Litografia Rosés S.A., Barcelona

MISTRESS FOR
A WEEKEND

BY
SUSAN NAPIER

Susan Napier is a former journalist and scriptwriter who turned to writing romantic fiction after her two sons were born. She lives in Auckland, New Zealand with her journalist husband, who generously provides the on-going inspiration for her fictional heroes, and two temperamental cats whose curious paws contribute the occasional typographical error when they join her at the keyboard. Born on St Valentine's Day, Susan feels that it was her destiny to write romances and, having written over thirty books for Harlequin Mills & Boon, still loves the challenges of working within the genre. She likes writing traditional tales with a twist, and believes that to keep romance alive you have to keep the faith – to believe in love. Not just in the romantic kind of love that pervades her books, but in the everyday, caring-and-sharing kind of love that builds enduring relationships. Susan's extended family is scattered over the globe, which is fortunate as she enjoys travelling and seeking out new experiences to fuel her flights of imagination.

Susan loves to hear from readers and can be contacted at PO Box 18-240, Glen Innes, Auckland 1130, New Zealand.

In memory of my Dad,
the little guy with the big smile.

CHAPTER ONE

BLAKE MACLEOD had been watching the young woman for some time before she became aware of his presence.

At first it had merely been out of idle curiosity. He'd happened to be glancing her way when she had tottered out of the lift and his attention had been caught by the paleness of her freckled face in the wash of the overhead light, and the abruptness with which she had halted, regarding the revolving floor of the restaurant with ill-concealed dismay. Her teeth had dug deep into her lower lip as her gaze resolutely avoided the circular sweep of floor-to-ceiling windows revealing the lights of the rain-washed city twinkling far below, fastening instead on the metal joints in the carpet where the fixed central column of Auckland's Sky Tower became the slowly rotating platform which formed the main body of the restaurant.

In any other circumstances Blake probably wouldn't have given the unprepossessing lone female a second glance, but he had been feeling dangerously bored and ripe for any form of distraction. He had only attended the party under pressure, as a courtesy to his host, a valued business client, and he was already calculating the earliest he could leave without giving offence. Once he would have relished the opportunity to rub shoulders with a room full of movers-and-shakers, but at thirty-three he was well past the stage where he felt the need to impress.

From his vantage point by one of the seamless windows, he had studied the latecomer over the heads of the party-goers as she hovered uncertainly in the elevated reception area, a folded umbrella clutched to her chest in a white-knuckled grip, her figure shrouded by the damp folds of a vo-luminous brown raincoat. She stood out from the colourful crowd like an ordinary house sparrow amidst a pride of peacocks. Her hair was a nimbus of brown curls frothing out around the blanched oval of her face and Blake guessed that, her style of coiffure notwithstanding, she had found the ride in the glass-fronted lift a hair-raising experience.

Tuning out the sycophantic conversation of his compan-ions, Blake speculated on the reason for the sparrow's shell-shocked state. He could eliminate the theory that she was a gatecrasher afraid of being caught—she never would have got past the tight security at the base of the Sky Tower if she hadn't had an invitation. The most obvious answer to her angst was that she had a fear of heights, but if that was the case why on earth would she have accepted an invitation to a party atop the tallest tower in the southern hemisphere?

One of the restaurant hostesses on cloakroom duty ap-proached her, and the twin brackets around Blake's hard mouth deepened in amusement as he watched the sparrow erupt into a flurry of awkward movements, getting both the umbrella and a large black-beaded evening bag entangled in the sleeves of the raincoat in her haste to shed her outer plumage. By the time she had freed herself from the bunched fabric, and picked up the umbrella and bag she had dropped in the process, her pale face was flushed with embarrass-ment. She thrust the trailing coat and umbrella apologeti-cally at the bemused hostess and walked jerkily towards the short flight of steps that led down to the fan of tables, tucking the beaded clutch bag into the crook of her elbow as she surveyed the glittering throng with a glazed expression that contained a curious combination of desperation and determi-nation.

Blake nearly choked on his drink when he saw the dress she had been hiding under the brown shroud. It was a plain black strapless number, blatantly sexy and sophisticated—and it didn't suit her at all. Rather than enhancing her femininity, it merely emphasised her flaws—making her bare freckled shoulders appear too wide and the rest of her body look too boyishly straight. Instead of smouldering sensuality, she projected all angles and elbows, her face looking oddly naked in spite of—or perhaps because of—her heavily made-up eyes. She was quite tall and therefore correspondingly leggy, but the hem of her dress finished too far below her knees to showcase what Blake suspected were her best assets. As she teetered down the staircase in shiny spiked heels, still nibbling at her pale pink lower lip, he thought she looked more like a fresh-scrubbed, freckle-faced kid playing dress-up, and from the way she kept discreetly hitching at the outer edges of the strapless bodice she felt no more comfortable than she looked.

Not his type at all, he thought wryly, as he watched her reach the bottom of the stairs and grab a wineglass from the nearest tray, sending the adjacent glasses skittering with her straying forearm and almost upending the entire silver platter down the waiter's impeccable white jacket. Her flustered apologies were accepted with a pained smile and her exposed skin was again bright pink as she attempted to melt inconspicuously into the crowd.

Blake got the impression that she spent a great deal of her time apologising.

Most *definitely* not his type.

Blake's taste in female companions ran to genuine sophisticates: beautiful, self-confident, worldly women who craved attention rather than interest, who never involved themselves in embarrassing situations—physical or emotional. Women who might tax his ingenuity in bed but who rarely challenged his independence, and who could be relied upon to accept an amicable parting of the ways when the affair had run its course.

Inexplicably, the downy-haired sparrow continued to bob

in and out of his wandering attention over the next half-hour.
At just over six foot, Blake had a reasonably unobstructed
view over the heads of most of the crowd and, since her high
heels made her almost his equal in height, it was easy to find
her at a glance. He noticed that, unlike everyone else, she
stayed well away from the windows, barely moving from the
spot where she had come in, quaffing the free-flowing wine
as she studied the passing parade of guests.

Even from a distance he could see the tension in the set of
her shoulders, the aura of suppressed energy that gave her
brooding watchfulness a sense of purpose. She seemed poised
to take wing at any moment—but for flight or fight? What was
it she was searching for amongst the crowd? Someone to rescue
her from her fear? Blake mocked his own whimsy as he turned
back to field the conversational ball that was tossed his way.
The answer was probably far more prosaic, and she was simply
looking for someone she'd arranged to meet at the party.

The next time he glanced her way she was scooting forward
to intercept another roving waiter, swapping her empty glass
for a brimming champagne flute. Blake unconsciously held his
breath until she safely negotiated the exchange, then watched
in fatalistic fascination as she stepped back on to a portly
matron's foot and spun around in dismay, elbowing her
victim's unfortunate escort sharply in the solar plexus and
dripping wine on his shoes. Recognising the head of a powerful
quasi-Government think-tank on foreign trade, Blake
winced…although, come to think of it, there'd been a time or
two during the industry consulting process when he'd been
tempted to take a slug at the pompous little windbag himself.

Perhaps the sparrow was the embodiment of his cosmic
revenge! he thought, a slight smile curving his hard mouth as
he looked down into the melting remains of his Scotch on the
rocks. Unfortunately, the ambitious young businesswoman at
his side who had been uttering flirtatious remarks took it as
a sign of encouragement, and he was forced to adopt a brutal
uninterest to convince her that she was mistaken.

When he looked up again it was to discover with a mild jolt of disappointment that his idle entertainment for the evening had disappeared. He turned his head and suddenly found himself staring straight into the brooding eyes of his former quarry. She had edged out of her comfort zone and was with a cluster of people helping themselves to canapés from one of the second-tier tables, close enough for him to see that he might have been wrong about her legs being her best asset. Her wide-set kohl-lined eyes were the sensuous colour of old gold, glowing with burnished brightness under their heavy-smudged green lids, dominating her otherwise unremarkable face. And they were currently trained on Blake with an arrested intensity. Big, luminous, disturbingly warm eyes, fringed with thickly coated black lashes; siren's eyes, that seemed to look straight through his polished shield of cynical sophistication into the hidden secrets of his soul.

To his astonishment Blake felt his body suffuse with heat, as if all his secrets had suddenly become X-rated. He gritted his teeth in disbelief as he felt the blood rising to his face, fighting to keep his expression impassive under that steadfast golden stare.

A clumsy freckle-faced kid was making him blush, for God's sake!

He shifted abruptly, using a comment addressed to him as an excuse to turn his back, but his mind was distracted by the disquieting realisation that he had, in effect, blinked first. He, who had never backed away from a challenge, who had outfaced kings of industry and princes of wealth, had flinched from a confrontation with a mere girl. Or was it himself he was unwilling to confront...and the underlying reason for his growing boredom with occasions like these?

Without turning around, he knew that he was still under surveillance, still being assessed by those golden eyes...but assessed for what?

The short hairs on the back of his neck began to prickle. A sure sign of impending trouble. Fortunately, he and trouble were intimate acquaintances. Handling strife was his chief talent and major occupation.

And the most important thing he had learned over the years was that it was far safer to meet the arrival of trouble head-on than to ignore it and hope it would leave you alone.

CHAPTER TWO

ELEANOR LANG'S fingers tightened around her wineglass as she made another visual sweep of the restaurant to check that she hadn't overlooked anyone.

Her eyes skipped impatiently over a face which could have belonged to a male model. She wasn't looking for the most handsome man in the room, nor even the most charming. She had discounted men who were obviously with their wives or significant others, which cut the field down considerably, and ignored the fun-loving party animals. She wasn't after character or personality, kindness or courtesy.

No, what Nora was looking for was much rarer. What she wanted was the most *dangerous* man in the room.

Her eyes returned to the broad shoulders which she had been studying a few moments before...the long, straight back encased in the faultless perfection of a tailormade suit. The man with the fierce grey eyes.

Blake MacLeod.

She hadn't known who he was when she had first caught a glimpse of his trademark scowl, but what she saw had made her spine tingle. She had immediately shifted closer to get a better look, squeezing her way over to the table of food which was directly across from the loose cluster of people around him.

Whoever he was, he certainly didn't look *safe*. In fact, he looked as surly as the devil and bored to within an inch of his life. One hand was thrust into his trouser pocket, ruffling the unbuttoned jacket of his light grey suit, the other lifting a squat glass of whisky to his mouth as he stared stonily over the rim at the attractive woman beside him, blatant disdain for whatever she was saying plastered across his harsh features. His collar-length hair was as black as sin, sleeked back to reveal a prominent forehead and thick black brows that gave the impression of a permanent frown riding astride his hawkish nose. He couldn't be classed as handsome but he was fully mature and formidably masculine. His face was long and narrow, his cheeks hollowed beneath jutting cheek-bones, and there was already a dark shadow blooming along the unforgiving line of his smooth-shaven jaw.

All in all, he looked lean, mean and hungry. The kind of man who would sell his own grandmother if it would turn him a profit, and give no quarter in a fight.

Not that Nora had any intention of fighting him! On the contrary...

Then their eyes had unexpectedly met, and she'd felt the same scary sensation that she had experienced coming up in the lift. Adrenaline pumped through her veins and sucked the blood from her head to fuel her racing heart.

Her first impulse was to pretend that she just happened to be casually glancing around, but she was forced to brazen it out when she found that she couldn't look away, fascinated by the molten flare of acknowledgement in his silvery eyes before they rapidly chilled to the colour of tempered grey steel. Curiosity unfurled inside her, spiked with a delicious thrill of fear at her own daring.

They must have stared at each other for only a second or two, but to Nora it seemed like aeons. When he finally turned away she went limp, and realised that during those few moments of suspended animation every major muscle in her body had contracted to a state of red alert.

She stiffened her wobbly knees, congratulating herself on her boldness. Danger Man knew she existed. For a split second she had forced him to notice her. That was a start, wasn't it?

Face it, Nora, you're not the sort of woman that men notice.

Her stomach clenched as she pushed away the intruding voice, reminding her that she hadn't had anything to eat since breakfast, her lunch break having been spent shopping for the elegant but annoyingly uncomfortable dress she was wearing. She tugged uneasily at the top of the low-cut bodice to make sure that it hadn't drifted down again. She didn't think she had enough cleavage to do justice to the style but Ryan had insisted that she wear something black and strapless, which he thought was the ultimate in feminine sophistication, to to-night's party.

He had given her some money and told her to buy a new dress for herself after work, but she had been so eager to make him proud of her that she had squeezed the task into a short-ened lunch break and worked like a maniac all afternoon so that she could leave early and rush home to try and pamper herself into the semblance of a glamour girl.

She had been such a gullible idiot, she thought, her throat tightening at the memory of the ghastly scene that had ensued at her flat. Her friends often chided her for being too trusting, and now she had wrenching proof that they had been right. Because it would never have occurred to *her* to be unfaith-ful, she had actually been pleased that Ryan seemed to be getting on so well with her young and trendy new flatmate.

A sudden stinging in her eyes threatened to ruin the make-up Nora had carefully applied to conceal her tear-swollen tissues. To think that she had naively imagined Ryan's unac-customed generosity over the dress had meant that he wanted to make the evening *really* special for her—maybe he was planning to suggest that they move in together! Instead, it had been a sop to his guilty conscience. She was only twenty-five and already she knew what it was like to be dumped for a younger model!

Anger boiled up like hot lava inside her, scalding away any

remaining urge to cry. She snatched up a succulent pink prawn from the table in front of her and bit it viciously in half. She had wasted five years of her life trying to mould herself into the kind of woman she thought Ryan could love. From now she was going to be her *own* woman. Starting tonight, she was going to prove that everything that Ryan had said about her was a self-serving lie!

A man likes a woman to take the initiative sometimes. But you're such a mouse when it comes to new experiences. At least Kelly knows how to have fun. You never want to experiment or take any risks....

Nora smouldered over the humiliating words that he had thrown at her as she had blundered her way out of the flat, numbed by the icy shock of his betrayal. He had been flattered by her feelings for him, but he had never meant them to tie him down. He was sure that if she looked around she would eventually find someone more compatible....

No one as fascinating as Ryan Trent, of course. No doubt he expected her to hook up with a man who was as timid and boring as herself!

Her eyes had remained trained on the man who looked like the absolute antithesis of all those things.

'Do you know who that is over there?' she asked a stockbroker acquaintance who was fishing in the same platter of prawns. 'The tall, dark man with the killer frown.'

The woman followed her sight-line and practically shivered when she said his name.

Blake MacLeod.

Ryan might accuse her of being more interested in computers than people, but even Nora had heard of Blake MacLeod...vaguely.

She remembered someone in the office reading aloud from a newspaper column about New Zealand's biggest domestically owned transport and communications conglomerate. Much of its current strong growth had been credited to the 'defiantly unpolished' MacLeod, who was said to be ferociously hard-working and ice-cool under pressure. He had been described as a maverick for his unorthodox views on business, and a brilliant opportunist for his ruthless, take-no-prisoners approach to acquiring ailing competitors. Much had been made of his working-class background, lack of formal qualifications and his cynical disrespect for the financial establishment.

He was also, she dredged up from the blurred fringes of her recall, an unrepentant bachelor.

'Isn't he the head of PresCorp?'

'Not yet. He's Prescott Williams's chief troubleshooter, but rumour has it that when the old man retires or kicks the bucket, the whole kit-and-caboodle will land fair and square in his lap,' her informant supplied obligingly. 'All the PresCorp shares are under Williams's thumb, but he never married and there aren't any children to inherit, you see.' She leaned closer and lowered her voice. 'MacLeod hadn't even graduated from high school when Williams took him into the firm and made him his pet protégé. Some say it's because he's really the old man's illegitimate son....'

Nora wasn't interested in his murky antecedents, only his current personal status. 'Does he have a girlfriend?'

The broker gave Nora's pale, absorbed face a sidelong look. 'You want to steer clear of the likes of him,' she warned kindly. 'He's got a bad reputation with women—great in the sack, but an ice-man out of it. Acquires mistresses rather than lovers, and none of them last longer than a couple of months. "Use 'em and lose 'em" seems to be his motto.'

In other words, he was every bit as dangerous as he looked. Perfect!

'He's not your type, anyway, Nora,' the other woman added as a parting shot. 'His women are all interchangeably gorgeous—and definitely not the kind to take home to Mother, if you know what I mean....'

She meant that Nora wasn't *his* type. No one had ever

come even close to calling her gorgeous. The words that had
haunted her all evening rang again in her ears:

*I'm sorry, Nora, but you must know this was inevitable. I
mean—you've been a good mate but, let's face it, the sex
between us has always been pretty pedestrian, hasn't it? You
take ages to get heated up and then you're only lukewarm.
I'm not blaming you—some women are like that—but I need
someone who physically excites me....*

As an apology it had been a slap in the face. So he wasn't
blaming her for being stodgy and undersexed—how kind of
him! She'd been a virgin when she met Ryan, so how had she
been supposed to know that 'the sex' was *pedestrian*? She had
never looked upon it as having sex, anyway, she had quaintly
imagined that they were making love, sharing more than just
their bodies. And he had never given any indication that he
was dissatisfied with her lovemaking...or her cooking, or her
frequent ironing of his shirts and tidying of his apartment,
or the amount of unpaid time she had spent after-hours at
Maitlands Consulting, where they both worked, helping him
meet his project deadlines.

Blake MacLeod might be a 'user' but at least he was
open about it.

And he was 'great in the sack'.

Nora was engulfed by a wave of heat. What she was contemplating was sheer madness, but she had earned the right
to go a little crazy. She was tired of people pointing out her
limitations. She had nothing to lose and everything to gain.

After all, what was the very worst that could happen if she
went over and tried out her womanly wiles on Blake
MacLeod? An embarrassing snub? Nora was living proof
that no one ever died of humiliation.

On the other hand, in the wilder realms of possibility, if
she actually succeeded...

Her imagination failed her, and Nora took a hasty gulp of
her drink to bolster her courage. She could do this. She might
not be beautiful but she was smart—smarter, in fact, than

Ryan, although she had learnt to downplay the fact when they were in company.

If only he wasn't standing next to a window....

'Those who are about to die, salute you,' she muttered, raising her glass in a fatalistic toast before forging her way through the crowd.

A passing waitress mistook her gesture for a request for another drink and Nora paused to accept her offer of a refill. She had a feeling that she might need it!

Progress in her spindly five-inch heels was slow, but given their inherent instability she didn't dare hurry for fear of twisting an ankle.

The nearer she got to that lean imposing back, the greater the number of butterflies trapped inside her chest. Her palms went clammy and her breath shortened. With every step she became more aware of the vast expanse of glass beyond him, and the fact that at any moment the dizzying vista could open up beneath her feet. Only by focusing fiercely on the solid breadth of his shoulders could she block out the incipient panic, and by the time she fetched up behind him she was wound as tight as a drum.

At the last moment, with her hand reaching out to tap him on the shoulder and what she hoped was a mysterious Mona Lisa smile pinned to her lips, her nerve failed.

She jerked her hand back and wheeled away, but the sharp movement dislodged the clutch-bag wedged under her armpit and it thudded to the floor, the faulty catch springing open to disgorge the contents.

'Oh, no!' Nora sank down on her knees amongst the forest of legs, trying to hold her wineglass on an even keel as she started to rake her possessions back into the yawning maw of the capacious bag with her other hand. To her mortification a floral-wrapped tampon had rolled up against the swivelling toe of a highly polished masculine shoe. She swept it up in her palm and thrust it into the dark recesses of her bag as the shoe flexed and the owner came down in a crouch beside her.

'Allow me…' Blake MacLeod's amused grey eyes met her horrified ones as he picked up a pair of low-heeled black velvet shoes wedged one inside the other, and handed them to her.

'You carry an extra pair of shoes in your handbag?' he said, under cover of the party noise which buzzed uninterrupted over their heads.

His voice was a deep, soft drawl that sent sensual ripples across Nora's exposed nerves.

'They're for driving,' she said quickly, avoiding his gaze as she stuffed them awkwardly into the bag. Thank goodness he had politely ignored the tampon!

'Really?'

Sensitised by her agonised embarrassment, she was quick to detect the lilt of scepticism. God, she was such a terrible liar. Why did she even bother?

'No, not really,' she confessed helplessly, sinking down on her folded legs. 'I—that is, I bought the ones I'm wearing on the way to the party.' She couldn't believe that he had actually stooped to help her. Was this fate's reward, or punishment, for her moment of cowardice? 'At the hotel boutique downstairs. I was passing and saw them in the window and, well…'

He tipped his head to look down at her feet, tucked beneath her bottom, and blinked, his hard mouth kicking up, revealing the unexpected fullness of his lower lip. 'Let me guess— you just *had* to have them….'

He made her sound wickedly self-indulgent, used to the instant gratification of her impulsive desires.

'Something like that,' she agreed vaguely.

Because Ryan was slightly shorter than her five-foot-nine, and unduly sensitive about it, Nora hadn't possessed any high heels…until tonight. She had been wandering through the complex, following the signs from the underground car park to the Sky Tower lifts, when she had spotted the frivolous, tall strappy pair she was now wearing in the glitzy boutique window…shoes that would have made Ryan look like a tiny insignificant speck beside her. She had immediately marched in and bought them. Only a vestige of her normal thrift had restrained her from binning her low-heeled pumps.

'I admire a woman who knows exactly what she wants... and goes after it,' he murmured, rescuing more of her scattered possessions from under passing feet.

She was perversely annoyed by his approval, the rage simmering just beneath the surface of her skin unconsciously seeking an outlet.

'Instead of expecting a man to get it for her, you mean?' she challenged, startled to hear that her voice was husky with suppressed temper. Heavens! She actually sounded provocative.

'Something like that.' He smiled, tossing her own phrase back at her, and she was swamped by a hot bloom of physical awareness. His eyes drifted lower, to the ginger-flecked expanse of skin that rose above the flattened curve of her bodice, and the speculative gleam that she glimpsed through his thick lashes made her nervously check the security of her dress with a discreet upward tug under one arm. His white teeth flashed as he innocently returned his gaze to her rosy countenance.

The fully fledged smile did fascinating things to his sullen face, warming the cold angles and austere planes and lending his mouth a sensuous softness. Close up, she could see the smooth grain of his olive skin, darkened further by the kiss of summer sun and the blue-black shadow on his chin and upper lip. She discovered that his deep-set eyes had tiny chips of green in them, hidden gems embedded in the grey sheet-rock, flecks of emerald fire that sparked in her a sudden lust for precious stones. When she inhaled she found that she was breathing in the spicy scent of his body, not an artificially astringent cologne, expensive and anonymous, but his own unique natural fragrance—musky and unmistakably male....

'You certainly seem to have the knack of acquiring things,' he was saying, helping her to gather up her notebook and calculator, wallet, eye-make-up compact, tissues, vial of perfume, keys, pen-knife, a card of fuse-wire, mini-torch, nail

file, comb, travel toothbrush, hotel sewing kit and tube of
breath mints amongst sundry other bits and pieces. Pivoting
from his splayed crouch he had the greater reach, occasionally stretching across her, the sleeve of his jacket brushing
goose-pimples along Nora's bare arm.

'I— Really, you've helped enough. I can manage the rest
myself,' she protested, trying to distract his fascinated attention from the embarrassing amount of personal clutter. She
saw him flipping through a small folder of family photos and
snatched it away as he reached the image of herself as a
plump, fuzzy-haired teenager.

'That was taken when I was sixteen,' she couldn't help saying.

'You don't look much older than that now.'

'Is that supposed to be a compliment?'

'Most women enjoy giving the impression they're
younger than their years,' he said, making her feel unutterably gauche.

'It's the freckles,' she sighed. 'They make me look like a
perpetual schoolgirl.'

He picked up her blood donor card. By the time he had
finished 'helping' her, Nora thought, she would be totally
stripped of all mystery. 'Please, don't let me keep you from
your conversation with your friends—'

'This is much more interesting,' he drawled, with the
teasing inflection which made her feel hot and edgy. 'And I
always finish what I start. It's sort of a trademark of mine.
Besides, they're acquaintances, not friends. My friends know
better than to bore me.'

'What happens when you're bored?' she dared to ask.

'I behave like a complete boor,' he said languidly.

'Oh…*Oh*!' A hiccup of startled laughter erupted from Nora
as she belatedly recognised his pun, her eyes crinkling into
merry crescents. 'The insensitive and ill-mannered person, or
the male pig?' she asked with pretended confusion.

'Actually a boar is an *uncastrated* male pig.' He corrected
her second option, and watched her eyelashes flutter and her

freckles fight against a rising tide of pink. 'I feel that's an important distinction, since my answer is...yes to both.'

'Really?' She wasn't about to let a man get the better of her— not tonight. 'Then you must have a lot of very tolerant friends.'

He laughed. 'Or a few very interesting ones.' He held aloft a yellow-handled tool and shot her a compelling lift of his dark eyebrows. 'A *screwdriver*?'

'I like to be prepared for every eventuality,' she told him, plucking it out of his hand, noticing that his fingers were long and supple and his nails beautifully manicured.

'So I see,' he murmured, as he spied the last stray item, almost hidden by a fold of her dress flaring away from her knee. He handed her the small foil package with grave ceremony.

She stared at it lying on the palm of her hand, stricken by a chilling thought. Thank God she was unable to take oral contraceptives and therefore had had to insist that Ryan always used a condom. What if Kelly wasn't the first woman he had slept with during the year that their relationship had been sexually intimate? She would have been forced to wonder whether her health was at risk.

With a jolt she realised that it had been ages since she and Ryan had actually made love.... He had been away on business, then he had gone on a skiing trip to Colorado with his rugby mates, and after he got back he had been busy with work, or she had, and their social life had got busier. There had always seemed to be a ready enough reason *not* to make love, and Nora admitted that she had barely noticed their extended bout of celibacy—on her side at least!

'It *is* yours, isn't it?' he said, intrigued by the parade of expressions across her abstracted face.

'What? Oh...yes.' She blushed, dropping it hurriedly into her bag. 'But don't let it lead you to jump to any hasty conclusions about me,' she added, putting her drink down carefully on the carpet while she fished about to find the fuse-wire and quickly wound a 15-amp strand in a figure of eight around the worn clasp.

'The only conclusion I've come to is that you're probably a highly organised person in a disorganised kind of way,' he said wryly, watching her complete the makeshift repair with a deft twist of the fragile wire. 'Shall we rejoin the party before people start wondering what we're getting up to down here?' He rose smoothly to his feet, showing no signs of stiffness from his prolonged crouch, whisking away her bag and wineglass and placing them on the edge of the window table behind him, next to his own drink, before stooping to offer both his hands to Nora.

His palms were slightly rough, the friction of his skin sliding against hers producing sparks of heat that fanned hotter as his fingers tightened, totally encompassing her slender hands, making her momentarily feel trapped and helpless and alarmingly vulnerable. A quick flex of his legs and he hauled her upright in one fluid, easy movement. Alarm turned to a rush of unexpected excitement, the sparks leaping from the point of contact to sizzle up Nora's arms and razzle-dazzle around her body with electrifying speed, making it difficult to breathe, let alone coordinate her movements. The force of her forward momentum plastered her against his shirt front and she flailed on her precarious heels to find her balance, gasping when she felt an ominous downward drag on her breasts.

'Oh, stop! Don't move!' she hissed at him as she realised what was happening. 'I think I've caught one of my heels in the hem of my dress!' she groaned, hopping on one wobbly foot like a drunken stork.

He uttered a smothered curse, threaded with laughter, obediently freezing in position.

'This isn't funny!' she whispered fiercely into his ear. 'I'll be topless in a moment if we're not careful.'

'And this would be a bad thing?' he chuckled softly, his breath stirring the silky curls that feathered her cheek. The deep vibration in his chest resonated against her squashed breasts and Nora was mortified to feel them begin to tingle, the nipples budding against the sheer fabric of her strapless bra, the top edge of which was now peeking above the satin band of her bodice.

'*Yes!*' Her chin was level with his shoulder, his tanned throat a tempting few inches from her mouth.

'For goodness' sake, stop laughing at me and try doing something *helpful*,' she gritted. She pulled her hands from his loosening grasp and looked down over her shoulder, arching back to try and unhook her spiked heel from the looped thread, but the twisting motion jerked her awkwardly bent leg and she gave a little squeak as she felt herself begin to pop free from the top of her dress.

Her squeak turned to a breathless gasp as his hands whipped to her sides, palms clamping around the front of her ribs with almost painful force, splayed fingers digging into her back, anchoring the straining fabric firmly in place, her dignity still intact. 'It's all right. I've got you. *Now* try,' he advised.

Nora was aware that she was teetering on the brink of social disaster. She licked her dry lips, her heart still pounding with fright, scarcely able to draw breath against the fierce compression of his grip. She stared up at the man holding her, her eyes wide and dark with doubt, her teeth sinking painfully into her bottom lip. She had already been betrayed by one man tonight. She had picked Blake MacLeod out as a dangerous man...what if it was an element of cruelty in his nature which gave him the dark aura she had found so appealing? What if he was setting her up for fresh humiliation?

'Go ahead—I won't let go.' There wasn't a trace of his previous mockery in his quiet voice and cool gaze. 'Trust me.'

His calmness and the continuing steady pressure around her ribs curbed her fears. In any case, trussed up as she was, she really didn't have any choice *but* to trust him.

It took her several flustered seconds to untangle the transparent thread from her snagged heel, and when she was finally standing on two feet again she uttered a ragged sigh of relief.

She was grateful that he had drawn her slightly away from the group he had been talking to, sparing her the embarrassment of introductions. 'Thank you.'

'My pleasure....'

The silky mockery was back and as their eyes met she was even more aware of his hands still firmly caging her ribs, his thumbs sloping up under her breasts so that with every exhaled breath she stroked herself against him. All he had to do was to alter the angle of his thumbs and he would find the stiff crests which pushed against the shiny satin, she thought hectically. She could feel the long muscles of his thighs bunching as they tensed against hers, the hard thrust of his hips still bracing the centre of her slender body, generating a primitive response that filled her with a furious elation. The social buzz around them faded from her consciousness, her breathing quickening in response to the sultry recognition that darkened his grey eyes. Her heart jumped inside her chest, throbbing against the warm pad of his thumb, and her sensitised skin crackled with energy.

'We haven't even been introduced,' she murmured faintly, having difficulty shaping the words on her thickened tongue.

'It's a little late to be formal. I'm Blake MacLeod.'

'I know.' She saw his eyelids give a wary flicker. 'After I saw you across the room, I wondered who you were, so I asked someone...'

'I see.' The brackets around his mouth relaxed. 'And?'

He obviously sensed there had been more to it than a simple identification. 'She said that you had a bad reputation with women and I should avoid you like the plague.'

'And yet...here you are,' he said in a neutral tone that was at odds with his smouldering eyes. 'Should I have asked someone about *you*?'

A rueful smile revealed Nora's disproportionately wide mouth and splendid teeth. 'It wouldn't have done you much good. I hardly know anyone in this crowd. I only got invited because I used to flat with the sister of the girl who's turning twenty-one.' Her eyes were almost on a level with his and it gave her a powerful kick to look directly into the windows of his deep, dark soul. 'I'm Nora.'

His impressive eyebrows lifted. 'Just Nora?'

'Eleanor, actually, but no one calls me that,' she breezed. No one except Ryan when he was impatient with her— grinding up the syllables in his gritted teeth!

Blake was silent, and she realised that he wasn't going to let her get away with the evasion. So much for hoping that she could cloak herself in alluring mystery for the evening.

'Lang. Nora Lang,' she said, adopting a flippant Bondian drawl. 'Does that make you any the wiser?'

He dipped his head, acknowledging the introduction. 'Not wiser, but certainly better informed. I always try to make informed decisions.'

'How boring,' she teased. 'Don't you like surprises?'

'It depends on the nature of the surprise,' he said, deliberately running his eyes over her captive body.

She felt her skin tighten in every pore. 'Are you always so cautious?'

'It depends on the nature of the threat.'

The verbal fencing was having a heady effect on Nora's battered self-confidence. 'Do I threaten you, Mr MacLeod?' she asked with a sweet smile.

'The idea seems to excite you.'

She felt a sluggish warmth move through her veins. 'I'll admit it has a certain raw appeal...'

'It's an interesting proposition, Nora, but I'm afraid I'm not into S&M.'

She blushed, not pink, but a vivid rose-red. 'I wasn't—I didn't mean *that*!'

'No? Sorry, I must have misunderstood,' he said with such patent insincerity that they both knew he was lying, and mightily enjoying her confusion.

'I'm not into anything weird!' she said firmly.

'How about mildly kinky?'

She thought of Ryan and Kelly in the bathroom. In the *bath* of all places, in the middle of the afternoon. *Nora's* bath! Boring, undemanding, unadventurous Nora who obviously didn't know what she was missing….

'Define kinky.'

He laughed, a deep masculine rumble of appreciation. '*Now* who's being cautious?'

'A woman alone has to take care not to raise expectations she's not prepared to fulfil,' she said primly.

'You're here alone?' In spite of the upward inflexion it was more of a statement than a question, and he didn't wait for an answer. 'I watched you as you came in,' he admitted unexpectedly.

'Did you?' Her smile widened for an instant before she remembered her ignominious entrance. 'Oh. And I suppose now you think I ricochet about the place like some sort of unguided missile,' she said with a sigh.

His fingers briefly contracted on her ribcage. 'Or perhaps a cleverly guided one.'

'Are you accusing me of dropping my bag at your feet on purpose, in order to meet you?' she demanded, clenching her fists against his chest.

'Did you?'

She tipped her chin and looked down her nose at him. 'That is *so* arrogant! Do you consider yourself so irresistibly attractive that you automatically assume that every woman is grovelling to attract your attention?'

His mouth ticked up at her haughty response. 'Well, not *every* woman. *Did* you?'

'No, of course I didn't!'

Then she recalled her chaotic thoughts in the moments before she had turned coward. 'Well…' She caught her lower lip between her teeth as she struggled with her over-scrupulous conscience. 'Maybe I *might* have been thinking of a way to introduce myself, but…no, I wouldn't have—certainly not consciously, anyway…'

His eyes were on that tell-tale worrying of her lip. 'You mean it was in the nature of a Freudian drop?' he said, with such suspicious blandness that her fists relaxed against his chest.

'Is that any different from a Freudian slip?' she asked, discreetly smoothing out a small crease she had made in his yellow silk tie.

'It's generally more revealing,' he told her, and paused before adding, 'Rather like that dress.'

She followed his gaze and uttered a stifled sound of annoyance when she saw that the embroidered edge of her black bra was still visible above the top of her dress. He beat her to the rescue, the backs of his fingers branding her with their searing warmth as they dipped beneath the fabric at the side of her breasts to gently hitch up her top by several freckles.

'Thank you,' she muttered, her hands automatically replacing his as he stepped back, leaving her bereft of his disturbing touch. She wriggled even more securely into the dress while he turned to pick up his neglected drink. 'I wish I'd never worn the wretched thing,' she grumbled. 'I knew it wasn't right for me.'

Unfortunately she'd had no choice since it was what she had been wearing when she had fled the flat. She had been trying on her dress and accessories when she had heard odd noises from the bathroom. Believing Kelly was out on a modelling job, she had snatched up a heavy lamp with which to clock the intruder if he turned nasty. In hindsight, she wished she had used it!

To Nora's chagrin Blake didn't disagree. He tucked her bag in the crook of her elbow and placed her wineglass in her hand. 'So why wear it?'

He had manoeuvred her to one side of a support pillar, his back to the room, discouraging anyone else from joining the conversation.

'It was a gift from a friend. He advised me that something black and strapless would make even *me* look elegant.'

'Some friend.' His sardonic drawl made Nora's eyes light up with militant agreement.

'*Former* friend,' she corrected him with savage relish.

'Personally, I think the shoes were the better buy,' he said.

'The dress was terribly pricy,' she murmured, with a twinge of guilt.

He shrugged. 'So were the outrageously sexy shoes, but they're a work of art in themselves.'

Outrageously sexy? Little thrills ran up and down her spine.

'How do you know what they cost?' As soon as the words were out of her mouth, Nora cursed the foolish naivety of her question. As a wealthy man he was probably used to paying his lovers' bills—and to making sure he got full value for his money!

His wicked smile suggested he had read her mind. 'Because they have a famous Italian name stamped on the sole…and you're still wearing the price tag.' He bent down and laced his fingers around her left ankle, lifting her foot and peeling something off the delicate sole of her shoe. Although she automatically gripped his shoulder for balance, he had acted so swiftly that he had replaced her foot firmly on the ground before she had a chance to wobble. 'I noticed it when we were kneeling down.'

Ignoring the lingering warmth in her tingling ankle, Nora stared at the small adhesive-backed paper square he had pressed on to the back of her hand.

'Oh, my *God*!' she breathed, aghast.

'Don't worry, I don't think anyone would class it as a major social gaffe—' he began in amusement.

'My God, this can't be the *price*!' Nora continued in an outraged whisper. 'This is wrong—it has to be a stock number or something. I can't have paid *that* for a pair of *shoes*! I wouldn't have! It's indecent!'

'Maybe they were on sale,' he murmured, watching her dusting of freckles glow vivid ginger against her blanched skin.

'Expensive hotel boutiques target high-rolling tourists— they don't *have* sales,' she said hollowly. She blinked her thickly mascaraed eyelashes, trying in vain to make the dollar sign in front of the figures go away. 'I don't believe it—they cost almost twice as much as the *dress* did!' She heaved a sigh, screwing up the price sticker until it was a tiny hard pellet and flicking it away.

'How much did you think they cost?' he asked curiously.

'I don't know. I didn't care. I was in such a temper I didn't even look at the price,' she admitted, closing her eyes as she frantically tried to remember what else she had put on her credit card this month.

'A temper?'

'Mmm?' Her eyes flew open and she became enmeshed in his intently curious gaze. Had he noticed that her eyelids were slightly pink and puffy under their lavish powdering of green shadow and gold glitter? She didn't want him to think she was a pathetic weepy female. 'Oh…' She gestured vaguely with her glass and delivered the understatement of all time. 'I was upset about something that happened earlier.'

'And when you're upset, you shop?'

'God, no. I hate shopping…for clothes, anyway.' She shuddered. 'All that standing around, staring at yourself. And I certainly don't get paid enough to buy shoes like this every time I lose my temper!'

'What kind of work do you do?' he asked, propping his arm against the narrow pillar, his wrist skimming the curve of her bare shoulder.

'I help people fix problems with their computers,' she said, deliberately down-playing her skill. She was all too familiar with the glaze that appeared on people's faces when she started talking about her job.

'Here in the city?'

'Our offices are just a few blocks away.' She didn't want to talk about Maitlands. Or even *think* about how she was going to cope with the strain of working in the same office as Ryan—and Kelly—after tonight. 'This is the first time I've been up the Sky Tower, though. Have you been here before?'

'I bring international clients to the restaurant and casino quite regularly. PresCorp has a permanent suite at the hotel. It's also useful for occasions like this, when my workload is so heavy that I don't want to waste time commuting.'

Prickles danced across her skin. 'You're staying here at the hotel?' she blurted huskily. He gave her a speculative look and she fought down a blush. 'Wouldn't a serviced apartment be more cost effective for the company?' she hastened to say.

'Even luxury apartments don't come with twenty-four-hour room service—' He stopped as she suddenly stiffened, the colour draining from her face. 'Is something wrong?'

'No—yes.' She ducked her head below the level of his shoulders, burying her nose in her drink. 'I just realised that I'm famished. I wonder when they're going to serve some proper food.'

'Not for some time yet.' He tilted his wrist so that she could see the face of his steel Rolex. 'Supper at ten-thirty p.m., the invitation said—and there'll be speeches to get through first. Didn't you eat before you came?'

She recalled throwing up in a rainy gutter somewhere, retching her heart out while the tears streamed down her face.

'I wasn't in the mood.'

'There're plenty of nibbles going around. Would you like me to get us some?' He dropped his arm and began to turn.

'No! Don't go!' She clutched at his jacket, her eyes sliding past him.

'I was only going to signal a waiter.' He looked down at her fixed expression, noting the way she had edged around to keep his body between herself and the room, while still keeping whatever was holding her attention in view. 'Someone you didn't expect to see tonight?' he asked shrewdly.

Someone she would be happy never to see again!

With growing outrage, Nora watched Ryan working the room as if he didn't have a care in the world. He had been enormously pleased at the prospect of mixing with some of the city's leading citizens, but he had only received an invitation to the party because he was *her* partner. He certainly knew how to market himself, she'd give him that, but now that the scales had fallen from her eyes she could see him for what he was: a noxious little opportunist!

CHAPTER THREE

'LET me guess…the *former* friend who mistakes fashion for style?' Blake MacLeod murmured, tracking her gaze.

Nora felt a spurt of spiteful amusement as she turned her eyes squarely back to her companion and his impeccably understated elegance.

'His name is Ryan.'

'Is he important?' The supercilious tilt of his eyebrows was a masterly put-down.

Nora smiled brilliantly. 'Not anymore.'

She raised her glass to her lips and was dismayed to see her hand tremble.

It was too much to hope for that the sharp-eyed man she was with wouldn't notice it, too. His eyes flickered down the slender length of her arm and his face turned to stone. 'Are you afraid of him?' he asked quietly.

'Ryan? No, of course not!' she scorned. He had already done his worst and she had survived.

'Did he beat you?'

'Only at squash—I always creamed him at chess and Scrabble!' she replied flippantly.

His expression remained guarded. 'Then how did you get these?' he said, lightly touching his fingertips to the fresh bruises on the inside of her forearm, blotchy shadows blooming through the smooth, translucent skin.

The tiny sizzle that accompanied his touch made her senses scatter. 'What? Oh…I banged my arm against a doorknob at home this afternoon,' she recalled reluctantly. It had been the bathroom door she had been backing out of—her eyes screwed shut against the sight of the guilty pair in the bathtub, scrabbling to separate themselves. The sharp jolt of physical pain in her arm had been a welcome distraction from the agony of her disillusionment as Ryan had followed her, dragging a towel around his hips, blustering in self-defensive anger, turning the blame for his behaviour back on to Nora.

'You walked into a door?' Blake said with blunt scepticism. 'Do you realise what a stereotypical answer that is?'

Her eyes widened as she realised that he was seriously concerned that she might be a battered woman. 'But I really did,' she protested. 'I would never let a man get away with being abusive towards me.'

'I thought they looked like fingermarks,' he murmured, aligning his fingers over the blue-brown smudges.

'Well, they're not. I have very sensitive skin. Bruises always show up quickly, looking worse than they are.'

The sight of his lean tanned fingers lying against her skin made her mouth go dry and her body throb with awareness. The contrast between his sinewy brown hand and her delicate paleness seemed starkly erotic. She couldn't believe that a stranger's touch could have such a dramatic impact. On the other hand, she had never before opened herself up to the possibility that another man could arouse her with a mere look, a touch…

She watched as he slowly splayed his hand, gently encircling her arm in a bracelet of warm flesh. She shivered.

'Cold?' he asked, in a knowing voice that said he knew very well what had caused her reaction.

Her eyelids felt heavy, weighted down by lashes as she lifted them to meet his gaze. 'It is rather cool up here.' She uttered the bald-faced lie in the nature of a challenge.

His lips and eyebrows quirked. 'Perhaps the altitude doesn't suit you.'

She wished he hadn't reminded her! 'Or maybe it's the fact that I'm more exposed than usual,' she said, with a hitch of one dappled shoulder.

'Would you like me to put my jacket around you?' he offered.

Nora's hectic emotions translated the private gesture of courtesy into a primitive act of public possession.

'No, you keep it,' she said huskily. 'I wouldn't like you to catch a chill.'

'I don't think there's any fear of that.' His thumb moved on her arm, sliding over the rounded inner curve of her elbow. 'I'm very warm-blooded.'

Her own spurted hotly in her veins. 'That's not what I've heard.'

'And do you always believe everything you're told?' he taunted.

Her pupils contracted to narrow dots, the only sign of her inward flinch. 'I used to.' She couldn't help glancing over to where she had seen Ryan. 'Now I prefer to rely on more tangible evidence.'

Blake's hand left her arm to tilt her head firmly back in his direction, demanding her full attention. 'Very wise. How hungry are you?'

She blinked at his *non sequitur*. 'I beg your pardon?'

'You said you haven't had dinner and, as it happens, neither have I. What say we blow this joint and find a restaurant that can serve us within the next half-hour?'

Blow this joint? His mocking slang made it sound invitingly dangerous, with the added bonus of allowing her to avoid any painful encounters with Ryan.

'But what about the party—?' she stammered, not sure whether he was joking.

'In a crowd this size, one or two less isn't going to matter.'

One or two? Did that mean that he intended leaving, with or without Nora? She felt a stab of disappointment, followed by a fresh surge of reckless determination. When she had singled him out in her sights she had had no idea where her flirtation would lead, or how far she was prepared to take her rash experiment. She still didn't know, but her fear and uncertainty was all part of the intoxicating excitement that jetted through her as she contemplated her next move.

'They might not notice *my* disappearance, but you're a lot higher up the scale of importance,' she felt compelled to point out.

A world of natural arrogance was expressed in his shrug. 'I've done my duty. I came. Waved the PresCorp flag in the necessary faces. Kissed the birthday girl and gave her a gift. More than enough to satisfy Scotty's festering social conscience. Now I'm back on my own time.'

It took her a moment to realise who he meant by 'Scotty'.

'You only came because Sir Prescott Williams asked you to?'

'The word "ask" implies choice. Prescott is far too shrewd to offer options that won't deliver his preferred outcome,' he replied drily. 'He knows exactly how and where to apply pressure. He's an expert in getting his own way.'

'Somehow I can't quite picture you as anyone's helpless pawn. You don't look like a man who enjoys taking orders.'

He threw back the last of his drink and acknowledged her tart remark with an insinuating smile. 'On the contrary, if I perceive a mutual benefit I can be extremely accommodating.'

His soft purr hinted at all sorts of intriguing wickedness. 'Are you saying you'd let *me* order you around?' she said, forbidden images swirling up from the unplumbed depths of her mind.

'Well, not here, obviously—I do have my ruthless image to protect,' he mocked, playing to the shocked curiosity that flared across her face, fascinated by the contradiction between the smouldering passion of those sultry painted eyes and the astringent freshness of her unpredictable personality. It was a long time since Blake had been surprised by anyone or anything. 'Perhaps I'll let you order *for* me in the restaurant, as a start...'

'Restaurant?' In her flurry of wild imaginings she had forgotten the original question.

'You'd rather wait and eat here?' He looked down into his empty glass, masking his expression as he mused, 'Maybe you're right. Even if you're not lucky enough to be assigned a window-seat, once everyone sits down you'll have an uninterrupted view from whichever table you're at, reminding you with every bite that you're in a nine-storey building perched atop a concrete shaft around three hundred metres high but only a bare twelve metres in diameter…'

Nora's stomach did a sickening loop-the-loop, a fine dew springing out on her brow.

'…whereas the restaurant I have in mind is only a quiet ground-floor place around the corner from the casino,' he continued smoothly. 'Good food, but one step down from the street…with absolutely *no* view—'

'Actually, that sounds rather nice,' Nora gulped, clutching gratefully at the dangled safety-line. 'Let's go there.'

Only when the words were out of her mouth did she realise what she had committed herself to, and her stomach performed another crazy loop, this time of excitement. Somehow, she had beguiled one of the city's most cynical bachelors into taking her out to dinner!

He gave her no chance to change her mind. 'Do you need to make any farewells, or do you want to just melt away?'

She should at least exchange a few words with Patty, her former flatmate, and thank her for the invitation. 'Well, I—'

Suddenly, out of the corner of her eye, she saw Ryan and felt a sharp spike of panic.

'Melting would be good,' she said quickly. 'Melting is *very* good—as long as we do it right away.'

If Blake was startled by the rough urgency of her tone he didn't show it. 'Don't you want to finish your drink?' he murmured, half turning to put down his empty glass.

Ryan's face was now a nasty white blot on the periphery of Nora's vision. Had he seen her yet?

Her overwrought imagination bubbled with horrifying scenarios. What if Ryan wanted to appease his guilty conscience with more shattering revelations? What if he decided that by approaching her in public he could compel her to listen to what he had to say?

Ryan knew how much she disliked being the centre of attention—he would be *relying* on it to prevent her from making a scene. He could be doggedly persistent and remarkably ingratiating when it served his own interests. He was even capable, she thought wildly, of following her from the party and turning Blake MacLeod's desirable companion into a dreary woman scorned!

She held out her drink. 'No, thanks, it's gone warm anyway—'

As Blake turned back, a group of chattering people pushed past behind Nora and she was shunted forward. The arm she had extended jerked, the contents of her glass splattering in an arc over Blake's jacket and tie and plastering a fist-sized patch of his shirt to his chest.

There was a stunned pause.

'Oh, God, I'm most terribly sorry!' Nora brushed ineffectually at the splashes on his lapel, which had instantly soaked into the pale sheen of the fabric.

'There's no need to apologise,' he said, taking away her empty glass and handing it to a sympathetic bystander, 'if it wasn't your fault.'

'Those people bumped against me,' she explained, sure her guilt must be written in fire across her forehead.

He looked at her from under his lowered brow. 'So I saw...'

'One of them must have jogged my arm,' she added unnecessarily.

'I suppose I should be grateful that you weren't drinking the Cabernet Sauvignon,' he commented with wry resignation, taking a white linen handkerchief out of his breast pocket and blotting at himself.

If she *had* been drinking red wine she would never have had the courage to do it! she thought, but desperate situations had called for desperate measures. 'I don't think it'll stain if you rinse it out immediately.'

'This suit is made of silk,' he pointed out.

He didn't need to add that it was very expensive Italian-styled silk. Nora had already guessed that it had probably cost more than her top-of-the-line office laptop.

'Oh, dear!' She bit her lip. 'And so is your beautiful tie,' she commiserated. 'If you don't want to risk them being permanently marked you really do need to do something as soon as possible…'

He dabbed at the splotches on his tie. 'What would you suggest?'

Her mouth went dry and she deliberately pitched her voice low to disguise her jittery tension. 'Well…we were leaving anyway, and you said you have a suite at the hotel. Why don't we go there and you can phone the concierge? I'm sure the hotel offers an emergency dry-cleaning service…'

His hand stilled.

'I'm sure they do,' he said, looking into her wide innocent eyes. 'If you're certain you don't mind taking the detour?'

She swallowed, fighting down a blush. 'No, no, not at all. You can't go to the restaurant like that. I'd feel dreadful if you risked ruining your suit because of me.'

It was all she could do not to hustle him along as they began to move across the revolving floor. Unfortunately their progress was slowed by people who sought to waylay Blake, and it was several minutes before they finally made it up the steps to the reception area by the lift bay. In the meantime a furtive glance over her shoulder showed her Ryan's startled face, mooning at her from the crowd as he set out on an intersecting course.

Nora stalked towards the glass doors, only to find herself stayed by Blake's polite command.

'If you wait here, I'll collect your coat and umbrella.'

'Oh, but—' She found herself talking to empty air. She

would gladly have abandoned the wretched things for the sake of a quick getaway. Stranded on elevated ground, she had no place to hide when the unwelcome voice sounded behind her.

'Nora? Nora—I know you saw me. I can't believe you're here! Thank goodness you're all right!'

She turned reluctantly, plastering a look of surprise on her face. '*I* was invited, remember? Why shouldn't I be here? Why are *you*?'

Ryan mounted the last step, his even features bearing a tentative conciliating smile. 'Well, we'd accepted the invitation. I thought at least one of us should come, and I didn't think that you'd make it all the way up here by yourself. You were so upset when you took off from the flat, I didn't know what to think! We were worried about you....'

He dared mention Kelly? As if either of them had cared a fig about her feelings when they were wallowing in her bath!

She stared haughtily down at him, unimpressed by his attempt to smooth things over. She had always seen him as a lovable, cuddly teddy bear—with his curly blond hair, button-bright blue eyes, square jaw and stocky physique. Now she could see his brash charm was a threadbare illusion, the careless affection with which he had captured her dreams no substitute for genuine passion.

'Well, you needn't have—as you can see, I'm fine,' she said abruptly. He must have remembered the system profiles that she had been creating for his current project, beavering away in her spare time for weeks so that Ryan could gain extra kudos from his boss—who also happened to be Kelly's uncle!

His eyes were puzzled as they travelled over her, trying to work out what was different—so different—about her. Finally it clicked and he looked down.

'My God, Nora, where on earth did you get those *ridiculous* shoes? You'll likely break your neck in them. Besides, they make you look like a beanpole.'

A few hours ago she might have meekly agreed with him, but Nora's blood was up.

'Look, Ryan, I'd love to stand around and chat all night,' she said with heavy sarcasm, 'but as it happens I have better things to do.'

His patronising confidence said he didn't believe her. What could be more important to Nora than the man she had been mooning over since she was twenty?

'Give me a break, Nora,' he appealed, producing the wheedling little-lost-boy smile that she used to think was adorable. 'We need to talk. You didn't give me time to explain what I meant this afternoon. I never wanted to hurt you, you know, Nora—'

'Then you shouldn't have slept with my flatmate!' she said icily.

'We all make mistakes, Nora. We've known each other for years. I'd still like us to be friends, especially since we work at the same place—'

Of course he would, because then he could continue to tap into her specialised talent to enhance his own career. When he had been at university and she had been working in the technology lab, he had noticed her unrequited crush and persuaded her to give him free tutoring to help him pass his computer and statistics papers. As well as helping him out with research she had also typed up his assignments and edited the bad grammar and fuzzy logic out of his essays, all for the sake of a few platonic hugs and kisses and the privilege of being accepted into his magic circle of friends. And five years later she was still helping him to make a good impression at the expense of her own needs.

'I've decided it's time I graduated to a better class of friend.'

He laid a heavy hand on her wrist. 'Come on, Eleanor, you don't mean that,' he said thinly. 'Everyone makes mistakes.'

'Yes, and you were mine,' she said, clinging to her self-control.

His hand tightened. 'If it wasn't for me you'd still be stuck in some dreary little cubicle somewhere—'

'Ready to go, Nora?' The deep voice resonated in her bones and with a start she realised that Blake MacLeod was standing behind her, holding out her open coat. Instead of feeling embarrassed at what he might have overheard, Nora was emboldened by his solid strength at her back.

Ryan's hand fell from her arm, his jaw going slack as he focused on the man taking her bag while he helped her into her coat. 'You're leaving with *him*?'

'I told you I had better things to do.' It gave her a malicious pleasure to say.

He didn't appear to hear her, hastily extending his hand to take advantage of the unexpected encounter. 'Uh, Mr MacLeod, we haven't met, but of course I know who you are—I'm Ryan Trent—'

To Nora's delight Blake ignored the eagerly outstretched hand, returning her bag and hooking her umbrella over his arm so that he could adjust the collar of her coat, his knuckles brushing with gentle deliberation along the tense line of her jaw.

'I have in mind something far more succulent for you to sink your teeth into,' he told her with shameless eroticism, pressing his thumb against the swollen lower lip she had been unconsciously abusing. 'I hope you're still as hungry as I am…'

'More,' she said throatily, falling in with his baiting game, her teeth briefly grating against his salty thumb which he withdrew to place between his lips.

Tasting her. His tongue flicked out, a provocative dart that only she could see, and suddenly it was no longer a game.

'Shall we?' he murmured, placing his flat hand low on her back, and Nora went warm all over, steaming up the inside of her coat.

'Eleanor!' Ryan's shocked voice held the hint of an aggrieved whine as she began to move. 'I thought we were going to talk—'

'Some other time, Ryan,' she tossed out carelessly. 'And, oh!' She paused beside him, savouring the advantage of her dominating height. 'I never noticed it before, Ryan, but maybe you should see someone about that thinning patch on the top of your head—it's a classic sign of premature male-pattern baldness….'

She sashayed on by, leaving Ryan, his hand smoothing

uneasily over his crown, staring after them, his face a blotchy rash of angry colour.

'Beautiful,' said Blake in admiration as they sauntered out through the glass door, and Nora knew he wasn't talking about her. 'Is he really going bald?' he asked as he summoned the lift.

'If there's any justice in the world. Ryan's very vain about his hair. He'll drive himself crazy worrying about it.'

'Probably feel insecure about it for the rest of his life.' The shiny metal doors hissed open and he indicated with the umbrella for her to precede him. 'You're clearly a dangerous woman to cross.'

She liked the sound of that. Even the hint of laughter in his voice couldn't dent her triumphant confidence as she stepped over the threshold. 'Yes, I am.'

'In that case I'll be careful to stay on your good side,' he said, following her in. 'Which is it, left or right?'

The wet patch on his shirt was low over his heart, the white cotton sticking transparently to his olive skin, showing the fine tangle of black hair on his chest. She thought she could also see his bronzed nipple, but she wasn't sure whether it was just a shadow of a curl.

'Nora?'

'Hmm?' Her coat rustled as she started guiltily, gesturing towards his open jacket. 'I'm awfully sorry about what happened with the wine,' she said, barely registering the sound of the door sliding shut, enclosing them in a hush of privacy.

He shrugged, dragging the dampened shirt taut across his skin. 'I'm not; it saved me from a slow drowning in a sea of social platitudes.' Definitely a nipple, thought Nora dizzily, feeling like a sleazy voyeur for noticing.

'Since it's still raining outside, and we're going to the suite anyway, perhaps you'd prefer to relax there and order dinner from the room service menu,' he continued, pressing the button for the ground floor and turning to face her.

Nora's breathing quickened under his quizzical gaze. They both knew there was nothing innocent about his casual offer.

It had not escaped him that she had virtually invited herself to his room, and now he was politely testing the waters, asking her to clarify her expectations in terms that a virtuous young lady was safe to misinterpret.

He was letting her know that all she had to do was refuse and the rest of the evening would be conducted under the conventional rules of propriety—a pleasant meal in a public restaurant, a light flirtation...final outcome: uncertain.

But Nora wasn't feeling virtuous or conventional. She knew that there was no respectable excuse for her to accept his loaded offer; she had already successfully evaded Ryan and salved some of her deeply wounded pride. But that 'beanpole' taunt still rankled, and no man had never looked at her in the way that Blake was looking at her now—with a blatant sexual speculation that ate her up with curiosity.

Her stomach flip-flopped as the lift began its rapid descent. She was conscious that he was watching and waiting as she hovered on the brink of the precipice. She hastily turned away, hugging her evening bag to her pounding breast with both hands.

'I think that sounds—' The words froze on her tongue as she found herself staring straight out through the rain-smeared glass front of the lift. Everything tilted, her blood roaring in her ears, a metallic taste flooding her mouth, her body going rigid, limbs paralysed with shock. The lights of the city blurred into coloured streamers that lashed back and forth, reaching through the glass, trying to pull her headlong into that rushing void, binding her chest until she was unable to breathe, to think, to save herself from falling, falling...

'Nora?' Blake's sharp voice pierced her consciousness but, encased in an icy block of fear, she was helpless to frame a coherent response, an indistinct mewing sound issuing from her bloodless lips, her fingernails bending as they dug into her bag.

She heard him swear fluently, cursing his own thoughtlessness. A protective arm whipped around her waist, turning her aside from the cold glass, drawing her against the reassuring warmth of human flesh.

'Don't look.'

He didn't understand, she thought, screwing her head sideways in order to keep the mesmerising horror in sight. She couldn't *not* look. Imagination was far worse than terrifying reality.

'Nora, it's all right, you're safe with me—you've only got to hold on for a little while longer. Close your eyes, if it helps….'

And let the nightmare of falling completely take over? She shook her head violently, a silent scream building up in her throat.

He cursed again and she dimly heard a rattling thud as he dropped her furled umbrella. 'Nora, stop looking down—' He grasped her jaw in his hand, far more roughly than he had at the party, and forced her eyes to meet his compelling gaze. 'Don't worry about what's out there…look at *me*.'

Her head jerked in mindless panic. 'I can't—'

Instead of impatiently snapping at her to pull herself together, as Ryan had done whenever she had revealed her weakness, he firmed his grip, his voice quiet, slow and forceful. 'Yes, you can. Focus on me. Concentrate. Breathe deeply and think of something else, something you want more than *anything*—'

'Like what?' she choked despairingly, her slender body beginning to ripple with chills, the blood draining from her extremities to warm her icy core.

His eyes fell to her mouth and blazed with a fierce determination. 'Like this…'

He bent his head, blotting out the world, his mouth crushing down on her cold lips, sealing in her ragged breath, invading her with his masculine heat and iron will sheathed in a wet velvet tongue. The arm around her waist slid down and tightened, arching her hips against the centre of his body, his other hand flattening between her shoulderblades, his palm hot against her bare skin as he locked her to his chest, trapping her folded arms between their bodies, leaving her helpless to resist his devouring hunger. The assault was sudden and brutal, an erotic smash-and-grab raid which swamped her fear in a flood of pleasure, robbing her of everything but the desperate need to feel him thrust harder, hotter, deeper inside her...

He cupped her head, changing the angle of his kiss to allow him deeper access, smothering her with his scent, his taste, sucking at her lower lip, scraping at her with his teeth, luring her tongue into a seductive battle inside his mouth, battering her with violently delightful sensations.

She squirmed to get closer, her chills turned to a raging fever, burning away her inhibitions, her awareness of time and place. She groaned as she felt him subtly pull back from the kiss, but it was only to allow her to free her arms. Her evening bag plopped unnoticed on top of her umbrella as her hands slid eagerly up under the back of his jacket, fingers clawing at the soft cotton of his shirt, her short-trimmed nails biting into his hot skin through the thin fabric.

His muscles tensed and he growled a warning deep in his throat, the sound of a hungry male predator staking claim over his captive prey. A new, entirely delicious fear feathered along Nora's nerves and she flexed her nails again, revelling in his lightning-swift response to the feline goad. She gasped, the sound lost in his plundering mouth as he unleashed another burst of aggressive passion, prowling her backwards until her shoulders hit the padded corner of the lift, caging her there with his lean, hard body while he greedily satisfied her feminine curiosity. His hands slid to her waist, anchoring her to the wall, then sliding up to splay over the slight curve of her breasts, his fingertips curling into the top edge of her dress as if he would wrench it down, his hard knee pushing between her legs, his strong, sinewy thigh jamming itself intimately against the melting centre of her body.

'Uh, excuse me...'

A polite cough had Blake wrenching his mouth from hers and for a few thundering heartbeats he stared at her, his breathing uneven, his grey eyes slightly stunned, his expression tight.

'Excuse me, Mr MacLeod, but I need to let the lift go. Were you intending to get off here—or um…?'

Blake spun around and Nora flushed to the roots of her hair as she straightened and met the brightly curious stare of the liveried young man who was politely restraining the twitch of the automatic doors.

She hadn't even been aware of the lift coming to a halt, let alone the doors opening. The whole journey had probably taken less than thirty seconds but she felt as if she had acquired the experience of a lifetime!

CHAPTER FOUR

To HIDE her blushing confusion Nora ducked to pick up her umbrella and freshly abused evening bag, sending up a silent prayer of thanks that it hadn't broken its makeshift wire catch. When she looked up again it was to see Blake tucking something into the young man's breast pocket, murmuring a low-voiced remark into his reddened ear before turning back to place a guiding hand under Nora's elbow.

'What were you saying to him?' she asked breathlessly, her heels wobbling to keep pace with his long impatient strides.

'I merely reminded him that as a regular visitor I know I can rely on his discretion,' he said, leading her on to the escalator that would take them up to the main entrance to the casino complex.

'You were paying him to keep his mouth shut,' she guessed, not sure whether to be admiring or disapproving.

'Merely a small token of my appreciation,' he demurred. 'I also suggested that he share his bounty with the person who monitors the security cameras.'

'Th-There was a camera in the lift?' she stammered, blushing anew as she imagined her passionate frenzy splashed across a flickering screen somewhere in the bowels of the building. 'I hope we don't turn up on some "caught on video" reality programme,' she muttered shakily.

'I don't think they'd be interested in anything so tame.'

'*Tame?*' Nora stared at him wide-eyed, her fingers tightening nervously on the moving hand-rail.

'We kept our clothes on,' he pointed out as they reached the top of the escalator.

'Oh, yes, of course…' she muttered, slightly reassured.

'Although I must admit it was touch and go there for a moment,' he added slyly, and Nora gave a little yelp as she mistimed her step off the moving pad, hooking her heel on the metal rim and lurching drunkenly against him.

'I'm sorry,' she said, ultra-conscious of the coiled tension in his flexing muscles. 'I—I guess I'm still feeling a bit weak at the knees—'

He didn't even break stride, his hand sliding from her elbow to her wrist, supporting the full weight of her stumble with his braced forearm. 'I'm flattered.'

His confident amusement ruffled her pride. 'I was talking about the lift!'

'So was I,' he drawled, negotiating what seemed like a maze of pillars and walkways at a pace which had Nora's loose coat billowing out behind her and rendered her even more breathless and light-headed. Blake MacLeod was clearly a very goal-orientated man, as decisive in his actions as he was in his ideas. Swept up in his whirlwind energy, Nora wondered darkly whether any woman had ever succeeded in making *him* weak at the knees.

He slowed down slightly, only because they had reached the plush hotel foyer and were approaching a bank of lifts. The door to one of the lifts instantly hummed open, as if to his silent decree.

'Open sesame!' Nora murmured, contemplating the empty, elegantly lit interior with a *frisson* of alarm.

'How fortunate for both of us that you know the secret password.' Blake distracted her with his sensuous purr, using his body to shepherd her gently over the threshold.

It was on the tip of her tongue to tell him that cracking passwords was one of her professional specialities, but that would be far too prosaic. 'I thought everyone did,' she said huskily.

'Only those conversant with *The Arabian Nights*. And knowing what words to say is useless unless you know where and when to say them. You enjoy romantic tales of the imagination?' he asked, moving over to the control panel.

'It beats reality any day,' she said with a wry twist of her mouth.

'Maybe your previous reality just hasn't been exciting enough to compete with your imaginative desires.' His deep lazy tone was an implicit promise to remedy the fact.

Her 'previous reality' had complained about her *lack* of imagination, but her disturbingly intense response to Blake's caressing words and flagrant handling put an entirely different slant on Ryan's taunts about Nora's sexual shortcomings. Now she wondered if it hadn't been her awareness of his impatience and an over-anxious desire to please which had inhibited her lovemaking. She wouldn't have to worry about pleasing Blake MacLeod in bed. She had complete confidence that he would please himself no matter what she did or didn't do!

She moistened her dry lips and his eyes narrowed on her tense face. 'If this is really a problem for you, we could take the stairs,' he said, flattening his hand across both door controls to prevent the lift from moving.

She was stunned by his thoughtfulness. 'N-no, I'm fine. I'm OK as long as I can't see where we are on the vertical scale...' An awful thought struck her. 'You aren't in the penthouse suite, are you?'

His head moved fractionally in the negative, his grey eyes absorbing her relief as she sighed. 'You must think I'm a terrible coward...'

'Must I?' His raised eyebrows expressed surprise that anybody should tell him what to think.

She lifted her chin. 'I know it seems irrational—'

'Feelings frequently are illogical—it doesn't make them any less valid.' He shrugged. 'Our primitive instincts and basic drives often cause havoc with our rational selves…we call it being human.'

She was wary of his understanding. 'I hope you don't think I'm weak and over-emotional just because I'm a woman.'

'God forbid,' he said drily, finally setting the lift in motion with a casual tap of a knuckle. 'Some of the strongest and most ruthlessly unsentimental people I know are women.' He leaned back against the wall of the lift and folded his arms across his chest, regarding her flushed face with a smoky satisfaction. 'And as a man I'm quite happy to admit that there are times when allowing one's primitive urges free rein is deeply rewarding….'

When he suddenly chuckled it was a stinging reminder of another man's belittlement.

Her eyes blazed at him. 'What's so funny?'

'I was just thinking…you'd make a good model for Boadicea right now—tall and queenly, feminine and fierce, draped in a flowing raiment and carrying your bag and umbrella clasped to your bosom like a sword and shield.'

To Nora's chagrin she realised that she was indeed clutching her accessories in front of her like defensive weapons. She forced herself to nonchalantly lower her arms.

'If I'm Boadicea who are you…one of my lowly English serfs?'

His eyes gleamed with appreciation. 'I rather saw myself as a Roman general accepting your surrender.'

Nora tossed her autumn-brown head in unconscious challenge. No man was ever again going to bemoan her passiveness. 'I don't think Boadicea ever surrendered herself to the Romans, did she?'

'Actually, I think she chose to take poison rather than bow her head in defeat,' he said, pushing himself off the wall as the lift pinged its arrival at the selected floor. 'You look as if you admire her courage. Is my captive warrior queen getting cold feet?' he murmured against the rumble of the opening door. The words were playful, but the underlying message was not.

Colour streaked across Nora's cheeks. 'I'm nobody's captive!'

'Very impressive, but that doesn't answer my question.'

She looked him straight in the eye, concealing her angry turmoil, determined to be bold and assertive.

'You're the one who seems to be having second thoughts, *General*. Afraid you can't handle me without a legion at your back?'

Silver light flared in his storm-dark eyes and hot blood pulsed through the vein in his exposed temple.

'I already have,' he reminded her with a lethal smile steeped in male arrogance. He braced his hand across the gap into which the sliding door had retracted. 'And, as I recall, you would have been on your knees if I hadn't been holding you up.'

'I thought that was where you wanted me to be,' she shot back.

'Oh, it is…but I'd prefer to wait until we're both naked.' He was swift to take advantage of her unwitting *double-entendre*. 'It's much more satisfying that way.'

She blushed from head to foot but valiantly battled on. 'Maybe *you'll* be the one brought to your knees.'

His eyelids lowered over his sultry amusement. 'I'd like that. I'm all for equal opportunity in the bedroom.'

Her mouth went dry as she thought of this aggressive and strong-willed male submitting himself to her every whim, his sleek, muscled body her erotic playground, his sexual expertise hers to command. 'And out of it?'

'I like to think of myself as a fair man. Is it relevant?'

Of course it wasn't. She was just wasting time. She swallowed hard, trying to work some moisture into her mouth so her voice wouldn't come out as a nervous croak. 'Which way is your suite?'

'To the right—the *right*,' he repeated, hooking her by the elbow as she veered in the wrong direction.

'Sorry,' she muttered, flustered by her mistake. 'I'm left-handed.'

'That explains everything,' he said, with a dry humour which made her feel a shade less foolish.

'Well, I'm right-brained, but ambidextrous when it comes to doing most things,' she expanded. 'That's why I get mixed up sometimes.'

He came to a halt in front of a panelled door and swiped the keycard across the lock, standing aside to usher her inside, flicking a switch to softly illuminate the long room. On their lowest setting, the lamps cast a mellow glow over the whipped cream carpet, plush sofas and art-strung walls. To Nora's surprised relief, Blake's next action was to cross to the full-length windows and draw the heavy curtains across what was undoubtedly a superb view of the city.

A little of her tension eased and she placed her umbrella and bag down on the narrow entrance table, moving further into the luxurious cocoon. There was a desk stacked with papers and files and an ultra-slim laptop computer blinking in sleep-mode; next to it a sideboard held a television and video game machine, coffee-making facilities and a heavily stocked mini-bar. A mahogany table with six ladder-backed chairs was angled to take advantage of the view. A large basket of fresh flowers and tropical fruits graced the coffee table between the cushioned sofas, and through the archway to her left the spill of light along the floor showed Nora a wedge of bathroom floor and, beyond that, the edge of a king-sized bed receding into the darkness, the turned-down sheet and plumped pillows at its head shimmering ghostly white in the gloom.

'I don't think it's likely to rain in here, do you?'

'I beg your pardon?' She tore her eyes hurriedly away from the beckoning fantasy to find Blake prowling back in her direction.

'Your coat. Would you like to take it off?'

'Oh…yes…' Anxious not to seem gauche, she hastily peeled the lapels, her fingers all thumbs, until he stepped around behind her, stilling her jerky movements with a light touch on her shoulders.

'Allow me.' Unlike Nora, he was in no hurry. His warm palms cupped her supple shoulders as he eased the sleeves free and slid them slowly down her arms, his fingertips trickling down her bare skin in their wake, caressing her from the tender crease in her armpits to her delicate inner wrists.

'Thank you,' she murmured, standing stiffly straight as he tossed the coat carelessly across the corner of the desk, his hands returning to bracelet her dangling wrists, trapping them at her sides. He bent his head, his silky black hair brushing her cheek as he rested his mouth against the smooth dip of her shoulder.

'My pleasure,' he said, his breath fanning over her skin, his lips stroking her as they shaped the words, making her wish he was more loquacious. Her head tilted to grant him greater access and he made a low sound of approval, shifting his mouth closer to the curve of her throat.

'There's something slightly barbaric about a woman showing this much bare skin without the civilising distraction of jewellery.' He feathered his lips along the ridge of her collarbone. 'Is that why you decided not to wear anything around your throat? Because you knew how temptingly naked it would make you look?'

Nora's hands involuntarily clenched at the gentle rake of his teeth, a shocking pang of sweetness spearing through her body. The thought of herself as a brazen temptress was wildly arousing but she didn't think she could sustain the role of calculating vamp, not when a simple touch of his mouth rendered her a jumble of confused longings. The exhilarating sense of danger was now even more acute, his stance shifting, his hips crowding her slim bottom, leaving her in no doubt as to the intensity of his interest. 'I—I left home in a rush,' she admitted thickly. 'I just didn't happen to have time to think about jewellery.'

'Then it's up to me to provide you with suitable adornment,' he murmured, nuzzling aside a veil of curls to string a necklace of slow kisses over her vulnerable nape, placing each one as carefully as if it was a precious jewel. The sharp rasp of his hair-roughened chin was a spine-tingling contrast to the velvet softness of his lips, and with each successive kiss her nerves tightened another notch. His hands moved down to enclose her balled fists, making her excitingly aware of his potentially crushing strength, his mouth ranging back out to the smooth roundness of her shoulder. 'Mmm, I've always wondered how freckles would taste…you have a very interesting cluster right here…' She felt the hot, wet stab of his tongue.

'I—I have freckles everywhere,' she pointed out shakily. No doubt his interchangeably gorgeous women were all creamy-skinned natural beauties, or sported carefully applied tans, and never had to worry about spots or blemishes on their polished complexions—certainly nothing so unsophisticated as a common freckle!

'*Everywhere?*' he teased huskily. She felt his teeth, followed by a moist suction against her skin. 'Is that my invitation to a private tasting?'

The image he evoked made her shiver, her eyes closing, her head falling back against his shoulder. She didn't care if she appeared to be surrendering too easily to his seductive technique. She had incited this, so she was the one who was controlling events. She felt gloriously empowered by his obvious arousal. She wanted—*needed*—to immerse herself in the dazzling sensations that were rolling over her, to prove that she was a woman of passion, worthy of a man's desiring. She wanted to have her womanhood reaffirmed in the most raw and elemental way. And not just by any man, but by this one—a connoisseur of women, a practised warrior in the eternal battle of the sexes, who could show her all she had been missing by clinging to a rosy delusion of love with a man who didn't want her—who had *never* really wanted her….

His hands tightened over hers in silent acknowledgement of her acquiescence, then flattened out against her thighs, smoothing slowly up over the front of her dress, her flat stomach, her trembling ribs, to come to rest just beneath her taut breasts.

To her shock he stepped abruptly away and she heard a slither of sound. Stricken with frustrated disappointment, she turned and saw that he had stripped off his jacket and was wrenching his loosened tie from his collar, flicking open the buttons of his shirt with his other hand, revealing a wedge of tawny chest dusted with blue-black hair and a belly that rippled with lean muscle as he twisted to free his shirt-tails from his belt. She could only stand and stare, her temperature shooting sky-high, while he shrugged free of the shirt, his tanned arms bulging with latent strength. If he had seemed formidably masculine to her before, bare-chested he looked like the very essence of male virility.

His expression was a dark mask of lustful intent, the skin drawn tight across his bones emphasising the intimidating harshness of his face. His eyes burned in their deep sockets, the coal-black shadow on his pugnacious jaw making him look uncompromisingly tough, his slashing widow's peak adding a faintly satanic air to his smouldering regard. He looked primed and ready to take her, body and soul.

Nora took an uncertain step back. His nostrils flared as if he scented her sudden doubt, and then he was reaching for her, gathering her up and driving her back until her legs bumped against the side of the desk. In the same forceful motion his mouth was swooping down on hers, drinking in her shocked gasp as she threw up her hands and they came into contact with the hot skin of his chest, her fingers automatically curling into the soft thicket of dark hair, hanging on for dear life as he deepened his plundering kiss. He tasted of wine—a rich, earthy, complex blend of flavours exploding on her tongue, an intoxicating vintage better than any *premier cru*. Nora melted into the ravishing assault, her senses reeling, her body swept into a tumultuous current that bore her violently away from the shores of logical thought.

His hands went under her arching back and she suddenly felt her zip parting all the way down to the base of her spine. She wrenched her mouth from his, instinctively grabbing at the loosened dress as it fell away, but her scrabbling fingers tangled with deft masculine hands that had other ideas.

'It's all right, this time there's no one here to see you but me…' he murmured, pushing the bunched dress down to her slender hips as her oxygen-starved lungs struggled for breath.

He looked down at the sheer stretchy bandeau bra covering her heaving breasts and his mouth tilted up.

'You don't really need to wear this at all, do you?' he said, toying with the lace-trimmed edge of the narrow black band.

She stiffened defensively, arching back against the arm around her waist, but then his finger dipped to delicately trace the outline of a rigid nipple where it had eagerly flattened itself against the transparent mesh. Splinters of painful pleasure prickled through her swollen flesh as he continued in a tone of honeyed admiration, 'They're as tantalising as ripe apples, so pretty and round and firm that you don't need any artificial support….' His fingers moved to the adjacent peak, chafing it lightly through the thin fabric as his other hand skilfully flicked open the plastic catch at her back. There was no clumsy fumbling, nothing to disrupt the erotic spell he was weaving with his hands and mouth and voice.

'See,' he whispered as her bra followed the path of her dress and her creamy tip-tilted breasts swayed and settled high against her slender ribcage. It was all done so smoothly that Nora didn't have time to feel shy, although her breasts grew rosy under his caressing gaze. 'Firm and round and speckled with warm little freckles.' He drew her briefly against his naked chest, rubbing her dusky pink nipples back and forth against his skin, his hands cupping her shoulderblades. 'Now, let's see if they taste as sweet as they look and feel….'

He bent his head and sipped at the swollen tips, lapping at her with a delicate greed that made her head swim. She couldn't believe she had come so far so fast. Instead of the long, slow build-up she was used to, everything was happening with breakneck speed. With a little moan Nora sank her hand into his thick black hair, the silky strands sifting through her fingers as they clenched in convulsive pleasure. The bevelled edge of the desk, lightly padded by the folds of her discarded coat, cut into her bottom and trapped her crumpled dress around her hips as he tipped her back, attempting to rid them of the annoying impediment to greater intimacy. Squirming to help, Nora gasped as her elbow knocked against a neat stack of files, sending them spilling across the desk and floor.

He stifled the apology that automatically rose to her lips with a fiercely impatient kiss, sweeping her off her feet and stepping over the scattered mess to perch her on the padded arm of the nearby sofa, her dress still twisted around her legs. Nora clung to his satin-smooth shoulders, her mouth eagerly responding to his fiery demands, her heart knocking as she felt his left hand touch her knee beneath the folds of her dress. His teeth tugged at her lower lip, his hand sleeking up the inside of her thigh, finding the elastic top of her stocking and exploring the petal-soft skin just above it. Liquid heat exploded in her belly and she tried to clench her legs together to ease the ache he was creating, but his heavy thigh intruded, forcing them further apart.

Nora could feel the tension quivering in his whipcord muscles, the carnal hunger crouching for the kill. His body exuded a musky male scent that drugged her senses, her hands slipping on the sheen of sweat which coated his tawny skin. She dimly realised that she was no longer in control, if she ever had been.

'Wait—' she panted, jerking violently as she felt the brush of his fingers against the thin fabric which hid the creamy heart of her desire, almost fainting at the gush of pleasure released by the brief contact.

'I can't—' His prickly jaw rasped across her skin, creating a stinging trail of sweet pain as he ate his way down to her throbbing nipple. He suckled hotly, pushing up his knee until she was astride his leg. 'I need this too much…and so do you,' he growled roughly. She felt his arm tighten around her waist, dragging her weight down against his contracting muscles, setting up a friction that turned the delicious pressure between her legs into an electrifying thrill. 'Come on, baby—ride me,' he invited hoarsely, rocking her against his powerful thigh until she adopted his urgent rhythm. Her breathing quickened, her fingers digging into his naked chest, her eyes glazing over as her body responded recklessly to his primal urging. He threw his head back, his glittering eyes darkly triumphant as she began to ripple with tiny convulsions.

'That's right, baby, ride me all the way home…. Let me make it happen for you…' he coaxed huskily, his knowing fingers finding again that secret sweet spot, tracing the blossoming dampness of her bikini panties in a way that made something inside her ripen and burst. Her world shattered into a million pieces, an exquisite avalanche of pleasure cascading through her, carrying her over the brink of a sweeping precipice and flinging her far out into star-studded space. Suddenly she was in a floating free fall…spiralling into nothingness, and yet there was no fear, just a soaring sense of release, the wondrous freedom of realising that she could fly…!

When her eyes fluttered back into focus the fractured world had re-formed around her, forever changed. She was conscious of the damp bloom of her skin and the small aftershocks which rolled over her as she eased back against Blake's locked arms and met his hooded gaze. She could feel the coiled tension in his muscles and felt mortified as she realised what had happened.

She bit her lip and winced at its swollen sensitivity. 'I'm—'

'I hope you're not going to say you're sorry,' he interrupted her with a growl.

'But I—you—' Her freckled face was so enchantingly dismayed that his rigid jaw flickered with sultry amusement.

'I said I couldn't wait. I wanted you wild for me,' he said in a voice like smooth dark chocolate. 'I got what I wanted.'

'I—you did?' Her golden eyes were still muddied with doubt.

'It was incredibly sexy seeing you lose control,' he said,

flexing his hips between hers, letting her feel the iron-hard proof of his words. 'Wanna play turnabout?'

Not exactly sure what he was suggesting, Nora nervously licked her lips and he uttered a sharp groan. 'I take it that's a yes,' he said, divesting her of the trailing dress with a few quick tugs and sinking into a crouch to slide her daring shoes off her unresisting feet. On the way back up he trailed his fingers over the front of her stockings and plain white panties, while he pressed kisses into her dappled skin. But as he rose between her breasts he froze, a frown thundering across his brow.

'My God, what's this?' He touched the crimson abrasions on the side of her breast, recoiling as she winced.

'It's nothing...I told you before, I have very sensitive skin,' she said dismissively.

He swore under his breath, his eyes following the tell-tale path of reddened patches. 'Damn it, stop trying to take the blame for something that's entirely my fault!' He dragged his hand across the coarse black stubble on his chin. 'I haven't shaved since this morning; no wonder I almost rubbed you raw,' he castigated himself.

He sounded so horrified that she almost smiled. 'But you didn't. Really, it's all right.'

'No, it's not,' he said grimly. 'I hurt you. I wasn't think-ing—' He gently stroked her reddened breast and she trembled.

'Neither was I,' she tried to convince him. 'How could I have—uh—*you know*...if I thought what you were doing was painful?'

His eyes flamed. 'I'm likely to be a great deal less re-strained in the throes of an orgasm,' he said bluntly, disdain-ing her feeble euphemism. 'I'm bigger and stronger than you are. I don't want to risk hurting you like that when I'm inside you—I'm going to have a shave before I touch you again,' he said, stepping back from temptation.

Nora immediately felt self-conscious, wrapping her empty arms around her semi-nude body to disguise her lack of curves.

With a smouldering look at her innocently provocative

pose, Blake bent and picked up his shirt, dropping it loosely around her shoulders from whence it hung almost to her knees, scooping her hair out from under the collar and fluffing it out around her oval face.

'Better?' he commented, drawing the open sides across her breasts where they peeked at him from her sheltering arms, not hiding the fact that he found her unexpected shyness arousing.

'Hadn't you better pick up your jacket, too?' she said jerkily. 'You're supposed to be arranging for your suit to be cleaned—'

'I thought that was just an excuse for you to get my clothes off,' he murmured, and she lowered her eyes guiltily.

'It's still going to need professional treatment.'

'Especially since we seem to be adding a new category of stain,' he goaded, drawing her attention to the damp spot on his trousers where she had straddled his thigh.

Nora blushed at the graphic evidence of her violent excitement, her flustered reaction turning his mockery into smouldering concupiscence.

'Maybe I should have that shave before this conversation goes any further,' he said, dropping a quick hard kiss on to her parted lips. 'Feel free to help yourself from the mini-bar; anything I have is yours…'

And with all my worldly goods I thee endow? Nora flinched at the interpretation that popped into her head. She knew he was talking about a glass of wine and a bag of nuts, not a lifetime of loving trust and mutual sharing.

Nora snaked her arms into the sleeves of his shirt as he headed for the bathroom, her eyes falling on the shambles they had made of the desk. In her confused emotional state it suddenly seemed vitally important to restore a sense of order to her physical surroundings. Perhaps that way she might bring some order to her chaotic feelings, find her way back to that liberating sense of *rightness* that she had felt whilst in his arms.

'What are you doing?'

She turned, papers slipping from her nerveless hand, her

eyes widening at his altered appearance. He wore a plush white three-quarter length towelling robe with the hotel's monogram discreetly embroidered on the breast pocket. He was frowning, but more in impatience than suspicion, and she waved one hand helplessly in the air.

'Just tidying up—trying to make myself useful…'

'Forget it,' he ordered dismissively. 'I didn't bring you here to play the domestic.' He caught her fluttering hand and tugged her towards him, lifting her palm to his still scratchy chin. 'I've decided I need a shower as well as a shave. I came to the party straight from work, in the same clothes I've been wearing all day.'

He lowered her hand to the burnished wedge of chest revealed by his loosely tied bathrobe, holding it there as he walked slowly backwards, drawing her along after him. 'If you have a compulsion for neatness, I'm sure you prefer your lovers to be freshly laundered…'

Nora could feel the heavy beat of his heart reverberating through flesh and bone. 'You don't have to bother on my account,' she said breathlessly, obliquely informing him that she liked his earthy male aroma.

He tipped his head to one side, his mellow voice caressing. 'For *my* sake, then.'

His eyes ran over her pale limbs, glimmering at him through the gaps in his shirt. 'I rather thought I might entice you to join me. You can make yourself useful as my soap bearer….'

He had reached the door of the steamy bathroom, the sound of the pulsing shower-head within almost drowned out by the thunder of blood in Nora's ears.

'Perhaps while I'm shaving you might like to wash my back—and anything else that takes your fancy…' he drawled.

He must know that she found *everything* about him wildly fanciable! The provocative admission trembled on the tip of her tongue, until she glanced past him and saw the gleaming empty bath next to the heat-misted glass shower cabinet.

In her mind's eye the bath expanded to take up the whole

room, her memory filling it with a kaleidoscope of flickering images that made her desire curdle in her stomach.

Nightmare reality crashed into her fantasy-fuelled dream world.

What on earth was she *doing*?

She fell back, slipping her hand out of his, flattening it defensively over her heart.

His eyebrows rose. 'No?' Clearly, rejection was a rather startling novelty.

'I—I think…I'd rather not, if you don't mind,' she managed lightly, edging further out of sight of the bath and the spectral frolics that had visited her with a degrading sense of *déjà vu*.

She braced herself for a backlash of wounded male pride, but Blake's grey eyes were merely quizzical.

'Don't tell me that you have a phobia about water, too?' he said.

Nora shook her head dumbly, tucking a curl behind her ear with a nervous gesture that caused his eyes to flicker upwards and an enlightened smile to dawn on his saturnine face.

'But of course…you don't want to get your hair wet—I quite understand.' His good-humoured resignation spoke of an intimate knowledge of the vanity of women. 'In that case, I'll be as quick as I can.' He turned her around and sent her on her way with a caressing pat of her sleek bottom. 'Meantime why don't you slip into something more comfortable? I'm sure you'll find the bed a perfect fit….'

Out in the hallway Nora put her shaking hands up to her hot cheeks. He was expecting her to be nestled on his pillow when he got out of the shower, eager and willing for another hot bout of mindless sex. Only this time he wasn't planning to restrain himself, and he had every reason to expect her to deliver the full bill of goods.

What had she been trying to prove with her craziness— that she had no more respect for herself than Ryan did?

She had never subscribed to the throwaway society. She

had secretly felt sorry for those people who drifted from partner to partner, substituting sex for emotional intimacy. And yet here she was, about to leap into bed with a total stranger. If she went through with this, Nora knew that she would utterly despise herself tomorrow.

She was shivering as she hurried back into the main room and scrambled into her own clothes, terrified that he was going to finish showering before she escaped.

She briefly thought about leaving him a note, but didn't dare take the time to hunt for pen and paper. Besides, what would she say?

Thanks for the mind-blowing orgasm, sorry I can't stick around to return the favour.

He was going to be furious enough that she had run out on him; there was no point in adding insult to injury by rubbing his nose in the fact. She couldn't even explain her behaviour to *herself*, let alone to *him*.

She snatched up her umbrella and bag and bundled her coat off the desk, her heart stuttering as she heard the low roar of the shower suddenly cease. Adrenaline pumped through her veins. 'Oh, God, oh, God, oh, God,' she chanted under her breath, darting for the door of the suite, shoes in hand. To her horror she discovered that Blake had flipped the security bolt when they came in and her sweaty fingers slipped on the shiny metal as she tried to disengage it without a betraying click.

Unfortunately, as she dashed out into the hallway, the inside door handle caught on the ankle strap of one of the dangling shoes, jerking it off her crooked finger. It banged against the wall and bounced back inside the room with a soft thump.

'Nora?'

Nora stared helplessly back at the stranded shoe as the door snicked closed in her face. It only took her a split second to decide to cut her losses. She ran down the hall and jammed the end of the umbrella on the button for the aeons that it seemed to take the lift to arrive, all the while casting panicked looks over her shoulder. He might glance out into the hall when he discovered she was gone, but surely he wouldn't bother to follow her? And, even if he did, he would have to dress first—that gave her at least a couple of minutes' grace.

A couple was all she needed. When the lift doors finally opened Nora blundered in, elbowing aside a clutch of Japanese tourists in order to take command of the controls.

For the price of a shoe, her freedom was won.

CHAPTER FIVE

NORA watched Kelly bounce out through the front door of their apartment building and down the short flight of damp steps to the footpath, her short shock of bright red hair glowing like a match in the bright morning sunlight.

Nora sank lower in the seat of her ageing Citroën, her hands whitening on the steering wheel, thankful that she had pulled in behind the line of parked cars near the end of the street to wait for her flatmate to leave for work…late, as usual.

Kelly was a PA in the public relations department at Maitlands, but her hours were hugely flexible thanks to the amount of social junketing with clients she was obliged to do.

When her previous flatmate had decided to move to Sydney a few months ago, Nora had posted an ad on the company's computer bulletin board. Kelly's outgoing personality and enthusiasm for life had persuaded her that the bubbly twenty-one-year-old would be fun to have around. It had only been after she moved in that Nora had begun to realise that their ideas of fun didn't always coincide.

She watched Kelly walk jauntily off towards the bus stop around the corner. It didn't seem fair that the hard-partying Kelly should be brimming with health and vitality, while Nora squinted through bleary red eyes, her mouth puckered with horrible dryness, her head squeezed in the vice-like grip of a vicious hangover. Of course, Kelly had been able to enjoy all the comforts of home last night, whereas Nora had had to make do with a depressing motel room and the spurious sympathy of a bottle of eighty-per-cent-proof vodka. And she didn't even *like* vodka!

The feeling, she had since found out, was entirely mutual.

As soon as Kelly turned the corner, Nora coaxed the Citroën's temperamental engine back into life and eased out from the line of cars at the kerb, driving down to slot into her usual parking place amongst the other residents' vehicles.

She got out of the car, moving carefully so as not to jolt her painful head, still brooding over the reasons for her enforced exile.

By the time she had reached her car last night she had been alternately sweating and shivering, almost semi-hysterical with relief. As she'd navigated her way through the saturated streets she'd vowed that she would never, *ever*, behave so irresponsibly again—no matter *what* the provocation. Or the temptation!

Operating on auto-pilot, she had instinctively headed for the security of her own home and had been shattered when she'd turned into her street and spied a familiar silver BMW parked outside the apartment and the lights in Kelly's corner bedroom glowing cosily behind drawn blinds.

Ryan certainly hadn't wasted any time, she had thought numbly. He must have left the party straight after Nora and raced over for more fun and games with Kelly. How many other times had the pair of them taken reckless advantage of Nora's absence?

Anger balled in her stomach. Ryan always liked to have the last word in an argument. What if he had arranged with Kelly to wait around and confront Nora when she eventually arrived home?

Home. That was a laugh. A home was supposed to be somewhere you felt safe, a protective fortress against the slings and arrows of misfortune.

And now that had been taken from her, too.

Nora had wanted to storm inside and scream at the pair to get out. The lease of the compact two-bedroomed ground-floor apartment had always been in her sole name, so she had every right to ask Kelly to leave, but she couldn't very well do it tonight—not in her current woefully vulnerable state; not until she had shored up her defences again.

She had several friends who would put her up, but most of them were friends with Ryan, too, and right now she felt too emotionally exhausted to run the gauntlet of the inevitable questions if she turned up distraught and begging for shelter.

So she had put her foot back down on the accelerator and sought out the nearest low-rise motel, a rather down at heel establishment which included an hourly rate on its dog-eared price card. Unlocking her door, she had noticed the neon-lit window of a liquor wholesaler across the road, in which a sexy female mannequin sported a sign promising a free T-shirt with every purchased bottle of famous-brand vodka.

When Nora had walked out of the store she'd been carrying not only the vodka and a black T-shirt but also the mannequin's fluorescent green leggings. She might have been stranded in the twilight zone but she wasn't going to spend a minute longer than necessary in the dress that had come to symbolise her stupidity.

And, having bought the vodka, it had seemed a good idea to stave off some of her misery by opening it. It would make a fine title for a reality TV show, thought Nora, as she opened the car boot: *When Good Ideas Go Bad!*

The vodka idea would certainly go down as famous in the annals of bad decisions she had made. She drank, but never to excess, and now she wondered why anyone would knowingly court this kind of physical torture.

Carrying the company laptop she had forgotten to take inside when she had eagerly rushed home to try on her new dress, and with the rest of her things stuffed into the liquor store carrier bag, Nora nudged the boot of the Citroën closed with her elbow, wincing as the heavy thunk rattled her aching skull.

A tall solidly built man in a rumpled white shirt was getting out of a black van across the road as Nora approached the steps, her mind concentrated on getting to the top without her head falling off. The first thing she was going to do when she got inside was make a huge pot of coffee, she thought longingly.

'Excuse me?'

Nora looked gingerly around at the politely forceful voice. The rumpled shirt had a face to match—fiftyish, lived-in, blandly unremarkable except for sharp periwinkle-blue eyes.

'Miss Lang?'

She was trying to work enough fur out of her mouth to answer, conscious of his arrested survey of her vodka-touting T-shirt and bilious leggings, when he added, 'Miss *Nora* Lang?'

There was a hint of amusement in his tone which rubbed at her raw nerves. 'Who wants to know?' she said with uncharacteristic rudeness.

'These are for you.'

He held up the sheaf of red roses he had been carrying half-concealed at his side, and Nora was startled into feeling a momentary lift of her spirits.

Her mouth began to curve into an involuntary smile. 'For *me*? Are you sure?'

'If you're Eleanor Lang from apartment 1A.'

'Yes, that's me.' Her elation died and her smile inverted itself. Only one person she knew had any reason to send her flowers. She recoiled as if they were plague-ridden. 'I don't want them!'

He seemed taken aback at the heated response. 'Look— I'm just making a delivery, OK?'

She glared. Any colour would have been unacceptable, but red was rubbing added salt in the wound. They were even more offensive considering that Ryan had never bothered to send her flowers before.

'Then you can just deliver them right back where they came from,' she declared, her contempt recharging her dwindling stores of energy. 'And you can tell that—that *snake* who sent them that he's a moron if he thinks he can bribe me with a measly bunch of flowers! He's never going to get back what he lost. And when this goes public I'm going to make sure that everyone knows how it went down. Maybe people won't be so quick to trust him in future, if they know his personal morality stinks!'

She stumped up the steps, feeling slightly better for having vented her spleen, even if only at an innocent by-stander. The poor guy had looked quite stunned by her outburst. She glanced back as she went into the building and saw him walking back to his van with the rejected roses, cell-phone plastered to his ear…reporting his aborted mission, no doubt, she thought with a bitter sense of satisfaction.

Entering the flat, Nora felt none of her usual welcome sense of homecoming. To her dismay she felt alien in her own envi-ronment, tense and resentful of all the signs of Kelly's occu-pation—the open fashion magazine left on the couch, the unwashed dishes in the sink, the pile of ironing draped over a chair, the drips of nail varnish on the coffee table. Usually Nora was tolerant of her flatmate's habitual untidiness, but now her thoughtlessness seemed insultingly close to contempt.

It had been too much to hope for that Kelly had already started to pack up her things, Nora brooded as she switched on the coffee-maker, but surely she must have realised that she would have to move out? Until she did, the atmosphere in the flat would be hideously strained and uncomfortable.

A prowl around showed no evidence that Ryan had ever been there, but venturing into the bathroom made Nora's gorge rise and she hastily snatched up her toothbrush and re-treated. For the sake of personal hygiene she knew she'd have to get over her atavistic horror at the sight of her bath. Maybe she should get the place ritually exorcised!

A quick brush of her aching teeth and an ingestion of freshly brewed coffee made Nora feel a trifle less like dying. Anxious to change out of the tacky clothes, she paused to look at herself in her bedroom mirror and grimaced. Her eyes looked glassy and sunken and the stubborn remnants of her mascara deepened the bruised shadows that surrounded them. She had washed her hair at the motel, using the meagre courtesy sachet of shampoo, but the establishment hadn't run to hair-dryers and now her curls were an uncontrollable tumble around her pale face, her bleached complexion accentuating the ginger freckles and the faint whisker burns glowing on her cheek as well as on the skin above the drooping neckline of the baggy hip-length T-shirt.

She looked like a woman who had been used and abused, she thought bitterly—which was pretty much the truth.

Only...she had done her share of using, too, Nora reminded herself in a smothering of guilt. She had shamelessly courted danger and almost been consumed by it.

She kicked off her shoes and hooked her fingers into the waistband of the bright green leggings. Perhaps once she was back in her own clothes she would feel more like herself.

She tensed at the sound of the doorbell, and then relaxed as she told herself that it couldn't be Kelly—and Ryan also had his own key, although he had never given Nora similar free access to *his* apartment.

Nora's mood swung from brooding self-doubt to angry anticipation as she walked to the door. If it was that flower delivery man back again he was going to get himself a fresh ear-blistering.

She whipped open the door, eyes sparkling with challenge. 'Hello, Nora.'

For an instant she gaped, paralysed with shock and embarrassment. 'Blake! W-what are you doing here?'

He bared his teeth in a lethally unpleasant smile. 'Guess.'

She didn't like the sound of the sibilant threat and instinctively tried to whip the door closed, but that first instant of unwariness had given him all the edge he needed.

A muscular hand slapped against the wood and slowly applied the pressure to widen the gap to a full body-width.

'I—I'm just about to go to work,' she lied, struggling to resist the inexorable pressure.

His eyelids flickered downwards. 'Dressed like that? I doubt if it'll meet the Maitlands dress code.'

'How do you know where I work?' she croaked, the muscles of her arm straining against the losing battle with the door.

'I asked around.'

She wasn't fooled by the laconic drawl. Repressed fury oozed from his every pore.

'Where have you been all night?' he demanded, as if he had every right to know.

She tried to gather her defences. 'Look, I'm sorry I left the way I did, but I really don't have time to discuss it right now—'

'Make time,' he said, leaning more heavily on the door. 'I have something that belongs to you.'

Yes—her innocence. Before she had gone off with Blake MacLeod she had quaintly imagined that she could handle the kind of risk he represented. But she had never dreamed that danger would turn up on her own doorstep!

'I thought you might want it back...'

He was dangling something from his other hand, distracting her from his savage expression. Her wildly expensive new shoe. Shades of a fairy-tale romance...he had tracked her down to return her lost shoe!

A rush of relief weakened her grip on the door and, before she could register the unlikelihood of him performing such an extreme act of altruism he rammed through it, kicking it shut behind him with his polished heel. His head swivelled as he made a scowling survey of the room, seemingly unimpressed with the serenely comfortable decor which reflected Nora's unfussy taste. This was certainly no gallant Prince Charming come looking for his Cinderella. In a dark blue pinstriped suit and navy shirt and tie he looked ominously like a storm cloud looking for somewhere to pitch his lightning and thunder.

He turned to face her and Nora fell back under the frontal assault of his molten silver gaze.

'H-How did you find me?' She knew it hadn't just been a matter of looking her up in the phone book. After a number of nuisance phone calls the previous year she had obtained an unlisted number.

He pitched the shoe on to her couch. 'Your credit card receipt confirmed your name; the rest was relatively easy, given my resources.'

Her stomach lurched. He had gone back to the hotel boutique? She didn't know whether to be flattered or horrified.

'You thought I might have been lying about who I was?' she croaked.

'Well, I didn't think you'd really be fool enough to try and screw me under your real name.'

She stiffened, fighting a hot wave of shame. 'There's no need to be crude!'

His mouth compressed to a cruel line. 'Oh, there's every need. After all, what you did to me was the essence of crudity.'

She put her hands to her blazing cheeks. 'So I changed my mind—that's supposed to be a woman's prerogative,' she said, her words muffled with mortification.

'The hell you did,' he grated, stalking closer, deliberately menacing her with his size. 'You got me precisely where you wanted me, and I played right into your hands by acting the gentleman. I won't make that mistake again.'

She swallowed hard, dismayed by her body's response to his nearness. Surely he didn't mean to pick up where they'd left off last night? She ran her damp hands down the uneven seams of the cheap T-shirt.

'I—I don't understand,' she said, bewildered by his strange intensity. Why was he making it sound as if *she* was the dangerous one?

'Tell me, Nora, is there some personal history between us that I don't know about? Did I reject you at some point? Have I dated someone you know or slept with your sister—?'

She backed further into the room, wide-eyed with confusion at his sudden change of tack. 'I don't have a sister.' Only a brother who was living in Florida, well out of range of any screams for help.

'There must be something—some reason that you're willing to go to such lengths to discredit me,' he said. 'Is this some kind of vendetta? What's so important that you were willing to prostitute yourself for the sake of getting even with me?'

The heat drained from her cheeks. 'Vendetta?' she repeated shakily, putting a hand to her throbbing head.

She knew she had acted like a reckless idiot, but a *prostitute*? The accusation was too absurd to be insulting. 'I don't know what you're talking about.'

'Come on, Nora, a woman doesn't call a man a snake and threaten to ruin him without some very personal feelings being involved—'

'I never called you a snake!' she protested.

His face tightened in contempt. 'If you're going to lie, Nora, at least try and make it believeable—'

'I am not lying!' she shouted at him, almost blowing off the top of her head in the process, her slight body vibrating with outrage.

A sneer curled the corner of his mouth. 'Doug reported your conversation verbatim. You want me to call him up as a witness? Or was that comment about a bribe a hint that you'd prefer to be paid? Unfortunately for you, my stinking *personal morality* draws the line at giving in to blackmail. I'll see you in hell before I give you a cent!'

Nora had the strange feeling she was there already. She pressed a fist against her churning stomach as a light belatedly went on inside her fogged brain.

The man with the roses! 'I— D-do you mean—the flowers were from *you*?' she stuttered weakly.

He stilled, his eyes narrowing. 'You told Doug you knew who sent them.'

'I thought I did—I thought it was Ryan,' she murmured,

collapsing down on to the oatmeal-coloured easy chair. 'Why did you send me roses?'

'I didn't,' he replied bluntly, shattering any romantic illusions she might have been building up. He planted himself in front of her, hands thrust into his pockets as if to physically restrain himself from putting them around her pale throat and throttling the truth out of her. 'That was Doug confirming your identity without putting you on the alert. I'd described you, but he wanted to be sure he had the right woman before he let me know that you'd turned up. I'm not surprised he had doubts—you look like hell.'

He had no need to sound so pleased about it!

'That's strange, since I'm feeling so fantastic,' she said in a voice that dripped with sarcasm. She tipped her head back and glared up at him. 'Wait a minute. Are you telling me that you had this Doug person watching the flat, waiting for me?'

He seemed to relish her outrage, answering her question with his own. 'Your flatmate said you hadn't been home, so where did you go after you left me, Nora? Who was it you had arranged to meet?'

She bristled with hostility at the mention of Kelly. 'Nobody. Not that it's any business of yours! Look, just because we almost—almost—' She found herself floundering and he supplied her with a crude word that struck her like a bullet.

'—*slept* together,' she substituted with ragged dignity, 'it doesn't give you the right to come around here and interrogate me.'

'Would you rather discuss it with the police?'

'The *police*?'

He looked grimly satisfied at her dismay. 'You either deal with me or deal with them.'

He had to be bluffing! 'Are you crazy? It's not against the law for a woman to decide not to be sexually intimate with you...' She trailed off, remembering just how very intimate things had got between them before she had lost her nerve.

The extraordinarily vivid memories of their passionate encounter had haunted her all night.

'It is, however, illegal to steal,' he said harshly.

Thinking about the pleasure that she had stolen from him without giving him anything in return, she blushed. She had melted like honey at each stroke of his skilful fingers, selfishly absorbed in her own gratification to the exclusion of everything else.

'I didn't take anything you weren't offering,' she denied feverishly.

'Is that going to be your defence in court?'

'Oh, don't be ridiculous. You can't sue me for not giving you an orgasm!'

'*What?*'

He looked as stunned as she had a few moments ago, and Nora was drenched in scalding embarrassment.

She jumped to her feet, her uncertain balance almost sending her reeling into his chest. He automatically reached out to steady her and a hot thrill shot up her arm. She snatched it away, rubbing at the tingling skin, humiliated to feel her nipples firming and the skin along her inner thighs tighten. Oh, God, one night of almost-sin and she was turning into a raging nymphomaniac! What on earth had made her think that he was talking about *sex*? She closed her eyes and felt the room revolve sickeningly around her.

'*What* did you just say?'

Her eyes popped open to meet his darkly incredulous gaze. He looked as if he couldn't believe his ears, and she hoped that he wouldn't.

'I—nothing,' she mumbled, wrapping her arms defensively across her chest. She felt the whisker-burns he had given her glowing like brands on her face and breasts. *His* brand. She couldn't help noticing that, this morning, the hard jaw which had rasped at her skin was as smooth and glossy as polished teak. 'I guess we were talking at cross purposes. I'm not thinking straight—I had way too much to drink last night,' she admitted feverishly, by way of diversion.

'Are you trying to claim that you did what you did to me because you were *drunk*?' His deep voice was coldly scathing.

She wished she could blame the booze, but she wasn't going to demean herself even further. 'I wasn't *then*, no.' She pushed the curls back from her face with a limp hand. 'I only started on the vodka later—'

His eyes dipped to the inviting slogan on her T-shirt. 'When you were celebrating your successful getaway?'

'I wasn't *celebrating*, damn it, I was trying to *forget*!' Her stomach contracted with the force of her protest and she groaned.

'What's the matter?'

Desperate to escape from that laser-like stare, she clapped a hand over her mouth. 'I think I'm going to be sick!' She started for the bathroom, only to abruptly change course for the kitchen, as yet blessedly free of dire memories. Her nausea was nowhere as bad as it had been when she woke up, but at least she would gain a few minutes of precious privacy in which to regain her composure!

Unfortunately Blake appeared unfazed by the prospect of watching her vomit. He followed close on her heels, blocking off the only exit from the compact galley kitchen. Silently cursing him, she turned on the cold tap and ran it over her wrists, splashing droplets on to her clammy cheeks as she bent over the sink, cringing as the sun streaming in the window stitched a line of red dots across her gritty vision.

'You do look rather green,' he commented maliciously, resting his hip against the edge of the white Formica bench. 'But I thought it was just the reflection of those ghastly pants you're wearing.'

'Oh, please—don't try and make me feel better.'

Again, her sarcasm bounced off his impenetrable hide. 'There's only one thing that'll do that. They do say confession is good for the soul.'

She could never, in a million years, see him as a priest. 'Are you offering me absolution?'

'Retribution is more my style.' He let her see the volcanic temper still simmering in his eyes. 'Here.' He had rinsed out a used glass from the bench and filled it with water. 'The best cure for a hangover.'

Given his crackling hostility, Nora was startled by the thoughtfulness of the gesture. 'I've already had some coffee—'

'Water is better for the dry horrors. Drink it.'

Because she knew he was right, and she was feeling too rotten to dispute his right to order her around, she obeyed, taking small sips to spin out the glass as long as possible.

As she tilted the glass for the last drops, a tiny rivulet trickled down her wrist from her wet hand and dripped on to the front of her T-shirt. They both looked down at the silver droplets streaking down between her breasts and Nora saw that her stiffened nipples were tenting the thin black cotton. She flushed and something hotter than temper flared deep in his eyes.

She hurriedly clattered the empty glass back on to the bench. 'Well, if you'll excuse me, I really should be getting ready for work now. It's after nine and I was supposed to have started at eight—' She made a tentative movement but he refused to shift, trapping her in the patch of uncomfortably bright sunlight.

'I doubt it.'

Her mouth was suddenly bone-dry again. 'W-what makes you say that?'

'Because you've already phoned in sick this morning.'

'How do you—?' Her mouth snapped shut. He or his tame snoop must have tried to call her at work. This was what she got for being a conscientious employee! 'They're not supposed to give out that kind of information,' she said sharply.

He shrugged. 'I said I was your lover and we'd had a tiff… It's amazing how indiscreet people can be when they think they're giving romance a helping hand.'

'You *didn't*!' she gasped, then realised how naive and gullible she sounded. He had probably only been winding her up. Would she never learn? 'Oh, very funny!'

Her withering glare had no effect. 'Do you see me laughing?'

She made one last attempt at reasoning him out of his implacable hostility. 'Look, I admit that I shouldn't have run off last night, but I made a mistake—'

'And now you have a chance to rectify it. Give me what I want and I'll consider us even.'

Her stomach quivered. 'Y-You mean...here?' she squeaked. '*Now*?'

She had a fevered vision of him taking her right there on her kitchen floor, in the full dazzle of sunlight, sliding her against the hard glossy vinyl as he drove ruthlessly for the satisfaction which she had denied him last night.

'Yes, now. Before things go any further. That is, if they haven't already...'

The implicit threat in his tone nipped her torrid fantasy in the bud. The thumping ache in her head almost obliterated coherent thought, but she had sense enough to decide she wasn't going to leap to any more embarrassing conclusions.

'Perhaps you'd better spell out exactly what it is you want from me,' she said warily.

His eyes ignited under the scowling black brows, scorching her with his fury. 'It's a bit late to try and act innocent,' he growled. 'We both know you're as guilty as sin. I want the property you lifted from my hotel room.' He straightened, exuding a powerful menace. 'So, are you going to hand it over quietly—or are we going to have to do this the hard way?'

CHAPTER SIX

'*PROPERTY*—?' Nora broke off, a smile of relieved enlightenment dawning on her pallid face. 'Ohh—oh you mean *that*…'

There was no answering humour in his expression. 'Yes, *that*,' he echoed grimly.

'I told you I wasn't thinking straight this morning, otherwise I would have clicked straight away,' she said, embarrassed by her obtuseness. 'Of course you want your disk back…I'm really sorry for the mix up. I'll just go and get it—'

She moved, confidently expecting him to give way, but he didn't and she walked straight into his solid chest. His hands closed around her upper arms as her bare feet stubbed themselves against his polished shoes. She gave a little squeak as he lifted her until her face was level with his.

'Go where, exactly?'

'To my bedroom,' she gasped, conscious of her dangling legs bumping against his iron thighs, of the effortless ease with which he had lifted her. 'If you'll put me down, I'll fetch it for you—'

'Like an obedient little bitch? I don't think so.' His acid words were etched with cynicism. 'I'm sure you'll understand if I insist on coming with you. I wouldn't like you to vanish on me again.'

'For goodness' sake, what do you think I'm going to do? Climb out the window?' she protested shakily, pushing against his iron shoulders to little effect.

'At this point, I wouldn't put anything past you,' he said, setting her back down on the ground, but keeping a firm grip on one slender elbow.

'Don't be silly,' she said, hurrying into the bedroom, trying to ignore his overwhelming closeness and the electric tingle of his fingertips against her skin. 'It's not as if I *meant* to take it. It must have got caught up in the folds of my coat when I grabbed it off your desk last night. I was going to courier it back to you today—'

'Really?' He drew out the word into a sceptical drawl.

Nora had always thought her bedroom was airy and spacious, but as soon as Blake stepped through the door the proportions suddenly seemed to shrink and the oxygen supply dip below the level of comfort.

'It's not usually this messy,' she was annoyed to find herself explaining, hastily gathering up the scattered clothing from the rumpled bedcover. 'I—I left in rather a hurry yesterday.'

His all-encompassing glance had taken in the orderly possessions on her mirrored dressing-table, the neatly coordinated clothes hanging in the open wardrobe and the tidy row of photo frames on her tallboy.

'Are these your parents?'

'What?' She looked up from rummaging in the bulging side pocket of the soft-sided case that held her laptop to see him studying a photo of herself aged ten, flanked by a blond couple exchanging laughing looks over her nut-brown head. 'Oh, no, they died when I was little—that's my father's sister and her husband—Aunt Tess and Uncle Pat—they brought my brother Sean and me up.' Her voice was coloured with unconscious warmth as she attempted to take the edge off his hostility by adding, 'They hadn't planned on having kids themselves, so we were a bit of a drag on their lifestyle, but they never made us feel unwanted—'

'Do they still live in Invercargill?'

She stiffened. She was sure she hadn't mentioned her origins last night. He must have discovered it while delving into her identity. It gave her a shivery feeling to think that he knew things about her that she hadn't chosen to tell him. Not that she had anything to hide, she consoled herself. The fact that she had lived the majority of her life in a small town on the southernmost tip of the South Island was a point in her favour as far as she was concerned.

'Yes, they do. As I'm sure your paid snoop will confirm,' she said tartly, pulling out the compact disk in its clear plastic protector. She had been a self-deluded idiot to think for even one second that Blake MacLeod's unfinished business with her was anything to do with what had happened between them in his room last night.

He turned. 'A wise man knows his enemies.'

'I'm *not* your enemy,' she protested, slapping the disk into his outstretched hand. 'And I don't steal,' she added with all the force of angry sincerity. 'When I found this lying on the back seat of my car last night, I had no idea where it came from—'

He stared impassively down into her wide-set eyes. 'Copies?'

'I beg your pardon?'

'I want any and all copies you've made,' he said, slipping the CD into the inside pocket of his jacket. 'And don't bother to tell me you didn't burn any, because I wouldn't believe you.'

She gritted her teeth. He made it sound as if good computer housekeeping was a criminal act. 'Since I didn't know what the disk was, of course I made a back-up copy before I tried to open it,' she informed him.

'Is that where you were last night…at your office, downloading my confidential data on to Maitlands' network? I suppose you were hoping I wouldn't notice anything was missing until today. Unluckily for you, I decided to do some more work after you ran out on me—'

'Don't be ridiculous! I never went near the office,' she said tightly, massaging her aching temple. 'Why would I? I told you, I didn't know what the disk was, and I couldn't very well return it until I found out who it belonged to, could I? I happened to have my laptop with me, so I used that to check it out.' She found the copy she had made and shoved it at him. 'There. Now, feel free to leave after you apologise!'

Her bitter sarcasm had little effect. 'Did you make a printout or email it to anyone?'

Her generous mouth thinned. 'Of course not. And, no, I'm not going to turn over my computer to you—you'll just have to take my word for it.'

'And why should I do that?'

'Because I'm a very trustworthy person,' she snapped.

His steely gaze was unrelenting as it inspected her shiny face. 'You expect me to believe this was all an unfortunate coincidence…? That you didn't seduce me in order to gain access to information in my hotel room—'

'Any seduction going on was entirely mutual!' she choked.

A faint gleam appeared in his grey eyes. 'You have an odd idea of mutuality. Or do you usually get your kicks from picking up strange men and skipping out on them as soon as you've taken your own pleasure?'

She clenched her hands at her sides. 'I don't *usually* pick up men at *all*,' she rebutted fiercely. 'I don't go in for meaningless one-night stands—'

His voice deepened into a dark drawl that wrapped around her like black velvet. 'Then why did you invite yourself to my hotel room? Why did you lead me on the way you did…let me undress you, touch you, taste you…?'

She shivered at his evocative words, her skin prickling from her scalp to her toes at the erotic memory of his sensuous skill, her limbs weighted with a strange heaviness that had nothing to do with fatigue.

'Look, you've got your disk back and I've apologised; what more do you expect?' she said raggedly. 'Can't we just forget about last night?'

'No, I'm afraid we can't,' he said, with an implacable gentleness that seemed more threatening than his former raging temper. 'Because we both know that you opened and read those files—didn't you, Nora?'

His soft words made it more of a statement than a question and her gaze dropped to the item in question, her thick brown lashes screening the guilty expression in her eyes as she watched him pocket it with its twin. 'It was security protected.'

A sceptical sound rumbled in his chest at her evasive answer. 'R-i-g-h-t. And you're a hacker from way back. You're one of Maitlands' resident computer whizkids, constantly manipulating the interface between man and the sharp end of technology.' He flaunted his newly acquired knowledge of her background with ruthless intent: 'You took papers at Otago University while you were employed there, but you never bothered doing a full degree course—you'd already proven yourself in the market-place, hawking your software skills since you were in high school. Coming up against a good security block like the one on this disk would be a challenge rather than a deterrent to someone like you.' His cool contempt was not unmixed with admiration. 'Given the time, opportunity and Internet access, bypassing it would be well within your capabilities. So don't insult my intelligence by pretending to be an innocent fluff-head.'

She winced at the accuracy of his insight, his accusing words pounding into her tender skull like hot nails. 'OK, OK—so I peeked at your boring reports,' she admitted sulkily. 'I know I shouldn't have—but, well—it was a choice of that or the porno channel.'

'What in the hell are you talking about?'

His abrupt scowl made her regret her loose tongue. 'I—I stayed the night in a motel a couple of blocks from here.' The words dragged themselves reluctantly out of her mouth. 'I couldn't sleep, the TV reception was dreadful and the in-house video channel was playing adult movies, so I decided to pass the time with my laptop.'

Finding that her computer was still in the car had been the saviour of her sanity through the long lonely hours. She had welcomed the company of a trusted old friend, one who was endlessly entertaining and who had never let her down. And the mystery disk had been a convenient distraction from her personal problems. With a complex puzzle to focus on, Nora had been able to shove her own misery to the back of her mind, her steady ingestion of vodka muffling any whispers of conscience.

'A motel? What were you doing at a motel?' Blake's face had tightened with renewed suspicion, his nostrils flaring with distaste.

Nora squirmed inwardly under his accusatory gaze.

'It's a long story.' she muttered. 'A very long, very *boring* story,' she hastened to emphasise as she saw his eyes flare with curiosity. 'And it really has nothing to do with any of this…'

He put his hands on his hips, his sleek dark suit cloaking a lean frame that bespoke both immovable object and irresistible force. 'Why don't you let *me* be the judge of that?'

She felt too fragile to keep battling his bull-headed stubbornness.

'If you'll just get me a couple of aspirin from the bathroom, I'll tell you,' she stalled, directing him with a limp wave of her hand. 'They're in the mirrored cabinet above the basin.'

She groaned as he remained welded to the spot. 'Oh, for goodness' sake—I'm not going to run away as soon as your back is turned. I have a thumping great headache and I don't want to go in there right now, OK?'

'Why? Is there a body in the bath?'

His sarcasm conjured up the images she was trying so hard to scrape out of her skull. 'In a manner of speaking,' she said, rubbing at her bloodshot eyes.

'Explain.'

She automatically baulked at the rapped-out order. 'Can't you get the aspirin first?'

'Stop whining and start talking.'

Nora had never whined in her life. Infuriated by his intransigence, she exploded and gave him an earful of her stored resentment, drawing a graphic picture of the sordid events of the previous day and taking a masochistic delight in painting all the gory details of her humiliating failure to satisfy the man she had honoured with her long-time affections.

'Is it any wonder that I didn't want to come home last night? I'd be happy never to see either of them ever again, but we all work for Maitlands so I'm stuck with having my nose rubbed in my stupidity five days a week.'

There was a crackling silence. 'So what was I supposed to be?' he asked with a distinct edge. 'Your revenge on the straying boyfriend?'

'No!' The instinctive denial came from the depths of her femininity, but was tempered by her innate honesty. 'Yes—no—maybe—I really don't know.' Nora slumped down on to the edge of the bed, closing her eyes and propping her elbows on her knees, resting her heavy head in her hands. 'Maybe it started out that way, but I don't know what I was thinking by the time I—we... It all seems so surreal now, like a bad dream....'

She heard him move away and was conscious of him using his cell-phone, but was too tired to strain to hear the low-voiced conversation and when next she opened her eyes it was to see him crouched in front of her, holding out two flat white pills and a half-filled glass of water. Disorientated, she blinked, wondering whether in her state of extreme tiredness she had dozed off.

'Thanks,' she said, and downed them quickly, puckering her mouth at the chalky taste. 'That wasn't arsenic, was it?' she joked weakly.

He eyed her pale face as he put aside the empty glass. 'Have you given me reason to want to murder you?'

She smiled weakly. Even if she had gained his sympathy, his trust was obviously not so easily obtained.

'Not that I can think of. I just thought—well—you might feel that I'd insulted your manhood...uh, the frail male ego and all that—'

He stood, towering over her. 'My ego is very healthy, thank you...particularly after last night. There's nothing more flattering for a man than to watch a woman come helplessly apart in his arms,' he mused in that dark and dangerous drawl. 'So violently aroused that she melts all over his fingers like sweet hot honey, and moans his name like a sexy mantra as she shudders to her first climax....'

Nora's lips parted, but not a breath of sound trickled out of her shocked mouth, a wave of heat chasing away her pallor.

'Or are you going to try and dismiss *that* as a bad dream, too?' he goaded silkily, his eyes riveted to her upturned face as he watched the wild flush creep up to her hairline. 'If you doubt my veracity as an eye-witness perhaps we could try a re-enactment to jog your obviously deficient memory....'

She shot off the bed as if the sheets were suddenly on fire. 'Uh, I think perhaps I will go in to work after all. I mean, I have to face up to Kelly and Ryan *some time*, don't I?' she babbled, raking the tangle of curls away from her hot cheeks.

'You're obviously still feeling pretty fragile right now.' He cut ruthlessly across her hectic tumble of words. 'Do you really think you're up to the *challenge* of confronting them in front of all your coworkers?' His subtle emphasis on the provocative word triggered a predictable bristling of Nora's pride.

'Of course I am,' she insisted thinly, despite a backbone that went to jelly at the thought. 'After all, *I've* done nothing to be ashamed of!'

'Quite.' Her gaze shot suspiciously to his and met an expression of such bland innocence that she frowned.

The brackets around his mouth deepened into a smile that made her stomach twist itself into fresh contortions. 'In that case, why don't you get dressed for work and allow me to drop you off?' he offered smoothly. 'It's the least I can do in the circumstances.'

She didn't want to dwell on the circumstances. 'Thanks, but I have my own car—'

'If you drank the amount you claim you did last night, then your blood alcohol level would still be well above the legal limit,' he pointed out sternly. 'What would have happened if you'd been involved in a car accident this morning?'

She was shocked to realise that the thought hadn't even occurred to her. She probably shouldn't have been behind the wheel last night either, given the several glasses of wine she had consumed on an empty stomach, she thought, appalled at her criminal self-absorption.

'Statistically, most car accidents happen within a few kilometres of home,' he said, piling on the guilt. 'I'd be reneging on my duty as a responsible citizen if I let you get behind the wheel again.'

She nibbled her lower lip. Why did the thought of the ruthlessly ambitious Blake MacLeod as a virtuous citizen set alarm bells ringing in the back of her mind?

'Does this mean that you've finally decided that I'm not a modern-day Mata Hari?' she ventured.

He gave her a measuring look. 'I suppose that depends on what you intend doing with the information you've unexpectedly acquired.'

'Nothing!' she was quick to assure him. 'It's of no matter to me if you want to acquire a *dozen* shipping companies—' She broke off as his fierce black brows snapped together. 'What?'

'I find that rather hard to believe,' he said, 'considering that one of Maitlands' leading clients is the preferred bidder for TranStar Shipping—the white knight elected to fight off big bad PresCorp's attempts to acquire a majority shareholding.'

'Is it?' She spread her fingers dismissively wide. 'I don't have anything to do with the acquisitions side of the business; I'm just a technician. Is *that* why you jumped to the ridiculous conclusion I was some sort of spy? Well, you don't have to worry about it, truly—because I really wasn't interested.' She pinned him with a hopeful look. 'Actually, my memory is pretty hazy on *everything* that happened last night.'

'But what you do recall of strategic value you'll no doubt feel honour bound to pass on to your employers.'

She frowned at his sardonic response. 'Not when the information was obtained unethically.'

There was a moment of stunned silence.

'You can't be *that* naive,' he said, in a voice so dry that it crackled.

She was stung by his obvious incredulity. 'It's not naive to have principles.' The tilt of her freckled nose indicated her haughty displeasure. 'Maybe if you were more trusting of people you might find yourself pleasantly surprised by the rest of humanity—'

'Like you were, you mean, when you stumbled in on your boyfriend and his busty blonde cavorting amongst the bubbles?'

She took the jab with a sharp intake of breath. 'It must be really depressing to be so cynical and pessimistic,' she counter-punched weakly.

'On the upside, I'm rarely disappointed in my expectations,' he parried. 'Shall I help myself to a cup of coffee while I'm waiting for you to change? Or do you intend to cut off your nose to spite your face and spurn my offer of a ride?'

He seemed to expect it, so she took perverse pleasure in disappointing his jaded expectations. 'Give me ten minutes.'

His mouth twisted downward as he backed towards the door. 'Don't make promises you can't keep. Women aren't programmed for a quick turn-around.'

Fifteen minutes later she stalked out of her room, bracing herself for a snide remark, and surprised Blake MacLeod delving in the laundry basket which sat on the washing machine at the far end of the kitchen.

'What on earth do you think you're doing?' she screeched, visions of perversion dancing in her head.

'Folding your clean laundry.'

She snatched the lacy black 36D quarter-cup bra out of his fingers and threw it back into the overflowing basket. 'That's not mine; it's all Kelly's—*my* laundry is over there!' She pointed to the neatly folded pile of fragrant clothes sitting on the fold-down ironing board. To her horror, lying on top was a pair of white cotton panties figured with cartoon rabbits, a pathetic contrast to Kelly's sexy wisps of lace.

'I see...' His voice was smoky with speculation as he turned to survey her boyish figure in the narrow buff skirt and creased short-sleeved white cotton shirt that she had hurriedly snatched out of her wardrobe.

'What do you *see*?' She regretted the snappish words the instant they were out of her mouth. She didn't need to be told she looked less than her best. She tightened her clammy grip on her laptop and hitched on the strap of her shoulder bag, trying to summon the stamina she would need to get through the rest of the day.

'I see that you're ready to go,' he said with an evasiveness that was more annoying than any critical remark. 'Are these your keys?'

Without waiting for an answer, he scooped them up from the bench where she had tossed them and smoothly shepherded her from the flat, locking the deadbolt and escorting her out into the dazzling sunshine. Nora's headache instantly flared as the hot needles of light stabbed into her brain and she submitted meekly to the firm hand in the small of her back which propelled her towards a long, sleek, low, wine-red coupé with tinted windows parked against the kerb. Eyes watering, she groped blindly in her shoulder bag for her dark glasses, muttering under her breath as they eluded her grasp.

He opened the passenger door of the car and she sank gratefully into the inviting dimness, still rummaging in her open bag.

'Here, let me put that in the boot for you and give you more leg-room,' he said, removing her laptop from her feet and suiting his action to his words.

He dipped his head as he returned to her open door. 'What's the matter?'

'I can't find my sunglasses,' she whimpered.

'I'm not surprised, given the quantity of clutter you seem to cart around with you,' came the unsympathetic answer.

She gritted her teeth as she tried to think up a suitably

scathing reply, only to be cut off by his impatient curse as he straightened, his hand tightening around her keys.

'Damn! I must've left my cell-phone on your table. Wait here—I'll be right back.'

'See if you can find my sunglasses, too,' she just had time to fling at him before the car door was closed firmly in her face and he strode back towards the flat with an energy that made her feel doubly exhausted. She slumped back in the butter-soft leather seat and discovered that her fingers were resting on the elusive eyewear. She debated calling after him, but couldn't work up the energy to reopen the door. Serve him right if he had to waste some more of his precious time on a fruitless search. Nora slid the sunglasses out of her bag and on to her nose. She clipped on her seatbelt and lay back in the soothing dimness, waiting for the painkillers she had swallowed to kick in.

She closed her eyes, the better to brood on the iniquities of men in general and one or two in particular, and only opened them again when she felt a vibrating thud from the rear of the car. She discovered she had slumped sideways in her seat and hurriedly sat upright as Blake MacLeod walked around from the back of the vehicle. He had taken off his jacket and tie and must have stowed them in the boot. She wondered why he had bothered for such a short trip.

He slid in behind the steering wheel. With the collar of his navy shirt unbuttoned he looked as comfortable as she felt grotty.

'What took you so long?' she needled.

He fastened his seatbelt and started the car, ignoring the provocation. 'I see you found your sunglasses,' he commented over the signature rumble of a V-8 engine.

'They were in my bag all along,' she admitted with sweet malice.

'Why didn't you phone your flat and let me know I could stop hunting?'

'Because I don't have my mobile with me. I left it at work yesterday,' she shot back.

'Really? A technophile without her phone? Isn't that a contradiction in terms?' he said as he glanced in the rear-view mirror and executed a neat U-turn, sending the cluster of black-on-white dials under the steering column jumping.

She concentrated on adjusting to the unwelcome motion. 'I was in a rush to get home,' she remembered sourly.

'Lucky for you.'

'*Lucky*?'

'Ignorance isn't always the bliss it's made out to be,' her companion commented. The car pulled out on to the main road with a bellowing surge of speed that sent Nora's stomach lurching back against her spine.

'Would you mind slowing down a bit? I don't think I can take too many corners like that,' she asked through clenched teeth.

He eased off the accelerator and the car instantly responded to his command, the aggressive bark settling back into a guttural growl. 'Better?'

Sweat prickled across her brow. She swallowed the moisture that had gathered under her tongue before she answered. 'Thanks.'

'If you're feeling too weak to do this, I could turn around and take you back home,' he offered.

Too weak? So he no longer saw her as a sexy seductress, a proud Boadicea to his Roman general, but an object of pity? 'It's just the sudden change in direction. Keep driving—I'll be fine.'

'If you say so.'

'Don't worry; I'm not going to throw up on your expensive upholstery.'

'It's you I'm worried about, not the car,' he said, showing a stunning disregard for the possessive pleasure with which his fingers caressed the steering wheel. 'Why don't you just try to relax—take a power nap for a few minutes? Here, maybe this will help.' She heard a muted click and a delicious breeze sprang up to whisper against her face and throat, chilling the perspiration on her exposed skin. A soft burr signalled the loading of a CD and quiet classical music began to flow around the sculpted curves of the sealed cabin.

'Mmm, that's lovely…' Her smooth brow wrinkled as she pursued an elusive familiarity. 'What is it?'

'Ravel's *Pavane*,' His voice was leaden with patience.

'Do you usually listen to music like this as you drive?' she murmured.

He was quick to detect the trace of surprise in her tone. 'Do you expect me to be a cultural barbarian just because I don't have a higher education?'

Behind her closed eyes she mentally blinked. Did he carry a chip on his shoulder about his background? If he cultivated the image of himself as a ruthless savage in the business arena then he could hardly complain when there was a spill over of that opinion into his private life. 'No, it's just that it doesn't really gel with your public image. I expected something more…more—'

'Crude?'

'*Elemental*.'

'Gangsta rap, perhaps?'

She blunted his sarcasm with a yawn. 'Why should I think that? Was there a lot of gang activity where you grew up?' she wondered.

'You could say that.' Ironic humour replaced the sardonic edge in his voice. 'If you're one of those people who think official trade unions are legalised gangs. As for street gangs—yeah, we lived in a fairly rough neighbourhood, but I was too busy to waste my time posturing about on the streets. Dad was a hard-line unionist with no time for slackers—a rough-as-guts waterside worker who died on the job when I was twenty. Mum's a union activist from way back. There were four of us kids and we were all expected to pull our own weight from the time we were old enough to hold down a job.'

'You have three brothers?' It would be no surprise if he was raised in a swamp of testosterone.

'Sisters. I have three strong and opinionated older sisters,' he corrected, squelching her theory about his macho origins.

'So you're the baby of the family.' She smiled dreamily at a startling vision of Blake MacLeod as a chubby toddler bossed about by a trio of females. 'Do you still see much of them?'

'Too much. They live to complicate my life.' His wry affection congealed into irritation. 'Now, why don't you give that insatiable curiosity of yours a rest and let me concentrate on my driving?'

'Surely not difficult in a car like this,' she scoffed, her consonants slurring slightly as a pleasant lethargy stole through her veins. 'What kind is it, anyway?'

'A ninety-six TVR Cerbera—a classic British sports car.' He sounded typically male, shedding the hard-bitten cynicism for an endearingly boyish enthusiasm.

'Really?' Her eyelids were far too heavy to lift. She conquered another cracking yawn. 'I bet it costs a fortune to run.'

'You sound like my mother.'

Great! Now she reminded the most dangerously sexy man of her acquaintance of his *mother*! 'Cerbera...isn't that some character in Greek mythology?' she mumbled vaguely, hoping to redeem herself.

'Cerberus is the three headed dog who guarded the entrance to Hades.'

'Mmm...hell and wheels—now what phrase does *that* particular combination of words bring readily to mind?' she teased drowsily, the leather of the padded headrest cool against her cheek as she sought a more comfortable position.

When he didn't immediately pick up the thread of the conversation, it slipped beyond her grasp. Nora's lightly drugged consciousness floated away with the music, weaving it into dreams, her weary body rocked deeper into the arms of Morpheus by the rumbling vibration of the car.

Her curls shivered in the breeze from the air conditioner as she slumped bonelessly in the cradle of her seat, her lips parted on a soundless sigh, her sunglasses sliding askew down her lightly freckled nose. When her companion reached out to tip them off and let them drop into her lap she didn't stir by as much as the flicker of a lash.

Blake's hard mouth kicked into a triumphant grin as he abruptly changed lanes and turned down a narrow side street. Snarling his way out of the prison of downtown traffic, he joined the steady flow of cars on the motorway and within half an hour was cruising on the open road.

Keeping a sharp eye out for the law, he exploited the road-hugging aerodynamics of the car as he wound up over the bush-clad Waitakere Ranges north-west of the city. Apart from the network of walking and tramping tracks in the dense native forest, the narrow dual carriageway was the only route to the isolated enclave of famously wild surf beaches on the other side of the ranges.

Blake's fierce satisfaction at the unexpected turn of events was charged with exhilaration. The Cerbera was a challenge to handle at higher speeds—a pleasure that he rarely permitted himself—but now he had the perfect excuse to put the car through its high-performance paces. Dust kicked up at the ragged edge of the sealed surface as he hurtled towards his destination, the leafy undergrowth and graceful ferns that fringed the roadside whipping and bowing in homage to his velocity.

The leisurely trip to his beach house from his home in central Auckland usually took just over an hour, but right now he wanted to get as far as he could, as fast as he could—before his unwitting passenger awoke to the fact that she had been hijacked.

Her story was so bizarre it was probably true, but there was too much at stake for him to risk giving her the benefit of the doubt. The fact that she had been pathetically easy to manipulate into assisting in her own abduction didn't automatically make her innocent of all charges. Unfortunately, at this point, wilful naivety could be just as damaging as malicious intent. Guilty or innocent, Nora was the equivalent of an unexploded bomb—one that it was going to be his very great pleasure to defuse....

A kick of anticipation tensed his muscles and his foot sank sharply on the accelerator. He had no doubt that once Nora recovered from her hangover her natural intelligence would reassert itself, turning her into a potentially dangerous opponent. But a fascinating one.

He glanced sideways at his dishevelled guest, deep in a trusting sleep. Far from disarming him, her vulnerability was unexpectedly arousing. Her shirt had slipped a strategic button and he could see a glimpse of smooth freckled skin above a white cotton bra, very different from the sheer black number she had flaunted last night. Perversely, he found the *faux* innocence of the opaque cotton even more of a turn-on.

A carnal image of Nora's pale body splayed out against the dark leather, her restless hands restrained by the tangled black webbing of her seatbelt suddenly flashed into his mind. It was so diverting that Blake over-steered a corner and almost clipped the crumbling clay bank.

Sweating and swearing, he spun the wheel to correct his mistake, shifting in his seat to relieve the sudden constriction in his loins. He was startled by the unruly reaction of his body to his erotic flight of imagination, and distinctly unnerved. He didn't usually indulge in fantasies of bondage and submission. His tastes were straightforward and earthy, and he had never felt possessive enough about any one woman to daydream about dominating her body and mind to the exclusion of all others.

This one was different. Unique in his experience. She had slipped under his guard with annoying ease: intrigued, amused, seduced, insulted and enraged him in swift succession. She had kicked him squarely in the ego and then had the nerve to appeal to his sympathies. As far as he and the rest of the world was concerned, Blake MacLeod had an ice-cool head and a heart to match, but all it had taken to explode that myth in his face was one ruffled brown sparrow on an emotional bender. This morning she had caused him to act on an impulse that was guaranteed to create havoc in his smoothly run life…and, to top it off, she had almost made him crash his cherished car!

CHAPTER SEVEN

NORA OPENED her eyes to see a wall of green rushing towards her.

She let out a little scream before she realised that it wasn't the wall that was moving at breakneck speed. It wasn't even a wall… Where there should have been the familiar concrete canyons of the city there was nothing but a blur of trees!

'What's happened? Where are we?' She winced at the painful crick in her neck as she turned a bewildered face to search out Blake MacLeod's fierce profile.

'Nearly there.'

His thick brows were lowered in their characteristic frown, but his hard mouth was chiselled into a self-satisfied smile which rang alarm bells.

'Nearly *where*?'

Nora gave another smothered shriek as Blake hit the brakes and spun the car down a roughly sealed side road cut into the side of the hill—a road so steep that it was almost vertical, and so narrow there seemed barely room for the car.

'Karekare Beach is just over to your right.' He nodded towards the flash of glittering sea that revealed itself between the bisecting hills.

'How can it be? You were supposed to be dropping me off at work!' she squeaked, instinctively bracing her feet against the floor in the vain hope of stopping their plunging descent.

'I changed my mind.'

'You can't do that!' she spluttered, clutching the edge of her seat as he rounded another tight corner.

His eyebrow shot up in an ironic slant that said he already had.

Outside her window, the forest fell away into a steep-sided valley and Nora blanched, her heart leaping into her mouth at the sight of the flimsy wooden crash barrier that marked the edge of the drop.

'Oh, God!' she groaned weakly. The music which had earlier soothed her now seemed to mock her fear. 'You lying rat!'

'A pity you had to wake up during this bit,' Blake murmured with abrasive sympathy. 'But once we get down under the bush canopy again you won't notice the elevation.'

'Don't bank on it!' She sucked in a nervous breath that did nothing to reassure her. 'Is it my imagination or is the air thinner up here?'

'We're not *that* high,' he replied with an admirably straight face. 'You needn't worry about me passing out at the wheel from hypoxia.'

She shuddered. 'What happens if we meet someone coming the other way?' she fretted.

'One of us has to back up until there's room to pass,' he said, with a calmness that told her he had done this many times before.

Suspicion congealed into full-blown certainty: this was no random drive to blow away the mental cobwebs. 'Where exactly are we going, MacLeod?'

'Somewhere nice and secluded—'

'—where no one will hear me scream?' she concluded with acid sarcasm.

'Where you can take time out—relax and unwind in the peace and quiet of tranquil surroundings.' His deep voice mingled with the sexy growl of the car. 'No stress, no pressure, no prying friends…. You can catch some sun and laze about in luxury while you consider all your options….'

It sounded achingly like heaven to Nora's bruised soul.

'One of them being to have you arrested for kidnapping!'

'What kidnapping?' he countered blandly. 'I suggested we spend the long weekend at my beach house. I didn't hear you object, so naturally I assumed that you were willing....'

'How *could* I have objected? I was *asleep*!' she blustered, her outrage at his blatant manipulation of the facts ambushed by a treacherous thrill of excitement.

His beach house? The long weekend? She had forgotten it was a public holiday on Monday. She was on the brink of being stranded for *days* in Blake MacLeod's sole company!

She didn't flatter herself that Blake was whisking her away to his private hideaway because he was crazed by love, but there was a certain provocative undercurrent to his threats that charged them with erotic meaning. Even knowing that he had some devious ulterior motive for wanting to keep her isolated for the next few days didn't stop her from feeling a rush of feminine triumph. Boring women didn't drive sexy bachelors to reckless acts of piracy....

'You're taking a serious risk, you know,' she told him. 'I could cause you a heap of trouble.'

'More than you have already, you mean?' he asked, unruffled by the threat. 'Perhaps I believe that the potential rewards far outweigh the risk.'

She wondered what kind of rewards he was talking about. They hit a pothole and the car momentarily swerved, jolting her out of her abstraction. 'Why doesn't the council do something to fix this road?' she gasped.

'Because it dead-ends at a beach with no public facilities and there are only a few private homes along the way. The road doesn't generate enough traffic to justify the expense of regular upgrades.'

'Are you sure it's safe?' she gulped as an overhanging fern slapped the windscreen.

'As long as you're with me, Nora, you're as safe as you want to be....'

That was what she was afraid of! 'And if I said I wanted to go back?' She knew it was what she *should* say.

'To what? You didn't really want to go anywhere near work today. You were just saying that out of misplaced bravado.'

She gritted her teeth at the accuracy of the thrust. 'I was actually trying to get rid of *you*.'

'Didn't work, though, did it? Face it, I'm doing you a favour. Remember, revenge is a dish best served cold.'

'I don't want revenge.' She had wasted more than enough time and energy on Ryan already.

'Then you must be unique amongst human beings,' he replied drily. 'If someone I loved betrayed me, I'd take great pleasure in stripping them of everything they valued in life, piece by painful piece.'

Nora shivered at the icy implacability of his words and the implicit passion behind them. The kind of passionate intensity that had clearly been lacking in her relationship with Ryan.

'Maybe I wasn't really in love with him,' she muttered. 'He seemed like an unattainable god at university—he had a rugby blue and was hugely popular with everyone, whereas I was a geeky teenager who'd never even had a real boy-friend. Most of the other girls threw themselves at him, but I was too shy, so I—I—'

'Contented yourself with worshipping from afar until he deigned to notice you?' He sliced cleanly through her self-pitying gloom. 'Sounds like a normal teenage crush to me. I had one on my biology teacher when I was thirteen. It's one of those things you outgrow and laugh about afterwards.'

She tried, and failed, to imagine an adolescent Blake MacLeod in the throes of unrequited love. 'Yes, well…I was obviously a late bloomer. When he moved up to Auckland to work for Maitlands and suggested there was a job for me there I thought it was because he missed having me around. I guess I didn't really have a chance to grow out of my infatuation—'

'Perhaps because Superjock didn't want you to. I bet he

fed off your innocent admiration. How many people who challenged his superior self-image remained his friends?'

'At least I can blame my idiocy on youth and inexperience—what's *your* excuse?' she jabbed back. 'Why are you *really* doing this? I doubt if you normally encourage people to run away from their problems!'

He turned his head to study her, his gaze taunting. 'Do you really want to get into it with me right now?'

'Keep your eyes on the road, for God's sake!' she yelled, clutching the seatbelt across her chest.

He obeyed her ear-splitting command, scouring around the next corner. 'Sorry, but I like to look people in the eye when I'm having a serious discussion,' he said with pious calm.

'Then you can save the discussion until we get wherever it is we're going!' she gritted, knowing full well she was being manipulated. And to think she had been on the verge of forgiving him for preying on her vulnerability!

She simmered and suffered in burning silence until Blake pulled off the steep road on to a long, even steeper, concrete driveway which drilled down through the thick screen of bush covering the coastal side of the hill.

'I thought you said your house was at the beach,' she said nervously as the green canopy meshed overhead, further hemming them into the leafy shadows.

'It is. The beach is directly below us.'

As soon as the words were out of his mouth Nora's heart began to sink and her palms dampen. 'But, but—beach houses are usually at sea level...'

His mouth twitched at her choked protest. 'I prefer not to run with the usual crowd.'

'I knew there had to be a catch,' Nora muttered as the driveway burst out into blazing sunlight and she found herself looking down at the red-tiled roof of a semi-circular house which jutted out from the side of the hill. *Way* out...over a very high, very sheer drop.

'Oh, God…!'

'The structural engineering was done by a highly reputable firm,' murmured Blake reassuringly as they swooped down to the broad paved turning circle in front of three double-width garage doors. A short bridge fed across the falling ground to one side to a wide door protected by a wrought-iron grille. 'If anything, it's been *over*-engineered—the cantilevered beams are strong enough to support several times the actual weight of the house.'

He touched a slim remote and one of the wood-panelled garage doors silently lifted to allow the car to slot in beside a boat-trailer loaded with an inflatable rubber surf dinghy. Further along in the huge internal garage Nora could see a shadowy black four-wheel drive, a motorcycle, a beach-buggy, a stack of surfboards and a surf-ski next to rack of assorted wetsuits.

She debated refusing to budge, but Blake had already sprung open both doors and slid out of the car, and she suspected that sulking in her seat like a defiant child would get her nowhere.

Only when she had scrambled out and walked haughtily around the car did she remember that Blake hadn't needed a key to start the car—he had just pushed a black button on the swooping dashboard. Her heart stuttered and she tucked her handbag under her arm as she sneaked a look at Blake's bent head, half concealed by the raised boot. How careless of him! He really was taking it for granted that she would fall meekly in with his plans. She wondered if he would feel quite so smug watching her drive off in his precious car! The thought of handling all that power on that skimpy road made her feel even queasier, but a foolish rush of adrenaline sent her diving to pull open the driver's door. Her seeking fingers collided with a smooth unbroken surface as she suddenly realised what was missing.

'Mind you don't damage the paintwork.'

Nora jerked around to stare up into Blake's sardonic face. 'This car has no door handles!' she spluttered.

Blake smiled. 'A very useful deterrent to thieves.'

'Then how do you open it?' she asked, endeavouring to project an air of innocent interest.

'You could try saying *Open Sesame*,' he said smoothly, and she blushed at the reminder of their last ride together, in a lift.

'I think it's more to do with modern engineering than magic incantations,' she said.

His deep-set eyes gleamed. In the periphery of her vision she was aware of him sliding a hand up over the gleaming wine-red curves as tenderly if he was caressing a woman, his fingers briefly cupping the jutting wing mirror. There was a quiet click and Nora's bottom received a gentle nudge from the warm metal. Before she could react she had been swung decisively out of the way and Blake had re-shut the door and locked it with his remote.

As the garage door thunked definitively shut behind them, Nora zeroed in on the mirror he had so lovingly stroked and located the discreetly placed button beneath.

'Very cunning,' she said, torn between admiration and frustration. Just once she would like to get the better of him!

'I thought so,' said Blake, sliding his electronic control into his trouser pocket and picking up the bag, draped in his jacket and tie, which he had dropped at his feet. He strode over to punch a series of numbers into the electronic keypad on the wall, his lean back shifting to block her view when she craned for a look.

'Is that an alarm?'

'And remote deadlocking—it's on password access now,' he told her smoothly. 'Would you like to come in?' He opened the internal door to the house and stood back politely.

She lifted her chin. 'You mean you're actually giving me a *choice*?'

'We all have choices—they're just not always the ones we'd like them to be.'

'You have a very glib tongue, don't you?'

It was his turn to try and look innocent. 'That's not what

my teachers used to say. They said I was so quiet in class they hardly knew I was there.'

'I bet half the time you weren't,' she sniped.

His wicked grin was supremely confident. 'How did you guess?'

'You're the type to have problems with authority.'

'And what type is that?'

She wrinkled her freckled nose, the only part of her that didn't actively ache. 'Arrogant.'

To her chagrin he seemed flattered rather than annoyed by her insult. 'Is it arrogance to have faith in one's abilities?'

'If it gives you an exaggerated opinion of your own importance, then, yes. Conceit like that could be your downfall.'

'Now you sound like my father. He didn't have any faith in my personal vision of the future either. He hated it when Prescott offered me a job.'

'Did he think you should have stayed in school?'

He gave up waiting for her to move and brushed past her through the doorway. 'No, he just didn't like the idea of his son betraying his origins by becoming an errand boy to The Bosses.'

Lured by the skilfully dangled bait, Nora automatically followed, hovering by a potted palm in the tiled entrance way as he re-engaged the deadlock, brooding over his words.

'Didn't he want you working for Sir Prescott?' she asked, recalling the woman at the party who had mentioned the rumour about Blake's paternity.

'Let's just say that Dad disapproved of my capitalistic yearnings,' he said, with an irony that suggested a radical understatement. 'He thought that multi-national corporate executives were the corrupt robber-barons of the modern age. He would have preferred to see me pursue a career in honest crime than assist in the legalised oppression of the working masses.' He put his free hand under her elbow and guided her up a wide flight of stairs, their feet sinking soundlessly into thick wool carpet the colour of bleached sand. 'We fought like hell about it every time we saw each other.'

'That must have been tough on your mother,' she murmured, her bleary eye caught by the paintings which enlivened the lime-washed plaster walls—an eclectic mix of signed prints and originals.

Irony turned into open amusement. 'She wouldn't thank you for saying so. Mum loves a good fight. She and Dad scrapped like cat and dog all their married life. Being a MacLeod meant you learnt from the cradle to stand your ground and fight tooth and nail to defend your beliefs. We were all extremely vocal.'

'Except in the classroom,' she said drily.

He shrugged. 'I wasn't interested enough to make myself heard there, and since I worked before and after school I had to catch up on my rest somehow. Thanks to large classes and inattentive teachers I perfected the art of dozing at my desk—and it didn't cost me a cent in lost wages.'

'It couldn't have done much for your school grades.'

His mouth held shades of the cocky kid. 'It wasn't my academic record that caught Scotty's attention; it was my willingness to hustle, to tackle anything that was thrown at me, to persist until a job was done...'

His fascinating frankness, Nora realised, had been a deliberate ploy to take her mind off their surroundings, but now that they had reached the top of the stairs she was hit by the full impact of his private eyrie.

The open-plan living area was centred around a square firebox enclosed in glass, capped by a stainless steel flue and flanked on three sides by long couches in vibrant dark blue, deep-cushioned and luxurious. Bifolding glass doors and windows ran the length of the house, opening out to a wide sun-drenched terrace flanked by roughcast walls smothered in a dark creeper, the outer edge of which fell away with heart-stopping suddenness into a zigzag shaped swimming pool. An aptly named infinity pool, for beyond the shimmering sheet of captive water was...*nothing*...striations of blue sea and sky dissolving into an indistinguishable horizon.

Nora's scalp tightened over her throbbing skull, her whole body going rigid with alarm. 'There's n-no guard rail out there—' she stuttered.

'Yes, there is. You just can't see it from here. There's a strip of garden a metre and a half below the far edge of the pool, closed in by a solid balcony wall...' Which provided safety, but no security against Nora's soaring imagination.

Her lips parted on a soundless mew of protest but Blake had already turned her smartly in the opposite direction.

'Don't worry, I've given you one of the guest rooms at the back of the house,' he said, his hand flat between her shoulderblades as he propelled her through an archway on the other side of the stairs and down a wide windowless hallway into a high-ceilinged room with walls of palest coffee and Persian rugs splashed across the bleached carpet.

'See—' he said, crossing to the bay windows and whisking back the filmy curtains to reveal the dense native bush which formed a natural screen on the other side of the glass. 'No view whatsoever. You're tucked right up against the slope of the hill here. If you don't want to use the air conditioning you can switch on the ceiling fans, and there's a home entertainment centre in that lattice-wood cabinet. Your *en suite* bathroom—which is minus a bathtub, by the way—is through that archway. I'm sure you'll find everything very suitable to your needs.'

Suitable wasn't the word which sprang immediately to mind as Nora's jittery gaze fell on the queen-sized platform bed draped in white mosquito netting which dominated the room. Flanked by huge glazed pots sprouting luxuriant palms, the bed seemed to float above the floor on its polished wood pedestal, and behind the folds of the gauzy hangings textured silk cushions in jewelled colours and dense patterns were piled on the white bedspread, adding to the aura of exotic luxury.

Talk about Arabian Nights! Nora visualised herself languishing in sensuous abandon amidst the mounding of pillows, the silk cool against her hot skin, a temptress worthy of a sultan's favour…a tall dark grey-eyed sultan with a hawkish face and a black frown that made everyone tremble before him—everyone, that was, but the woman who could bring him to his knees….

'Well, what do you think?'

She blushed, tearing her mind from her silken fantasies, seeking refuge in cool flippancy.

'What—no bars on the window?'

He let the curtains drift back into place. 'Why should there be? I thought we'd agreed that you're a guest here, not a prisoner.'

His innocent expression fooled neither of them. 'You and I obviously have different definitions of the word "guest",' she sniffed. 'Which reminds me—you were going to tell me why you brought me here.'

'Of course. But why don't I let you get settled in first?' His grey-eyed gaze slid over her crumpled figure. 'You might feel more disposed to relax if you change into something more casual….'

He placed the small bag he had been carrying on top of the squat wooden chest at the end of the bed—and for the first time Nora noticed the distinctive home-made tags.

'Hey, where did you get that? That looks like mine!'

He gave a wry shrug and suspicion turned to fresh outrage as she elbowed him out of the way to unzip the lid and throw it open. A very familiar pattern of cartoon rabbits stared back up at her.

She flushed to the roots of her hair. 'You stole my laundry!'

He shrugged, unrepentant. 'I was being a good host. I doubt you would have wanted to spend the entire weekend in the same set of underwear.'

She was ransacking the contents, recognising several things that hadn't been in the plundered laundry basket. 'You went through my chest of drawers, too!' she accused.

'I thought you'd want a reasonable selection of your own things to wear. I know how women are about their clothes—'

'I bet you do,' she muttered darkly.

'Growing up with three sisters, I could hardly help but gain an insight into the female perspective,' he reminded her.

Her flush deepened. She doubted that his insight was solely due to sisterly influence. 'That's not the point. I didn't give you permission to go into my things—'

'Are we going to have an argument now over who first invaded whose privacy?' he drawled.

Her anger deflated like a pricked balloon. 'I already admitted that was a mistake,' she said.

'Which you're now going to rectify by behaving like the perfect guest,' he said smoothly.

'My laptop's not here—' she realised.

'Sorry, I must have left it down in the car—I'll bring it up later. Now, if you'll excuse me, I'm going to get changed myself. Meantime, feel free to explore. My room is at the opposite end of the hall.'

Was that a warning or a tacit invitation? Nora wondered with a shivery *frisson* that led her to close the door with a slight snap at his departing heels. Either way, her first inclination was to do the exact opposite of whatever it was he wanted.

However, she had no intention of cutting off her nose to spite her face, so she peeled off her hastily donned office battle armour and substituted an amber sleeveless T-shirt and a pair of loose white cotton shorts, both still fragrant with sunshine and washing powder, from her open bag. Then she ventured into the compact luxury of the *en suite* bathroom to splash water on to her face.

She nosed shamelessly into the drawers of the marble-topped vanity and found a mixture of used and new make-up and feminine toiletries of various brands. Evidence of sisters or his string of Insignificant Others? she wondered moodily.

Back in the bedroom, she couldn't resist crawling under the voluminous mosquito netting to find out if the bed felt as gorgeous as it looked.

It did. Soft, yet resilient, the mattress sank under her testing weight. Sliding her bare toes over the nubby silk, Nora experimentally stretched out to her full length, draping limp arms over the mound of cushions and letting her tired bones melt into the welcoming depths of the downy softness. Her puffy eyelids felt as if they had little weights attached and it was an effort to keep them open. Motionless, Nora became aware of the heavy silence hanging over the house, absorbing the continuous muted roar of the ocean and transforming it into a lullaby of white noise. Perhaps if she didn't move for a few minutes the warring factions within her body might make their fragile peace, she thought hopefully, and render her fighting fit for another round of verbal fisticuffs with Danger Man.

Her mouth curved into a bitter smile. Blake MacLeod might think that because she had let herself be temporarily swept away by his aggressive arrogance she would be putty in his hands, but she was no longer a naive soft-hearted idiot who trusted people to act with honour. No, she was a hardened cynic. From now on she would be a taker rather than a giver—smart and ruthless. And beautiful, of course…. She snuggled deeper into the gratifying fantasy of herself as a voluptuous sexy *femme fatale*, a fascinating woman of passion and mystery, an irresistible and unconquerable challenge to men everywhere.

And to one infuriating man in particular….

CHAPTER EIGHT

NORA DIDN'T BELIEVE in ghosts, but the white shrouds swirling around her in the smothering darkness made her rear up with a cry of alarm.

As she lashed out at the floating phantoms, the ghosts abruptly transformed themselves into billowing folds of mosquito netting dancing to the slow beat of the ceiling fan chopping quietly overhead.

She blinked and her vision cleared. Waking up in a state of horror seemed to be an ongoing feature of her relationship with Blake MacLeod, she thought wryly, batting away the wispy veils and scrambling off the wide bed. She could have sworn she had only closed her eyes for a few minutes, but her cramped limbs were telling another story.

Groping through the gloom, she located the familiar shape of a switch on the wall. The mellow glow of uplights sprang to life, but her relief turned to dismay as she stared at the dark rectangle looming behind the sheer curtains at the window.

She looked down at her watch in disbelief, verifying what her disordered senses were telling her. It was well into the evening. She had been crashed out all day!

A mortified groan rusted across her dry lips as she realised who must have turned on the fan. The thought of Blake looking in on her as she slept made her feel shivery inside.

Of course he had seen her asleep in his car, too, she

reminded herself—but his disciplined mind would have been totally focused on his driving. This was different—even though she was fully dressed, the surroundings were far more intimate....

Crushing down her embarrassment, she ventured out, following the faint sounds of a tap gushing and utensils clattering, underscored by some mellow jazz. The kitchen, she recalled vaguely, was at the far end of that huge open living space....

She marched into the almost dark room and came to a halt with a stunned gasp.

There was a sharp movement off to her far left, where angled halogen spotlights bounced off polished surfaces.

'What's wrong?'

Nora pressed her hand to the fluttering pulse at the base of her throat, a foolish reaction to the sound of his voice. 'Nothing... For a moment I thought there'd been some kind of volcanic eruption out there,' she said sheepishly. 'It looks like the whole rim of the earth is on fire!'

The wall of glass on to the west-facing terrace had been folded open, and far out in the darkness a thin line of molten red bled across the width of the sky, radiating hot colour up into shadowy clouds boiling with crimson, orange and gold: the last throes of the dying day. A velvety blackness, already pricked with stars, bore down from above, poised to smother the final rays of the red sun.

'Another minute or so and you would have been too late. The sunsets here are always spectacular—no smog to diffuse the light particles.' Even as Blake spoke, the last sliver of fire was swallowed by the black glitter of the sea and the hot crimson cooled to a golden-pink blush.

'I wish I'd had a chance to see it properly,' Nora murmured. When was the last time she had paused to appreciate the splendours of nature? Since she had come to Auckland she had allowed Ryan's scorn for such unsophisticated pastimes to stifle her enjoyment of the simple pleasures of life.

'There's always tomorrow night....'

The cool assumption in the gravelly voice spun her around.

Blake was leaning behind the curving granite-topped breakfast bar that divided the big kitchen from the rest of the room. With a shock, Nora saw that he was bare above the low-slung waist of his white drawstring pants. His raw masculinity was like a punch to the stomach, a violent reminder of the last time she had seen him stripped for action. A faint glistening of moisture dotted the dark hair on his tawny chest and imparted a glossy sheen to the streamlined muscles which rippled in the arms braced against the gleaming granite. Not an ounce of surplus body fat marred the ridged lines of his abdomen or the taut curve of his waist where it tapered to meet his lean hips. Nora hurriedly lifted her gaze from the tantalising streak of damp hair that arrowed down from the flat scoop of his navel to disappear beneath the loose gathers of white linen. The hair on his head was also wet, gleaming blue-black under a halogen halo and slicked back from his hard forehead to emphasise the dramatic widow's peak. The thick straight brows cast his grey eyes into shadow, but Nora could tell that he was amused at her flustered reaction.

'Excuse my state of undress, but I've just had a swim,' he said lazily. 'The pool is solar-heated but it's cool enough to be refreshing, if you want to take the plunge...'

Nora had the feeling that she'd already plunged in way over her head. He must have shaved very recently, she noticed with a fresh tingle of awareness, for the long masculine jaw was invitingly smooth and glossy.

'Uh, no, thanks.'

'I did pack a swimsuit with your things,' he continued as if she hadn't spoken, 'but you might prefer to do as I do and not bother with any encumbrance. There's no one overlooking us here, so you don't have to worry about peeping Toms—'

'Only peeping Blakes,' she said, walking self-consciously towards him, the soles of her feet shrinking at the change from soft carpet to the slick hardness of the unglazed tiles.

'Ah, but there's not much I haven't seen of you already, is

there, Nora?' he responded lazily, looking her over from sleep-creased cheek to dainty toes. 'You have nothing to be shy about, as I recall—you have a very nice body.'

She could feel her freckles popping at the blatantly patronising phrase. *Nice?* There was that damning, dull-as-dishwater word again. She had a good mind to peel off all her clothes and prance out into his pool just to show him that being *nice* was no longer on her agenda!

'Thank you, but I don't feel like a swim right now,' she said primly. Much less in a pool that dropped off the edge of a cliff!

He shrugged, a supple flex of his shoulders that drew her attention back to his tapering torso. Why had she ever thought that Ryan's thick and chunky rugby player's physique was the height of attractiveness? This man, nearly ten years his senior, had a honed sleekness which made Ryan's slabs of gym-inflated muscle seem like puppy fat, and a potently mature confidence in his own strength and sexuality which was more persuasive than any boast.

'How are you feeling?' he asked, and she ran a self-conscious hand through her rumpled locks, wishing she had stopped to look in the mirror before she had come marching out.

'Fine,' she said, pleased to realise that it was only a slight exaggeration.

She glanced around. The breakfast bar stepped down to a working bench that ran around two sides of the kitchen. Beneath the windows overlooking the terrace was a double sink and on the opposite wall twin ovens topped with a fearsomely professional-looking gas cook-top interrupted the smooth flow of the granite surface. Lacquered grey cabinetry complemented the brushed stainless steel of the appliances and hooded extractor.

It was a well-planned kitchen. One with a definitive style and a serious purpose. Just like Blake MacLeod. She would do well to remember that he reputedly never made an uncalculated move.

'I checked up on you several times through the day, but you were so deeply asleep that I thought it best to leave you to wake up naturally—you obviously needed the rest,' he told her. 'I only turned on the fan when I decided your skin felt overheated—'

'*Felt?*' Her tangled dreams suddenly rose up to haunt her. 'You mean you came in and *touched* me?'

The little shrill of guilty alarm in her voice goaded him to say innocently, 'You were very flushed and sweaty. I was concerned you might be suffering from more than just a hangover—dehydration can cause some nasty complications.'

Her imagination ran riot. 'You should have woken me—'

'As befits a Sleeping Beauty? I tried, but the evil spell of the demon drink must have been too strong.'

The riot became a rampage. 'You k-kissed me?' she said, her eyes instinctively falling to his firm mouth.

'Actually, it was vice versa. I just put my hand against your cheek and you grabbed me and wrestled me down on to the bed.'

Her hazel eyes jerked back to his, flaring with embarrassment. 'I did not!' she protested.

'You were all over me like a rash,' he drawled. 'I worked up quite a sweat myself, trying to fight you off without hurting you.'

She clutched at the edge of the breakfast bar to support her wobbly knees. 'I wouldn't! You're making that up!'

'How do you think I got these scratches?'

He touched a hand to the right side of his chest. Nora's fingers curled into her palms as she stared in appalled fascination at the four parallel pink lines scoring the smooth skin just below his flat brown nipple.

'You can examine me inch by inch if you like…. You branded me in other places, too,' he prompted softly.

She flushed, tearing her compulsive gaze from his hard chest. 'That doesn't prove anything. You could have scratched yourself for all I know, or it could have happened last night—' She broke off, aware of her tactical error.

He took full advantage of her confusion. 'Ah, yes…so it could. Some women are all teeth and claws in the sack, honey—here's proof that you're one of them.'

'We never got as far as the sack,' she growled.

'Until today.'

That was definitely mockery in his tone. Nora tossed her caramel curls, more certain of herself. 'Nothing happened. Or, if it did, it was only because I was having a nightmare.'

'It seemed more like an erotic dream to me—'

'And you would be an expert on those, I suppose?' she shot back unwisely.

Another distracting shrug of his superb shoulders. 'What can I say? I seem to attract women who like to talk to me about their sexual fantasies....'

A hot tingle streaked from the pit of Nora's hollow stomach to the tips of her breasts. She could feel her nipples begin to bud against the stretchy cotton of her bra and hurriedly hitched her bottom on to the nearest bar stool, planting her elbows on the granite and folding her arms to shield the front of her snugly fitting T-shirt.

Her apparent nonchalance was a dismal failure.

'You're starting to look overheated again, Nora,' he murmured, a thread of open amusement in the deep voice. 'Here, perhaps this will help.' He poured her a tall glass of amber liquid from a jug tinkling with ice cubes. 'I made it for you earlier.'

'What is it?' she asked suspiciously, curling her fingers around the frosted glass, keeping her gaze firmly above his neck as he resumed his former position.

'Iced tea,' he said.

She took a cautious sniff, then hesitated, with her lips touching the icy rim. 'Why aren't you having any?'

'Because I'm drinking something else.' He tilted his head towards a glass of red wine standing on the kitchen window-sill above the double sink.

Still she hesitated, and he made a rough sound of impatience. 'What's the matter? Afraid it's spiked? Do you really think I brought you here with the sole purpose of keeping you drugged and helpless?'

Her eyes widened and he gave an exaggerated sigh.

'I've already had ample time to have my wicked way with your unconscious self—remember? I try never to repeat myself!'

She felt foolish. But it was his fault for making her so jumpy. 'You can't blame me for being suspicious after the way you carried on this morning. How do I know what's going on in your devious male mind?'

He shot her a cynical look from beneath drooping eyelids. 'Oh, I think if you try very, very hard you could make an educated guess....'

She blushed. 'I—you—'

'Drink your drink and stop trying to pretend you're not as curious as I am.'

'About what?' she said, fighting to keep her end up.

'About what it would be like to finish what you started when you deliberately poured that glass of wine all over my jacket.'

Nora was tempted to bluff it out, but her conscience wouldn't let her. While she tried to think of a clever answer she buried her pinkened face in her drink. It tasted innocuous. She swilled more of the icy beverage over her tongue; in fact, it tasted quite delicious!

'You said you *made* this?' She gulped greedily, her parched mouth and throat absorbing so much moisture that only a trickle seemed to make it as far as her stomach. 'From scratch?'

'Don't sound so surprised,' he murmured, topping up her empty glass. 'I'm quite competent in the kitchen.'

He was much more than competent if he knew how to make iced tea. It wasn't a common Kiwi beverage.

'You just don't seem the domesticated type,' she said.

He turned to the bench by the sink where an assortment of partly sliced vegetables were strewn across the big chopping board. 'What type am I?'

She eyed the flashing knife, wielded with lethal precision against a defenceless red pepper. 'Rich single male—the type who eats out a lot and delegates all the grunt work to someone else.'

The knife turned expertly on an unwary onion. 'You think I'm lazy?'

'Quite the opposite. I think you're probably far too busy to bother with the mundane details of life.'

'Wrong. The devil is in the detail, Nora. It can make men's fortunes—or break them. The fact that I'm rich and single makes it more, not less imperative that I maintain my basic survival skills. Actually, I like to cook; I find it relaxing.'

To Nora, who found it a chore, he sounded insufferably superior.

'I suppose you're going to claim you do all your own cleaning, too?' she said sceptically.

'I'm self-reliant, not stupid,' he said, pausing to sample his wine. 'My eldest sister runs a co-operative of domestic cleaners—she gives me a good deal on a contract for my home in town and this place gets done for free, since the whole family uses it....'

A chip of ice caught in Nora's throat. 'Your sister's a *cleaning lady*?'

Her choking disbelief induced a grin that exploded the harsh angles of his face. 'Don't let Kate hear you call her a lady, she'll be insulted—she's a working woman. She started up a business which now supports her and her kids, not to mention giving other solo mums a chance to earn a decent wage without having to pay for childcare. I consider that a pretty admirable achievement, don't you?'

'Well, yes, of course it is...I just thought—'

'What? That because I'm wealthy my family must live in the lap of luxury?'

'It's a reasonable assumption,' she defended herself. 'Most people like to share their good fortune with their loved ones—'

'Not if the loved ones are pig-headed idealists who would throw the offer back in his condescending teeth,' he said wryly. 'You forget, the MacLeod roots are staunchly working class—I'm the renegade in a bunch of social reformers. Mum would take every cent I had for one of her causes, but for herself she doesn't believe in soft living or idle hands. She's a union activist who sees it as her duty to remind me that the average working Joe's health and welfare depend on men like me sacrificing a few points from the bottom line.'

A belated recognition clicked in Nora's brain. 'Your mother's the Pamela MacLeod who chained herself to an official limo during the Commonwealth trade talks in Wellington!'

'Actually, it was *my* official limo, and, yes, she managed to get herself arrested on primetime news. *Again.* Much as she's against the globalisation of industry she seems to have no problem using the information highway to globalise her fight against oppression. That artistic photo of her plastered against my grille was all over the Internet within minutes of it being taken.'

There was amused exasperation in his tone, a rueful respect that told her more about his feelings for his mother than any amount of words.

'She doesn't sound very oppressed.' Nora chuckled.

He rolled his eyes. 'I wish!'

She didn't believe it for a moment. 'Would you prefer to have the kind of mother who cooed and clucked over you and believed her darling boy could do no wrong?'

He shuddered—a very distracting ripple of that long, lean masculine back. Was he that same melted honey colour all over? she speculated helplessly. Her gaze slipped lower down his profile and she couldn't help noticing that the finespun fabric of his drawstring pants clung patchily to his damp flanks in a way that suggested he wore little or nothing underneath.

He turned towards her and her eyes shot hastily up to his face.

'Chicken.'

What was he? A mind-reader? 'Of course not!' She was embarrassed to have been caught sneaking an ogle.

He looked taken aback by her vehemence. 'If you don't want chicken, I could defrost some prawns…'

'Oh!' She fought down another blush, determined not to encourage the speculation stirring in his hawkish gaze. 'I—uh—chicken is fine, but really, I'm not very hungry—'

'You will be,' he said, cutting through her defensive babble. 'By my estimation, you haven't eaten in over twenty-four hours. You'll run out of steam very quickly if you don't put something solid in your stomach.'

At the moment the inner heat she was generating was enough to power a small city! Nora fumbled to pour herself another drink, her damp hand slipping against the handle of the jug, almost shattering the lip of the glass. 'Sorry,' she muttered, leaping to her feet as iced tea spilled on the counter. 'Let me get that.' She snatched up a handy cloth and mopped up the pooling liquid.

'Thanks,' he murmured. 'May I have my shirt back now?'

She looked down at the crumpled white cloth in her hand and noticed a button poking out between her thumb and forefinger. A tiny embroidered polo player, now stained with brown, stared accusingly up at her. 'Oh, God! I'm sorry—it was just lying there—I thought it was a dishcloth!'

'So much for my taste in clothes,' he said wryly. 'You really are hell on a man's wardrobe, aren't you, Nora?'

'I don't suppose it's a cheap knock-off rather than the genuine article?' she said with a sigh.

His trademark scowl wiped the amusement from his expression. 'Now you're adding insult to injury. Do I seem like the kind of cheapskate who would buy fakes when I can afford the real thing? Or do you think I'm just too undiscriminating to be able to tell the difference?'

'I think your inferiority complex is showing again,' she told him. '*I'm* the one who can't tell the difference. What do I know about designer labels? I used to sew all my own clothes before I came to Auckland, and I still get most of my stuff from chainstores.'

He cocked his head. 'Is money a problem for you?'

She wasn't fooled by the casual way he tossed out the

question. Her soft mouth tensed. 'Why bother to ask? I'm sure your snoop ran a full credit check on me.'

'And you came up clean as a whistle. But, as Doug pointed out, some debts don't show up on official files—'

'I'm not being blackmailed, I don't have a drug or gambling habit or any other form of secret addiction,' she declared, her voice rising above the smoky jazz. 'With me, what you see is exactly what you get!'

His mouth kinked, his gaze flicking over her slight figure. 'That's very generous of you, Nora, but I think we should eat first...'

She spluttered, as he'd known she would. 'That's not what I meant!' She glared in frustration as he carried the board of chopped vegetables across to the hob, watching him line up bottles of cooking oil, soy and sweet chilli sauce within easy reach of the wok.

'You're not going to cook like that, are you?' she felt compelled to say. 'What if the oil spits when you add the food? Here, maybe you should put this back on.'

He turned just in time to catch the balled shirt—thrown with a little more force than was necessary—as it hit his bare chest. 'Thanks, but I think I'll go and get myself something less clammy,' he said with a grimace.

She averted her eyes from temptation as he strolled past her, and while he was gone she decided to make the most of her opportunity to poke and prowl. She was rifling the telephone table at the top of the stairs when a voice sounded in her ear.

'Are you looking for something in particular?'

Nora jumped, her knee knocking against the open drawer, trapping her groping fingers inside.

'Ouch! I—uh—' She pulled her hand free and sucked on her stinging fingertips, flustered by Blake's sudden reappearance in a tight black T-shirt that was but a small improvement on the distraction of his bare chest.

'I was just wondering where the telephone was,' she mumbled.

'Why?'

'I thought I'd ring home…' she confessed, further unnerved by his looming intensity.

His eyes narrowed. 'You want to call your flat? I thought you said your flatmate had gone to work. Who was it you expected to pick up?'

She nibbled at her lower lip, presenting an unwitting picture of guilt. 'Nobody.'

The straight black bars of his eyebrows rose above eyes steely with suspicion and she sighed.

'I just thought I'd better leave a message on my machine, saying where I was and when I'd be back, that's all. You know—contact details in case of emergency.' She tugged at her wrist and his fingers tightened.

'You mean as insurance against any plans I might have to make you *permanently* disappear?' He invested his words with a silken menace.

'Yes—I mean, no! I'm sure you're a very law-abiding citizen,' she added hurriedly.

His eyelids drooped. 'I'm flattered by your faith in my honour.' His sarcasm was designed to intimidate.

'The phone?' she reminded him with dogged persistence.

'There isn't one.'

'No phone?' She was startled as much by what he said as his tone of grim satisfaction. 'But…there are phone jacks all over the place—'

'To be functional they have to be connected to a network,' he pointed out, stalking back to the kitchen. 'I come here to get *away* from all that—to have some uninterrupted down-time.'

Nora trailed after him. It sounded like an excellent theory, but…

'I don't believe it,' she muttered. 'I bet you didn't get where you are today by working nine-to-five five days a week. It would be tantamount to professional suicide for you to totally cut yourself off here, especially when your boss happens to be in the middle of a hostile takeover bid—'

'Which is why I regularly check for messages on my mobile,' he said, abruptly curtailing her speculative musing.

'Oh,' She felt foolish for forgetting. 'Of course. Then... may I borrow it for a minute?'

'Unfortunately, the battery's very low and I forgot to bring a charger down with me,' he continued smoothly. 'I'm sure you don't expect me to risk professional suicide for the sake of giving your untrustworthy flatmate a heads-up on your whereabouts?'

Nora mistrusted his bland expression. 'Then I suppose you'll have to drive me out to the nearest public phone booth so I can make my call,' she persisted.

His trademark scowl descended as he silently debated the extent of her stubbornness. Victory was sweet when he reluctantly fetched a slim state-of-the-art phone, bristling with all the latest software bells and whistles.

'Gee, thanks,' she said with a grin.

'Make it short,' he ordered, and flagrantly eavesdropped as she delivered her self-conscious little message to the answer-machine at the flat.

'Satisfied that I didn't pass on any state secrets?' she said when she finally slapped the phone back into his outstretched palm.

'You could have been speaking in code,' he pointed out.

She sucked in a frustrated breath. 'My God, you're suspicious—' she began furiously before noticing the provocative slant to his mouth. She lifted her chin and flounced past him to pick up her drink.

To her secret disappointment he meekly lapsed into bland amiability, delivering a smooth line in unthreatening patter as he expertly finished cooking the prepared food. He finally scooped the glistening contents of the wok into two white porcelain bowls and picked them up, along with his wineglass.

'I usually dine *al fresco*, weather permitting, but I thought you'd prefer us to eat inside,' he said, seating her at the polished slab of wood which dominated the dining alcove around the corner from the kitchen. Here the bifold doors were firmly closed, screened by wooden shutters slanted to obscure the view of the darkened terrace. Cutlery gleamed against the woven placemats grouped intimately at one end of the long table, burnished by the light from a row of tea candles in a tortured metal holder.

'You needn't have bothered to change your habit for my sake,' she said stiffly. 'I would have managed.'

He sank into the chair to her right 'It was no trouble.'

She bristled. 'Then why mention it?'

'Why, to make you feel indebted to me, of course,' he said, playing blatantly to her suspicions. He picked up his fork. 'And for the purpose of hearing you express your gratitude so prettily....'

Her freckles glowed, mini-beacons of mutinous embarrassment, as she shook out the paper table napkin and draped it across her lap. 'You're not exactly the most gracious of hosts,' she muttered.

'Shall we duel over our manners later?' he suggested. 'We may as well eat our food while it's still hot.'

The fragrant chicken was scrumptious, and after only a few bites Nora felt her spiky hostility melt away.

'This is really delicious,' she said, her voice an unwitting purr of sensual appreciation.

'I'm glad you like it,' he responded, watching her golden eyes haze with pleasure as she licked an enticing drop of spicy red sauce from the corner of her wide mouth. She ate with a delicate gluttony that sparked his own baser appetite.

'You missed a bit,' he said.

'Where?' she asked innocently, and he mirrored her actions with his tongue against his own cheek to demonstrate the spot. To his banked amusement, her gaze fixated on his mouth while a forgotten load of vegetables slid off her fork and landed with a splat on the table.

'Oh, dear!' She tore her gaze from his lips and jerked back, dabbing at the sticky pile with her napkin. 'Oh! Oh, *no*!'

'Don't worry about it,' he said, snuffing out the flaming edge of her napkin where it had drifted into one of the tea candles and ignited with a soft 'whuff'.

'I'm so sorry—' She frantically chased an elusive wisp of blackened paper as it broke away and floated in the air between them.

'It's only paper, Nora,' he said, capturing the ash as it settled into his drink. 'The napkins are *designed* to be disposable.'

'Not by incineration at the table,' she said, rubbing at the burnished surface, searching for scorch marks.

'Nora—'

'I don't think there's any permanent damage,' she discovered, thumbing up a tiny pile of soot.

'Nora!'

Her mortified eyes skittered up to meet Blake's winter-grey look of amused exasperation.

'Relax!' He pressed a folded replacement into her restless hand. 'Everything's fine. Just be thankful the smoke alarm didn't go off and bring the local volunteer fire brigade battering down the door. They're always eager to get some practice in.'

Her face registered a brief flare of horror before she realised he was teasing. 'I'm sorry. I don't know why these things keep happening to me.' She sighed, turning her attention back to her food.

'Chemistry. You're a natural catalyst,' he added when she looked puzzled.

'Should I take that as a compliment or an insult?' she asked wryly.

'Well, it means that life around you would rarely be boring.'

She pulled a face. 'That's not what Ryan said.'

'A catalyst is wasted on an inert substance. From what I overheard at the party, I would guess that *he* was the one with the boringly conventional mind. And the bathroom high jinks certainly suggest a sad lack of imaginative flair. A shower stall is so much more versatile than a narrow cramped bathtub—

as you would have discovered last night if you hadn't been in such a hurry to run off....'

Nora almost choked on a slice of red pepper and hastily gulped at her fresh glass of iced tea. 'Which reminds me, you still haven't told me the real reason you're so keen for me to hide out here for the weekend,' she said to cover her blushes. 'I wonder what it is you think I know that would make me a danger to you if I went back to Auckland?'

The seductive amusement was wiped off his face as he studied her brightly innocent expression from under lowered brows.

His long fingers toyed restlessly with the stem of his empty wineglass.

'I'll answer your question if you'll answer one of mine,' he offered, with such smooth guile that Nora almost grinned.

In fact, the knowledge that she was innocent of all his suspicions put her in a position of hidden strength when it came to bargaining with the truth. It was Blake who had secrets to protect.

'As long as it doesn't involve me giving you confidential information about my employer,' she stated firmly.

He gave her a bland look. 'I would never try to compromise your integrity.' At her disbelieving snort, he added, 'I have the greatest admiration for people who fight for their ethical principles.'

'Even as you try to circumvent them,' Nora murmured, although, strangely enough, she believed him. 'So, what's your *one* question?' She propped her chin on her hand, the reflection from the flickering candles creating dancing flames of mischief in her honey-brown eyes, her sharpened wits ready to repel any attempt at subtle trickery.

'Why are you afraid of heights?'

CHAPTER NINE

NORA'S BODY JERKED in surprise and her chin slid off the back of her palm, her teeth meeting with a sharp click that made her head hum.

'That's it? *That's* your question?'

'I'm curious,' he said, hooking one arm over the back of his chair, angling his body towards her, his eyes intent on the startled oval of her face. 'Is it a bad case of vertigo, or a genuine phobia?'

'I don't know what you mean by *genuine*,' she flared defensively. 'I'm not putting it on, if that's what you're implying—'

'I think you're confusing me with your *former friend*.' Once again he displayed an alarming ability to read her mind. 'I was in the glass lift with you, remember? I know you weren't faking that panic attack…although if it was a full-blown phobia I doubt that I would have been able to distract you as completely as I did….'

Nora suspected he was seriously underrating his sexual impact, but she wasn't going to pander to his already healthy ego by saying so.

'I thought that fake florist you sicced on me—'

'Doug is actually my Chief of Security,' he said.

'I thought *Doug*—' she pinched out the offender's name with disdain '—had ferreted out everything there was to know about me. Didn't he mention how my parents died?' Finding she needed to do something with her hands, Nora stood and began to clear the table.

'Only that they were killed in an accident when you were four years old—I assumed it was a car crash.' He circled her slim wrist with implacably gentle fingers as she reached across for his plate. 'Leave the dishes,' he ordered with rough impatience, tugging her around the edge of the table until she stood facing him. 'What happened, Nora?'

Why was she resisting? It was old news, after all…

She sighed. 'We were picnicking at a regional beach park and Mum and Dad went for a walk up a track over the headland. It was the day after some heavy rain and my mother slipped and went over the edge of the cliff. When my dad climbed down to help her they both fell to the rocks below.'

His lean face tightened with shock. His fingers slipped from her wrist to enclose her hand in a compassionate grip. 'My God, you saw all this? No wonder you were traumatised—!'

'Oh, no!' She was chastened by his shaken response to her stark description. 'Sean and I never saw anything—we were with my aunt at the far end of the beach where there was a sand-castle competition for kids. I didn't know the details until years later. I can't remember what they told me at the time. Sean was nine, old enough to understand what had happened, but I don't even have any real memories of life with Mum and Dad.'

'But you've been afraid of heights ever since?' She glanced yearningly at the dirty dishes, but he caught her other hand and drew her reluctant body further between his splayed knees. 'Nora?'

She sighed at the unyielding set of his jaw. This was the part she was *really* reluctant to talk about.

'No, only since I was fourteen, if you must know. It was just a silly overreaction…' She trailed off, but he waited patiently for her to continue. 'I went on a biology field trip with my high school class. I didn't realise until we got there that it was the same regional park. I'd never been back there, but we were up on the cliffs looking at nesting sites and I felt this compulsion to take a quick look over the edge—to—I don't know—just to *see*.'

He leaned forward and she was aware of the hard column of his splayed thighs, the utter intensity of his gaze, the latent strength in the lithe body. It was both alarming and alluring to be the focus of all his concentrated attention, almost as if he really *cared*…

'So I looked down—and I saw—a woman was sunbathing on one of the slabs of rock at the base of the cliff… She was lying on her back on a red towel with her long hair spread out around her head—for a moment I actually thought that all the red was her blood! I didn't realise some of the guys in the class had been rough-housing around behind me, and right at that moment I saw her—' Her breath grew choppy. 'Well, do you know that silly trick where a person sneaks up and grabs you around the waist with a violent jerk that seems to shove you forward but really just rattles you in place—?'

Blake cursed, surging to his feet, flattening her captive hands against his chest before roughly enclosing her in protective arms.

'Goddamned idiots,' he growled into the nimbus of curls at her temple, his hand moving up and down her rigid spine.

Nora tilted her head back so that she could see his face, his ferocious scowl brightening her heart. 'They didn't know my history; they were just boys being boys. Any other time and place and I probably would have been able to laugh it off,' she said, striving to be fair.

'As it was, I totally freaked out. Completely lost the plot, right there in front of the whole class. It was so-o-o humiliating. I knew what was happening but I just couldn't seem to stop myself—screams, tears, throwing up—and worse…' She bit her unruly tongue, dropping her gaze, hoping that he wouldn't pick up on that mortifying detail. For a shy overweight teenager, losing control of her bladder in front of her peers had been a deeply shaming experience.

'Anyway, I avoided high places completely for a while, but I eventually taught myself ways to cope.'

Going to university in Dunedin, she had had little choice—the city was much hillier than Invercargill and boasted a daunting number of multi-storey buildings. And, of course, by then there'd been Ryan to adore and impress…

'I can usually handle the anxiety OK now, as long as I get the time to psyche myself up beforehand,' she added. 'Thank God, it's never been as bad it was that first time.'

He looked down at her restless fingers, smoothing and re-smoothing his T-shirt, and slowly let his arms drift down to settle around her narrow hips. As he had suspected, the ruffled sparrow had the heart of a gamecock. When she was knocked off her perch she didn't lie in the dust waiting to be rescued. She rescued herself.

'Because you're no longer that young impressionable girl.' He brushed a stray curl back from her cheek, tucking it behind her neat ear, taking his time smoothing it into place until her skittish gaze darted back to his. 'Maybe your fear at the time was exaggerated by a form of post-traumatic stress—delayed feelings of grief and loss, especially the loss of your mother.'

Nora frowned at him, her hands spreading wide over his chest in instinctive protest. 'But Tess is the only mother I remember having—'

'That doesn't mean the memories aren't there.' His fingers had lingered on the sensitive skin behind her ear, toying with the lock of hair, his knuckles grazing her delicate lobe. 'Until you were four you were bonded to your birth mother, and then suddenly she vanished from your life. It must have been profoundly bewildering and frightening. You were obviously able to transfer your maternal bond to your aunt, although I notice that you don't call her *Mum*, or share her surname—'

'Sean still called her Aunt Tess so she thought it would be less confusing if I did, too. Lots of people call their parents by their first names,' Nora murmured, distracted by the little trickles of heat sliding down the back of her neck.

The strong supportive hand that had been in the small of her back had somehow moved south, his fingers curving down over the gentle flare of her bottom, the warmth of his hard palm tilting her hips against the cradle of his thighs, while her small breasts grazed his chest.

She struggled to pretend that she hadn't noticed, in case she was obliged to object. 'Anyway, Tess and Pat didn't formally adopt us, and Dad's father wanted Sean and me to carry on the family name—Dad was an only child.'

Nora's breathing was breaking up again, but not from the echoes of panic. That Blake was naked under his thin trousers was becoming more obvious with each passing moment. She could feel the unmistakable masculine shape of him against the hollow of her groin, the soft bulge of muscle slowly firming into a distinct ridge.

'What makes you such an expert on young girls, anyway?' she heard herself babbling wildly. 'I thought your sisters were all older than you.'

His fingers abandoned her ear to trail lightly down the side of her neck, his thumb dipping into the small indentation at the base of her throat.

'Four nieces.'

'Oh!' An unexpected laugh began to bubble up inside her, mingling with the intoxicating fizz brewing in her blood. 'No nephews?' she guessed.

He answered her with a mocking glower of discontent. 'My life is a plague of women. Kate's seventeen-year-old twins are reckless tearaways who need firm and frequent squashing.'

An effervescent giggle escaped Nora's compressed lips, unconsciously relaxing her guard. The new information had put the ruthless predator male in an entirely different light.

'Why are you looking at me like that?' he demanded

She had screwed up her honey-gold eyes, her freckled nose wrinkling. 'I'm trying to visualise you as a father figure,' she dared to tease.

'Oh, please don't!' His thumb flicked up under the point of her chin, lifting it to meet her punishment in the form of a smouldering gaze and sultry purr. 'Incest is not one of the sins I had in mind for you to commit...'

'I— Really? W-what sins?' she said, trying hard to maintain her brazen air and realising from his glint of satisfaction that she wasn't doing a very good job.

His head dipped, his face so close that she could see the faint throb of the blue vein on his temple and count the tiny green flecks that gleamed like buried gems in his eyes.

'Well, let me see...' he murmured, his warm breath caressing her flushed cheek. He swooped down to graze a soft kiss against her jaw, moving up to settle lightly on her pale pink mouth before she had time to do more than draw a shaky breath. Even braced for more of his outrageousness she was surprised by the violent kick of her heart when his tongue briefly slid against hers, only to withdraw with a tantalising flick that left her tastebuds craving more....

He now employed his clever tongue to even greater seductive purpose. 'I think lust, gluttony and covetousness are definitely on the list of our transgressions...' he nibbled suggestively at her lower lip '...with possibly a long, lazy stretch of voluptuous sloth afterwards. What do you say?' He rubbed his hawkish nose gently over hers, slanting his head to take her mouth with another, frustratingly light, languid kiss.

'Of course, if you're really hung up about the father thing,' he whispered, 'you could ask me to be your sugar-daddy—I'm sure we could arrange a mutually enjoyable exchange of favours....'

Nora's brief flirtation with sexual sophistication went up in flames as she wondered what favours he had in mind. 'Don't be ridiculous! I— You— Y-you're too—'

'Perverted?' he breathed into her stuttering mouth. 'Insulting?'

'Young!' she blurted, and went crimson at his deep

chuckle, a hot charge running through her nipples where they were pressed against his vibrating chest.

The sensation increased when his arm went around her back, only her braced hands preventing their upper bodies from melting together.

'Well, I confess I'd be a virgin in the role,' he admitted silkily, 'but there's a first time for everyone—isn't there, Nora?'

'Yes. I mean—no! I don't want you to play *any* role.' An X-rated vision of a cruel grey-eyed sultan and his languishing favourite suddenly revisited her imagination, causing her freckles to join up with rosy guilt.

'Shame!' His knowing grin damned her for a bare-faced liar. 'I could have delivered you an Oscar-winning performance.'

'For acting or special effects?' she muttered through her blushes.

He made another deep sound in his chest, half laugh and half groan. 'We do seem to have a rather special effect on each other, don't we?' The hand on her bottom moved down to cup one taut rounded globe, lifting her more tightly into the heavy fullness of his groin. 'What do you think we should do about it?'

She shuddered. The hot thrust of his desire ignited an answering fire deep within the core of her being. A molten heaviness gathered low in her abdomen, sending thick spurts of scalding excitement pulsing through her body, a turbulent mixture of fear and delight that threatened to burst the flimsy barriers of her control.

'I don't know…' She tried to remember all the reasons she should resist Blake's potent allure, but they seemed to be slipping from her increasingly hazy mental grasp.

He would be a dangerous enemy, but Nora had an uneasy premonition that he might be an even more dangerous friend! Despite all the suspicion and mistrust that lay between them, Blake made her feel things that she had never felt before, not even with Ryan. Her comfortable life had been thrown into chaos and the painful emotional upheaval was proving oddly liberating. She had *wanted* Ryan, but was beginning to realise that she had never really *needed* him....

'I can't think properly—' she gasped, arching her throat as Blake nuzzled into the warm crease of her neck, surprising her with yet another previously undiscovered erogenous zone.

'Then don't!' His rough urgency invited her to surrender to the moment. 'Just go with what you feel...'

But feelings could be treacherous, too. They put the generous, loyal and loving at the mercy of the cool-headed and self-serving. Did Blake even know what it was like to suffer betrayal on such an intimate level—to the extent that he could no longer trust his emotions?

Nora pushed her braced hands against the rock-hard chest, holding his overwhelming physicality at bay with trembling arms. She was right to be nervous. His harsh face was drawn into a mask of arousal, flesh stripped back from the bone, his mouth full and slightly reddened, a dark and hungry look prowling in the glittering grey eyes—the epitome of a dominant male.

'Have you ever made a total fool of yourself over a woman?' she wondered wistfully.

He hesitated, eyes narrowing, instinctively wary: a predator alert for hidden traps.

'No, no of course you haven't!' she said, her voice wry. Blake might be an acknowledged expert in the bedroom but, discounting his teenage crush, he was no authority on love. He had been too well armoured by his ambition to allow himself to be sidetracked by his emotions.

'What makes you so damned sure?' he pounced. He seemed to have taken her answer on his behalf as a challenge. Perhaps he resented the fact that she could read him so easily.

'Well, you haven't, have you?' she said, the confident upward arch of her dark eyebrows making his own plummet to new depths.

A lethal smile peeled away from his teeth, baring his wolfish determination.

'Maybe that's about to change…' he murmured, contracting his powerful arms with an explosive jerk that collapsed Nora back on to his chest. He raked his open mouth over her parted lips, letting her feel the sharp grate of his teeth, forcing her soft squeak of surprise back down her throat with long, deep, drugging kisses that caused an instant sensual overload.

While the hot male taste of him ravished her senses and stole away part of her woman's soul, her mind spun sugar candy fantasies from his words. Was he implying that *Nora* might have the power to make him act foolishly?

Her heart fluttered up into her throat when she suddenly realised that they were no longer beside the dining table. His soul-stealing kisses had blinded her to the fact that he had been slowly walking her backwards, manouevering her with instinctive skill around the scattered furniture towards the plush blue couches that lay in wait in the shadows of the big room. At some stage her protesting arms had wound themselves around his neck, her fingers fisted in the cool dampness of his midnight-dark hair.

Dizzy and breathless, she felt her legs bump to a halt against the low arm of one of the couches, the plush velvety pile creating a delicious friction against the sensitive nerves at the back of her knees. She imagined being tumbled back the short distance into the safety net of deep squashy cushions, crushed into the softness by that lithe, hard body, dominated and controlled by his clever hands, which had already slipped under her T-shirt to explore her bare back and the satin smoothness of her seamless bra. His fingers looped under one narrow strap, dragging it to the side so that the cool fabric peeled down from the silky curve of her breast, exposing the taut button of her nipple to his rasping thumb. His tongue dipped and curled enticingly in her mouth as his fingers gently played with his find, drawing the delicate bud out to swollen fullness, milking it of pleasure with smooth, measured strokes, then squeezing with a ruthless finesse that made her shudder in violent delight.

'Yes, you like that. I know you do...' he affirmed with crushing satisfaction as he turned his carnal attention to her other breast, circling her begging nipple with a taunting scrape of his nails. He bit at her tender earlobe as he whispered, 'Do you remember how you felt at the hotel when I suckled your lovely breasts? You almost climaxed when I took your nipple inside my mouth. Shall we do it again now...?' His fingers tightened to illustrate his shockingly explicit words.

Nora thought she was going to faint.

'Oh, God—! No— I— Wait!' She panicked, teetering on the brink of a new emotional precipice, afraid, not of falling, but of actively flinging herself over the edge. Her hands dug into the thickly bunched muscles across his shoulders as she strove to cling to her fast-eroding resolve. 'You said you'd answer my question if I answered yours!'

His hands froze against her breasts. 'You've *got* to be kidding!' he groaned in her burning ear.

She shook her head, her curls bouncing against his cheek. 'We had a bargain,' she gulped.

He drew back. 'You'd really rather talk than—' He offered her a string of erotic variations that made her burn with curiosity. Was it really possible to do all those things? *In one night?*

She shook away the wicked thought and his mouth compressed, his eyes flaring with a ferocious impatience. She half hoped he might arrogantly ignore her shaky resistance, but instead she felt his whole body ripple with a series of pulsing contractions, as if he was fighting to rein himself in, muscle by individual muscle. His hands abandoned her aching breasts to encircle her smooth waist just above the band of her shorts, keeping her firmly compressed between his hard thighs and the soft side of the couch.

'All right, ask your damned question,' he said, with a clipped precision that signalled his rigid self-control.

She was dismayed to find that she was suddenly reluctant

to put him to the test. There were some things she might be better off not knowing…

'I just don't understand why I'm such a threat to you,' she blurted, aware from his rigid face that she was putting it badly. 'I mean, why hacking some stupid disk makes me so important. Because if it wasn't for that, you wouldn't have bothered to find me again, would you? Let alone bring me into your home. We wouldn't be here, doing *this*…' Her voice petered out as his rigid mask slipped to reveal a banked fire.

'Maybe not here and now, but make no mistake, Nora. *This*—' he rocked his flamboyant erection against her quivering belly '—would have happened between us sooner or later. Circumstances dictated the urgency but not the impetus…. You created that when you gave me that sexy look of wide-eyed innocence across a crowded room.'

Nora's body thrilled to his sensual threat, even as her mind shied at the picture his words were creating.

'Only it wasn't so innocent on your part, was it, Nora? You were marking me out for your experiment. And when the instant physical attraction between us went too far too fast, instead of dealing with it like a mature adult, you simply bailed.'

She squirmed, unable to deny it. But he was making it sound as if he had been nothing but a helpless victim!

'I hardly knew anything about you, and what I did know wasn't exactly reassuring,' she protested, discreetly wrestling her bra back into position over her tingling breasts. 'I'm not very good with confrontations—'

He gave a snort and she glared up at him in righteous indignation. 'I'm not! I'm usually very even-tempered and easy to get along with. But you have an extremely forceful personality, and it can be very overwhelming for an ordinary person like me,' she said, the spirited challenge in her glowing eyes unconsciously giving the lie to her words. 'Look at how you steamrollered over my protests this morning! And every time I ask you a question you don't want to answer you find a way to distract me—'

'When the stock market opens on Tuesday morning PresCorp intends to buy the rest of the TranStar shares it needs to take a controlling interest in the company,' Blake interrupted bluntly, shocking her to silence with his unexpected openness. 'We're confident we'll succeed in spite of the board's resistance because we have what we believe to be watertight deals with a couple of major stakeholders. The only way we can possibly lose out now is if a rival bidder manages to leverage one of our deals out from under us over the weekend, or can lock up a strategic shareholding by off-market lobbying of minority interests....'

Nora's eyes began to glaze as his frankness blossomed into talk of conditional bids and buy-backs and cross-holdings, but when he paused with a frown, she hurriedly rearranged her features to indicate intelligent life within. An ironic twist of his mouth suggested he wasn't fooled, and she was not to know that her glassy-eyed uninterest had done more to persuade him of her innocence than any of her heated protestations.

Fortunately for Nora he seemed to have finally arrived at the relevant bit—the bit that *was* interesting. 'PresCorp got the jump on everyone else because they expected we would wait to do due diligence before launching a bid, but we'd already run our own confidential investigation. That disk you took—'

'Innocently acquired ' she interjected.

'*Accidentally misappropriated*—' he allowed with a stern look of reprimand '—was loaded with highly sensitive financial information about TranStar, and PresCorp's share-buying strategy and tactics, and plans for future restructuring. There were also files containing some extremely compromising and potentially actionable personal material about past and present TranStar shareholders and directors. If some, or all, of that information were to leak out before we make our stand on Tuesday—even a *hint* that we'd had a breach of security and the knowledge was out there to be scavenged—it could wreck months of planning and create havoc in the market, not to mention damaging a number of reputations....'

'I see why your man Doug is such a favoured employee; you must keep him awfully busy.' Her vodka-blitzed brain remembered tedious graphs and dreary stock projections interlaced by screens of crackling-dry prose, but nothing of any personal scandals. She must have nodded off before she even got to the juicy stuff! 'You've actually *blackmailed* people into selling you their shares?' she commented incredulously.

A muscle flickered in Blake's cheek, but his voice remained cool. 'There's always cut-throat manouevring and mud-slinging behind the scenes in situations like this. Fortunes can turn over on a rumour. Grudges and loyalties get played out, especially in third generation family-founded companies like TranStar. Knowing who's sleeping with whose wife or who's over-extended himself buying a new yacht can give you an edge in negotiations. I don't break any laws, but there are always plenty of loopholes in the rules and regulations for the lawyers to dispute afterwards. Meantime everyone scrambles to protect their own personal positions and maximise their financial gains.'

'In other words it's every man for himself,' Nora said disapprovingly.

'Or woman. There are plenty of women out there ready to slit a company's throat for the promise of a seat on the board.'

'And you think I might be one of them?' she said, using scorn to disguise her stab of hurt.

His thumbs stroked her hip-bones, a glint of humour resurfacing at the sight of her furiously fluffed feathers. 'Somehow I don't see you as boardroom material,' he murmured.

More bedroom material? Nora bit the tip of her unruly tongue to prevent the old cliché from spilling out, but from the lucent spark in Blake's eye she might as well have uttered the provocative words out loud.

As an oblique form of apology it had bordered on a pretty good insult, she thought, trying to whip her hurt into a defensive outrage. She might not be brimming with management savvy, but she was clever enough to learn to run a company if she put her mind to it, albeit something small and interesting, like maybe her own IT business....

'So I'm here because you're afraid that my venal nature is going to get the better of me if I'm not under twenty-four-hour guard, and to make sure I can't escape with my ill-gotten gains if it turns out that I've already been corrupted! I'm surprised you want to sleep with me if I'm so obviously untrustworthy,' she said bitterly.

He met her stormy gaze with a compelling calm. 'There's a wider issue of trust involved here. I have to deal with the facts as they stand here and now, not as I want them to be. I have a responsibility for those I work for and with—a lot of people have put their faith in the soundness of my judgements. Every day they take huge risks based on my recommendations. If I start to make critical business decisions based on my personal feelings rather than best practice, then I wouldn't be worthy of their trust. And this buyout is set to cost Scotty several hundred million dollars, so he's not going to be very sympathetic if it all suddenly turns to custard and my excuse begins, "Sorry, but there was this bewitching young woman with stunning golden eyes..."'

Several hundred million dollars? Nora's stomach jumped at the notion. God, no wonder Blake was so paranoid! 'Personal feelings?' she ventured tentatively.

'*Extremely* personal,' he answered with a tantalising shift of his hips. His eyelids drooped, giving her a brief warning he was about to say something calculated to unsettle. 'And, by the way, Nora, I never said I wanted to sleep with you....'

'*Oh!*' Elation turned to instant mortification and she tried to wriggle out from between his thighs, only to have him bend to hook his arm behind her knees, sweeping her off her feet and up against his chest with a deep satisfied laugh.

'Because sleep will definitely be the *last* thing on my mind when I finally get you into my bed,' he concluded in a wicked undertone, carrying her across the room as if she weighed no more than a feather. He turned down the hall, adjusting her more securely in his arms, and Nora's head fell back against his shoulder as she contemplated her choices, knowing that there was only one she really wanted to make. Had wanted ever since she met him. This fascinating, infuriating, impossibly complex and wholly desirable man was like an elegant encryption, designed expressly to test her mettle.

'Where are we going?' she asked, her voice husky with nervous anticipation, convinced that she knew.

'My mother always taught me to escort my date to her door,' he teased in that same low, intimate tone.

Her door? Hadn't he mentioned *his* bed?

But of course every bed in the house was technically his, she supposed, her body suffused with warmth.

He set her down gently, in a slow, erotic, mutual caress of bodies, at the darkened entrance to her exotic room, and Nora willed her wobbly legs to support her as she prepared to take the scariest leap of her life. A leap into the dark. A leap of faith.

She swayed to meet Blake's lingering kiss, but when her hands moved eagerly up to cup his face he gathered them to his lips in a gallant, but chaste, salute.

'Sweet dreams, Nora. I'll see you in the morning,' he said, and with another brief goodnight kiss on her stunned brow he strolled back down the hall without a backwards glance.

CHAPTER TEN

THE THIRD TIME that Nora woke up in the big white-swathed bed on Sunday morning, it was with a smile of rapturous bliss. Instinct told her it was still early and her eyelids fluttered dreamily open as she rolled over on her side, reaching out to run a lazy hand over the sun-burnished body of her thoroughly decadent sultan.

Instead of warm bare muscles toned by energetic bouts of lovemaking under the hot Arabian sun, Nora found cool, crisp one hundred per cent Egyptian cotton.

With a groan of frustration Nora continued rolling until her face was buried in the depths of the smooth, undented pillow that lay next to her. She couldn't believe that Blake had once again sent her to bed with only her erotic fantasies for company. She was starting to wonder if he had any intention of living up to his bad reputation!

She had bounced out of bed on Saturday morning with the firm conviction that Blake's gentlemanly conduct at her bedroom door had merely been his clever way of ratcheting up the sexual tension between them. She had been sure that, having asserted his dominance, he would swiftly make good his sensual threats and seductive promises.

Instead she had spent the day with a man who had been by turns infuriatingly casual and maddeningly friendly.

He had fed her breakfast while chatting about the difficulties involved in the building of the house five years ago, and how it had been designed by the same architect who had built his home on Auckland's waterfront.

Afterwards he had given her a guided tour of the sprawling upper level, whisking her in and out of his aggressively masculine bedroom without a single suggestive comment, seemingly more interested in her opinion of the architecture and furnishings than in seduction.

Then he had chivvied her into changing and going for a run with him along the beach, taking her down the winding gravel road in the jaunty beach-buggy.

'My nieces tortured me into buying this!' he shouted above the roar of the engine and the wind in their ears as they shot on to the beach, but Nora could tell from the white grin that gashed the hard face below the black wrap-around sunglasses that he hadn't taken much persuading.

The tide was only halfway up the wide sweep of black sand and apart from a few hardened surfers out amongst the waves the beach was empty but for a family with a dog out on the rocks by the point.

They jogged the kilometre or so to one end of the beach on the hard-packed sand just below the high-water mark, but when they got back to the dune where he had parked the buggy, and Blake showed no signs of stopping, Nora collapsed panting into the sand and waved him on. With an insufferably superior grin he took off towards the other end of the beach at double their speed and did another couple of complete laps of the beach in the same pounding rhythm, while Nora fetched a towel and water bottle from the bag he had stowed in the cockpit of the buggy. Kicking off her sneakers, she stripped down to her pale bronze bathing suit, a sleek one-piece with a deep V neckline and detail around the high-cut hips.

When Blake returned, his tank top and shorts clinging to his sweat-soaked body, it was to find Nora sitting on a towel absorbed in conversation with a sun-bleached young surfer who stood, his wetsuit peeled down to his waist, his muscled arm holding his upright board to one side of his smooth, deeply tanned torso.

'Steve.' Blake's voice was as curt as his nod.

'Blake.' The surfie nodded back, grinning down at Nora.

'Going out?' Blake demanded even more curtly.

'Coming in.' The flick of a calculated hand through his long blond hair made Nora gasp as a glittering arc of cold drops splattered over her hot skin and slid down between her breasts.

'Sorry. Shall I lick that off for you, darlin'?' he offered with a playful grin that had her smothering a giggle.

Blake took a menacing step closer. 'Beat it, kid. You're playing out of your league. Especially if you want that summer internship you've been pestering me for....'

The fearless grin widened. Steve tipped a wink at Nora as he tucked his surfboard back under his arm with a flourish and lowered his voice to a stage whisper. 'Just remember, I'm the first on the left going up the road if the old man pegs out on you—I have a soft bed, a great stereo and a fully stocked drinks cabinet....'

Nora turned her stifled giggle into a choked cough as the young man sauntered on his way up the beach.

'You didn't have to be so rude,' she chided. 'He was just being friendly.'

'I suppose you were so busy simpering up at him you didn't notice he was leering down your suit,' he said tersely. 'You do realise that's his *parents'* liquor cabinet he's boasting about!'

Secretly encouraged by his dog-in-the-manger attitude, Nora stretched her legs out in front of her and leaned non-chalantly back on her braced arms.

'So he said.'

'Did he? What else did he say?' He dropped to his knees, removing his tank top and mopping his forehead, throat and chest with it. His brows twitched together. 'What were you two talking about?'

'I was telling him all your TranStar secrets, of course,' she said sweetly. 'We were plotting a way to get rid of you and take over the company ourselves.'

The snatched eyebrows melted into a laugh. 'Did you happen to mention I'd brought you here against your will and beg him to take you back to Auckland? I mean, this was your big chance to escape my wicked clutches and cause me maximum pain and embarrassment.'

Wicked? If only!

'I— He— As you pointed out, he's only a boy. It wouldn't have been fair to involve him,' she floundered, trying to disguise the betraying fact that it hadn't even occurred to her. 'And, anyway, since you're neighbours and he's obviously applied to you for some sort of holiday job, I doubt he would have risked crossing you—'

'But you didn't know that when you spoke to him.' Blake twisted the top off a second water bottle and she watched, fascinated, the rippling of his strong throat as he drank. Then he tilted his jaw to one side and splashed some of the water down on to his sweaty chest, causing the skin to tighten and his nipples to visibly contract. The muscles in Nora's arms went lax, and to hide her sudden weakness she lay flat on her back, wriggling her bottom to form a comfortable hollow in the sand beneath the towel.

Blake froze, the bottle still held high, watching the shimmy of her hips and the matching shimmer of her breasts against the thin covering of Lycra.

'The colour of that suit is almost the same shade as your freckles. From a distance you look as if you're not wearing anything at all.'

She forced herself not to move. 'I do not!'

'How do you know?' he goaded. 'I bet that's why Steve came hotfooting over—he thought you were sunbathing in the nude. Did he look wildly disappointed when he got up close?'

'No, he didn't!' she gritted, although, come to think of it, he had given her a rather sheepish grin. 'I've had this suit for ages; no one's mentioned anything before—'

'Maybe lover boy enjoyed the view too much.'

'We hardly ever went to the beach together—or the pool,' she recalled. 'Ryan doesn't like swimming.'

'Except in bathtubs.' He took another cool swig of water. 'I forget, was it the breast-stroke he was doing—or the crawl?'

Nora's voice suddenly trembled on the verge of a laugh and her riposte was correspondingly weak. 'You're an insensitive pig!'

'And he apparently never cared enough to do with you the things that *you* liked to do. You're a genuine water-baby, aren't you? Doug said that you used to swim as a teenager and you still do lengths at the local pool several times a week, summer and winter.'

'I only took it up because I wanted to lose weight,' she found herself confessing. 'And then I kept on because I loved it—the swimming part, I mean, not the competing.'

'I didn't see it at first because of that ghastly dress you were wearing,' he said, 'but you have the classic swimmer's body—strong shoulders, high breasts, slim hips and long slender legs that look as if they have a real kick in them.'

He was leaning over, his shadow falling across her like a cool, dark caress, and for a shattering moment Nora hoped he was actually going to follow through on his softly flattering words but he suddenly rocked back on his haunches and jack-knifed to his feet, tossing the water bottle into the sand.

'I usually cool off in the surf after a beach run.' He started towards the line of breakers, casting a careless invitation over his shoulder. 'Join me if you want to give that suit a workout....'

His tantalising advance and retreat set the scene for the entire day. They spent the morning on the beach and went back up to the house for a lunch which meandered into mid-afternoon, then lazed around on the terrace, with Nora in a sun-lounger firmly wedged up against the glass doors of the house, her heart in her mouth every time Blake rolled indolently into the pool to disport like a seal in the silky blue water. Envy and a much fiercer emotion burned in her breast, but no amount of subtle encouragement or needling, or outright flirting on Nora's part, succeeded in provoking the desired response. His eyes intermittently smouldered with banked fire and he made plenty of excuses to touch her, but any impulse to turn the fleeting contact into anything more intimate was firmly diverted into conversational channels.

Not that Nora was bored. She learned all about his mother and his sisters—thirty-seven-year-old Kate and her Terrible Twins, whose father had dropped out of sight before they were even born; Maria, the thirty-five-year-old union lawyer who resided with her live-in lover and was following in her mother's activist footsteps, delighting at nipping at her brother's corporate heels; and his youngest sister, Sara, who worked at the restaurant managed by her husband, and whose two daughters were sports mad.

'I don't know why you need nephews; it sounds like the family females have all the bases covered,' she kidded.

'It'd be nice to have at least *one* of the next generation of MacLeods who sees the world from my perspective,' he said wryly.

'Well, it's obviously being left up to you to provide the masculine branches on the family tree.'

Something shifted behind the hawkish features, the steel-grey eyes darkening as they registered a seismic shift in his perceptions, then the cynical mask snapped back into place. 'Wondering if I've left any stray twigs lying around, Nora? I haven't, I assure you—I take *all* my responsibilities seriously.'

It was only natural that Blake's relaxed talk of his assorted relatives should lead Nora into comparisons with her own family, and stories of growing up in Invercargill and how Tess had been a great substitute mother, just not very domesticated. While her aunt and uncle were busy running their sales business it had fallen to Nora to manage the family household and do most of the shopping and cooking.

She was eager to boast about Sean, especially when Blake showed a genuine interest in her brother's career as a marine salvage diver and sometime Caribbean treasure-hunter. Over pre-dinner cocktails she confided that Sean's tales of his treasure-seeking expeditions had inspired her to start designing a computer programme which would help him more accurately predict the break-up and dispersion pattern of ancient wrecks in any given combination of sea-floor topography and wind and sea currents. Chin propped on his hand, Blake listened with such rapt absorption to her enthusiastic description of her ideas that she stopped worrying about his unfathomable behaviour and gave in to the sheer joy of being in his company, licensing herself to ignore the whispered warnings from her vulnerable heart.

Cocktails flowed almost seamlessly into another delicious home-cooked dinner, but in spite of Nora rifling her meagre cache of clothes for her one and only dress—a simple floral wraparound with a flirty flimsy skirt—the combination of excess sun, sea, fresh air and nervous tension took their inevitable toll and she actually yawned when Blake walked her along to her room and took her tightly in his arms.

He had *finally* got around to kissing her again and Nora had *yawned*! Worse still, instead of being offended or annoyed, he had *laughed*....

Nora groaned more deeply into the pillow, pounding it with her fists and kicking her feet against the confines of the top sheet, which had been tangled into damp skeins by her sweaty, dream-shot night.

Her mini tantrum over, she went into the bathroom, opening the frosted window, the better to enjoy the chorus of bird-song and the earthy scent of the bush while she brushed her teeth. Her mouth was full of foam when she heard the rumble of a high-performance engine floating up through the window. Was that the TVR in the driveway? She doubted Blake would be sneaking off to church!

She rinsed her mouth and gave her face a smear with a

dampened flannel, running her fingers through her wildly kinked hair as she hurried out to the stairs. She flew down the first flight, her bare feet silent on the thick carpet, and came to a skidding halt by the rail on the landing as she saw Blake with his back to her, one arm braced high against the open front door and security grille, greeting someone crossing the entry bridge. The back of his head was still bed-ruffled, he was barefoot, the belt of his black jeans dangling from the tabs at his hip, and—why hadn't he put on a shirt? His room was at the front corner of the house… He must have dashed down here as soon as he heard the car.

Nora crept forward for a better view, sidling up to a large ornamental urn stuffed with dried flowers so that she could see but not be seen.

The car was a late-model silver Mercedes convertible, the driver a *very* late-model blonde, her generous curves shrink-wrapped in a glittery pink crop-top and black leather mini-skirt. Her sequinned pink high-heeled sandals matched the wide leather belt that cinched her waist and her long straight hair was razor-cut to frame a youthful face boldly made up to seem older. From the way she was smiling as she stepped off the bridge on to the tiled porch she was supremely sure of her welcome. Was this one of Kate MacLeod's notorious twins?

'Hi, Blake.' The greeting was accompanied by a coy wiggle of coral-tipped fingers. Having got to the doorstep and finding that he wasn't stepping aside, the wattage of the smile increased. 'Surprise, surprise!' She placed her fingertips on Blake's chest and walked them provocatively up towards his unshaven chin. 'Happy to see me?'

Whoa!

Not very niecely behaviour, Nora fumed, watching Blake jerk his head back and catch the wandering fingers in his free hand.

'What are you doing here, Hayley?' His voice was neutral but Nora's straining ears detected a hint of deep unease.

The young woman gave a throaty laugh that made Nora revise her age up a few years. 'We had a date last night and you didn't show. It was a fantastic party, too; you really missed some fun.' She pouted a playful lower lip, slick with gloss, to show there were no hard feelings. 'I was *so* disappointed, but when Uncle Prescott explained all the pressure you were under and told me you'd snuck away for the weekend I realised that you just weren't in the party mood.'

Uncle Prescott? Nora's brain went on red alert. Hayley was the niece of Blake's boss? And she and Blake had been *dating*?

'Poor Blake,' Hayley was commiserating, snuggling up to his side with a nauseatingly kittenish air. 'Uncle Prescott said he was sure you didn't mean to let me down—you know how he likes to see me happy—so I decided to give you another chance. I thought I'd come and provide you with my special brand of stress relief....'

The kind of 'relief' she was talking about was obvious from the way her hand was creeping up Blake's thigh.

Nora's suspicions went ballistic. A red mist covered her vision and for a moment she thought she was going to be sick. For the first time she faced the real truth about her feelings for Blake. The dangerous attraction she had felt from the moment she first saw him wasn't just physical, but her painfully mixed up emotions had refused to believe she could have fallen for him so completely, so fast. Even when she had mistrusted his motives, she had still respected him and, yes, *admired* the fierce commitment he brought to everything, whether it be his lovemaking or his ruthless pursuit of his goals.

Only maybe his *real* goal was marrying the boss's niece!

At least this resolved any question of his paternity, she thought sickly. If Prescott Williams was keen on promoting a match between Blake and Hayley, then Blake couldn't be his son.

The red mist became a fog of fury. Kelly and Hayley—two spoilt young madams, both nieces of men who could pull company strings for their lovers!

Silently Nora fled back up the stairs and ducked into the first room she came upon—Blake's bedroom. Her wrathful gaze fell on the racks of clothes in the huge open wardrobe and her mouth curved in a vicious smile. She tore off her nightie and threw it on to the unmade bed. Naked but for her cotton briefs, she stormed over to the wardrobe and pulled a crisp white business shirt off its wooden hanger. She twisted it in savage fists and dragged the crumpled result on, rolling up the cuffed sleeves to her elbows and fastening five of the small pearlised buttons that marched down over her midriff. She looked at herself in the full-length mirror next to the bathroom door and undid the top button to reveal more cleavage. Leaning in to the mirror, she pinched roughly at her cheeks and chewed at her bottom lip. Her hair was sufficiently wild not to need any help in looking as if she had just climbed out of a passion pit!

Barely a couple of minutes had passed and when she reached the top of the stairs again she could hear the murmured conversation still going on at the door.

Let him talk himself out of *this*!

She took a deep breath that cleared some of the choking rage from her throat. Then she called out, using the sugar-sweet whine she had heard Kelly use when she wanted to twist a man around her manicured finger.

'Bla-ake! Where are you? Come on, Babycakes, what's taking you so long? You must have got rid of whoever it was by now!'

She heard the muted talk downstairs come to a sudden halt. 'Bla-ake! I'm getting cold and the champagne is getting warm!' she sang in a sexy lilt.

Dead silence. Nora began to trip down the stairs, changing her voice to a teasing sing-song. 'Oh, Bla-ake! Are we playing another of your kinky games of hide and seek? Then... coming, ready or no-ot!' she trilled, making the familiar playground call sound wickedly adult.

'Oh!' She came to a sudden stop halfway down the final

flight, one hand on the railing, the other covering her open mouth as she pretended to see the couple below for the first time. They were still standing in the doorway, Blake holding both of Hayley's hands in his.

'Oh, dear,' Nora gurgled. 'I didn't realise there was someone still here! I'm sorry, Blake. Have I let the cat out of the bag? I know we weren't supposed to let anyone know I was here....'

She waited expectantly for him to explode, but instead he appeared to be transfixed by shock as Hayley wrenched her hands out of his and said shrilly, 'Who's *she*? Why isn't anyone supposed to know? What's going on, Blake?'

'Yes, aren't you going to introduce us, Blake?' simpered Nora, slinking down the last few steps and sauntering up beside him.

'I don't think so,' he said with a tight-lipped grimness that gave her spiteful pleasure.

She mimicked Hayley's sulky pout and it must have been successful, for the younger girl took a step back, clutching her pink handbag to her glittering breasts, and sent Blake an angry look of scorching reproach.

'I'm Nora—Nora Lang,' said Nora helpfully, stirring the pot. 'Blake and I—well, we...' she ran a hand through her tousled curls, drawing attention to the suggestive pink marks on her cheeks and her sensuously bitten lips, as well as the brevity of her attire '...I suppose I *could* say we were just good friends, but in the circumstances that would be rather silly, wouldn't it?'

Hayley glared disdainfully at Nora with hard china-blue eyes, showing no hint of apology or discomfort.

'Uncle Prescott told me that you came down here *alone*,' she insisted stridently to Blake, wielding the name as an implied threat with such practised ease that Nora, who had been suffering a pang of empathy, felt her sympathy wither.

'Yes, well, "Uncle Prescott" isn't privy to everything that goes on in my personal life,' Blake replied coolly. 'Nowhere in my employment contract does it say that I have to clear it with the Chairman of the Board if I want to spend the weekend with the special woman in my life.'

Hayley's bee-stung mouth fell open and Nora sensed her own jaw sagging in stunned disbelief. She started to jerk away, experiencing a thrill of alarm, when Blake's arm snapped across her lower back, his heavy hand settling on her hip-bone, locking her against his hard flank. 'As I was saying before Nora so charmingly interrupted, you should have talked to me before driving all the way out here, Hayley. I could have saved you the trip.'

Hayley went pale with anger. 'You never seemed to mind me dropping in before!' she said petulantly, digging around in her handbag to produce a bright pink cell-phone. 'And anyway, I *did* call. I texted *and* left a message on your mobile to say I was coming, because every time I dialled it kept cutting straight to the answerphone!' She brandished the phone in his face.

'Perhaps the fact that I wasn't responding to my messages should have warned you that I didn't want to be disturbed.' Blake's cruel bluntness added to Nora's growing fear that she might have just made the biggest mistake of her life! 'I *have* asked you to stop turning up unannounced—to avoid just such an awkward situation as this,' he continued. 'I know that, as his late brother's stepchild, Scotty wants you and me to be friends, but even my family respects certain boundaries in my life. Naturally, I wouldn't have chosen to have you find out about Nora like this, but perhaps it's best that it's out in the open—'

'Then why did *she* say no one was supposed to know? You've never bothered to try and hide your mistresses before.' Hayley slashed wildly out at Nora. 'I suppose she's married or something!'

'Or something,' murmured Blake, his hand tightening warningly on Nora's hip as she stiffened. 'And Hayley—you and I *didn't* have a date last night. You told me last week that you were hosting a party on your uncle's yacht and invited me along. I said I'd see if I could make it. I didn't know then what Nora was planning to do for the weekend. As you might have gathered, I find her utterly irresistible and our time together is precious…'

'*Blake!*' Nora was jolted out of her dumbstruck silence by his outrageous embroidery, realising how thoroughly he had turned the tables. Instead of trying to talk himself *out* of trouble, he was intent on digging them in deeper, blatantly using Nora as an excuse to extricate himself from the sticky tentacles of an inconveniently possessive woman!

Before she could articulate her thoughts, he had pulled her up on to her toes and kissed them out of her head with devastating efficiency. He hadn't yet shaved and the scrape of his beard brought back torrid memories. By the time he let her go her brain was so oxygen starved that black dots danced in front of her eyes.

Through the mist of darkness she saw Hayley watching them with a disturbingly malign intent. She still had the shiny pink cell-phone clutched in her talons as she backed across the porch.

'You won't care if I tell Uncle Prescott you're here with her then!' she threatened, still refusing to dignify Nora with a name.

'That's up to you,' said Blake, relinquishing Nora to her uncertain balance as he moved to see his unwelcome guest on her way, 'but before you blow this trivial encounter out of proportion, you might want to consider whether you want it known that you intruded into my love-nest under the mistaken impression that you'd be welcome. It might be less amusing for your more bitchy friends if we can simply agree that this never happened.'

Nora's last glimpse of Hayley was of a blonde fury flinging herself into the convertible, a vindictive glitter of thwarted rage in the sullen blue eyes.

Suddenly recalling that discretion was the better part of valour, Nora felt silently for the tread with her bare toes as she began to back stealthily up the stairs.

The security door clanged into place and the front door

swung closed with a definitive thud. Nora froze into wary stillness as Blake turned in a fluid ripple of muscle, his laser-like gaze zeroing in on her apprehensive face.

'I hope you're planning to iron that shirt when you've finished with it,' he said mildly.

'O-of course I will,' she stammered, smoothing the badly crumpled front, disconcerted by his calm. She would have been furious, *had* been furious, whenever he had questioned *her* honour.

'It *is* my shirt, isn't it?' he enquired, coming to stand at the bottom of the stairs, leaning a casual hip against the carving that decorated the end of the bannister rail.

She tensed. 'Um…yes, I—found it in your wardrobe….'

He didn't immediately demand to know what she had been doing rifling through his possessions. His inscrutable grey eyes dropped to her toes, curling to grip the stair carpet, then meandered slowly up her tense legs and over the creased white cotton to where the rumpled collar sagged to one side, almost sliding off her shoulder and revealing the small swell of one freckled breast.

'It suits you.'

'Oh!' Her eyes widened and she unconsciously clamped her thighs together to suppress the warm tingle that surged through her lower body at the unexpected compliment.

'Especially with nothing underneath…'

Uh-oh! Nora gulped as she remembered that this was one of Blake's masterly tactics—soften up your trembling victim with distracting trivialities and then pounce with tooth and claw when the guard drops. Best to try and get her explanations in first!

'Look, Blake, I'm sorry. I…I didn't mean—I overheard what was going on and I misunderstood—I—I just thought—'

'You thought I was an unscrupulous brute who'd callously seduce the boss's spoiled stepniece in order to feed my insatiable lust for money and power,' he said pleasantly.

'N-no—' Nora casually shifted her weight to disguise the tentative placement of her foot on the stair behind her.

'You were jealous,' he accused softly.

'*No!*' She instinctively protected her battle-scarred heart.

He straightened to his full height, half-naked…all man. 'Oh, yes—and so you decided to spike my guns by showing me up as a two-timing bastard with a secret taste for bold brassy tarts!'

He was still using that exquisitely calm voice, but Nora was no longer deceived. He was watching her like a hawk.

'FYI: Hayley and I have never been intimately involved,' he said quietly. 'She likes to play hostess for Scotty, but I stopped accepting invitations to social events with them when I realised that she was using them to persuade herself and others that we were a lot more than friends. I've been trying to discourage her without being offensive to her or to Scotty, but subtlety hasn't worked, and lately she's been verging on the obsessive.'

Conscious of his coiled tension, Nora hastened to repair the damage she had wrought. 'I—I lost my temper. I'm sorry. I hope it won't damage your relationship with Sir Prescott. If you like, I—I can go to him and explain—'

He stretched out his arm, placing his left hand flat on the bannister, parallel with the first step. 'Why don't you come down here and explain it to me first?' he invited with silky menace.

Nora licked her lips, her nerves stretched like piano wire, her breasts budding against the white cotton at the look in his eyes.

His nostrils flared, as if he had caught the alluring scent of her helpless excitement. He smiled.

'*Come on, Babycakes, what's taking you so long?*' he mocked.

Her nerve broke and she started to swivel on to her back foot. Her only warning was the green flash in his eyes a heartbeat before he exploded up the stairs, two at a time. She screamed and turned to run, managing to make three steps before she felt his fingers grab at her flying leg, slither down her calf and latch around her ankle. Clinging to the rail, she twisted her body and kicked out, all thoughts of modesty forgotten, and felt a connection with hard muscle, heard his curse, and was free to stumble up to the landing, where she dodged nimbly behind the tall stone-fired pottery urn.

Blake, hot on her heels, backhanded it casually out of the way and Nora gave another small scream as it crashed against the wall and spun around on the floor, spilling dried stalks across the small stretch of carpet between them.

They stared at each other across the debris, motionless, panting.

'You could have broken that,' Nora scolded piously.

His eyes flamed with unholy delight. 'Spank me!' He grinned and launched himself across the scattered flowers to snatch at the trailing edge of the white shirt.

Nora squeaked and skipped backwards, batting it out of his fingers. Seizing the bannister rail and whirling around, she vaulted herself up on to the next flight of stairs. They seemed to stretch for ever and Nora was already oxygen-depleted, her heart pumping furiously. Blake was stronger, but she was lighter and jet-powered by such a delicious terror that she managed to keep ahead of him for several breathless moments, until a mistimed step had her stumbling and this time when his hand clamped around her ankle, he wasn't letting go. His upward momentum carried his body up and over the back of hers, toppling her forward on to her knees, her hands still desperately clinging to the vertical rails supporting the bannister as he flattened her against the stair-treads and she felt in danger of becoming a human toboggan.

'Get off me, you oaf!' she gasped as the carpeted ridges bit into her squirming thighs.

'Hell-cat!' He let go her flailing ankle to grab her wriggling hips, his knees straddling hers, the heat of his heaving chest burning through the back of the shirt, the zip of his jeans pressing against her bottom. 'That's no way to talk to your lover!'

'Thug!' she said, trying to buck him off.

'Spitfire!' he groaned, and she realised the hardness against her bottom wasn't his metallic zip, it was what was behind it.

'Deviant!' she spat. 'Do you get turned on fighting helpless women?'

'Helpless? You nearly unmanned me with your kicks, you virago!'

'Well, I obviously didn't succeed, did I?' she said, pulling on the balusters to try and lever her body out from under him.

An insufferably arrogant chuckle fanned down the back of her neck as he merely caged her more closely with his arms and legs. 'If you wanted to turn me off you shouldn't have come prancing out in only my shirt, offering to play kinky games.'

'I said I was sorry—' she panted, the breath whooshing from her lungs. Somehow one of his hands had insinuated itself underneath her trapped body, sliding between the gaping buttons of the shirt and finding her breasts, suspended like firm, ripe fruit from her arched torso. He palmed each warm swaying mound in turn, thumbing the little stiff crests and enjoying her thready squeaks of unconvincing protest.

'Don't be sorry—this time you created exactly the right kind of trouble,' he murmured, rhythmically nudging her with his hips as his fingers trailed down to her quivering stomach to rim her belly button. 'I think this lesson in humility was just what Hayley needed to shock her out of her delusion that I'm hers for the asking—' He broke off as his fingers ran into an unexpected barrier.

'Well, well…not as wicked as you pretend to be, are you…?' He withdrew his hand to flip up the tail of the shirt and splay his hand over her exposed panties. 'Why, it's Mr Rabbit!' he exclaimed in deep tones of fond recognition, smoothing the printed cotton fabric over the plump curve of her blushing bottom. 'And look, there's a Mrs Rabbit, too, both primly dressed in their Sunday best. But bunnies are notorious for their lack of restraint. I wonder what naughtiness the pair of them get up to down here when the lights are out….' He stroked with his finger where Nora *knew* no bunnies frolicked, and she jerked violently.

'*Blake*…'

'Yes, Nora?' He leaned over her again, his mouth hot on the straining cords of her neck, the sharp prickle of his dark-blooming beard an exciting contrast to his warm wet tongue, his playful humour evaporating as his blind touch worked up under the band of elastic at the top of her thigh to slide against her creamy velvet centre. 'Oh, yes, you want me quite badly, don't you, Sparrow?'

She gave an incoherent choked cry that mingled with his hoarse sound of pleasure as he felt the slickness of her desire coat his fingers and explored the hot swollen folds of her womanhood where they curled protectively over the hidden kernel that had ripened into secret prominence.

'Sweet, sweet honey,' he murmured with impassioned reverence as he gently parted the petal-soft pleats of sensitised flesh between her legs, opening her moist heart to his exquisitely skilful and oh-so-delicate touch. 'Let it flow for me, baby…. Show me how sweet and hot and ready you are….' He nudged the tight little bud with the very tip of his finger and Nora felt it pulse with pleasure, sending a stream of sensation showering through her body, cascading over her breasts and belly and thighs like stinging sparks of incandescent fire.

Her spine arched, the rotation of her hips pushing her deeper back into the cup of his loins and he reacted violently to the invitation, dragging her panties roughly down her legs and tossing them carelessly over the bannister to flutter to the tiles below.

Nora felt the pressure of his denim-clad thighs suddenly ease on the back of her legs and heard a rustle and the rasp of a zip, the soft metallic hiss sending a flutter of apprehension beating along her singing veins.

She didn't want it to happen like this; she wanted to be able to *see* everything that he was feeling, to look into his eyes as he came into her, to touch him and fully participate in every glorious moment of anticipated bliss, not merely accepting, but loving, *sharing* in his mysterious male essence…

'Please—' She tried to twist an arm free and cried out

with pain when she banged an elbow against an overhanging tread.

'What's the matter?' He instantly shifted, rolling her over and frowning down into her watering eyes. His mouth twitched when she confessed that she had hit her funny bone.

'It's nothing to laugh at!' She practised her brand new pout. 'I'm probably going to have a lot of bruises later.'

His eyes darkened. 'I'm sorry; I'll kiss them better,' he said, lifting her slender arm and pressing his mouth to the tender curve of her elbow. His gaze fell to her bent legs. 'Every single one of them—wherever they might be,' he added gruffly, making her aware that he was lying propped between her splayed knees, and the bottom of the shirt had wiffled up around her waist. She blushed furiously and tried to push it down but he got there first.

'Here, let me help you with that.' He gripped the lower edges of the shirt and reared upwards, ripping them violently apart, scattering buttons in all directions, leaving Nora quivering with delicious shock and quite forgetting her physical discomfort.

'That's better!' he announced with raw satisfaction as he studied her blush-pink and cinnamon-speckled nudity draped over the stairs, lingering longest on the downy triangle of autumn-brown curls which sheltered the treasure he had already begun to plunder.

Nora felt as if she was burning up under his fiery inspection, her limbs too heavy with molten desire to rise in defence of her modesty, fascinated by the ragged rise and fall of his deep chest and the compact ripple of his flat abdomen where it arrowed into the open fly of his unzipped jeans. Wanton curiosity led her to discover that his tan *did* go all the way, disappearing into the bold black thicket of hair that filled out the base of the 'V'.

'You're not wearing anything under your jeans,' she blurted, and he looked down at himself, indecently amused by her prudish surprise. This, from a sexy sparrow without the remaining wisp of a feather to fly with!

'Shortly to be remedied!' he murmured with a shameless smile, reaching into his back pocket to produce a slim wallet, from which he extracted a small familiar-looking package.

Bracing himself on one arm, he leaned forward until the ends of his loosened belt brushed her inner thighs, the cold kiss of the buckle making her skin jump. He dipped his head to place a kiss between her tip-tilted breasts, at the same time placing the feather-light gift in her hand. She blinked at it uncomprehendingly and he urged softly, 'I want you to put it on me….'

Her eyes widened. 'Oh! But I— Sh-shouldn't we wait until we get into the bedroom?'

'Not when we're going to need it right here. Right now,' he advised her with hoarse intensity, letting her feel the fine tremors of barely leashed tension that racked his body, his hand silking over the hollow of her hip to toy pointedly with one of her dewy-damp curls.

Make love on the stairs? How outrageous, how reckless, how daring! How very un-Nora! Her eyes skittered down to the blatant invitation of his open jeans, and up again. Incurably honest, she had to try, 'I'm not very…' She tailed off, thinking better of mentioning that Ryan had always been in too much of a hurry to waste time with her inept fumbling! 'I— It may take me a bit longer than you're used to, to put it on,' she confessed awkwardly.

'Oh, really?' His eyelids drooped, turning his eyes into glittering slits of smouldering approval. 'You promise?'

Her flustered response gave him licence to torment her with more sizzling suggestions. 'I'll help you, then, shall I? It might even take longer that way….'

And with that he threaded his fingers around the back of her head and slanted his open mouth fiercely across hers, flooding her with the rich taste and scent of aroused male, inciting her to new levels of excitement with low, throaty sounds of carnal hunger. The insecurity of their awkward, slanting position and the odd protrusions and difficult angles only heightened the erotic intensity, emphasising the voraciousness of their need. Nora gloried in the textures of his turbulent loving—the prickly roughness of his jaw, the silkiness of his tongue, the oiled sweep of his muscles, the feathery stroke of his hair. Caught up in the passion of the moment, she was hardly aware of him picking up her empty hand until he forced it down into his open jeans, moulding her fingers around the thick shaft that tucked down one leg, tenting the heavy fabric. Nora gasped as she touched the swollen hardness she had secretly fantasised about—hot and smooth as satin-wrapped steel, yet pulsating with life, with the promise of eternity, of *new* life...

He gave a clotted moan of pleasure as her fingers fluttered curiously down to find the lightly lubricated tip, trapped against his thigh by the cut of his jeans, measuring his full length as more than the span of her hand. His grip on her wrist tightened involuntarily, his hips thrusting to increase the friction of her palm, and he groaned.

'That's right, Sparrow... Now take me out,' he begged roughly, and it was Blake, the expert, who was fumbling as he guided her to free his swollen flesh from the prison of denim and sheath him in the snug new covering. True to her warning, she was not very deft, afraid of hurting him and a little awed by his size. She handled him with gentle care, until the prince of sexual self-mastery was sweating and shaking and gritting his teeth to stop himself coming like an inexperienced schoolboy before she even had the damned thing halfway on! It didn't help him that he could see she was just as aroused herself, her rosy breasts tight and swollen as they dipped and swayed, the pert nipples yearning for his mouth.

'That's enough,' he shuddered at last, pushing her hands away and kicking off the confining jeans so that he could scoop her bottom to the edge of the stair and drive gratifyingly deep at his first thrust.

Nora was seduced, invaded, conquered and won in that first instant of possession. The blunt force of his entry was almost painful, but it was a sweet, savage, soul-satisfying pain that she sought again and again, the liquid heat of her body quickly adjusting to his daunting size, accepting him, welcoming him, drawing him deeper with tiny rhythmic convulsions of muscle which resonated in every nerve and cell of her being. His face was tight, his expression tense with concentration, his grey eyes intent on reading the unspoken signals that told him of her intoxicating enthusiasm for his every move.

Her rapturous response unleashed an insatiable demand, his increasingly urgent thrusts lifting her body, driving her sideways with every cycle of surge and retreat until her back was jammed against the balusters, the small of her back riding the ridge of a stair. Her hands slipped on his perspiration-slick shoulders and she anchored herself by wrapping her arms around him, splaying her fingers over the thrilling bunch and flex of his long back, trying to relieve the pressure on her back by twining her supple legs around his plunging hips.

He must have seen the gathering cloud in her golden eyes for suddenly he gave a convulsive heave and the world was awhirl and when she recovered her equilibrium she found herself on top of him, seated astride his lap as his broad back took the brunt of their combined weight against the stairs, his legs drawn up behind her back, providing her with extra support. Startled, she began to push up on to her knees, but he caught her hips and re-seated her with a jolting thrust.

'Don't leave me,' he ground out, the earthy plea paralysing her heart, making her faint with wild and foolish hopes.

'I don't want to hurt you—' she whispered shakily, leaning her hands against the stair on either side of his straining shoulders to try and redistribute the load on his back, conscious of him pressing up against the entrance of her womb, stunned by the ravishing feel of all that unrestrained power riding between her thighs.

'The only way you can hurt me now is if you stop,' he gritted, rocking his hips to tilt her further forward so that he could reach her breasts with his mouth. Stretching out to eagerly cooperate with his wordless demand, Nora watched the sides of the shirt billow out around his head, enclosing them in an erotic haven of filtered light, thickly perfumed with mutual desire. Thick pulses of liquefied pleasure spurted between her legs as she watched him lapping at her painfully distended nipples with his skilful tongue before drawing them fully into his hot mouth to suckle hungrily.

The end, when it came, was sublimely shattering, yet even that was infused with his unique blend of passion and devilry. As her hips began to churn and Blake's body to quake with uncontrollable spasms he tore his mouth from her breasts and threw back his head to meet her tempest-tossed gaze.

'Coming, ready or not...' he rasped with impeccable timing, and Nora's explosion of violent delight was intensified by paroxysms of helpless laughter. Which made it all the more inexplicable when, sprawling full length in his arms, weak with exhausted pleasure, she surprised them both by bursting into raw tears, sobbing into his heaving chest.

Gentle hands stroked and soothed up and down her shaking back while she apologised, shuddering hiccups causing interesting sensations in their still-joined bodies as she sought to explain away her foolish tears without embarrassing either of them with rash declarations of love, and spoiling what should be a perfect moment of post-coital bliss. Of course, a sophisticated lover like Blake would be appalled at all this excess emotion. He might even begin to fear that he had another potential stalker on his hands....

She fished beside him for the shirt which had been wrenched off in the throes of their final climactic eruption and dragged it to hide her face and blot her tears.

'It was my first time on top,' she said inconsequentially, sniffing into the crumpled folds.

The hand patting her back stilled. 'And it was so awful it made you cry?'

She wrenched the shirt away from her dismayed face,

causing him to utter a stifled groan as she dislodged him by squirming to sit up and impress him with her earnest reassurances. 'No! Oh, *no*—it was *beautiful*!' she said. 'It's just… Oh, I don't *know* why—'

'I would think it was obvious,' he said kindly. 'I've just given you the most spectacular orgasm of your life, and now you've realised what you've been missing out on all these years.'

'Why you arrogant—!' Realising he was teasing to help banish her hectic embarrassment, Nora broke off and tried to stuff his shirt into his laughing mouth. Thank God he didn't know how close to the truth he was!

He sprang up and chased her, shrieking, up to the top of the stairs, where he snatched her up and carried her ceremoniously to his big bed, tumbling them both down on to the unmade sheets.

'Now that I've finally got you where you belong, I think there's something you should know about me,' he said, pinning her to the luxurious mattress with a warm hairy thigh.

She ran her hands over his rough jaw, exulting in her new freedom to touch. There were other ways to express love. It didn't have to be in words.

'What should I know?'

He bent and nipped at her shoulder. 'That I really am an unscrupulous brute with an insatiable appetite…for *you*.'

CHAPTER ELEVEN

As LOVE-LETTERS went it was a fairly pathetic effort:

> *Nora,*
> *Sorry, but I had to do it this way.*
> *Have arranged for someone to collect you.*
> *Call you later.*
> *Blake*

God forbid that he should have signed 'love, Blake' after they had just spent two whole passion-saturated days—and nights—making love with each other, Nora thought wistfully. She apparently hadn't even ranked a 'Best wishes' or 'Kind regards', although in the circumstances a 'Yours faithfully' would have been nice!

He had been insatiable in more ways than one—an exciting, witty, wonderful companion, flatteringly interested in her thoughts and opinions and free with his own. He had shown her that laughter and fun could be an integral part of lovemaking and had showered her with words of passion and praise, and even tenderness, but he had been scrupulously honest. He had made no reckless promises.

Still, at least he had cared enough to leave a note, rather than just abandoning her while he raced off to oversee his all-important stock market bid. And he *had* lingered until after dawn to bring her breakfast in bed…a breakfast which he had proceeded to share with an ardent enthusiasm that had left his sheets gritty with toast crumbs and sticky with honey. It was while Nora was showering off her syrupy body and donning Friday's blouse and skirt in expectation of having to scurry to work as soon as they arrived back in Auckland, that Blake had made his discreet exit.

Call you later? How reassuring! How *vague*. Was she just supposed to hang around at home waiting for him to bother to contact her? And what about his cavalier attitude to her job?

Turning over the square of expensive paper and finding the security alarm code scrawled on the back, Nora wondered if she was supposed to feel gratified by this example of his trust. His faith in her seemed to be sadly limited to trivialities. He would trust her with his beach house, but not with his honour? She wanted, no, she *deserved*, far more from him than that! She wasn't going to let him assume that she could be packed tidily away in a convenient box until he was ready to take her out and play with her again!

Unfortunately, her search for a telephone proved fruitless—thanks, she was sure, to the one room he had kept locked. But when she went down to look through the garage she had been surprised to see the TVR still parked in its spot. For some reason Blake had taken the four-wheel drive back to town rather than his beloved sports car. A wicked little light went on in Nora's brain. A further, more detailed, search of his bedroom turned up the car's electronic key and after some experimentation she managed to unlock the doors and boot without setting off the alarm.

Carrying her laptop back upstairs, she plugged it into the supposedly unconnected phone line and powered up to the site of a broadband link to an ISP who also happened to be her own. She wouldn't even have to re-configure her modem!

'Hah! I knew you were lying,' she crowd, tapping at the keyboard. First item on the agenda: an Internet phone call to her boss at Maitlands.

Half an hour later her hands were slipping sweatily on the steering wheel of the TVR as she finally jerked out of the gravelled side road and on to the Waitakere dual carriageway. There had been no manufacturer's booklet in the car but after she had downloaded the results of her Internet search on the Cerbera she thought she had all the information she needed.

She now knew why Blake had chosen not to drive it back to Auckland. From the noises it was making there was something seriously wrong...unless it was just her driving. For a ghastly moment Nora wondered if she'd crept all the way up the steep gradient with the handbrake on. She glanced down to check and in doing so must have turned the wheel, for the steering reacted with the quickness for which it had been fashioned and the car headed obediently into the clay ditch at the side of the road.

With a graunching of its low-slung rear, the TVR settled at a drunken angle in the shallow depression. Quickly Nora punched the red button under the steering wheel and there was instant silence from the engine. She closed her eyes in stricken disbelief.

She didn't know how long she sat there, her head bowed over the steering wheel, but she was roused from her misery by a tap on the window. A car had stopped on the opposite side of the road and a tall dark-haired woman had crossed over to bend down and peer in at Nora's wilting figure. Nora searched for the little button on the side pocket which opened the door and climbed gingerly out.

'Are you OK?' The woman looked to be in her mid-thirties, wearing mirrored sunglasses and a smart suit which made Nora feel drab.

'Fine.' She smiled shakily. 'I don't think the car is, though.'

To her outraged astonishment the woman started laughing when she walked around to study the rear of the car. 'I'm afraid not! Boy, is he ever going to be ticked!'

She came sauntering back, removing her sunglasses and Nora found herself staring up into a pair of very familiar-looking grey eyes.

'On the other hand, it could just strengthen your hand if you want to make a personal grievance claim.' The woman's eyebrows snapped together thoughtfully as she tapped her folded sunglasses against her mouth. 'You do know you could sue him for what he's done? You could make megabucks if he detained you without your consent—and then there's the question of restraint of trade…I mean, his actions prevented you from working at your job, right?'

'Right! You must be Maria,' Nora said drily, recognising more than a superficial family resemblance.

'How did you guess?' The older woman grinned, arching her thick black eyebrows. 'And you're Nora. I just know we're going to get on like a house on fire.'

'I think I've caused enough damage for one day without adding arson to the list,' Nora said glumly. 'Did Blake send you to give me a lift home?'

'Hell, no!' Maria looked swiftly around as if her brother might rampage out from the bushes. 'He'd have a fit if he knew I knew! No, I just happened to be at Mum's when he rang and asked her to do him a favour. He gave her a quick run-down on the situation—' she laughed at Nora's appalled face '—expurgated, I'm sure!' She turned and waved at the other car and Nora saw a slim grey-haired version of the woman beside her waving back.

'He asked his *mother* to come and get me?' she squeaked.

'Yeah, I guess you don't know yet what a terrible Mamma's boy he is! He didn't mention that you might be using his TVR, though.' She looked at Nora's guilt-stricken face and skated briskly on. 'Anyway, let's transfer your stuff and lock up. I'll make a call to Blake's mechanic and we can leave this heap of expensive junk for the tow-truck to pick up.'

Nora wasn't sure what to say to her lover's mother, but Mrs MacLeod soon solved the problem. She directed her daughter to take the wheel and joined Nora in the back seat, getting down to brass tacks by dismissing Nora's garbled attempts to tell her about the car as irrelevant to the key issue. 'So…how do you feel about my son?'

At least her eyes weren't that haunting grey that sent shivers up Nora's spine. They were a very kindly, but very insistent blue. 'I— We only met last Thursday—'

'That wasn't what I asked.' Pamela MacLeod smiled. In jeans and a sweatshirt, she didn't look very intimidating, but Nora had a feeling that tenacity was another common family trait.

'I…well—' God, how did you describe a man who was great in bed to his *mother*? With his sister listening? Nora could feel herself pinken. 'He's very—very um—'

'Interesting?'

That would work! 'Yes, Mrs MacLeod, he's very interesting.'

'Call me Pam.' The grey head tilted enquiringly. 'In what way would you say he was interesting?'

Nora began to sweat. 'Well, he's a… He's very complex…. He has a very…er…forceful personality….'

'Yes, he's very like his father in that respect,' said his forceful mother. 'No looks or charm to speak of, so he has to make up for it in charisma!'

What planet was this woman living on? 'Blake's an extremely attractive man!' contested Nora hotly.

'Oh, I didn't say he wasn't *attractive*,' Pam replied with a twinkling smile that softened her angular face into maternal smugness. 'Just that he's not pretty in that metrosexual way that's so popular these days. His father was a big, gruff, crude man—but I like a bit of the primitive in a man, don't you?'

Nora wasn't going to touch that one with a ten-foot pole. 'His father?' she stumbled. 'You mean your husband?'

'Yes. Neil. Who else would I mean?' Unfortunately Blake's mother was as alarmingly perceptive as her son. 'Don't tell me you've heard that silly story about *Prescott*.' She looked amused. 'Have you ever *met* Prescott Williams?'

Nora tried to ignore the snickers floating over from the driver's seat. 'No.'

'Well, let me put it this way. If I'd ever been tempted to

cheat on my Neil, it wouldn't have been with a skinny runt he could have picked up with his little finger! Now—' She settled more comfortably in her seat, her sharp eyes on Nora's embarrassed face. 'Blake tells me he whisked you away without so much as a by-your-leave this weekend, but he didn't really explain why…. Just some nonsense about you getting tangled up in some deal he was doing. What line of work are you in, Nora?'

Nora was a limp dish-rag by the time the two women dropped her off on the front steps of her apartment building, wrung dry of explanations, excuses, evasions and her personal history from the year dot.

'Thanks for the lift Maria, Mrs—er, Pam,' she croaked, searching out her spare door key while his mother held her laptop.

'You can thank Blake,' said Pam. 'I was just his stand-in. He seemed very anxious that you didn't get the impression that he was trying to get rid of you by fobbing you off on some paid minion.'

Nora, who had thought that very thing, smiled weakly.

'He also told me I wasn't to put you on the spot by asking any embarrassing questions about the two of you,' admitted Pam, without a flicker of shame. 'So, perhaps you'd like to leave it to me to tell Blake about his car getting a tiny scuff?' she continued, blatantly indulging in a little friendly black-mail. 'These things are much better coming from one's mother. I shall make sure he knows that it's all his own fault for acting like a caveman in the first place. If he had any social conscience he wouldn't be driving such a glaring symbol of conspicuous consumption, anyway!'

Nora was spinelessly quick to accept the quid pro quo, and for the rest of the day she grinned whenever she thought of Blake being scolded by mother into accepting the blame for the accident.

She found precious little else to smile about. Kelly had def-initely moved out some time over the weekend, taking not only all of her own things, but several of Nora's as well, leaving a pile of unwanted junk strewn in her wake. Having already made the phone call from the beach house to let her boss know that she would back to work by the afternoon, Nora turned her back on the mess and drove to the office, where she conscientiously tried to compress everything she should have done on Friday into half a day's schedule. It didn't take her long to find out that Kelly had moved into Ryan's apartment on Saturday and that she was now flashing a brand-new diamond ring on her engagement finger. Nora was proud of herself when she came unexpectedly face-to-face with Ryan in the coffee room and cheerfully congratulated him on finding his perfect match, adding in dulcet tones that Kelly could keep the set of crystal wineglasses she had taken, as an engagement present.

At one stage she did peek at the on-line financial news and was unsurprised to see that the headliner was PresCorp's successful stand in the market for TranStar shares. Had Blake ever failed at what he set out to do? PresCorp had apparently reached its targeted holding within minutes of the start of morning trading. So her exciting career as a suspected *femme fatale* was officially over, Nora thought wryly as she logged off.

Then, when she answered her cell-phone not recognising the caller's number, she got a delicious shock.

'What in the hell are you doing in at work?' a voice snarled in her ear.

'And good afternoon to you too, sir!' replied Nora briskly, all too aware of the drawbacks of working in an open-plan office.

'My mother said you refused to let her call an ambulance, or take you to the A&E clinic to get you checked out.' Blake had no time to waste on pleasantries. 'She said she thought you could have delayed concussion—'

Nora closed her eyes. He sounded furious. 'Uh…your car—'

'To hell with the car!' he swore. 'Are *you* all right? Mum

said you were as white as a ghost and she thought you were limping….'

To hell with his car? Oh, thank you, thank you, Mrs MacLeod! Nora took a deep breath. 'I'm fine, really, it was nothing—!'

'If it was nothing then why does your voice sound so weak and wobbly?' he snapped suspiciously.

Because she was trying not to laugh. She cleared her throat. 'Look, can we talk about this later? I'm not supposed to accept personal calls at work and my boss is glaring at me.'

She paid for her insouciance later that evening when Blake coolly let himself into her flat with her keys and made very short work of extracting a full and frank confession.

'I swear it wasn't deliberate, Blake,' Nora gasped apologetically, as he finally completed his very thorough, and ferociously intimate, inspection of her body. 'It was just a lot harder to handle than I thought it would be when I started out….'

'I know the feeling,' he muttered, rolling off her and collapsing on his back, taking up most of her narrow single bed. 'I should have known it was dangerous to leave you on your own. And then to toss Mum into the mix—I should have realised you'd gang up on me!'

Nora almost felt sorry for him. Almost. 'I'd offer to pay for the damage but your sister said I shouldn't admit any liability,' she teased huskily.

'It was going in for an overhaul, anyway. I didn't like the sound of it when I turned over the engine this— Wait! Liability? Maria! *Maria* was there, too?' He raised his head to scowl at her. 'Damn it! I told Mum this was to be kept *low-key*—'

Nora felt a freezing touch kill the delicate tendril of hope that had begun to unfurl in her breast. She scolded herself for her naivety and maintained her warm tone of amusement. 'Maria said I should sue you for restraint of trade.'

His frown turned into a sexy grin as he took her back in his arms. 'Make it *lack* of restraint and I might be willing to deal!'

If Nora thought it was challenging to try and maintain a 'low-key' affair with a dynamic and powerful man, by the beginning of the following week she was faced with the far more difficult prospect of living in a high-profile scandal.

'But you can't fire me; I haven't done anything wrong!' she protested to her boss.

'You're not being fired, just suspended,' Ruben Jensen said uncomfortably. 'Sorry, Eleanor, I'm just following orders. The Acquisitions and Takeovers people are in a flap and TranStar's chairman is screaming dirty tricks to the Market Surveillance Panel. You must admit this doesn't create a very good impression.' His lined face looked harassed as he tapped the tabloid which had hit the news-stands the previous day.

Nora snatched it up, glaring at the two photographs of the half-clad couple under the splashy headline. In the larger picture the woman locked in Blake MacLeod's embrace in the doorway of his beach house could have been anyone, but the smaller inset showed the moment the kiss had broken off and Nora's back was no longer to the camera, her face clearly identifiable. No, not camera, she thought furiously—*cell-phone*. The furious Hayley had had the last word after all. She must have taken the photos with her phone, and now the PXTs were in the public arena.

Nora scanned the copy with rising ire. The story was heavy on conjecture and light on facts, concerned mainly with drooling over Blake's reputed past bedding of several celebrities and how close-mouthed he generally was about his affairs. But it did identify Nora by name—oh, why had she foolishly introduced herself to Hayley?—and a little journalistic rummaging had mis-identified her as a stock analyst for Maitlands and threw up the connection between the company she worked for and TranStar.

'This is all total rubbish!' she declared, flinging it back down on Ruben's desk.

'Yes, well, unfortunately one of our employees brought it to the notice of management and all hell has broken loose,' he said. 'And someone has confirmed that you and MacLeod *did* spend that weekend away together, including the Friday you were supposedly home sick…'

Nora's heart plummeted. Kelly! Or Ryan. Or both of them. She, who had never made an enemy before, suddenly seemed to be besieged with influential foes!

'But they're saying I might have passed on inside information! That's just ridiculous—I didn't know anything about the takeover to pass on,' Nora cried.

'I know, but with your security clearance you have access to a lot of sensitive stuff, and maybe you didn't even realise what he was doing. You know, you're way too trusting, Nora. Do you really think he's just interested in *you*…?' Ruben probably thought he was being supportive; he didn't even realise how insulting he was being, to Nora as well as to Blake.

'Don't I get a hearing first? What if I refuse to accept this suspension?' she said angrily.

But no amount of argument could budge her boss.

'Nora, under the terms of your contract, I'm afraid you don't have a choice.' Ruben was beginning to looked alarmed by her unaccustomed fierceness. 'If you'll hand in your keycard and your laptop, I'll get a member of the security staff to escort you out.'

A short time later Nora stood in front of the towering PresCorp building on the fringe of the city's wharf district, buffeted by a stream of lunch-time workers exiting the building. She had not only burnt her bridges, she feared she had set fire to her entire transport system with her explosion of outrage.

She shouldered her capacious bag—the one which had been searched by security before she left Maitlands—and stalked across the marble foyer to the information desk.

'Where do I find Mr MacLeod's office?' she asked the bored-looking man who was signing for a delivery.

'Executive suite's on the seventeenth floor,' he informed her, without looking up from the clipboard. 'Take the lift over there to the tenth-floor lobby, turn left and follow the signs. The executive lift will take you the rest of the way.'

Nora was so busy stewing over what she was going to say if and when she got in to see Blake, that it was only as she was stepping out on the seventeenth floor that she realised that 'executive lift' had been a euphemism for one of the fashionable glass-sided monstrosities, and that she had ridden up looking out over the city without even registering the fact. Smoothing down her navy skirt and making sure her fuchsia blouse was tucked in, she approached the executive receptionist, who exhibited the polished sympathy of a hardened professional as she listened to Nora's request for a personal meeting with the most sought after man in the building.

She obviously didn't read the tabloids because, before Nora had even finished speaking, she launched into her stone-walling routine.

'Hi, there! Here to see Blake?'

Nora turned and for a moment didn't connect the smooth-faced young man in the Hugo Boss suit with the bristly, bronzed surfer.

'Oh, hello, Steve. Have you started your internship already? That was fast work.'

He grinned. 'I got suspended from school for smoking and persuaded Blake to take me on early. You might say we exchanged favours. He rang me down at the beach last Tuesday afternoon, foaming at the mouth about his TVR being in a ditch somewhere up in the hills and asking me if I would ride back to town with the mechanic to make sure he didn't treat her too harshly.'

Nora blushed. 'Oh, dear. Did he say how it happened?'

'Funny thing, he never did. He was as touchy as hell about it!' Steve gave her a familiar wink that suggested he knew more than he was telling. He was *definitely* a tabloid reader! 'Hey, you want me to take you along to his office?'

The receptionist intervened with stern talk of back-to-back appointments, but the upshot of his friendly interference was that she eventually conducted Nora into a spacious office with a huge picture window that looked out over the glittering Waitemata Harbour.

Her stomach lurched, not at the sight of the bobbing ferries docked far below, but at the wizened sprite of a man with a thick shock of white hair who was seated behind the huge wooden desk in front of the window. A man whose portrait hung prominently in the waiting area.

'I think there must be some mistake—' She started backing out.

'No, no!' Sir Prescott Williams leapt to his feet. 'When Sandra said you were waiting for Blake I told her to bring you in here. Wanted to meet you.' He limped around the desk, his dark suit jacket flapping open, and seized Nora's hand, shaking it with a vigour that made her teeth rattle. 'Prescott Williams—you can call me Scotty—Blake always does. It's Nora, isn't it?'

'Yes, but—'

'Sit down! Sit down!' He led her over to a buttoned leather couch and urged her into it, standing over her, rocking on his heels, brows beetling over his black-button eyes. 'I can get Sandra to bring some tea, if you like. Or what do you say we both have a *real* drink? Sun well over the yard-arm and all that!' He sprang across the room and whipped open a bulging drinks cabinet, rubbing his hands together as he looked over his shoulder at her. 'Join me in a whisky? Or do you prefer that rot-gut vodka that Blake drinks?' He spun around, his face creasing with sudden inspiration. 'Or we could open a bottle of champagne—make a proper toast.'

The thought of vodka made Nora feel green, and why she would want to toast the smoking ruins of her career and reputation was beyond her. She decided to try to assert some ownership of the situation. 'Sir Prescott, I don't know what you've read in the papers, but—'

'Oh, no need to worry about the *papers*.' He waved a knobbly blue-veined hand in contempt. 'Blake has all that well in hand. Told me the whole story. Silly girl Hayley got the wrong end of the stick! Typical—not the sharpest tool in the box! Whisky, was it you said you wanted?' He clinked the glass hopefully and Nora knew that if she didn't say yes he would gallantly refuse to have one himself.

She agreed, dying to ask exactly what story he had been told to make him sound so cheerfully unconcerned.

He limped across with the glasses and plonked himself down on the couch beside her, extending his leg in front of him. 'Damned hip—they tell me I have to have a new one put in next month. Cheers!' He clinked his glass against hers. 'Drink up! Drink up!'

Nora sipped cautiously and coughed politely into her hand, blinking rapidly to try and clear the tears in her eyes.

Sir Prescott chuckled. 'That'll put hair on your chest!' He settled back, black eyes snapping. 'Work for Maitlands, do you? Computers and all that rigmarole. Pity!'

Nora wasn't quite sure what she was being pitied for, so she took another sip of her whisky, which encouraged her to admit bravely, 'I don't... work at Maitlands any more, I mean. I quit. Today.'

The black eyes lit up. 'Good! Good! Blake persuaded you to come to us, has he? Cunning lad. Says you're a top brain. Talked you up a storm. Mentioned that you're working on something of your own that could be just up our alley... software for use in sea-bed salvage work.' He took a long, satisfied gulp of his drink, not noticing Nora's stunned expression. 'That's how I started this little empire of mine, you know— in the marine salvage business.' He chuckled. 'That programme of yours sounds as if it might have uses in the underwater construction and drilling fields, too. Maybe you should be thinking of getting some investment capital behind you to help develop your ideas and diversify them into commercial applications. And if it's finance you're after, well, I'm always on the lookout to invest in up-and-comers with bright ideas. Of course, if we negotiated our way into doing some business together, that would be over and above any salary you make with PresCorp....'

Nora lubricated her frozen vocal cords with a warm trickle of whisky. 'Sir—uh…Scotty, I haven't really even thought about—'

Suddenly the door crashed open and Blake strode into the room with a thunderous scowl. 'What the devil is going on?'

'Ah, there you are, boy. We were wondering where you'd got to, weren't we, Nora?' Sir Prescott said blandly.

Blake's eyes took on a strange glitter as they whipped suspiciously back and forth between the pair on the couch. 'Were you? How strange, then, that Sandra never bothered to tell me that Nora was here to see me. I had to learn it from some pimply intern.' He prowled over to frown at the older man. 'I thought the doctor had told you to cut down on the hard stuff until after your operation?'

Sir Prescott's bony knuckles whitened on his glass, as if he was afraid Blake would snatch it away. 'This is a special occasion.'

'Yes, Scotty was just offering to back me in a business venture,' said Nora, nervously defiant. 'Apparently you've been telling him all about the sea-bed project I'm working on—'

'*Scotty?*' Blake folded his arms across his chest as he loomed over her, looking magnificently menacing in his black suit, black silk shirt and steel-grey tie. 'I had no idea you two were such friends.'

'Come off it, Blake. I may have jumped the gun but I thought this was what you wanted.' Sir Prescott chuckled at his stony expression. 'It was your idea to offer this clever fiancée of yours a job. And, lucky for us, she says she's already quit the other mob—'

Fiancée? Nora scooted forward on the couch. 'Oh, but we're n—'

Blake abruptly shifted his stance, a black-clad knee

bumping her arm, upending her whisky glass in her lap. She jumped to her feet with a shriek, brushing at the sodden linen, which had sucked up the liquid like a thirsty alcoholic and now clung drunkenly to her legs.

'What a waste of good Scotch,' mourned Sir Prescott, picking up her empty glass.

'I don't think it'll stain if you rinse it out immediately,' murmured Blake and Nora froze as she recognised the words she had said to him on the first night they met. He took her elbow, propelling her to the door, barely giving her time to grab her bag. 'Come on, you can use the bathroom in my private office.'

'Good idea. Can't have you going round smelling like a distillery,' chipped in Sir Prescott helpfully, limping after them. 'Tell you what—you go off with Blake and get cleaned up and I'll round everyone up and open a few bottles of that champagne so we can properly toast your engagement when you come back. I'll get Sandra to send out for some food, too, shall I, Blake? May as well go the whole hog. Perhaps even a cake—'

'*You!*—' Blake halted his Chairman with a disrespectful finger poked into his chest '—have done enough. Thank you, but I'll take this from here.'

He slammed the door on Sir Prescott's expression of injured innocence and hustled Nora back through the reception area, scowling at anyone who dared approach.

'Why did you do that? What was he *talking* about?' Nora burst out when she had been frogmarched into a luxurious blue and grey office which mirrored the layout of the one they had just left. 'Oh, for God's sake, don't bother,' she said impatiently, as he picked up the remote control from the desk to close the vertical blinds. 'If I came up in that wretched glass box of yours without turning a hair, I'm hardly going to keel over now! I want to know what you've been saying to Sir Prescott, and why he thinks we're engaged!'

'Did you?' He dropped the remote and spun around to study her.

'Did I what?' she asked distractedly, wrinkling her dainty nose as she lifted the saturated skirt away from her damp tights.

'Handle the lift without panicking?'

She shrugged, trying not to be disarmed by the warmth of encouragement in his eyes. 'I had other things on my mind,' she said.

'Like quitting your job? You've really left Maitlands?' He slipped off his jacket and hung it over the back of his chair.

'They tried to suspend me, so I told my boss he could make it my period of notice,' Nora said, her temper flaring all over again as she described the encounter. 'Ruben was even talking about honey traps—'

'Mmm, well, I do seem to recall at least *one* occasion when honey did feature rather prominently in our relation-ship,' said Blake with unblushing calm. 'Otherwise their in-vestigation is going to be a waste of their time and money. Now, why don't you take your skirt off and I'll get my sec-retary to send it out to the one-hour laundry service. That wet patch is far too big to try and blot with a towel—'

'And whose fault is that? What on earth am I supposed to do in here without a skirt for an hour?' she snapped unthink-ingly, and went the same colour as her blouse as he started laughing. 'Damn it, Blake—'

'I'm sorry, Sparrow, I can't help it—I love seeing you with ruffled plumage.'

Still laughing, he fetched a long black towelling robe from the adjacent bathroom and, flustered by the rare endearment and by his casual use of the 'L' word, Nora put it on, wrig-gling out of her skirt under his amused eye and stripping off her tights to drape over the bathroom rail while he spoke to his middle-aged secretary. When his poker-faced employee had left, he remained leaning against the closed door, looking at Nora as she nervously tightened the belt of the bulky robe.

'I'm sorry about your job,' he said gravely. 'But I was serious about wanting to offer you one here. PresCorp has a big IT de-partment and they're always aggressively head-hunting for experienced staff of your calibre. I also regret I didn't handle the problem of Hayley earlier, and protect you better from the inevitable fallout when our relationship went public...'

'I don't think I was going to stay on at Maitlands anyway,' she admitted with a sigh. 'It would have been too awkward. Ryan and Kelly have just got engaged—' She broke off, suddenly remembering the reason she had been given a whisky bath. 'Why did you want to stop me talking to Sir Prescott?' She tensed in alarm as she foresaw a potentially cringe-making scene. 'He wasn't serious, was he, about getting everyone in for a champagne toast to our engagement?'

Blake's shoulders lifted under the black silk. 'Unfortunately, when Scotty gets his mind fixed on something it's well nigh impossible to change it. He's ferociously stubborn and a rampant opportunist—'

'Gee, now who does that sound like?' said Nora wryly, receiving a potent glare for her interruption.

'I just didn't want him putting words into my mouth. I prefer to speak for myself.' He squared his shoulders against the door, as if facing a firing squad. 'He's been at me for years to settle down and marry. He thinks it would make me a better CEO, more loyal to the idea of staying with the company for life. He doesn't want me making his mistake and having no one of the blood to carry on his legacy....'

'So he was keen for you to marry Hayley,' she dared to say thinly.

His head tipped back arrogantly. 'He knew that was never on the cards. Besides, it wouldn't have made any difference—she's no more of a blood relation to Scotty than I am.' The dry tone confirmed that he knew of the slanderous rumours.

Nora was beginning to picture a very demeaning scenario. She bit her lip. 'So when that newspaper came out, you told him we were engaged as a temporary way of getting him off your back and defusing the likelihood of a scandal...' she said hollowly.

Blake snibbed the lock on the door and walked across to where she stood, her slender back to his heavily laden desk.

'There is no scandal as far as I'm aware, and I certainly didn't tell Scotty that I'd asked you to marry me.'

'Oh!' Her cheeks flaming, she deflated into mortified silence. Sticking her hands into the deep pockets of the robe, she forced herself bravely on. 'You mean…he just assumed—'

'I mean that I merely said I was *thinking* of asking you to marry me. Scotty being Scotty immediately advanced to the next step. Modesty should forbid me to say it, but it doesn't seem to occur to him that any woman would refuse me….'

Nora's breathing had stopped somewhere in his first sentence. 'I—you—I don't understand,' she choked.

He reached up to gently finger the lapel of the robe, adjusting it where it folded across her breasts with meticulous hands. 'Don't you? And here I thought you might be feeling some of the things that I was feeling. It's all happened so fast for us, though, hasn't it? That's what makes it so scary,' he murmured, his eyes on his fingers rather than her pale face, and it came to her that he was as nervous as she was, that his hands weren't *quite* steady….

'It gives me a tiny inkling of what it must feel like for you when you're somewhere up high, at the mercy of an uncontrollable force inside you that seems to be pushing and pulling you at the same time.'

He described the feeling so exactly that Nora shivered. His eyes flicked up to her face, dark and intense.

'I've never asked a woman to marry me before, so I'm sorry if I'm not doing a very good job,' he said softly. 'We need each other, Nora.'

Her vulnerable mouth quivered, her golden eyes huge as they clung to his face, her hands stealing from her pockets to still his restless fingers.

'Y-you're talking about a sort of—marriage of convenience—?'

He looked thunderstruck. 'The hell I am! I'm obviously not doing this right...' He drew a breath, trying to curb his savage frustration. 'You told me once that I can be very overwhelming, so I've been trying to hold back, to give you a chance to feel comfortable with me, rather than helpless or overpowered—'

'Liar!' she said, exultation battling her disbelief. 'You've done your best to overwhelm me since the day we met!'

'Only because I was so overwhelmed myself,' he admitted with devastating sincerity. 'You always gave as good as you got.' His mouth quirked reminiscently. 'Better, sometimes...I admire that.' His voice dropped to a quiet, almost boyish, awkwardness. 'I admire *you*.'

The simple declaration was unbearably moving. 'Oh, Blake—'

His jaw clenched, as if she was daring to disagree. 'Life happens, Nora. Sometimes when you're least expecting it, fate throws a fantastic opportunity your way and you have to grab it with both hands, or risk losing it for ever.' He turned his hands over, interlacing his fingers with hers. 'I know you think I don't trust you, but it was myself I didn't trust, my own judgement that I had to question. I rarely act on impulse and yet with you I've been nothing but impulsive. But then, that's what love is, isn't it? Meeting someone you feel an instinctive connection with, someone who excites and surprises you, someone who rouses you to passion and makes you laugh, someone who makes you feel good about them and about yourself, who convinces you that the world is actually a wonderful place....'

Nora made a soft, inarticulate sound which he was quick to interpret as assent. He tucked her hands against his heart, a slight edge entering his voice as he talked fast, his face close to hers as he ruthlessly worked the most important deal of his life. 'Some people go through their whole lives never having that feeling about another person. I thought I would, too. Until I met you, Nora....'

'But we hardly know each other,' she murmured weakly.

He cupped her cheek, strong yet tender. 'Do you love me?'

'It's been less than two weeks—' she said, drowning in his eyes.

'And we've been lovers for almost as long. Do you want me?'

Her lips turned to his palm. 'You know I do,' she relented.

'Then take the jump with me, Nora. Marry me.'

'Because you told your boss this morning that you were going to ask?' she said, from behind the last flimsy barrier of resistance.

Steel melted into a green-flecked tenderness. 'Actually I told him that day I came back from the beach that I'd met the woman I wanted to spend the rest of my life with…. He's been champing at the bit to meet you ever since, but I didn't want him to scare you off. I told my mother, too, when I asked her to pick you up. Thank God she kept that titbit from that big-mouthed sister of mine.'

'Blake, you didn't!' Her retrospective embarrassment was huge.

'If you take me, you get it all—my love, my children, my ever-loving, ever-annoying family, my interfering boss… I'll admit I come with plenty of extra baggage, but you need a lot of baggage for a long haul, Nora. And that's what it's going to be for us.'

'But still—' Her freckled face crinkled anxiously as she strove to be sensible in a world gone deliciously mad. '*A week and a half*…. We can't really know if we're compatible after such a short time….'

'That's what long engagements are for,' he said persuasively. 'With my ring on your finger we can have a proper courtship. You can move in with me when you're ready. Live with me for weeks, months, years—however long you need to feel safe in your choice of husband.'

His tone of martyred self-sacrifice made her want to laugh. 'As long as that ultimate choice is *you*,' she said wryly. He was so very big on offering her choices that had only one outcome!

'Yes…' He began to toy with the knot of the robe in a cunning way that made it suddenly fall apart. 'And, having said that, I'd naturally prefer that we married before our first baby is born,' he added, unable to resist the urge to negotiate better terms for himself. 'My mother is very tolerant of modern morality but Scotty would have fifty fits if his god-children were illegitimate.'

With a little giggle and a sly shimmy, Nora let the robe fall open. 'I suppose I can accept those terms.'

'You mean it?' he murmured, looking both delighted and indecently smug at his success.

'I love you; why wouldn't I love the idea of being your wife?' She laughed joyously as he whirled her into his extravagant embrace. 'And I especially love the idea that my indulgent new husband is going to let me drive his super-cool sports car whenever I want!'

Fortunately the champagne-fuelled celebrations had already begun down the hall and nobody heard the shrieks and growls that gradually dissolved in the sound of pure joy.

MISTRESS ON DEMAND

BY
MAGGIE COX

The day **Maggie Cox** saw the film version of *Wuthering Heights*, with a beautiful Merle Oberon and a very handsome Laurence Olivier, was the day she became hooked on romance. From that day onwards she spent a lot of time dreaming up her own romances, secretly hoping that one day she might become published and get paid for doing what she loved most! Now that her dream is being realised, she wakes up every morning and counts her blessings. She is married to a gorgeous man and is the mother of two wonderful sons. Her two other great passions in life – besides her family and reading/writing – are music and films.

CHAPTER ONE

SOPHIE had woken up with an awful presentiment that the day wouldn't go well. From the moment she'd squirted toothpaste all down the front of her pyjama top, to the near disaster when she'd just narrowly escaped spilling a whole mug of coffee down the front of the 'posh' frock she was reluctantly wearing to her friend Diana's wedding, her nerves had been jangled. Okay, so she didn't like weddings—*hated* them, in fact, but Diana was her closest female friend, and after a tumultuous year when her volatile relationship with Freddie was on one minute, then off the next, the least Sophie could do was show up and bear witness to the occasion.

But her luck, if she was going to be blessed with any at all today—and Sophie was beginning to think that she wasn't—just seemed to get worse and worse. She'd made three-quarters of the journey to the register office in her car when there'd been an awful spluttering hiss from the engine, then a pop, then…*nothing*, as it had finally given up the ghost and come to an undignified end by the side of the road. Sophie had had no alternative but to grab her coat and start walking to the register office. There was nobody she could ring for help because she wasn't covered for breakdown and, besides, *wouldn't you know it?* she'd left her mobile phone on the hall table *along with her purse* as she'd rushed out through the door. So she hadn't even been able to get a taxi.

Now, as she hurried across the grey London pavements grimly clutching her umbrella because it had been raining all morning, and was *still* raining, and just when she believed her luck couldn't get any worse, a gleaming black Rolls Royce swept past her into a puddle, which resembled a small reservoir, and all but drowned her in the backwash. Coming to a furious standstill as cold, muddy water dripped like sludge down the side of her fawn-coloured coat and turned her expensive matching shoes to a darker, grimier version of the concrete pavement, Sophie swore out loud. *Not just once—but three times, in quick violent succession*, each passionate utterance giving undisputed vent to her fury and indignation.

Narrowing her gaze, she saw to her surprise and satisfaction that the stately vehicle had slowed, then stopped at the side of the kerb. Not hesitating, she hurried towards it, her heart pumping with rage and her breath tight, her only concern that whoever was in there got a piece of her mind that they wouldn't soon forget. If Sophie had to arrive at her best friend's marriage ceremony looking as if she'd slept in a puddle beneath Waterloo bridge, then the occupant of that damned Rolls Royce was going to know that she prayed the same bad luck which had been visited on her today would dog the rest of *his* day.

She didn't for one moment doubt that the car's owner would be male. Only a thoughtless, insensitive *oaf* would deliberately drive through a puddle when he could clearly see her walking on the pavement beside it. But when she reached the car, a silver-haired chauffeur stepped out and looked immediately contrite.

'I'm so sorry, miss. We were in a hurry and I didn't see that confounded puddle until it was too late.'

'Well, *I'm* in a hurry, too, but you don't see me ruining someone else's day with my thoughtlessness, do you? You should have been more careful! Now what am I supposed to do?' Her freezing fingers curling stiffly around her umbrella handle, and the puddle that had soaked her shoes turning her feet to twin blocks of ice, Sophie had trouble keeping her teeth from chattering.

'Get back in the car, Louis. I don't have time for this. We're going to be late as it is.'

It was only at the sound of that coolly imperious voice that Sophie glanced into the passenger-seat window at the back of the car. Catching a glimpse of precision-cut wheat-blond hair and eyes as hard as flint, she felt a shiver run down her spine that had nothing to do with the cold or damp conditions she currently found herself in. The man's rapier-like instruction to his chauffeur, delivered as if he didn't give a damn what had happened to Sophie as long as he got to where *he* was going, made her blood boil.

'How dare you?' she shouted. 'I'm standing here soaked to the skin, my outfit ruined, because your stupid car happened to drive straight through a puddle the size of the River Thames, and all you can do is think about yourself and your own comfort! Well, I hope you have the worst day ever, I really do! You don't even have the guts to step out and face me, do you? Never mind apologise!'

'Miss…let me help you. I'm sure we could give you a lift to wherever you're going. We could—'

As the mortified chauffeur did his best to make amends for the ignorance of his boss, the passenger door suddenly opened and the man seated in the back of the car stepped out to gaze at Sophie with unconcealed disdain, as if she was an annoying drone buzzing around his dinner. He was very tall, and his height and breadth of shoulders alone, beneath his formal black coat, should have intimidated her. Green eyes, as crystal-clear and sharp as unflawed emeralds, studied her indignant features without so much as a flicker of emotion. *None.*

'What is it you want from me? You shouldn't have been walking so close to the kerb, and wearing such ridiculous shoes in this weather, too. You have only yourself to blame.'

Ridiculous shoes? Sparing a brief wounded glance down at her too-expensive open-toed cream high-heeled sandals, which she had splashed out on purely in deference to her friend's wedding, Sophie almost spluttered with rage.

'How dare you? What kind of footwear I put on my feet isn't your damned business remotely! I happen to be attending a special occasion... Not that that's any of your business, either. Am I supposed to have foreseen that some idiot would drive by and almost drown me? You have a bloody nerve, you know that?'

'I repeat...what do you want from me? Do you want me to reimburse you for the shoes or pay for your dry-cleaning? What? Tell me quickly so I can be on my way. I have already wasted valuable time standing here listening to you scream at me like a fishwife.'

He had some kind of accent, Sophie realised from his clipped speech. Dutch perhaps? But, more than that, she was reeling that he should dare to call her a fishwife just because she'd stood up for herself and hadn't let him simply get in his car and be driven away without making her feelings known.

Seeing him take out his wallet and extract some notes, she all but blanched. 'I don't want your damned money! Didn't it even occur to you that a simple gracious apology would do? I feel sorry for you...you know that? Driving around in your expensive car, hiding behind your tinted windows, acting like you run the world! Well, go on your way, Mister Whoever-you-are, and God forbid you're as late for your precious appointment as I'm clearly going to be for mine! But if you are— just remember the reason why, huh?'

About to turn on her unaccustomed high heel, Sophie was shocked into speechlessness by the blond giant's hand clamping suddenly around her more fragile wrist.

'If you don't want my money then perhaps a lift to wherever you are going would be more appropriate? Louis can drop me off at my own destination, then take you on to yours. Will that suffice?'

Knowing that it probably almost choked him to offer her a lift, and because her anger made her feel perverse, Sophie snatched her hand free and glared back at him with a distinct challenge in her large blue eyes. 'In the absence of an apology then a lift will have to suffice under the circumstances.' Biting her lip to prevent the more polite 'thank you' which threatened to follow her little speech, Sophie folded up her dripping umbrella and, at his instigation, preceded her reluctant host into the opulent hide-seated interior.

Feeling mutinous when her folded umbrella dripped muddy water all over the floor, she deliberately pursed her lips and stared out of the window while he settled himself as far away from her as possible at the other end of the seat. *Perhaps he thought he might catch something contagious?*

As the door slammed he said in a terse, reluctant voice, 'You may tell Louis where you are going when I get out.'

Not believing a reply to be necessary, Sophie glanced down at the time on her watch, then back out of the tinted glass window at the rainy London street. She couldn't help wondering if Diana was ever going to forgive her for turning up to her wedding late, and not only that, but looking like something the cat dragged in, too.

Minutes later, when the Rolls Royce purred to a halt outside a familiar-looking building, with wide curving steps leading up to its twin front doors, Sophie knitted her brows in confusion. She hadn't yet told Louis where she was going, so how come he'd just pulled up outside the same register office where Diana was getting married to Freddie? As she saw the blond Adonis beside her open the passenger door next to him, she frowned again. 'Wait a minute. This is where *I* need to be dropped off. I'm going to my friend's wedding.'

Cool green eyes assessed her confusion with the kind of haughtiness that was normally associated with royalty. It made Sophie bristle, as well as causing hot, indignant colour to flood into her cheeks.

'You are going to Diana Fitzwalter's wedding?' he demanded.

Now, how did he know that? And, more to the point, how did he know Diana? Sophie froze, as though she'd just lost her nerve on a tightrope walk, as the most obvious conclusion seeped slowly into her brain. *Was he going to Diana's wedding, too?*

'You know Diana?' she queried, her shock barely allowing her vocal chords to function.

'She is my personal assistant so, yes, obviously I know her.'

He was Dominic Van Straten? The billionaire property developer Diana worked for? The man who, according to her, found it hard to raise a smile even when the value of his stocks and shares had just shot through the roof and made him even richer? *But why on earth would Diana invite him to her wedding when Sophie and*

*one of Freddie's friends were supposed to be the only
witnesses because the couple wanted to keep the whole
thing low-key?*

Even her confident, outgoing friend had admitted to
Sophie that the man just plain intimidated her, and the
only reason she stayed working for him was that her
salary far exceeded most personal assistants', thereby allowing her a very comfortable lifestyle indeed.

Her legs feeling drained of strength, Sophie climbed
out of the car behind him to finish speaking. 'Well, I'm
Diana's friend…Sophie.'

Dominic didn't smile. Neither did he introduce himself. The light grooves bracketing his forbidding mouth
stayed obstinately still, without the merest suggestion of
a surprised or conciliatory gesture such as a rueful smile.
Well, what did she expect? The man was about as warm
as a frozen joint of beef straight out of the freezer.

Pushing her fingers through the short damp strands of
her hair, Sophie glanced down at her watch, barely registering that they were five minutes late for the ceremony
already because she was suddenly feeling drained of
every bit of pleasure or hope of an enjoyable afternoon.
She visibly shivered, and Dominic Van Straten's glacial
glance flicked across her face with a flash of impatience
before he turned and negotiated the wide concrete steps
which led to the entrance of the building with an imposing long-legged stride.

In the vestibule they were greeted by a radiant-looking
but anxious Diana, and her relieved and handsome fi-
ancé, Freddie Carmichael.

'Sophie! Thank God! What on earth happened to
you?' Diana's eyes widened in disbelief as she took in
the dark greying stains on Sophie's fawn coat and the
mud splashed up her cream hosiery and shoes.

Glancing briefly at her brooding and so far silent companion, Sophie shrugged. 'Car broke down and I had to walk. I'll tell you all about it later. Is it time to go in?'

'It is. Oh, God, I'm feeling nervous! How nice to see you, Dominic. I'm so glad you could come at such short notice. Trust Freddie's best pal to come down with flu! So good of you to act as stand-in. Shall we go in? I believe the registrar is waiting for us.'

All through the touching ceremony, it seemed to Sophie that Dominic expressed very little emotion of any kind. Not even a smile. His presence unnerved Sophie tremendously, she had to admit. When they both had to sign the marriage certificate as witnesses afterwards, he bent his blond head to the task as gravely as though he were signing someone's death certificate.

Diana had told Sophie that they were all going to lunch at the Park Lane Hilton where other friends were joining them, and Sophie found herself praying hard that Dominic wouldn't be accompanying them. Having to maintain a pretended civility towards a man she instinctively disliked would be like being forced to wear a tight Victorian corset that constricted her breathing for the afternoon.

She hadn't prayed hard enough. Half an hour later, holding a glass of crystal champagne in the foyer of the plush hotel to toast the bride and groom, her stained coat at last relegated to an obliging assistant in the cloakroom, and Dominic standing beside her, she gulped down her champagne too quickly and had an immediate coughing fit. The hand that clapped down on her back to try and ease her discomfort was surprisingly Dominic's.

'Here,' he said, 'let me take your glass until you compose yourself.'

'Oh, Soph! Are you all right, darling?' Diana appeared

at her other side, her hazel eyes full of concern. Smiling through the tears that had embarrassingly sprung to her eyes, Sophie nodded. Retrieving her glass from Dominic's large square hand, she wished the ground would open up and swallow her. She was having a pig of a day and no mistake! If anything else went wrong for her she vowed to herself she would simply go home, lock the door and devour a large box of chocolates, as recompense.

'I'm fine, thanks. Just went down the wrong way.'

'Oh, look who's just arrived! It's Katie and David. Will you excuse us for a moment, you two? We'll be right back.'

Before she could say anything, Sophie watched Diana glide away with her attentive new husband to greet the newcomers she had spotted in the foyer's entrance. Disconcertingly, she was left alone with Dominic. It was a little like being left alone in a sealed cage with a boa constrictor and a man-eating tiger, and probably twice as intimidating.

'The ceremony went well, don't you think?' Inwardly Sophie groaned as soon as the words were out of her mouth. *Now I sound like a character in an old English farce!* She thought with annoyance. It would probably be better if she stopped the pretence of civility right there and then, and simply ignored the hateful man. And she'd never forgive him if his taciturn and condescending manner ruined Diana's wedding day.

'Do you like weddings?' he asked her, surprisingly.

Seeing that there was still no hint of a smile or anything remotely friendly on his severe but handsome face, Sophie stared back at him defiantly. 'No. I hate them, as a matter of fact.'

'Why?'

Never having had to express her feelings about the subject before to a stranger, Sophie honestly wasn't sure how to explain her aversion. 'I find them…awkward. In my opinion Diana and Freddie did the right thing, keeping things simple. There's always some kind of horrible tension when families get together at these sorts of occasions, don't you think? Plus, you have to talk to people you'd rather not at the reception, and it's all very difficult.'

She reached the end of her sentence and clamped her mouth shut in horror at what she'd just said. Talk about putting her foot in it! But, to her consternation, Dominic didn't appear at all offended. Instead, a smile started to lurk around his lips, completely transforming that gravely serious face of his into something much more humane.

'I take it you are not married yourself, Sophie?'

'That's correct.' Her own manner now a little stiff, because she thought he must be thinking, *I'm not surprised*, she couldn't help flushing a little in embarrassment. She knew she wasn't exactly *plain* but she was hardly extraordinary, and the fact that he had already called her a 'fish wife' when she'd lost her temper with him didn't exactly help her case.

When he appeared not to be going to make any comment whatsoever, but simply studied her as though she were an interesting alien specimen that had flown in from Mars, Sophie honestly just wanted to go to the cloakroom, collect her ruined coat and flag down a taxi to take her home. She could pay for it when she got there. But, even though that was her strongest urge, she knew she would grit it out, for Diana. She wouldn't be the one fly in the ointment that spoiled her friend's wedding day. She would leave that particular little trick to Diana's very superior and aloof boss.

'You must let me reimburse you for your spoiled coat and shoes,' he said eventually, and Sophie squirmed with discomfort.

She didn't want to accept his money, or his sudden inclination to give it to her. She just wanted to get away from this horribly embarrassing situation that she found herself in as quickly as possible. Would Diana buy her story that she was up to her eyes in marking essays for her five-year-old pupils? *No. She didn't think so…*

'Look, Mr Van Straten. You don't like me, and I don't like you, so you don't have to reimburse me for anything, and we don't need to stand here making polite conversation when we'd both clearly prefer to be somewhere else! Why did you agree to be Diana's witness, by the way?'

If he was taken aback, either by her outburst or her question, again Dominic gave no sign. 'She asked me as a favour and I was happy to comply. That obviously surprises you, Sophie.'

It surprised the hell out of her that he even deigned to call her by her name, let alone pursue any further conversation with her after what had happened between them.

'Frankly, it does. You don't strike me as the kind of man who easily dispenses favours.'

'Oh? And so what kind of man *do* I strike you as, Sophie?'

Now she'd done it. The words *cold, remote, insensitive and superior* hovering on her tongue, she forged recklessly ahead instead with, 'Too self-contained and self-interested to notice others' needs if you want to know the truth.' Those words were probably worse.

Much worse, going by the glower that had suddenly replaced his previously more benign expression.

'You don't believe in mincing your words, do you? It does not surprise me that you are not married. A man likes a little verbal jousting, from time to time, Sophie, but he does not like a *shrew.*'

'I'm not a shrew!' It was true she had a temper, but it was only really roused by injustice of any kind. Like earlier, when Dominic's expensive regal car had splashed muddy water all over her nice clothes. Clothes that she was hard-pushed to afford on the ridiculously inadequate pay of a primary-school teacher.

Pursing her lips, Sophie held onto that temper by a thread, wishing that Diana would quickly come back and join them, to help alleviate the now increasingly uncomfortable tension between herself and this man.

'I'm not a shrew, but neither am I a woman who is scared to speak her mind. If it weren't for the kindness of your chauffeur, Mr Van Straten, you would have left me stranded and bedraggled by the roadside while you made your way to my best friend's wedding. Nothing you have said or done since makes me think that you have any redeeming qualities that I may have missed!'

'Even when I stopped you from choking?'

Sophie's blue eyes flew indignantly wide. 'You did not stop me from choking! My champagne went down the wrong way, that's all.'

'So I am too "self-contained" and "self-interested" to help someone in obvious distress? That is what you think?'

'Actions speak louder than words, so they say.'

'Then you need not worry that I will be joining you for lunch. I will not inflict my company upon you any longer.'

And, with that, Dominic abruptly turned his back on Sophie and left. With her heart throbbing beneath her ribs, she watched him cross the plushly carpeted foyer and go over to speak to Diana. Clearly seeing the surprise and dismay reflected on her friend's attractive face as he spoke to her, Sophie could have kicked herself for being the reason that Dominic was leaving. Obviously Diana wanted him there, or she wouldn't have asked him to stand in as a witness in the first place.

If only Sophie had been able to contain her temper! This day wasn't about her own comfort or discomfort. It was about Diana having one of the best days of her life. Now her best friend had thoughtlessly gone and ruined it!

Even though she disliked Dominic Van Straten with a passion, she still felt terribly guilty at driving him away. As soon she managed to get Diana on her own she confessed her feelings to her friend.

'I scared him off.'

She took another sip of champagne and screwed up her nose at a taste she wasn't sure she would ever become accustomed to. She needn't have worried. On a teacher's salary buying champagne was not exactly a dilemma.

'What do you mean, you scared him off?' Looking puzzled and beautiful, with her carefully styled blonde hair and her fitted ivory suit, Diana frowned. 'Nobody scares Dominic Van Straten away from anything! More like the other way round! He told me something important came up that he had to attend to. I thought that might happen. The man barely ever takes a break from his work. What a shame…especially as he's paying for all of this!'

'Your boss is paying for your wedding feast?' Now

Sophie was aghast. *You don't strike me as a man who dispenses favours easily...* she had said to him.

'He insisted. Including all the champagne we can drink. He's not the easiest man in the world to work for, but you can't fault his generosity.'

'Really?' Sophie's eyes slid guiltily away as she told herself it wasn't *her* fault if he was so easily offended. He *had*, after all, called her a *shrew*. Had he really expected her to forget that and carry on as normal? But this *was* Diana's special day, and she had clearly wanted her boss to be a part of the celebrations. *Why wouldn't she when he'd been decent enough to pay for everything?*

Honesty behoved Sophie to emphasise the truth more forcefully. 'Diana, listen, it really *is* my fault that Dominic left! We got off to a bad start. His car inadvertently splashed me with muddy water; that's why my coat was in such a state. Anyway, I'm afraid I lost my temper with him. Just now, before he left, things just went from bad to worse and I ended up insulting him rather badly.'

At the appalled look of disbelief on Diana's face, another surge of horrible guilt washed over Sophie. 'I didn't realise he'd paid for your wedding feast or I would have held onto my temper a bit better. I'm really sorry.'

'Oh, Sophie, what have you done?' Diana groaned, digging through her satin purse to find her mobile phone. 'I'll have to ring him and apologise. If I can persuade him to come back you've got to promise me you'll be on your best behaviour, or you and I won't stay friends for much longer! Do you understand?'

'Perhaps it would just be best if I left now?'

Knowing she was taking the coward's way out,

Sophie told herself that if Dominic conceded to return to the reception, and Diana enjoyed the rest of her day, then the fact that her best friend wouldn't be there would be worth it.

'Oh, no, you don't!' Grabbing her hand before she could take even one step towards the exit, Diana looked furious. 'You are going to stay here and face the music! If Dominic expects an apology from you then you are going to give it to him—do you hear me, Sophie? I am not having my wedding day ruined because you were rude to the one person I can't afford to let you be rude to!'

CHAPTER TWO

EATING humble pie had never been so painful. Later that evening, round the dining table, she deliberately avoided eye contact with Dominic.

After making her stammering apology, Sophie had lapsed into a painful and angry silence. The man hadn't even had the grace to accept her apology like a gentleman. Instead, he'd arrogantly replied, 'I will accept your apology, Sophie...for Diana's sake,' then continued to talk to Freddie—Diana's husband—as though Sophie no longer existed.

Sophie had never felt more belittled or disgruntled in all her life. He had got the upper hand again, and it was clear he was going to make Sophie suffer as a consequence. Right then, as she studied his handsome, hard-jawed profile, she honestly *despised* the man. She was glad for Diana's sake that he had relented and returned to the reception, but she almost would have preferred ex-communication from Diana's friendship than endure the vehement discomfort that she was currently having to endure.

When the guests moved into the bar area, where a tuxedo-attired pianist was entertaining the hotel residents with some gentle jazz, Sophie wondered how long in all conscience she should stay, before telling Diana she was leaving? Standing alone as she sipped the glass of wine she had brought with her from the table, Sophie glanced up startled as she suddenly found herself face to face with Dominic.

For a long moment he just stared at her, saying nothing. Her spine prickling with resentment, Sophie remembered that she had promised Diana not to let her temper run away with her again. At least as far as *this* man was concerned. *But, God, it was hard!* Swallowing razorblades would surely be easier?

'Having a nice time?' she asked, then coloured as she realised he could easily interpret such a remark as facetious.

'I can tell you are not happy that I came back, Sophie.' One corner of his mouth curled back into his smooth cheek. She focused her gaze on the two black buttons on his jacket instead of being persuaded to look into his eyes, unreasonably annoyed that his eyes should be so disagreeably hypnotic and so unrelentingly *green*.

'Whatever gave you that idea?'

Now she *did* sound facetious. Dammit! It was nigh on impossible to be agreeable to this man when he clearly thought himself so much better than everyone else. Stealing a look over Dominic's broad shoulder, in its perfectly tailored jacket, Sophie caught a pointed glimpse of Diana's definitely raised eyebrow. It was as if she were silently saying to Sophie, *Remember your promise? Don't go ruining anything else!*

Sophie swallowed hard, and somehow managed to persuade her mostly uncooperative lips into a smile up at Dominic.

For a moment he registered surprise. Then he glanced round, saw that she'd been looking at Diana, and turned back with a slight disapproving tilt of his jaw. *She had to be the most difficult and argumentative woman he had ever come across,* Dominic thought. But she had pretty eyes, and a torturously sexy mouth, and even though her ill manners exasperated him she stirred a surprising heat inside him that he couldn't deny. In fact, as he took another careful sip of his wine Dominic let that heat sizzle a little in sudden concentrated anticipation that he might turn his verbal conflagration with Sophie into a conflagration of a very *different* but much more pleasurable sort. If she wasn't passive by nature, there was no way that the woman would be passive in bed.

Quite unexpectedly, the thought became urgent and goal-orientated, until Dominic found he could think of nothing he'd like more than getting Sophie between the sheets and indulging in the kind of sexual sparring that excited him most. Before the night was through, he vowed to have her purring rather than wanting to scratch his eyes out!

'Your glass is almost empty, I see. How about some more champagne?'

Before Sophie could even register his intention, Dominic had deftly removed her glass from her hand and, glancing round him, signalled a nearby waiter to give him her glass and an order for more drinks. When he turned back to Sophie, levelling his disturbing gaze on her eyes and then her mouth, as if he would devour her down to her very bones, her senses were suddenly besieged by a wave of desire so ignitable that for a moment she couldn't think, let alone form words.

Rocked to the very toes of her expensive cream sandals, she wondered what the hell was wrong with her? *She disliked this smug, arrogant man intensely, never mind desired him! She must have had too much champagne and wine. That was the only logical conclusion she could come to right then.* She had better slow things right down before she committed one more act of utter and complete folly, and so thoroughly made a fool of herself that she wouldn't be able to live with herself again.

'I really don't think I ought to have any more alcohol,' she confessed, aghast at the fact that her composure had been thrown so off kilter by his too-intimate cynosure. 'I'm not really used to drinking.'

'If not drinking, then surely you must have other vices, Sophie? I wonder what they might be?'

Her attention trapped indisputably by the suggestive honeyed tones of his mesmerising voice, Sophie couldn't look away. She wanted to make some clever or cutting little quip, to put a dent in his too-confident leer, but her throat and her thoughts seemed to dry up at the same time, and nothing sprang helpfully to mind.

'Sophie? Are you all right?'

He touched her; laid his hand on her bare arm and gave it a definite *squeeze*. There was no question in Sophie's mind that he had somehow *branded* her. Now her senses were jumping around all over the place in utter and wild confusion, and the place where he had lain his fingers felt as if it were on fire. *Why was it that when she looked into that intimidatingly handsome face of his she knew she hated him? Yet when he had touched her just now she had almost swayed with the sheer intoxicating pleasure of it?* Today was turning out to be one of the most bizarre days in recent memory that was for sure!

'I'm fine. I was just—I just felt a little cold...that's all.'

'Cold?' A surprised eyebrow lifted towards Dominic's crown of blond hair, accompanied by a very wry and disbelieving smile. The room was almost too hot. And he could plainly see that Sophie's cheeks were burning. In that very moment Dominic knew without a doubt she was having trouble diverting her attraction towards him. Just as he was having trouble doing the same thing with her. *In his mind there was only one solution to their mutual problem.*

'How were you planning on getting home this evening?' he asked, his voice deceptively casual as his eyes met the startled blue of her anxious gaze.

'Home?' *Good God! Now she had completely lost the ability to converse at all. She'd turned into a monosyllabic idiot!* Determinedly Sophie made herself focus. Was he going to offer her a lift? she speculated.

'Oh, I'll probably cadge a lift off one of Diana's friends, or get a taxi.'

'I was wondering…as an alternative…' Dominic moved closer, and his fingers found their way beneath Sophie's chin and lifted it up a little. Her bones were so delicate and fine that she felt the strong imprint of his fingers acutely. Inside, her heart felt as if it was just about to go into cardiac arrest, and she waited for him to finish speaking all thoughts of Diana, Freddie, and their friends vanished as if they no longer existed. The only two people left in the room were herself and Dominic. '…whether you might like to stay the night in the hotel, with me?'

'Sta—stay the night?' she repeated, once more appalled at how this man could affect her so acutely with just one smooth, confident glance. *Was he serious?* The thought that he might be stringing her along, to pay her back for insulting him earlier, struck a very loud alarm bell in Sophie's head. He had turned on the charm, reeled her in, and now he was going to dump her in an even bigger metaphorical puddle than the real one that had drenched her earlier!

She circled her fingers around his wrist and threw his hand away. 'You must think me completely stupid if you

think I'm going to fall for that kind of obvious little ruse!
I'm on to you, Mr Van Straten! I know all you're trying
to do is pay me back because I spoke my mind earlier,
and didn't bow and scrape like you usually expect people to do in your exalted company!'

Dominic couldn't help but laugh. It simply hadn't occurred to him that she might think his invitation to bed
was some kind of game he was playing to repay her for
insulting him! She was a defensive little creature, that
was for sure. He would have to convince her he meant
no offence at all—*quite the opposite in fact.*

'You have it all wrong Sophie. There was no affront
intended. Nor do I expect you to "bow and scrape" in
my company. I *do*, however, desire very much that you
share my bed tonight. I am perfectly serious about this,
and there is no trick up my sleeve with which I am trying
to hoodwink you. Understand?' He saw the confusion in
her eyes, the slight flush that rushed into her cheeks, and
the way her hands nervously went to her hair. Feeling
his desire grow, Dominic slid his hand around the curve
of her cheek and jaw, and gently stroked the skin that
was as beguiling to the touch as the most opulent velvet.

'Understand?' he repeated more softly.

Dominic had taken off Sophie's shoes. Sitting on the
bed, with its rich claret-coloured satin counterpane, her
hands intertwined in her lap, it was hard for her to stop
trembling like a shivering kitten that had been left out
in the rain as he knelt before her. *She wanted him to kiss
her. Wanted it so badly that her very bones ached with
longing.* Instead, she watched entranced as he divested
himself of his jacket and tie, opened some buttons on
his shirt and—with his gaze fixed firmly on hers—slid
his palms up the outside of her stockinged thighs.

The blue silk of her dress rippled like a gentle flowing stream as he edged it further and further up her legs. She was wearing a cream-coloured suspender belt with little embossed daisies on it to hold up her matching cream hosiery, and Sophie wondered what Dominic would think of her undoubtedly sexy underwear? *Would he imagine she'd worn it just in case she got lucky?* Because this was so far from the truth, and she was unable to keep her pained thoughts to herself, she inadvertently released a groan. Dominic smiled at her with a slow, engagingly sexy smile of acknowledgement, and a spark of molten heat burned back at her from his darkened green eyes as he flipped open the fastenings that held her stockings up and slowly…very slowly…peeled them down her bare legs.

Excitement and all-consuming need thrummed commandingly through Dominic's blood. Seducing a beautiful woman was one of life's most exquisite pleasures, after all, and he knew the seductive arts as well as he knew how to make a million dollars without exerting himself. The skill had become innate. Knowing how to take things slowly—how to drive a woman's passion to such a crescendo that she would beg him to take her, to ease her agony—he was perfectly acquainted with bestowing sensual delectation.

But, right now Dominic was the one who was in desperate need of this woman's touch. He needed it—no, *craved* it, as if he would lose his mind if he didn't have it soon. With her eyes blinking back at him like a startled owl's, Dominic registered her tension—her *excitement*—and, linking his fingers expertly around the sides of the scant silk panties she was wearing, he gave them a gentle tug downwards. Quickly removing them, he settled his body nearer hers on the bed, whilst still kneeling on the carpet, and this time slid his palms up the insides of her trembling legs.

Hearing her deeply in-drawn breath, Dominic caressed the fine dark curls at her apex, then worked his fingers inside her. At the sensation of hot moist heat, that drenched him, he could not prevent his own gasp of violent pleasure.

Oh, God, yes! More please more! Don't stop. Sophie's thoughts were desperate and wild as Dominic worked his magic, making her climax almost before she even knew that was her destination. Feeling heat saturate her, and her aroused nipples rub acutely sensitively against the flimsy material of her bra inside her dress, she expelled her breath in soft urgent gasps of deliciously lustful pleasure. Tipping back her head, she shut her eyes in ecstasy as erotic waves rippled powerfully through her, one after the other.

She'd never known release like it. Such mind-spinning pleasure had only been pure fantasy for Sophie up until now.

Opening her eyes again, she saw that Dominic had discarded his shirt and was doing the same to his trousers. Her gaze devoured him greedily. *His body was amazing.* Broad, beautifully muscled shoulders and chest, an iron-hard stomach tapering down to lean, tight hips, a sprinkling of fine blond hairs disappearing tantalisingly down into his black silk boxers. Sophie inadvertently dampened her lips with her tongue.

Dominic honed in on the unknowingly erotic gesture with such a possessive, hungry glance that she almost climaxed again, right there and then. Then, rising over her on the bed he tipped up her chin and brought his lips down hard and hot upon hers. His tongue was a seductive instrument of velvet torture as he played with and teased Sophie's mouth, nipping and stroking her tender flesh with ruthless prowess.

His expertise took kissing to a whole new dimension. The taste of him was the most destroyingly addictive nectar her lips had ever experienced, and she wasn't ashamed to silently admit she wanted more. Reaching for the hem of her silk dress, he lifted it over Sophie's head in one quick, fluid movement, then undid her lacy cream bra in the same expert fashion.

'You are perfect,' he breathed in wonder, as his hand cupped the soft swell of one full pink-tipped breast and then the other.

'Not as perfect as you,' Sophie couldn't help replying, putting her hand out to touch his bare, flat stomach. Her fingers touched velvet steel, and she sucked in a deep breath in purely sensual satisfaction.

'Yes,' Dominic agreed, his voice a silken rasp, 'touch me, Sophie. I *want* you to touch me.'

His command opened the floodgates of need inside her. Greedily she slid her hand down, past his perfect navel, past the springy clutch of fine blond hairs, and grasped his hard, hot erection. *He felt like satin.* As her fingers curled around him Dominic groaned, then bent his head and kissed Sophie again, drinking from her moist, plundered lips with increasing urgency and ardour. She offered no protest when he guided her firmly down onto the bed and positioned his strong, muscular thighs either side of her.

Just before she lost the power to think of anything else but the intense gratification to come, Sophie knew she ought to tell Dominic that she was n the Pill. She took it more to help regulate her period. than for more obvious reasons, but even as she opened her mouth to speak she saw him reach into the trousers he had discarded and withdraw a small blue packet.

As he slipped off his boxers and sheathed himself in the protection she saw for herself how generously endowed he was, and her mouth went dry as chalk. She forgot the fact that they were supposed to be enemies, that they didn't have a single thing in common between them except this: *this wild, inexplicable sexual attraction that had flared up between them hotly and unexpectedly and compelled them to go to bed together.* And when Dominic brought his mouth down upon her breasts, attending to each one in turn with hot, demanding caresses, urging her towards the most intense delectation she had ever known, Sophie decided not to fight her conscience at all, but simply just to enjoy the experience instead.

Didn't her friends do that all the time? Not the ones who were looking for Mr Right, but the others, who believed it was a woman's right to take sexual pleasure wherever she could find it and suffer no guilt.

'Are you ready for me, Sophie?' Dominic whispered against her ear, as he slid his hard, fit body along hers. 'Are you going to let me inside now?'

Was that husky little whimper really hers? Was that soft, needy voice really the same vehemently strident one that had levelled all those insults at him just a few short hours ago? As he urged her slender thighs apart, and pushed slowly but firmly inside her, Sophie ran her hands down Dominic's back, pressing her fingernails into his toned muscled flesh with increasing need as he thrust deeply inside her.

'That's it, my little cat... Let me feel your pretty little claws.'

Dominic had always been blessed with a healthy libido, but even *he* had not experienced sexual need so intensely passionate as this. His lips became intimately acquainted with every inch of her flesh in a hungry search to sate himself with her body. *Even her sweat tasted sweet to his beguiled mouth.*

Holding back his own desperate compulsion to reach a climax, Dominic thrust into Sophie again and again, until she came undone in his arms. As she quivered and moaned, and slid her hands down the now slippery wetness of his back, he succumbed to a wave of ecstasy so powerful and glorious that he was left breathless and stunned in its aftermath. Before he rolled away from her, Dominic stared down into Sophie's lovely blue eyes and smiled at her with the most deeply satisfied smile he had ever bestowed on a lover before.

'You have nothing to say to me now my, little cat?' he taunted gently, green eyes brimming with amusement and fierce, fierce pleasure.

Staring up into the hard, lean contours of his mesmerising face, her body already needing him again, and throbbing with unashamed anticipation, Sophie sighed softly up at him.

'Sometimes words aren't necessary...don't you think?' she whispered, her glance already sliding away from his, in case she exposed herself too deeply to his hot, examining gaze...

About to race out of the door because she was late, Sophie was delayed by the appearance of a courier with a large package that she had to sign for. Puzzled by what the contents could possibly be, she nonetheless signed the delivery note quickly, left the box on the table just inside the front door, and dashed down the road to catch the bus that would take her to the primary school where she taught.

The local garage did not hold out much hope for her beloved car, so she had no choice other than to use public transport to get to work. The young mechanic who had looked over it for her had shaken his head and cheerfully told Sophie that it didn't have much value other than scrap. His blasé conclusion pained her deeply. Any repairs she might instruct them to undertake would apparently cost her almost twice that of the value of the car itself. Her heart sinking, she'd agreed to let them tow it away, and resigned herself to getting used to either Shanks's pony or the unreliable delights of the local transportation system. She certainly wasn't in the market for a new car—second-hand or otherwise.

Diana's wedding and the whole difficult day on Friday—culminating in the most surprising event of all, when she and Dominic had ended up in bed together— he'd vowed not to think about too much.

How had she allowed herself to behave like such an unbelievable little hussy? Even now she couldn't quite believe she had succumbed so easily to the ruthless charm of Diana's handsome boss. Coming to her senses in the early hours of Saturday morning, she had been careful not to wake him in the bed beside her, and instead had paid a brief visit to the bathroom, dressed quickly, then left the hotel without so much as saying goodbye to him. *What was the point?* In the harsh, cold light of morning she knew they'd both only regret their passionate fling.

No…Sophie had *definitely* done the right thing where Dominic Van Straten was concerned. She'd saved them both the embarrassment of confronting each other again.

No doubt he'd been nothing but relieved when he'd woken to find her gone.

Now, on Monday morning, Sophie found that she actually welcomed the chattering voices of her class of sixteen lively five-year-olds in preference to ever enduring such an uncomfortable occasion as Diana's wedding ever again. Whenever her unguarded mind recalled Dominic's intoxicating presence, her stomach reacted with an anxious, confused flip, and she was surprised yet again how one beguiling yet infuriating stranger could make her respond with such violent emotion.

She'd never had a one-night stand in her life before, and to have one with her best friend's boss, and on her wedding day, too, was probably the most uncharacteristic and reckless thing she'd ever done.

It was a good job Diana and Freddie had left before they'd found out that Sophie had agreed to spend the night with Dominic, or else she'd never have gone through with it in the first place. But even as she tried to reassure herself she would not willingly have embarrassed her friend—she knew she could not have resisted Dominic's invitation that night—not when his eyes had undressed her and openly made love to her even before they had reached the hotel room!

'Finish the story, Miss!'

'What?' Snapping out of yet another recollection of the Dutch billionaire who seemed to be dominating her thoughts with alarming regularity that morning, Sophie flushed guiltily, adjusted the illustrated book in her lap, and smiled warmly down at the group of children gathered round her seat on the floor. 'Where were we?'

'The big bad wolf was just about to gobble up the grandmother!' a little girl with blonde bobbed hair offered enthusiastically.

Sophie didn't miss the irony that she should be reading the story of Little Red Riding Hood and the Big Bad Wolf when her mind was preoccupied with thinking about Dominic…

The first thing she saw when she came through the door that evening was the package. Carrying it into the living room, Sophie shucked off the navy-blue duffel coat she'd been wearing over her skirt and sweater and laid the box down on the coffee table to examine the contents. There was a label on the back that announced the name of a well-known and expensive store in Knightsbridge, and Sophie frowned as she looked at it, wondering who on earth would be sending her anything from such an exclusive shop.

She came from an honest, hard-working, working-class family, and certainly her mum or dad or even her brother Phillip wouldn't dream of sending her expensive presents totally out of the blue.. and neither would Sophie want them to. As she opened the box and stared down at the contents she sucked in her breath in astonishment.

It was a coat…the same fawn colour as her own, but made from cashmere, with a luxurious cream silk lining. Lifting it out to examine it more closely, Sophie saw to her amazement that it was the perfect size and length for her shape and height. Laying it down carefully on her threadbare burgundy couch, she searched around in the elegant tissue paper for a note of some kind, even though by now she had a pretty good idea who had sent it.

By the time she'd located the small gold-embossed business card, with 'Dominic' scrawled across one side in an impressive flourish, her heart was just about ready to burst out of her chest. Sophie couldn't remember telling him her address, but at some point in the evening she guessed she must have. After they'd made love they'd had more champagne brought to the room, and Sophie had been uncharacteristically giggly and talkative because of it.

She groaned out loud as she remembered. *But why was Dominic sending her such an expensive coat when all they'd had was a one-night stand?* Was it meant to be some kind of veiled insult or a reproach to make Sophie feel cheap? Was that it? He'd said he'd meant no affront when he'd asked her to go to bed with him, *but what if he'd lied?* Her heart plummeted like a stone. *What if he was teaching her a lesson? A horrible and despicable one, but a lesson in his eyes all the same?*

He might have been an expert lover, and he might have made her blood zing, but it was still a fact that Dominic Van Straten was completely out of Sophie's sphere. *What would demonstrate that fact more completely than sending the 'poor little working class girl' an expensive coat in payment for her 'services' at the hotel the other night?* Just because he'd made love to her, it didn't mean that he wasn't still arrogant, and even possibly cruel.

Her first instinct was to fold the coat back into its expensive packaging and mail it right back to him, and even as the thought came into her mind Sophie found herself arranging the coat back into the box in a fever of indignation and rage. Reading the card again, she looked for an address and found it. Surprisingly, it wasn't his office address, but his home one: Mayfair, London. Where else would a property developer billionaire live?

Seeing that there was a telephone number included beneath the address, Sophie went to the telephone in the hallway with thumping heart. If he thought she'd given him a piece of her mind on Friday, he'd better watch out! What did he think she was? Some kind of loose woman who'd gladly accept his no-doubt insulting gift of an expensive coat without a murmur? If he thought that, then he had a very big shock in store!

'Mr Van Straten's residence,' announced a cultured male voice at the other end of the line.

'I'd like to speak to Mr Van Straten,' Sophie announced as a flood of adrenaline shot through her system and almost made her sway. He was probably conveniently out.. or if he was at home no doubt he would instruct his butler, or whoever it was that had answered the phone, to tell her he wasn't available as soon as he knew it was Sophie.

'Whom shall I say is calling?' the voice at the other end came back.

Licking her suddenly dry lips, Sophie stared blankly at the picture on the wall, a well-known Degas print of ballerinas at the barre, going through their exercises. Shocked that he was actually at home, she told herself to keep her head and not give way to shrillness of any kind when she told him what he could do with his expensive gift. He'd already accused her of being a 'shrew' and a 'fishwife,' and if he insulted her with any such labels one more time, he'd rue the day!

'Sophie Dalton.'

She'd been about to explain that she was a friend of his assistant, Diana, then had thought, How ridiculous! If Dominic didn't condescend to remember her after what had occurred between them on Friday night then he was even more arrogant and despicable than she'd thought, and therefore even less deserving of any respect.

'Sophie. What a pleasant surprise!'

His voice shocked her into silence. It was disconcertingly familiar, and much too compelling to ever be taken lightly. On the telephone, his tone was sexier and much more troubling to her peace of mind than it had a right to be. It made her remember him asking seductively, *'Are you ready for me Sophie?'* Hot embarrassed colour surged into her face at the recollection.

'I wish I could say I felt the same, Dominic, but I can't. About the coat you sent me, I—'

'I trust it's the right size? I confess I had to guess your measurements, but then I do pride myself on being uncannily accurate when it comes to such things.'

He meant women...and their bodies. Was she just one of *many* female bodies he had undressed? Furious and hurt at the same time, she had to take a moment to compose herself. 'Whether it's the right size or not doesn't concern me! You had no right to send it to me in the first place. Especially when I know you are only trying to insult me!'

'Insult you?' Dominic said something beneath his breath that she didn't quite catch, and Sophie smoothed her hand down over her hip and reminded herself to keep her temper.

'Yes, insult me! Why else would you send it? You were making some sleazy point, no doubt, to thank me for services rendered. Well, you know what you can do with your expensive cashmere, don't you? I'll be mailing the coat straight back to you tomorrow! Just as soon as I can get to the Post Office.'

'My chauffeur accidentally splashed your coat with cold muddy water, Sophie...remember? I was merely trying to make amends by sending you a new one.

Anything else is completely a figment of your over-sensitive imagination.'

'Why make amends now, when you seemed not to care one jot about my situation on Friday, at Diana's wedding? Just because I was foolish enough to sleep with you, Dominic, it doesn't mean I'm a complete fool! I don't want your expensive gifts, do you hear? Whatever your reasons for sending me the coat, I have no intention of accepting it, or being beholden to you in any way.'

Dominic didn't know many women who would be insulted by the gift of a very expensive coat from one of the country's top exclusive stores. No—he had to re-phrase that. He knew for a fact that there were *no* women of his acquaintance that would have reacted in such an unexpected way. The women in his life had always adored the fact that he had the wealth and taste to pur-chase such expensive gifts for them—even the ones who came from money themselves.

Again, in spite of his irritation with Sophie for think-ing he was trying to insult her, Dominic sensed the blood heat in his veins as though it were being pursued by a fire. The memory of flashing blue eyes the colour of cornflowers started an ache inside him that suddenly made moving too quickly a hazard. He knew she was passionate and principled...if misguided...and she had been a totally responsive and highly provocative lover. He had not arranged for the coat to be sent as an insult in any way. He had certainly not sent it as *payment* for sexual services. He had most *definitely* sent it as a reason to speak to Sophie again.

When he'd woken up on Saturday morning and found her gone he'd barely been able to believe it. No woman had left him that way before...*ever*! Initially irked, he'd told himself she must have had some appointment to rush off to. Why else would she not have waited at least to say good morning? When he'd calmed down, and reflected on the sensational sex they'd enjoyed the night before, Dominic had also known that Sophie hadn't left because they hadn't hit it off together. Whatever her reasons for leaving, one thing he hadn't doubted was that she would naturally want to see him again. *Why wouldn't she?* When she rang him to thank him for the coat, as he'd fully expected her to do, Dominic had been planning on inviting her out for dinner. *The sooner the better, as far as he was concerned, because he hadn't been able to get the woman out of his mind.* Which was why he had included a card with his home address and telephone number on.

'How does accepting my gift make you beholden to me?' *If only it did*, Dominic thought, in frustration. It had been a long while since a woman had commanded his attention in such an emphatic way. He probably just needed to go to bed with her a few more times, to get her out of his system, he acknowledged with typical male frankness. *If she gave him the chance…*

'It just does.'

Suddenly tired of verbal sparring, and with her growling stomach letting her know that she hadn't eaten a thing since lunchtime, Sophie had it in her mind to end their fruitless conversation there and then. Tomorrow she would send Dominic the coat back, and that would be that. Her time and her thoughts would surely be better served this evening in working out how she was going to afford another car to get to school in. She couldn't rely on the vagaries of public transport. The head of the primary school in which she worked was a real stickler for punctuality, and Sophie knew it. It wouldn't do to get on the wrong side of him and blot her so far un-blemished record.

'Anyway,' she added, once more examining the print of the pretty ballerinas on the wall, 'I'll have to say goodnight. I've just got in from work, I'm tired and hungry, and I've got schoolwork to arrange for tomorrow.'

'Schoolwork?'

'I'm a teacher.'

'Diana didn't mention it.'

Not believing even for a second that a man so high up in the echelons of wealth and personal achievement would deign to discuss something as mundane as his assistant's friends, with her, Sophie sighed. 'Why should she? Goodbye, Dominic.'

'Why did you rush off like that on Saturday morning?'

Sophie wished he would leave the subject of Saturday morning *and specifically Friday night* alone. She felt bad enough about succumbing to her baser instincts so recklessly, *and* with the most unsuitable man she could imagine!

'You may find this hard to believe, Dominic, but I'm not the kind of woman who usually goes in for one-night stands. In fact, this was the first...and I hope the last one ever. It was an emotional day for me, and I—my judgement wasn't at its best. You can rest assured I won't be bothering you again in any way.'

Dominic doubted that. Just thinking about the way she had curled her slender legs around his back and driven her nails into his flesh, in the throes of passion made him almost too hot and bothered for words! And what did she mean her judgement hadn't been at its best? Was she suggesting that making love with him had been a mistake? Now, that *did* hit at the heart of his pride.

'If you won't accept the coat, why don't you bring it

to my house instead of mailing it?' Dominic suggested smoothly, his calm tone belying the myriad of feelings flooding through him.

Her senses hijacked by surprise and shock, Sophie bit down on her lip. 'Bring it to your house?' she repeated, not sure that she'd heard him correctly.

'Tomorrow—after work. You have the address on my card?'

'Why are you doing this, Dominic?'

'I would like to talk to you about Diana,' he replied.

'Diana?' Drawing her brows together in confusion, Sophie glanced down at the floor. Some of the maroon carpet tiles were curling at the edges and needed replacing. A sudden wave of irritation and uncharacteristic despondency briefly descended. She totally loved her job— teaching for Sophie was a vocation—but she wished not for the first time that it paid better and allowed her to maintain a slightly better standard of living.

'I want to buy her a wedding present…something special. I thought perhaps you could advise me.'

Taken aback, Sophie really didn't know what to say.

'Well?' Dominic prompted into the heavy silence that ensued.

'Aren't you supposed to buy a present in time for the actual event?'

'I was away in Singapore on a business trip the week leading up to her wedding, so I did not get a chance to arrange a suitable gift for her.'

But he'd paid for her wedding breakfast just the same, Sophie reluctantly recalled. Diana had said he was generous. She immediately discarded the thought with irritation.

'I'm sure you don't need me to advise you what to buy Diana.' She shrugged, wondering why he should suggest such a surprising thing when she had already professed herself insulted by his gift of the coat. *She would have thought he'd be glad not to get himself further entangled with Diana's 'unsuitable' friend.*

'You are her close friend. You know her tastes, her preferences. That information could help me a lot in choosing a gift she would really like.' His voice was almost hypnotically persuasive, and Sophie couldn't believe she was actually hesitating over her natural instinct to refuse.

She'd told herself that Friday night had probably meant nothing very much to a man like Dominic, other than sexual gratification with an available, attractive woman. She'd told herself she could handle it, despite feeling somehow 'used' when she received that beautiful coat as a gift. Now her feelings were all mixed up, and even more confused.

'Isn't there anyone else you could ask?' Even as she uttered the question Sophie knew she was clutching at straws. Dammit! She was nervous about going to Dominic's house. Who wouldn't be? It wasn't every day that an ordinary girl like her got invited to a billionaire's home! *Especially one she'd had a hot one-night stand with!* She'd be nervous even if they *hadn't* slept together.

'Is it too much to ask that you might do this for your friend?' Deftly and without remorse, Dominic slid home his advantage.

'No. No, of course not. I'll come, then. What time?'

'I will send Louis to collect you at about eight o'clock. I will see you then, Sophie.'

CHAPTER THREE

DETERMINEDLY clutching the large box containing the coat she was returning, Sophie glanced nervously through the stained glass panels on the swish and elegant Regency front door, and willed the butterflies in her stomach to cease their incessant fluttering just for a moment.

She wasn't looking forward to seeing Dominic Van Straten again one little bit. Right now she felt as if she'd voluntarily agreed to step up to the guillotine and have her head separated from her body. *That* was how much she hated the idea of even being here—no matter how beautiful or imposing the house in front of her, or how exclusive the address, or the fact that she'd just been transported there in a chauffeur-driven car.

Sophie could find no pleasure in any of it. She just wanted to return the damn coat and get out of there as fast as her legs could carry her. But when the door opened graciously before her eyes, and an elderly man dressed in a dark suit with neatly combed grey hair stood before her with a smile that was inordinately polite, she forced herself to speak and go forward.

'Hello. I'm Sophie Dalton. I have—I have an appointment with Mr Van Straten.'

'Of course. Please come in, Miss Dalton. Mr Van Straten is waiting for you in the drawing room. Shall I take your coat?'

Quickly unbuttoning it, while the man briefly held her package for her, Sophie wished she could have refused.

But it seemed churlish and ignorant to be deliberately difficult with a man she'd never even met before, so she handed it to him and gratefully took back the package. Trying not to goggle at the magnificent entrance hall, with its elegant air of grace and opulence and its fine, grey-veined white marble floor, Sophie obediently allowed him to lead her to Dominic. After announcing her arrival at the entrance to the room, the manservant discreetly withdrew, and closed the doors behind her.

It didn't take her long to locate the man she'd come to see. He was standing by the white marble fireplace, a drink in his hand, his lips slightly curving in a smile that appeared without question to be self-satisfied and slightly smug. What was he thinking? Was he gloating that he'd been able to persuade her to do as he'd asked?

Sophie almost retreated back the way she'd come. Although the room was gracious and elegant in the extreme, the most intimidating, magnetic element in it was Dominic himself. He was the pivot around which all that exceptionally good taste revolved. Even at the not inconsiderable distance between them she couldn't fail to see that it was his very presence that marked their surroundings more than anything else.

As his emerald eyes examined her with cool detachment and, yes...perhaps arrogance, Sophie told herself she must have lost her mind to have come here. Wasn't it enough that she'd shamed herself by sleeping with him the first day they had met? Was she really so eager to entertain even more embarrassment?

Feeling her lip quiver slightly with nerves, Sophie clamped down her teeth to quell it. 'I brought the coat...like I—like I said I would,' she announced, desperately trying to rescue her rapidly dwindling confidence.

'So I see,' he said.

An awkward silence descended. Sophie had just about decided to make her excuses and leave when Dominic put his glass down on the mantelpiece, moved away from the fireplace, and gestured towards the long white couch behind her. 'Why don't you sit down? We can discuss the coat later.'

'There's nothing to discuss. I don't want it, so I'm returning it.'

Defiant, and determined not to let him get the better of her in any way, Sophie placed the box down on the glass table in front of her, and did not shy away from the definite irritation in his gaze that he directed back.

'Nevertheless…I still think you should sit down. What can I get you to drink?'

She didn't want a drink, and she didn't want to sit down. All Sophie really wanted to do was leave. But, quelling her almost overwhelming desire to escape, she forced herself to sit down on the couch, and folded her hands neatly in front of her on her lap. Glancing around the beautiful room, with its exquisite antique furniture and imposing art on the walls, she was suddenly seized with uncharacteristic self-consciousness.

She hadn't dressed up in any way, shape or form for this little interview with Dominic. She'd kept on what she'd worn to school that morning: a red V-necked wool sweater, and a black calf-length skirt with matching low-heeled boots. And she'd deliberately not fussed with her usual minimal make-up either. She hadn't even reapplied her lipstick. There was no way that she was going to make Dominic imagine for one moment that she'd make any sort of effort with her appearance for his benefit. Sophie wasn't interested in what the man thought about what she looked like, or even if he thought about it at all. The sooner they discussed what they had to discuss the sooner she could be out of there, and heading home again.

'I'm fine,' she replied coolly. 'I had a cup of coffee before your chauffeur arrived to pick me up.'

'I didn't mean coffee. Will you have a Scotch or a brandy? It's cold outside. It will help warm you up.'

Even as he said the words, Dominic doubted very much whether any amount of alcohol could effect a thaw in Little Miss Frigid sitting over there on his couch. He hadn't expected this coldness after what had transpired between them on Friday night, and the fact that she clearly took no pleasure in either his company or his beautiful house seriously bothered him. Whatever people said about him, when he invited them into his home he wanted them to feel welcome.

Seeing her again, Dominic realised how much he'd been anticipating her visit. With her vivid blue eyes and her short, dark hair curling becomingly round her small ears, she was even prettier than he'd remembered—despite her frostiness towards him. And he couldn't deny the warm little charge of electricity that was surging through him just by being in the same room with her. He'd thought he'd let his feverish imagination run away with him where Sophie's appeal was concerned, but now he saw that he hadn't. He just couldn't understand this wild desire he was harbouring for a woman who was now displaying all the signs of complete uninterest and none of the passionate attraction she'd demonstrated on Friday. It certainly pricked his pride.

'I'd rather not, thank you. You said you wanted to talk about a wedding gift for Diana?'

Reaching into the discreet side pocket in her skirt, Sophie withdrew a folded piece of paper and, getting to her feet, handed it to Dominic. 'I've scribbled down some ideas that might help. Of course, not knowing what kind of budget you had in mind, my suggestions might be somewhat limited.'

A smile touching his lips at the mere idea of a 'budget', Dominic accepted the slip of paper and dropped it onto the table as if it barely concerned him at all. Seeing the gesture, Sophie felt her stomach execute an anxious cartwheel. Indignant that he hadn't even glanced at what she'd written, she sat back down on the couch with definite trepidation.

'You're not even going to look at it?'

'Later.'

What did he mean, 'later'? Wasn't that why he'd invited her round in the first place? To discuss ideas for a present?

'About the coat...' Dominic began.

Hot colour poured into Sophie's cheeks. 'What about it?'

'Did you even try it on?'

She was ashamed to silently admit that she had. It had felt wonderful, too—a perfect fit. She'd loved the way the expensive fabric had swished round her legs and made her feel like a million dollars. But there was no way she was going to let him know that.

'The point is, Mr Van Straten—'

He couldn't believe she'd referred to him so formally. *Why was she now trying to erect fences between them when they had already been so intimate?*

'Dominic. We surely know each other well enough to use first names?' he interceded smoothly.

Startled blue eyes met slightly mocking green ones, then quickly glanced away again.

'We hardly know each other at all! Despite...despite

what happened between us. I told you on the phone that I couldn't—*wouldn't*—accept the coat. What happened, happened, and now we should both just forget about it. Diana is married and on her honeymoon, and hopefully having a good time. That's all that matters now.'

'Do something for me, Sophie, if you will? It would please me greatly if you tried on the coat.'

To Sophie's astonishment he was taking it out of the package and holding it out to her by the shoulders, ready for her to slip into, as though nothing she'd said previously had got through to him at all. The idea—the very *thought* of letting him help her on with his expensive unwanted gift was tantamount to agreeing to strip naked in front of him. Sophie blanched.

'Dominic, I—'

'What is it, Sophie?'

'I don't want to try on the coat!'

'Why not? What can it hurt?'

'Are you always this persistent?'

'When I want something badly enough…yes.'

'Oh, this is just too ridiculous for words!'

Seeing that he clearly had no intention of discussing anything else until she submitted to trying on the coat, Sophie suddenly felt very foolish at making such a fuss. He was right. What *would* it hurt? She could slip it on quickly, remind him she had no intention of accepting it, then take it off again and insist that he kept it. After that, she could make her excuses and leave.

But as Sophie grudgingly got to her feet and stepped around the table towards Dominic, turning at the last minute so that he could slip the garment onto her shoulders, she was so overwhelmed by him that she felt herself tremble. His heat and his nearness, and the dynamic, powerful presence he exuded as easily as some men wore cologne, was a heady cocktail for any woman. The effect it had on her was like some kind of powerful opiate that sent her spinning off into a whole other stratosphere.

As he settled the material around her, her trembling would not cease, and she was mesmerised as, with his hands either side of her arms, he directed her slowly round to face him. Something in his eyes transfixed Sophie, and bolted her feet to the floor. A scorching look so hot and desirous that beneath the luxurious coat she'd reluctantly tried on for his benefit, her limbs had all the strength of cotton wool.

Dominic was staring at her mouth. With the barest hint of raspberry lipstick, her pretty lips were temptingly ripe and plump, and too inviting for words. Knowing the delights that they promised, he wanted to plunder them, taste them, *ravish* them, until a rising tide of passion swept over them both, consigning them willingly to a little divine madness that they wouldn't soon forget. Lust rose up inside him so strongly that for a moment it was all Dominic could do to remind himself that if he capitulated to such desire Sophie would—in all likelihood—run a mile, and never see him again.

Or would she?

Realising that she was trembling, and that the blue irises of her lovely eyes had turned fascinatingly dark, Dominic quickly reassessed his opinion. She wasn't as *immune* to his attraction as she clearly wanted to convey. His little brunette spitfire still desired him as much as he desired her—only she was apparently determined to ignore it.

The knowledge ignited an almost dizzying satisfaction deep inside him—a victorious gratification that right then gave him far more pleasure than any multimillion-dollar property deal. *He would have her in his bed again soon, and the result would be even more sensational and breathless than the first time; an electrical storm that would not so soon die out.*

Keeping his desire and his intention deliberately in check, Dominic stood back to admire Sophie wearing the beautiful cashmere coat. It suited her without a doubt, as he'd known it would, and all of a sudden he was determined that she should keep it—despite her protestations to the contrary.

'See how well it looks.' He led her over to the large gilt mirror above the marble fireplace and saw that a rosy hue had invaded her cheeks and heat had made her eyes sparkle. *The betraying heat of sensual awareness...*

Gazing back at her reflection in that huge mirror, unable to hide from the slowly dawning truth that her attraction for this man had deepened more than it had diminished, Sophie wondered how on earth she even kept her balance. Her shocking feelings had betrayed her, as if paying her *will* no intention at all. How had she come to find herself in such an unbelievable situation? With Dominic's hard-angled and handsome face staring at her from behind, his large square hands firmly on her shoulders in the luxurious coat so reluctantly donned, it was hard to think of anything except to recall how those self-same hands had felt when touching her bare skin. She almost swayed.

More affected than she wanted to be by her wild, racing thoughts, Sophie spun round, determined to make herself come to her senses. Stalking back to the couch, she felt a tide of embarrassed heat wash over her making her body feel awkward and too self-conscious to be natural.

'I've got to go. Really...I have to.'

The coat came off and she laid it over the arm of the couch. Then she straightened, and stared at Dominic with her arms folded protectively across her chest—if only to hide the fact that her aching, tingling nipples were fiercely pressing against the cool cotton of her bra, and would no doubt betray her desire more emphatically than words ever could.

'I want you to keep the coat.'

His voice was husky, clearly affected by the shocking charge of primal electricity that had just ebbed and flowed between them. His hooded emerald eyes looked drowsy and heavy...*aroused*.

'No.'

'Yes, Sophie. I bought it for you and I want you to have it.'

If she made any more fuss about the infernal coat she was going to embarrass them both, Sophie realised. Reluctantly, hesitantly, she picked it up, and stroked over the soft wool with the flat of her hand. 'Very well, then. I...thank you. But I want you to know that I don't make a habit of accepting expensive presents from men.'

'Good. Then perhaps I am the first? That pleases me. Now, tell me—do you have a boyfriend? Are you seeing anyone?'

Her mind whirling with all the possible implications of such an unexpected question, Sophie stared. 'No. But why should that—?'

'Come to my house for dinner tomorrow night. I will send Louis for you at seven-thirty.'

'I've already made you the list you wanted regarding Diana's present. Why do you want me to come for dinner?'

Dominic's arresting green eyes narrowed. 'Don't pretend to misunderstand me, Sophie. You know very well why I have invited you to dinner.'

The unspoken erotic tension that Dominic hinted at lay between them, hardly managing to stay beneath the surface of the polite civility they both struggled to maintain. Realising it, Sophie was genuinely terrified. She'd convinced herself that Dominic meant the gift of the coat as an insult to make her feel cheap, because she'd slept with him, and now she had to reassess the situation completely, because he seemed to be expecting something more from her than a one-night stand.

'You didn't invite me,' she retorted, her eyes bright with renewed indignation, welcoming the emotion to hide behind. 'You *ordered* me!'

'I do not particularly care how you interpret my invitation. I just want you to be ready when Louis comes to collect you at seven-thirty. Am I making myself clear?'

She saw then the steel that his business associates and clients must regularly come up against, and her knees threatened to buckle. When this man wanted something, was there anything or any*one* that would even *dare* to stand in his way? she thought in fright. Probably not, considering his vast wealth and influence in the world that he moved in.

Diana had mentioned on more than one occasion that when it came to property Dominic Van Straten had the same awesome expertise and authority in the arena as a certain renowned media tycoon had on newspapers. Sophie only had to glance round the room at the probably million-dollar paintings so liberally lining the walls to know that. The man was successful beyond imagining.

'You have made yourself perfectly clear. But nobody

orders me to do anything I don't want to do! Do I make *myself* clear?'

Dominic laughed, and Sophie's already compromised knees almost *did* give way at the sound. That laugh immediately and worryingly provoked fantasies of naked bodies entwined on sheets of pure luxurious silk and, to her consternation, Sophie found that the images she'd conjured up, were not so easily dispelled.

'All right, Sophie. Since you are so anxious to leave, I will let you go. But you will come back tomorrow with Louis at the time I suggested… Yes?'

She wanted to be able to rewind the tape. To go back in time to the moment she had given him Diana's list. If she could go back to that moment, Sophie knew with certainty that she would not have stayed or been persuaded to try on the coat. Not now she was only too aware that the powerful undercurrent of attraction that she was being propelled upon towards this man was too strong for her to fight.

Unable to deal with this new, highly unfair tactic of unbelievable charm, Sophie released a pained sigh, wondering what price fate would exact on her for relenting to such a crazy attraction for even a second. 'Just dinner, then. Afterwards I'll go home, and that will be that.'

'Do you think so?'

Dominic's voice was gently derisive, and a small shiver of delicious awareness, like a shower of soft summer rain, cascaded down Sophie's spine.

'I *do* think so.'

'Sophie?'

'What is it?'

She had reached the door, her hand about to grasp the doorknob. When she turned her head to glance back at Dominic he was smiling, and the sight of that arresting, ruthlessly in control, undoubtedly sexy gesture almost snatched her breath away. She knew he was using it to illustrate to her that *he* was the one calling the shots, not Sophie. She should have left, right then, not waited for him to speak.

'Tomorrow, please wear something a little more feminine to dinner. *For me.*'

Biting her lip, lest she retaliate with something *not* so 'feminine', Sophie left the room, and the house, without another word.

The following day Dominic flew to Manchester on business. He was negotiating a deal to purchase some premier land in the city, on which to build three blocks of penthouse apartments with prime views. In a bidding war with a rival developer, Dominic had done his homework, considering all the angles and loopholes where he might gain an advantage over his rival.

Maintaining his customary cool, he emerged from the meeting five hours later, with the deal tied up and a sharp appetite for lunch. He ate at one of the best restaurants in town, met for drinks afterwards with the heiress daughter of a wealthy friend—owner of that same restaurant and several others round the country—declined her hopeful offer of going on to somewhere 'a little quieter' afterwards, and jumped on a plane back to London.

Throughout the day, behind the sharp dealing and the ruthless determination to come out on top in a deal he'd decided months ago would be his, Dominic's thoughts had strayed briefly from time to time to Sophie. Every time they had done so, a warm buzz had filled his body, making him long for the day to draw to a close and slide into evening so that he could see her again.

It had been a while since the possibility of a heated

sexual encounter had filled him with such desire and anticipation—but then he had already had a taste of what was in store. Together, he and Sophie were combustible. *Even if the little schoolteacher seemed to resent him with a vengeance.* It would make her complete capitulation to their mutual desire all the sweeter. But, that said, it was not in Dominic's mind to rush things, like a bull at a gate. He would take it very slowly this time: tease her a little bit, play with her, harness in his own needs with just the right amount of check—so that after a while she would be as crazy in lust for him as he was for her...

By the time he arrived back at the house in Mayfair he was in a *very* good mood indeed.

CHAPTER FOUR

TWICE during the day Sophie had slipped out of school, once in the morning and again at lunchtime, to ring Dominic's phone number. Both times all she'd got was the response of an answering machine, and both times she had decided against leaving a message. To leave a message on his machine telling him that she was declining his dinner invitation after all seemed cowardly in the extreme, and would probably earn her nothing but his undying scorn. She had her weak points, but cowardice was not one of them.

When Sophie reflected back on last night she could hardly believe that she'd been so hypnotised by the man that she'd agreed to see him again. Now, when she thought about it in the cold light of day, the whole idea seemed like madness. A disturbing and hot sexual attraction had briefly taken the edge off her dislike, and had hoodwinked her into thinking she'd actually like to experience more of the same with this enigmatic man. An extremely wealthy and powerful man, so far above her up the ladder of success that Sophie couldn't even see the soles of his shoes.

They were so mismatched it was laughable! She couldn't even afford to replace her clapped-out old car with a second-hand one, much less jet off to another part of the globe at the drop of a hat. And as well as the chasm-size gap in their social conditions, she didn't even *like* him. She really didn't. She told herself the only reason he was interested in her in any way was probably because he saw her as grateful and an easy conquest. Now and again perhaps he thought it a novelty to slum it a little, with girls from 'downtown' instead of 'uptown'. No doubt he played such games with women all the time…just because he could.

No. The more Sophie deliberated on the matter, the more she was utterly convinced she should just tell him to his face that she wasn't interested.

If only she'd told him that she *did* have a boyfriend. But lying was not something that came naturally to Sophie, either—even if it meant protecting herself from billionaire predators like Dominic Van Straten. So she decided she would go with Louis at the appointed time, when he came to collect her, then ask if Dominic could come to the door and confront him head-on with the fact that she'd made a mistake in agreeing to see him again, that she'd thought about it, but decided it wouldn't be a good idea.

Feeling pleased with the innate good sense of her proposal, Sophie returned to her class of enthusiastic five-year-olds, and threw herself with relish into an afternoon of finger painting.

A soft spring rain was falling as Sophie waited outside Dominic's front door that evening. He'd asked her to wear something feminine, but beneath her ordinary black coat—she'd deliberately not worn the one he'd gifted to her—she was wearing a plain, nondescript black sweater and jeans. She had not dressed up at all. What was the point when she'd only gone there to tell him that she'd changed her mind?

But when Dominic answered the door himself, filling the very air with the force of his charisma and looks, arrestingly handsome in a black tuxedo, his light-coloured hair gleaming beneath the chandelier-lit entrance hall behind him, Sophie's resolve about not seeing him again was swiftly blown away, like fragile autumn leaves clinging precariously to a branch.

'I won't come in,' she started, flustered by the fact she'd deliberately dressed down. 'I only came to tell you that I won't be joining you for dinner after all. In the cold light of day I've had some—I've had some doubts.'

Her cornflower-blue eyes were enormous in her pale oval face, and the rain had bestowed a myriad of crystals in her glossy black hair. Disappointment cut a deep swathe through Dominic's chest, along with fury that she should reject him so easily. And underlying both those emotions was a desire that could hardly be contained. He'd waited all day to see her again, and now she was telling him that she had some 'doubts'. No woman had ever rejected his advances before, and he was adamant that Sophie wasn't going to be the one to ruin such a long-standing record.

'Come in,' he told her, holding the door wide. 'You're getting wet, standing out there in the rain.'

Turning down her coat collar, Sophie reluctantly stepped inside. The warmth and light of the magnificent entrance hall enveloped her in a different world entirely from the one that denoted her own daily existence. Great wealth had a certain 'scent', she decided, even without all its more obvious trappings. And Dominic Van Straten exuded that scent.

As he closed the door and turned back to study her, his green eyes assessed her figure as thoroughly as if she were a painting he was considering buying, then hovered with slow deliberation on her face.

'I have friends waiting to meet you, Sophie,' he remarked, indicating the closed double doors of the drawing room at the foot of the beautiful winding staircase. 'Will you deprive them of your company as well?'

'Friends?' Sophie repeated in alarm, astonishment making her light-headed. 'But I thought that it would be just you and—' Biting off the end of her sentence as Dominic narrowed his emerald gaze with a slightly mocking glint, she swallowed hard. 'You didn't tell me it was a formal invitation.'

Her cheeks went from alabaster-pale to a vibrant rose-red in the space of just a few short seconds. Her unspoken belief that Dominic had been planning dinner for just the two of them hovered treacherously in the air, making Sophie feel like the biggest of fools there ever was.

'Were you hoping it would just be the two of us?' Soft-voiced, Dominic alarmed her even further by moving closer to her, so that Sophie was suddenly on intimate terms with every straight blond eyelash and each beautifully carved plane and angle of his arresting face.

He smelled good too…too good. Under siege, her heart began to race.

'No!'

Denying the charge with a passion, she wished the opulent marble floor would do her a huge favour and part like the Red Sea beneath her feet. Anything to save her further ghastly embarrassment beneath this man's all-seeing, mocking gaze.

'I wasn't ''hoping'' for anything. Would I have come here to tell you that I was declining your invitation if that was the case?'

'I'd like you to stay, Sophie.' He said this in such a way that Sophie had no doubt that it was practically an order.

But there was no way on earth that she wanted to meet

his more than likely equally well-heeled friends dressed as if she'd just walked out of a dusty classroom...which she practically had. There were even stubborn traces of coloured paint left under her fingernails from her afternoon with the children! Remembering, Sophie curled her hands and immediately dropped them down beside her.

'I really can't. Thank you for asking, just the same, and for—for sending Louis to collect me. I didn't want to just leave a message, you see. I wanted to tell you in person.'

He admired her integrity, he really did. But he wasn't a man readily to concede defeat—no matter what the odds. Not when he knew for a fact that the little schoolteacher was fighting as strong an attraction as he was. She was scared, that was all.

'Let me take your coat.'

To Sophie's astonishment, he worked his way deliberately down her buttons, popping open each one through its matching buttonhole with consummate ease. 'Dominic, I told you that I wasn't planning on staying!'

Impenetrable green eyes surveyed the plain black sweater she wore beneath her coat, the thin material hugging her breasts in a way that drew attention to the delightfulness of her shape. At the bottom edge of her sweater about half an inch of taut sexy midriff was on display above the plaited tan belt of her jeans, and Dominic's admiration intensified immediately. The outfit she was wearing might not scream designer chic, or be the most 'feminine' of clothing he could envisage, but he couldn't deny it was as sexy as hell.

'And I'm not dressed for dinner... You can see that!'

'You'll soon discover that being a friend of mine brings with it a certain amount of licence, Sophie. No one will bat an eyelid.'

Even if Sophie had believed him, which she didn't, walking into his grand drawing room looking as if she hadn't even bothered to think about what she was wearing, was not something she would do willingly. If any of his guests were women—and they were bound to be—of *course* they would bat an eyelid. They'd probably think that Dominic had seriously taken leave of his senses—entertaining a nobody like her, who couldn't even trouble herself to dress properly for dinner.

'I don't think so. If you knew how women can be, you wouldn't say that.'

'I do know women, I can assure you, and the only thing they will be is envious of your youth and beauty.'

About to protest, Sophie clamped her mouth shut, her pulse skittering as Dominic leant down and brought his face within the merest inch of hers. Closing his eyes, he deliberately breathed her in, his seductive cologne and body heat stirring the tiny space that separated them, making every tiny hair that covered Sophie's skin stand on end.

It was agony being so close, not free to touch him as she longed to, and for a dangerous second she almost raised her hand to stroke it down the side of his face. But he opened his eyes before that happened, and glinted down at her as though he could set her passion alight with just a glance. *Which he could*, Sophie admitted silently, again secretly admiring the generous blond lashes that gilded those amazing eyes of his.

'Andrews!' he called out, suddenly stepping back, and the manservant who had answered the door to Sophie yesterday appeared from a side door and walked smartly across the marble floor towards them.

'Yes, Mr Van Straten?'

'Take Miss Dalton's coat, if you please.'

'Dominic—I told you, I'm not staying!'

'I *want* you to stay,' he told her firmly, even as he helped her out of her coat and handed it to Andrews.

'What about what *I* want?' she asked feebly, feeling as if she were standing on stage, with a single spotlight trained deliberately on her and every vulnerable emotion and gesture brutally exposed for public delectation.

Glancing down at her figure-hugging jeans, she wished she had at least put on a skirt. But it was too late now, and anyway it was her own fault that she found herself in such a dilemma. She should have been firmer with Dominic. She should have—

'This way.'

Sliding a possessive arm around her waist, he led her towards the ominous double doors. And although Sophie vehemently wanted to resist his persuasion to accompany him into that room she found herself curiously unable to do so. It was as though her very will had somehow taken up residency somewhere else.

They entered to find Dominic's guests standing around with drinks in their hands deep in the throes of conversation. Their animated faces clearly denoted their enjoyment, and the sight immediately made Sophie feel excluded from that elite little circle. She knew instantly that even though she stood at Dominic's side she wasn't like them in any way. She didn't move in the same privileged strata that they did, and even if she'd had the inclination or desire to convince them differently both her obvious unease as well as the way she was dressed would reveal her to be a usurper.

As several heads turned towards her she longed to break free from Dominic's light hold on her waist and escape. But it was too late for that.

'This is Sophie, everyone. She dropped by to tell me

she was declining my invitation to dinner, but as you can see I've managed to persuade her to stay.'

Immediately taking umbrage at the surprising frankness with which he explained both her presence and her somewhat casual appearance, Sophie was nevertheless glad that at least now explanations for her attire would hopefully not be required. As to an explanation of what she was doing there at all—well, she would just have to pray that people would respect her privacy.

But, enduring the not-inconsiderable speculation in the glances of Dominic's other well-dressed guests, she seriously doubted it. Someone passed her a glass of wine from a tray and she glanced up and smiled her thanks. The man who'd undertaken the task was distinguished-looking, about fifty, and could not conceal the open curiosity in his frank gaze.

'I must say Dominic has kept very quiet about you, little Sophie. Where on earth did you two meet?'

'At a wedding,' Dominic interceded, the look in his eyes plainly conveying to Sophie that he would take care of things.

'Oh?' The man quirked an interested eyebrow. 'Someone we know? I heard that Lord Barrington's daughter Jemima got married to some stockbroker in the City the other week. Emily and I didn't go, of course. We were in Barbados for Roddy's twenty-first.'

As other people came to join their little group, the conversation proceeded, concerning people Sophie neither knew nor cared to know, their names bandied about like upmarket confetti and the mostly superficial exchange of words absolutely convincing her that she didn't belong there. Either with Dominic himself *or* his upper-class friends.

She found herself longing for the familiar and easy

comfort of her little maisonette, with her music playing on the stereo while she read or ate her dinner, her candles lit and her incense burning. The customary ritual was always a signal for her to shake off the cares of the day and relax. When a girl lived alone things like that became important cornerstones on which she could rely.

When she felt Dominic's hand clasp her own to his side, Sophie glanced up, startled to find him smiling back at her. The dimly lit lamps that burned in the room made his already arresting gaze even more troubling and unsettling to her peace of mind.

'Marcus was just asking what you do for a living, Sophie.'

'I'm a teacher,' she said clearly, her chin raised a little as if to say to the man standing opposite her, *Make of that whatever you will.*

'Lucky pupils,' Marcus remarked, laughing, but Sophie could find no humour in the condescending comment. 'What subject do you teach, Sophie?'

'A bit of everything,' She shrugged, and deliberately pulled her hand free from Dominic's. 'I'm a primary school teacher.'

'Of course. That makes sense.'

'What do you mean?'

'I only meant that you look far too sweet to be teaching big rough boys and girls, my dear. Don't you agree, Dominic?'

'Don't be fooled,' he replied, his green eyes openly teasing as they swept her indignant expression. 'She's a veritable tigress beneath that innocent little exterior.'

Gulping down a bit too much wine, Sophie sensed the alcohol delivering an intoxicating surge into her bloodstream, and for a moment her head swam.

'Dominic.' She addressed him, the expression in her

eyes as meaningful as she could make it. 'Could I have a word in private?'

'Certainly.' Without hesitation he slid his hand beneath her elbow, excused them both from his guests, and led her back outside into the entrance hall. 'What is it?'

Straight away Dominic knew that she was uncomfortable in his home, and was hating every second she had to spend with pompous individuals like Marcus. But Marcus's wife Emily was a warm, very liberal person, who accepted people just as they were, and she'd been a good friend of Dominic's for years. Unfortunately Emily had had to decline dinner at the last minute, and now Dominic wished he had put off the little dinner party he'd spontaneously arranged in preference for taking Sophie out to dinner or merely entertaining her on his own at home.

'I really can't stay for dinner. I have to go.'

'You mean you don't want to be here?'

Reddening a little round her jaw, Sophie spied a small table a couple of feet away and went to stand her wine glass on it. When she straightened again, Dominic was watching her intently, his expression unsmiling.

'Your friends aren't exactly my kind of people,' she told him. 'You must know that. I don't have a thing in common with any of them.'

'You sell yourself short, Sophie. You are a schoolteacher—an educated woman. Surely it is not beyond you to engage in a little meaningless conversation for…what?…a couple of hours at most?'

'Look, Dominic… I'm *tired*. I've had a busy day, and all I really want to do is put my feet up and unwind a little. It was kind of you to invite me to dinner, but, like I said when I first arrived, I had my doubts all along.'

He didn't want her to go. Now that she was here, with

her very tempting little body and her enormous blue eyes causing almost painfully acute little parries of desire throughout his body, Dominic wanted to keep her there. Once again he silently cursed his decision to have the dinner party instead of keeping Sophie all to himself.

'When can I see you again?'

His question, direct to the point of bluntness, completely took Sophie by surprise. *Was he serious?* Or was he only pursuing her because since they had slept together she had seemed to cool towards him?

'I'm sure you must be a very busy man. I think I—'

'I am not interested in discussing my schedule with you, Sophie. You can no doubt understand my frustration that this evening has not proceeded as well as I'd hoped. If you tell me when you are next free, I will *make* time for us to meet.'

A tiny muscle throbbed in his forehead, denoting a surge of emotion that surprised Sophie. As she studied his dauntingly good-looking visage, a fierce awakening of need and want throbbed through her body and made her head spin. She *did* want to see him again, because even when she wasn't with him she could not stop her incessant daydreaming about him. More than just a little overwhelmed by his highly potent charms, nevertheless Sophie instinctively knew that she had to protect herself—by keeping that knowledge to herself.

'Friday night,' she told him, rubbing her suddenly chilled arms. 'I'm free Friday night.'

'What time do you finish school?'

'What do you mean?'

'When do you finish teaching on Friday? I will come with Louis to pick you up. I have a meeting at a hotel in Suffolk from six until eight. I have already planned to stay there on Friday night. You can stay with me.

You can take a leisurely bath, get ready, and then we can dine together at around eight-thirty. What do you think?'

What do I think? Sophie silently repeated in panic. *I think I've just discovered a completely reckless side to myself that I didn't know existed until now! Surely I must be crazy to agree to spend another night with this man?* And not just *any* man. A man who could not only *buy* the hotel they'd be staying in a hundred times over, but who was completely out of her league in every way! *And what will Diana say when she finds out?*

'Dominic...I appreciate the invitation, I really do, but—'

'You are not going to turn me down?'

She could see immediately that the idea was anathema to him. Of all the women he could see, why had he picked on Sophie? She just couldn't understand it. Okay, so they had practically set the sheets on fire in bed together, but she didn't kid herself. For Dominic it was probably a regular and commonplace occurrence. He must meet beautiful women all the time.

It wasn't that she didn't value herself, or that she was putting herself down. It was merely Sophie's belief that men like Dominic Van Straten, who could have every single thing their heart desired—including their pick of stunning women—weren't generally known for dating ordinary, unassuming primary-school teachers. And especially not ones who lived in a run-down part of London and occasionally grabbed a Pot Noodle for lunch to eat on the run because they were either too busy or simply too disorganised to arrange anything else.

The kind of women that Sophie fully believed inhabited Dominic's world would eat in fancy restaurants and nibble lettuce leaves to keep their weight down. They'd go to plastic surgeons in Harley Street and have Botox and any number of nips and tucks to stay beautiful. But, regarding Dominic now, his emerald eyes blazing back at her with undisguised need, Sophie suddenly ran out of excuses to turn him down. The scary truth was, she didn't *want* to turn him down. No matter how unsuitably matched they were in reality.

'You really want to pick me up from school?' she asked, tucking a glossy dark curl behind her ear.

Dominic allowed his shoulders to relax. Relief ebbed through him with force. 'I am not accustomed to saying things I don't mean, Sophie.'

'Well...' Sophie shrugged. 'I don't know what my colleagues are going to think when you turn up in that chauffeur-driven car of yours on Friday.'

A genuinely amused smile curved her lips at the thought.

'Do you mind what they think, Sophie?'

Staring back at him, her smile disappearing as sensual heat flared hotly inside her, Sophie shook her head. 'No,' she admitted, defiance making her lift her chin. She didn't tell him then that she generally held herself a little apart from her colleagues, and didn't believe in gossip or getting too friendly. 'It's none of their business what I do or who I see outside of school hours.'

'Good.'

'I have to go now.'

'So you said.' Dominic's eyes glittered, as if he would hold her there and make her stay with just the sheer force of his will alone.

'Three-thirty,' Sophie told him, suddenly both nervous and enthralled at the idea of seeing him again, and spending the night with him on Friday.

'What?' He looked at her like a man who'd just woken up from a very erotic dream.

'You asked what time I finish…it's three-thirty.'

'I'll find Andrews and get your coat.'

As Sophie watched Dominic stride down the hall ahead of her, she couldn't help admiring the broad, undoubtedly muscular shoulders beneath his tuxedo, and the tall, imposing bearing that exuded such innate authority. A little frisson of pleasure danced down her spine and made her hug her arms tightly across her chest as her nipples tingled in guilty sexual awareness. It was hard to believe, but she suddenly found herself realising that three-thirty on Friday afternoon just couldn't come quickly enough…

CHAPTER FIVE

HURRYING out of school, with a heavy knapsack weighing down her shoulder and carrying her overnight bag, Sophie saw the car, its Rolls Royce insignia at the head, gleaming and stately, waiting by the kerb. Her heart skipped a beat, then, before she could catch her breath, promptly skipped another one.

Catching a glimpse of Louis behind the wheel, Sophie wondered if Dominic was observing her from behind those tinted windows at the back, and self-consciously slowed down. The last thing she wanted to appear was eager, and the only reason she had been hurrying was that she was actually ten minutes later than she'd said she would be.

Just before she reached the car, a colleague of Sophie's—a maths teacher called Barbara Budd—caught up with her, her curious gaze clearly trying to work out whether the gleaming vehicle had anything to do with Sophie.

'So, what are you up to this weekend Sophie?'

'Going to see friends. How about you?' Feeling a rush of colour flood her cheeks, Sophie tried to appear nonchalant, but guessed by the speculation still mirrored in Barbara's inquisitive hazel eyes that she hadn't quite pulled it off.

'That's never your lift, is it?' the other woman persisted, ignoring the question.

'I'm sorry, Barbara, I have to go. I'm already late. Have a good weekend, won't you?'

Knowing that her nosy colleague was still observing her as she reached the car and Louis stepped out to relieve her of her bags, Sophie wished that Dominic had chosen a less conspicuous place in which to wait for her. The street that the little Church of England primary school was situated in was hardly home to the kind of expensive vehicles that inhabited a billionaire's world, and no doubt it wasn't just her colleague Barbara who was looking on and wondering. On Monday morning, no doubt, the teachers' staffroom would be rife with gossip about Sophie's lift on Friday.

The car door on the passenger side opened kerbside. Dominic leant out to survey her coolly and Sophie got even hotter. 'You're late,' he said finally, his impervious green gaze travelling over her figure in the long black skirt, boots and sheepskin jacket.

Was he annoyed? Had he changed his mind about wanting her to join him on this trip? Sophie hovered on the pavement, furious with herself for capitulating to her ridiculously inappropriate need to see him again—and convinced now that the social gulf between them was far too wide ever to be bridged.

'The headmaster wanted to see me about something,' she explained, her pulse racing as his handsome face continued to study her from the car.

'Nothing serious, I hope?'

'Oh, no. He just wanted to warn me about reading subversive literature to my five-year-olds.'

Seeing the sudden confusion on Dominic's face, despite her anxiety, Sophie couldn't help but grin. 'I'm only joking.'

'Very amusing. Why don't you get in the car, then we can go?'

Did he have a sense of humour? As Sophie settled

back into the luxurious hide seat, her gaze re-acquainting itself with all the seductive features of that incredible car—from the burr walnut veneer to the deep-pile carpets and rugs beneath her feet—doubt overwhelmed her. At that moment she honestly would have jumped out of the car again had Dominic not smiled at her. That smile of his would have made the ground beneath her feet disappear if she'd been standing. The heat it stirred in Sophie's body started from the tips of her toes and ended in a series of fiercely electric tingles in her scalp.

'Did you have a good day?' he enquired politely, the man himself a sensory experience that far outweighed the seductive attributes of the famous car.

'Busy and…noisy,' Sophie grinned. 'Have you ever spent a day with a group of enthusiastic, chattering five-year-olds?' But even as she spoke, her lips had turned strangely numb, and she couldn't have said whether her smile would appear to him as a grin or a grimace. All she knew was that Dominic seemed to have a kind of explosive effect on her that she'd never experienced with another man before. From the tips of his expensive hand-made-leather shoes to the top of his silky blond hair he was in a class all of his own. A very *expensive* élite class.

Telling herself to try and relax, Sophie knew there was fat chance of any such thing if she continued to react as jumpily as a cat walking on burning coals around him.

'No,' he said without a smile. 'I have never spent a day like that.'

Relieved that she hadn't backed out of their arrangement, Dominic relaxed in the passenger seat next to Sophie and contemplated the drive and the evening ahead. He didn't know how such an unexpected, unlikely thing had come about, but he was feeling as smitten as a moonstruck youth with a severe case of unrequited lust around Sophie Dalton. All day he had anticipated her appearance with quietly excited stirrings deep in his belly, refusing to imagine for one moment that she would disappoint him and let him down at the last minute. After all, most women would jump at the chance of going on a date with him.

If doubt had surfaced at all he'd quickly and determinedly tried to bury it—yet, frankly, in all his thirty-six years Dominic had experienced nothing like the uncertainty he was presently suffering over this woman. And beneath the deliberately cool façade that belied the intense excitement running like a powerful river through his veins, Dominic *loathed* that uncertainty like nothing else.

For a man who was used to winning million-dollar deals before breakfast with stunning ease, feeling all at sea with a woman was not something he was used to at all. Having had the added advantage of being the progeny of already wealthy parents, even before he'd made his own fortune, Dominic had been used to the delights of the opposite sex since he'd been sent as a sixteen-year-old schoolboy to a prep school in England. Basically, he'd only had to cast his gaze at a pretty girl for her to fall at his feet.

Growing into a fully adult male, with the allure of not only handsome Viking-blond good looks but also wealth, dating women had been akin to being let loose in a treasure trove of sweet delights and told to help himself. It had been almost impossible to pick just one when there was always the enticement of several more should the flavour start to wane.

However, as Dominic's business acumen had honed into a more and more lethal skill, and the challenge of becoming one of the most successful property developers in the land had taken over, he'd mostly replaced his fascination for beautiful women with his work. For almost two years now he had been relationship-free, and had not minded the fact terribly much. Out of necessity he'd occasionally satisfied his healthy libido with a purely sexual encounter or two, but basically he actively welcomed the lack of distraction and demands of a relationship, if the truth were known.

But now, as his quietly ravenous gaze examined Sophie's beguiling profile, noting with pleasure the fierce sheen on her short ebony-black hair and the delicate turquoise studs in her perfect ears, Dominic was assailed by a wave of need so strong that it was almost beyond endurance.

His assistant, Diana, had often mentioned her friend Sophie, in passing conversation, but she'd never given him the slightest clue that the woman's appeal would be as dangerous to his equilibrium as it was. Now all Dominic could think of was the time he'd wasted being oblivious to her existence, when he could have been indulging in the passionate sensory delectation of having the sexy little teacher in his bed…

'Why Suffolk?' she asked him now, as she opened the buttons on her jacket and slipped it off in the warmth of the car.

For a moment Dominic honestly could not think straight. By rights, a plain red polo-necked sweater had no business being as alluring as satin and lace lingerie, but on Sophie it was. The soft wool clung to her breasts, outlining their undoubted perfection in a way that could trap a man's breath deep inside his chest. Dominic swallowed hard before he could get his lips to work.

'A client of mine I'm currently doing some business

with owns the hotel. The surroundings are picturesque, it's a lot quieter than London, and the food is first-class. Enough reason to hold our meeting there, wouldn't you agree?'

'It sounds…very nice.'

As Sophie folded her jacket and laid it across the fold-away armrest in the space between herself and Dominic her purse fell out of one of the pockets onto the lamb-swool rug that covered the floor. As she bent her head to retrieve it Dominic did the same, and for a timeless second, as their gazes met and held, Sophie was swamped with exhilaration and longing. Feeling the car start to glide away from the pavement, and the softly discreet hum of the engine helping to cocoon them in a private world all of their own, Sophie couldn't deny that it was one of the most sensually charged moments of her whole life.

He wanted to kiss her. How he'd held back from do-ing so Dominic didn't know, but in the space of just a couple of electrifying seconds he had fantasised hotly about melding his lips with hers. About commanding her to open her mouth. About becoming intimately ac-quainted once more with her sweet, entrancing flavours as only a lover dared.

If they had been anywhere else other than in his car, with Louis driving—in his apartment or his house, maybe—he would have definitely persuaded Sophie out of a few items of her clothing as well. As it was, they *were* in his car, with Louis driving, and so—painfully, and with great difficulty—Dominic willed his over-whelming desire back to a more manageable notch on the dial, and picked up Sophie's purse instead. As he handed it to her he saw a telling hint of red stain her smooth cheeks, and he sat back in his seat, intoxicated and enthralled by the brief sexual encounter, anticipating more, *much* more of the same, as soon as they could be alone together.

Telling herself that she might as well make the most of the wonderfully old-fashioned yet exquisitely appointed hotel room housed in this lovingly restored Tudor building on the edge of a timelessly beautiful Suffolk village, Sophie stripped off her clothes and immediately took a long, leisurely soak in the claw-toothed bathtub.

Dominic was going straight from his room to his meeting, and she wouldn't be seeing him again until eight-thirty, when they'd agreed to meet in the dining room for dinner. It gave Sophie some much-needed time to ponder how she was going to handle this unexpected excursion of hers into the lifestyle of the seriously rich. She knew that Dominic was fully expecting to sleep with her—why else would he bring her here?—but just for a second or two could she help it if her foolish heart longed for him to find pleasure in her company as well? She desired him, too. Just the thought of him *kissing* her again, never mind doing anything else, gave her serious goosebumps. But at the same time she wanted to make it clear to him that this wasn't the kind of encounter she indulged in on a regular basis.

She'd had her share of boyfriends—what young woman of twenty-six hadn't?—but Sophie had only gone 'all the way' with one of them. *Stuart.* And he had repaid her trust and devotion by having a drunken one-night stand with his best friend's girlfriend. Even though he'd begged her to forgive him, and had sworn to her that it would never happen again, Sophie had been unable to either forgive or believe him.

She'd told herself time and again that the experience

hadn't scarred her, that it had only made her naturally wary of involvement with men, yet beneath her brave assertions she knew that it *had* left its mark. Why else had she not seen anyone else for over a year now? She wasn't being conceited when she recalled that she'd had plenty of opportunity to meet other men. She'd even been asked out by two of the younger male teachers at her school. Yet *fear* of committing to another relationship had underscored every potential foray into that volatile, uncertain arena. *Until now.*

But Sophie wasn't some naïve schoolgirl. She knew with absolute certainty that Dominic wasn't likely to be looking for a relationship with her…just a hot little sexual dalliance in a hotel room to satisfy the itch of a rich man's fancy…

When nine o'clock came and went, and Dominic had still not appeared in the dining room to join her for dinner, Sophie picked up the paperback she had automatically popped into her handbag in case he was late and opened it at the page where she'd left her bookmark.

Endeavouring to concentrate on words that seemed to have the disconcerting ability to dance on the page, she couldn't get into the story no matter how hard she tried.

When the waiter appeared five minutes later and presented her with Dominic's apologies, explaining that his meeting had unfortunately run over time and that she should go ahead and order without him, Sophie put down her book with relief. Casting a surreptitious glance around at the other diners, she reluctantly picked up a menu.

She had initially been starving, but now her stomach simply felt uncomfortable—knotted with nerves. The longer she had to wait for him the more tense she grew, and the more time she had to tell herself that coming here at all with the Dutch billionaire had been one horrendous mistake. But suddenly he was there beside her, gazing down at her with the practised smile of a man who sometimes had to bestow that gesture in the course of a day's work to appease professionally, yet who did it with little sincerity or pleasure.

Sophie's stomach sank to her boots as she realised he would probably rather be dining alone than having to entertain a woman he knew very little about. She'd chosen her clothes this evening with such care, too. There was only one really smart outfit in her possession: this little black velvet dress with a matching bolero jacket and a choker with a fake ruby. The red of the ruby contrasted dramatically with her sable hair and blue eyes which this evening Sophie had carefully emphasised with plum-coloured eyeshadow and black mascara.

'I am sorry I am so late. Have you ordered yet?'

As he pulled out the opposite chair, Dominic's remote, preoccupied glance flicked over Sophie's appearance with no sign of any obvious pleasure, and again her heart flooded with doubt at the wisdom of joining him.

'No. I was just about to look at the menu. Didn't your meeting go well?'

Her astute observation sent an acute shaft of surprise hurtling through Dominic's system. Usually he was able to disguise his feelings better...*much better*. But this evening he had allowed himself to be rattled by a rival who had more than once snapped at his heels, over the years, and the encounter had left a bad taste in his mouth, leaving him questioning the wisdom of ruthlessly pursuing endless success for success's sake alone. He had seen desperation and greed so baldly reflected in that other man's eyes that he had felt sick to his stomach.

Was that how *he* appeared to other people who were less outwardly successful than he was?

So, no. His meeting had *not* gone well. He most definitely had not welcomed the introspection that had been forced upon him. But now, as he allowed his gaze to settle fully on Sophie's pleasingly pretty features, briefly dipping to examine the modestly low-cut neckline on her dress, displaying a hint of softly rounded feminine flesh, he experienced a strong surge of profoundly sexual pleasure that wouldn't be denied.

'I make it a rule never to mix business with pleasure, Sophie, so we will not discuss my dissatisfaction at my meeting and potentially spoil our evening together. You look very pretty in that dress, by the way.'

The way he delivered the unexpected compliment made Sophie shiver. All her muscles tensed as though she'd just emerged from a steam room into the shock of icy-cold rain. The man undid her with his eyes and at the same time scared her rigid with the raw, unfettered desire she saw reflected in them.

'Thank you. I bought it last year in the sales…' *She could have cut out her tongue.* Confessing she'd bought her best outfit in a sale to a man of Dominic's wealth and calibre was akin to inviting him to lunch and taking him to a workman's café for a fry-up! Where was her mind? She wasn't sitting cosily with some close girlfriend, having a chummy little chinwag! She was in a five-star hotel dining room with a man to whom the word 'portfolio' clearly didn't mean a case to carry around amateur attempts at artwork!

'Nevertheless,' Dominic commented, unsmiling, 'it complements your colouring and figure very well.'

His coolly voiced reply did not help Sophie's discomfiture one bit. Her silly *faux pas* had merely been another illustration to point up the vast and untenable social distance between them. Suddenly she couldn't even find it in her heart to *pretend* to be hungry.

'I think I should just go home. You're clearly regretting asking me here, and to be honest it wasn't such a great idea in the first place. I'm a primary-school teacher who leads a very ordinary type of life, Dominic. I don't mix with the kind of people you mix with, and I know nothing of your world. I know I'm probably a bit of a novelty to you, but that doesn't do a hell of a lot for my confidence either. So, to save both of us from further embarrassment, it's probably just best if we call the whole thing off. Don't you think?'

The last few words came out in a heated rush, and Sophie blushed and glanced away as Dominic began to smile. This particular smile bore no relation whatsoever to the coolly professional one he had worn when he'd first come into the restaurant.

'You are labouring under a very misguided assumption indeed if you believe that I'm regretting asking you to join me. I very much want you to be here. Apart from my meeting this evening I have thought about nothing else all day. And you insult both yourself and me by suggesting that I think you are some kind of 'novelty'. I only date women who interest me, Sophie—and not just physically. I am not so shallow that I could endure unintelligent or boring conversation just for the sake of gazing at a pretty face! Although in your case I think I might be prepared to make an exception. *Especially* when we go to bed. Although of course I wouldn't expect us to be indulging in much conversation then.'

Sophie's already heated blush grew even hotter, making her feel as if she were being slowly grilled under a sunlamp. Her lower lip trembled.

'You have nothing to say to this?' he goaded.

It was rare that Sophie was at a loss for words, but she acutely felt at such a loss now. Her racing thoughts just couldn't seem to make a connection with her vocal cords. 'Then…then I should…*stay*?' she asked, small-voiced.

'You should *definitely* stay.' He smiled again, that lethal, unfettered, destroying smile of his, and casually picked up his menu.

Inside the hotel room the curtains had been drawn and it was dark. When she reached for the light switch Dominic immediately pulled her hand away before she could turn it on. His cologne and his sheer male heat whispered over Sophie's senses like a powerful sensory drug, making her feel oddly disorientated and boneless with need.

'I am glad we skipped dessert,' he said teasingly, sliding his hand round her nape and tilting her face up to his.

His warm breath softly skimmed her face, like the brush of a butterfly's wing, and Sophie wondered what had happened to the ground, because suddenly she didn't seem to feel it beneath her feet any more. She told herself it was the wine she'd drunk at dinner, but knew in her heart she would be just as intoxicated if not so much as a drop of alcohol had touched her lips. This man's presence made her feel *drunk* with pleasure, unravelled with need.

'Sexy little Sophie.' He smiled, and touched his mouth experimentally against hers.

It was a mere brush, but as soon as the unrivalled taste of him exploded on her lips Sophie groaned a little and opened her mouth beneath his. The unpremeditated movement was as natural and as essential to her as breathing. Dominic needed no further entreaty or encouragement from her to take what he so voraciously longed for. He dived in without apology or hesitation, captivating her with his tongue, his ministrations ruthlessly exquisite, making her drown in desire as he explored the softly velvet surfaces inside her mouth.

As his hands caressed Sophie's body, acquainting themselves unhindered with her breasts, her hips, her bottom, he cupped the cheeks of her derrière in his palms and pulled her hard against his own aching manifestation of desire. She was in no doubt that he wanted her, and wanted her with the kind of passion and ardour that made her legs almost buckle in disbelief.

She stumbled a little as he guided her across what seemed to be miles of plush deep-pile carpet to the large, inviting king-sized bed with its plump cream duvet and crisp cotton sheets which the maid had turned down for the night. She heard the rustle of clothing being removed as Dominic slipped out of his jacket, tore at the buttons on his silk shirt, and bent his head to her neck to suckle on her exposed flesh. Feeling his teeth nip her, she put her hands up to grab onto the broad muscular banks of his shoulders for fear of falling, barely registering that his hands were unzipping her dress and dragging it down her body along with her jacket.

Time seemed to slow, taking on an almost unreal quality. *Oh, God…since when had she become so terrifyingly weak in the face of a man's desire?* So weak that she'd consider giving him anything he wanted? *She didn't do this.* She didn't sleep with men on a whim—no matter how attracted she was. But the man guiding her purposefully onto the bed was no whim. He set her blood pounding in her veins, like a throbbing, searching river, making her ache for him right down to her very marrow.

Falling with her onto the bed, Dominic covered Sophie's trembling flesh with his hard, impressive musculature, making her body burn wherever it came into contact with his. He kissed her deeply and voraciously, impatiently releasing the fastening on her bra and just as impatiently disposing of the flimsy garment altogether.

Feeling cool air awaken the naked flesh of her breasts, teasing her nipples into stinging buds of acutely sensitive steel, Sophie reached up and wrapped her arms around Dominic's neck, then slid her fingers through the thick blond strands of his hair, silently thrilling at the sensuous contact. She was desperate to touch him, and her longing knew no bounds. Feeling hungry and daring, she let herself explore the tempting outline of his hard body, feeling the taut flesh of his buttocks tense beneath her eager hands and his burgeoning desire press ever closer into the apex of her thighs.

Barely able to contain his rapidly growing lust, Dominic found the silky scrap of lace she wore that passed for panties and, pushing it aside, slid his finger into the searing moist flesh between Sophie's slim thighs. She arched her body against him like a cat and he drove deeper, withdrew briefly, then continued his lustful exploration with two fingers. Her scent undid him, hitting Dominic hard with its powerfully provocative sensuality and its erotic promise of pleasure unmatched. So much so that he found himself shaking with need as he endeavoured to find the sealed condom he had slid into his trouser pocket and undo it with any kind of finesse. That he managed it at all was a miracle, and as he unfurled it onto the throbbing, aching length of his manhood he was almost dazed by the fierce, ravenous hunger that ruthlessly possessed him.

How could she entrap him so? he asked himself heatedly, as he positioned himself at her entrance and thrust inside. Her soft moans almost finished him there and then. *How could this slim, fiesty scrap of a girl turn him on almost past bearing?*

Right then, Dominic wasn't actually looking for answers. But as he lowered his eager lips to her exposed breasts, palming one as he suckled the other, filling her with every hard inch, he did wonder how he had survived without this amazing and wild gratification for so long.

The pleasure he had received from his previous sexual encounters was like a calm breeze in comparison to this stormy cyclone. How had he possibly been satisfied by such soulless forays when it was clear to him now that he had an ache inside him for profound contact with *passion* so deep that it scarcely bore thinking about? That he had accepted mediocrity in his love life, and had laid aside the search for something more compelling in preference to becoming more and more successful in his work, truly astonished him.

But now that he had much more of an insight into what he really wanted sexually, Dominic had no intention of relinquishing it any time soon. If Sophie imagined that this tumble in a hotel-room bed was the mere whim of a rich man who could have anything he wanted, then her assumption was very quickly and earnestly going to be proved wrong.

'Dominic,' she breathed wildly as she writhed beneath him. 'Dominic, you're making me crazy... I can't... I can't stop myself from...'

'Let go, Sophie.' Thrusting harder and deeper,

Dominic revelled in the sweet joy of feeling her velvet muscles enfold him, contracting fiercely again and again as though she would never let him go. Her gaze was stunned and her body trembling uncontrollably as Dominic lowered his mouth to hers once again. Then, with one more savagely possessive, searing thrust, he heard himself cry out in amazement and joy before sinking down onto her trembling figure, his hands combing through her short dark hair as tenderly as if she were someone very important to him. Her dewy skin was so soft and her body so warm and inviting that Dominic wanted to spend the whole night making love to her, extracting every drop of pleasure he could, knowing that even then his desire for her would not be sated.

'You are glad you did not go home?' he teased, his expression somewhere between a smile and a frown.

Had she ever been so acutely conscious of every single thing before? So minutely and exquisitely aware of her heart beating with such untrammelled delight? As though every molecule of air she breathed were infused with wonder? Closing her eyes momentarily, to stop herself from crying, Sophie knew she had not. It wasn't as though she had never experienced moments of great pleasure or joy either. It was just that she had never known what she had been missing, what her body had been secretly *yearning* for, up until now.

Dominic might be able to get up out of this bed and carry on with his life without feeling as though a glimpse of heaven had just been snatched away from him, but Sophie seriously had to wonder if she could do the same.

CHAPTER SIX

TO SAY he was surprised to wake up and find the space beside him in the bed empty again would have been to seriously understate the power of the shock that pulsated through Dominic at the realisation. Rising up out of bed, checking the bathroom and finding it empty, he could not believe that Sophie had not woken him but had got up, instead, showered, and gone about her day as if the very *thought* of his own needs or wants had not even crossed her mind. He was unaccustomed to such cavalier treatment by a female, and for long moments he couldn't contain his anger.

As far as his own memory of the night before went, they had made love until the early hours of the morning when reluctantly, but out of necessity, both of them had finally succumbed to sleep. Used to waking early, and knowing that he had some unfinished business from yesterday's unsatisfactory meeting to take care of, he'd fully intended to let Sophie sleep on undisturbed, then join her for breakfast at around nine. *Had he not told her as much?*

It was hard to deny his fury at the thought that she had rebuffed his suggestion, and now, as he paced the floor outside the cosy and intimate dining room, Dominic wished that he'd stated his desire for her company more firmly. His body throbbed and tingled in the aftermath of last night's wild and urgent passion, and he was impatient to see her again this morning.

But even as the thought surfaced, something told him

that Sophie Dalton was a law unto herself…a woman as surprising and unpredictable as a snowfall in summer. He had—after all—pursued *her. Not* the other way round, as was often the case as far as he was concerned. But, that being true, Dominic was still anxious to assert who held the upper hand in their fledgling relationship. He was totally unaccustomed to being on tenterhooks around a woman, and did not like it one bit. He certainly did not intend to allow it in the future.

Sophie walked with her head down, barely noticing the pretty white swans that swam in the river alongside the lane that she was heading down. She barely noticed anything at all, in fact. Not even the luxurious scent of blossom that hung in the air—a perfume that she normally revelled in, come the spring.

There was no way she could have faced Dominic across the breakfast table this morning.

Pass the marmalade, please—and, oh, by the way…thank you for the three orgasms.

An embarrassed groan escaped her as she walked. *What had she done?* And what was she supposed to do now, when she'd compounded the folly of sleeping with him not just once, but *twice? And with such inhibition and reckless passion too?*

She had no idea what was going to happen next. This whole unbelievable scenario was so out of her day-to-day experience that she barely knew what to think. She had never slept casually with a man before simply for sex, then walked away as if all they'd done was have tea and a platonic chat together. How did some women *do* that?

If her bags hadn't been back at the hotel she would have found the nearest station and made her way home by train. She could have left Dominic a note saying *thanks for a lovely evening and see you around some time*—or something equally casual, to let him know she was a woman of the world who understood this kind of lightning attraction that flared one minute and burned out the next.

Only Sophie had the niggling feeling that what she felt for Dominic wasn't very likely to burn out in an instant. In fact, the opposite was most likely true.

By the time she decided to head back to the hotel she couldn't honestly say she felt one bit better about things. The truth was, she was even more troubled than ever. *And what on earth was Diana's reaction going to be when she found out that her best friend had slept with her boss while she and Freddie were on their honey-moon?*

Her expression preoccupied as she pushed open the door and encountered the welcome warmth of the hotel foyer, Sophie didn't immediately see Dominic, sitting in a cosy alcove nearby drinking coffee and reading a newspaper. He, on the other hand, saw her instantly, and put down his paper and his cup of coffee and strode across the deep blue carpet towards her with unquestionable purpose.

'Did we not have an arrangement to meet at nine for breakfast?'

The admonishing glance he bestowed upon Sophie was so devoid of warmth that she literally shivered. *He looked so good, too.* Lean and muscular and handsome in his dark blue sweater and black jeans. For a moment she was completely distracted. Even though the clothes he wore were undoubtedly casual, they were stamped with an irrefutably expensive air that conveyed to whoever glanced his way that for their owner money was no object.

'You said you were going to work first! Anyway... I wanted to go for a walk, so I just had a quick cup of tea and a slice of toast. Sorry.'

'You might have asked me if I was in agreement with such a decision. When I make an arrangement I am not accustomed to having it broken without so much as a message to let me know that things have changed.'

He sounded so serious and irate that for a moment Sophie wanted to laugh out of sheer embarrassment. Not many people could make her feel like one of the five-year-olds she taught at school.

'And I am not accustomed to having to report my movements, or indeed ask for permission to go for a walk should I so desire!' Her blue eyes flashed up at him with little sparks of fury in their cornflower depths.

'I did not say that you needed to ask my permission. Where did you go?' Dominic caught the male receptionist throwing them an inquisitive glance, and sliding his hand beneath Sophie's elbow, deliberately moved her out of earshot, back to the alcove where his coffee and newspaper sat waiting.

Glancing resentfully back at him, Sophie shook her arm free of his hold and dug her hands deeply into the pockets of her coat.

'I don't know *exactly* where I went! To tell you the truth I didn't pay much attention to it. I just needed to get out and get some fresh air. Is that such a crime?'

'Do you normally overreact to such a simple and innocent question?' His calm voice—although tinged with irritation—made Sophie feel slightly stupid.

To tell the truth, she didn't *know* why she was reacting to him so badly. She only knew that she had no idea how to handle the passionate intimacy that had taken place between them. Even now, when there was obvious dissent between them, her breasts were tingling like crazy, wanting to have him touch them, to have him squeeze and pull and—

'Sophie?'

Heat suffused her in a gushing torrent, and she had to wrench her glance away before he read the pure naked need that she knew must be reflected in her eyes.

'I'm feeling a little on edge. I'm sorry.'

'Why don't you take off your coat and sit down? I'll order us some more coffee.'

Not answering, Sophie did as he suggested, leaning back into the soft velour chairback, the idea of coffee suddenly sounding like the best idea in the world. Her bloodstream needed a shot of something, that was for sure!

When Dominic returned to the alcove after speaking to the receptionist, arranging his fit, muscular body in the chair opposite with relaxed ease, Sophie was finally forced to face him. To be honest, she was surprised that he seemed to want to linger. On the way back from her walk she'd convinced herself that he would be more or less ready to leave and anxious to return to London when she got back. He was a busy man, in much demand, and clearly his time was at a premium. Or so Sophie believed.

'Perhaps you would like to tell me why you are so on edge?' he suggested calmly,

'I really don't have any experience of this kind of thing, if you want to know the truth. It's not something that I do very often,' Sophie responded, her voice soft. 'Well...I mean when I say not very often I mean—what I mean is...*never,* really.'

'You mean making love with a man you have only just met?'

Licking her lips, Sophie nodded.

'I am glad to hear it.'

There was definitely a proprietorial air in his tone, and Sophie's head snapped up in surprise. As Dominic studied her, trying vainly to tamp down the desire that was quietly but indisputably rising like sap in his veins, he experienced a sharp sting of jealousy at the mere idea of her sleeping with anybody else but him. It was an unfamiliar feeling for him, and for a long moment he simply let the thought sit and gather quiet purpose, running with it as he characteristically did when the excitement of a new challenge beckoned.

'But you have had boyfriends, yes?'

'Yes but I didn't—that doesn't mean that I—'

'Are you telling me that you need commitment before you sleep with a man, Sophie?'

That wasn't what she was telling him at all! Sophie thought, a little desperately. This was the very thing she had wanted to avoid! Dominic believing that she felt the right to make some kind of claim on him now, because they had slept together. She might not be a *femme fatale* by anybody's standards, but she wasn't completely naïve.

'I'm not telling you that at all. Can we change the subject?'

'You are uncomfortable talking about intimacy?'

Dominic couldn't believe she was actually blushing after what they had done last night! The observation made him warm to her even more...not to mention made him hungry to have her back in bed with him. Already in his mind he was rapidly going over his schedule for the week, trying to work out when and how soon he could steal a couple of hours away from matters of business to be with her.

'I think—Oh, coffee…great!' Saved by the sudden appearance of a slim young waiter arriving with their coffee, Sophie busied herself placing cups on saucers and arranging the sugar bowl and cream on the table in front of them. She sensed that Dominic's gaze very rarely left her, even to thank the waiter for the coffee, and tiny prickles of intense awareness skimmed up and down her spine in quick succession. 'Shall I pour?'

'Sophie?'

The glance he gave her was both insistent and commanding, and Sophie stopped fussing with the coffeepot and put it down again on the tray. When she returned his glance her eyes were very blue and very wide.

'What?'

'I am getting the impression that you believe that after today I will not want to see you again. Is that right?'

It was not only right but so spot-on to what she'd actually been thinking, at that precise moment, that Sophie had to shake off the uncanny feeling of someone walking over her grave.

'You must be a very busy man, Dominic. Diana told me that in the past year it's been rare for you to even be in the country for more than a week at a time. And I…I have a busy life too. Obviously not at the same high level that you do, but just the same…I don't really have time for relationships.'

'You don't have time or you are anti-relationships?' A blond eyebrow lifted speculatively towards his scalp.

Stuart. To give yourself to a man in the most intimate way and then find out that he could quite casually give himself to another woman when he was having a relationship with you—well…that was quite *unforgivable* in

Sophie's book. This betrayal had stung worse than a hundred razorblades slicing into her flesh. And if she wasn't in a hurry to risk the same thing happening again, could anyone honestly blame her?

The Dominic Van Stratens of the world were playboys. Men who changed their women as regularly as they changed their cars. It didn't matter that he had the power to set her body aflame with just a hot, hungry look. What mattered to Sophie was honesty and integrity in a man, and above all…reliability too. Women who would trade that for a brief passionate fling were asking for trouble, in her view. And she had just walked up to trouble and invited it in!

'It's not that I'm "anti-relationships". I just told you that I have a very busy life. Shall I pour the coffee now?'

Her hand shook slightly as she poured the steaming beverage into their cups. *He should be grateful,* she considered, with feeling. Grateful that she wasn't one of those women who would cling on to a tenuous association in hope of something more. He'd had his *fun.* Well…they had *both* had a good time in bed, Sophie admitted silently, feeling hot. Why couldn't he just leave it at that and stop quizzing her about relationships?

'You are wrong if you imagine that I do not want to see you again.'

The innate authority in his voice made Sophie glance up in surprise. His expression was very serious, and for a couple of disconcerting seconds Sophie remembered a very *different* expression…in the throes of his passion, when he had made her rejoice in her womanhood and gasp for joy as his hands touched her everywhere…

'I have commitments for the next three days, but I have a slot free on Wednesday evening. You can come to my house for dinner.'

Did he have any idea how cold and uninviting such a command sounded? As much as her body betrayed her at just the slightest touch from him, Sophie was not going to succumb to such an emotionless dictate, like some kind of eager little puppy.

'I'm not free on Wednesday,' she replied coolly, raising her cup to her lips. 'I'm working late at school, getting my classroom ready for Easter.'

Dominic felt impatience surge through his bloodstream like a cursed virus. Was she deliberately being difficult, or was she speaking the truth? For her to reply to his invitation as though she could easily take it or leave it—and in this case obviously *leave* it—made him furious. Did she have any idea how many women would love the chance to be alone with him, for just a few hours even? Clearly she didn't. But what got to Dominic even more was the idea that even if Sophie *did* know how much in demand he was by the opposite sex, it wasn't likely to sway her decision one jot. The woman must be obsessed by her job. That was the only explanation that made any sense to him.

'Well, what about Thursday evening?'

He had an invitation to meet a colleague for dinner at his club, but as far as Dominic was concerned right now his need to see Sophie was far greater.

There was still no warmth in his voice, and Sophie squirmed uncomfortably in her seat. She wouldn't go running to him just because he willed it! If he thought she was one of *those* weak-willed, infatuated females who would drop everything for a man, then he was definitely barking up the wrong tree!

'I'm going out on Thursday night with a girlfriend, to celebrate her birthday.'

It was perfectly true. But as Dominic sat glowering

back at her she knew he was convinced she was lying. He swore. At least Sophie *thought* he was cursing, because he'd suddenly switched languages as easily as breathing.

'So when *will* you be free again to see me?' he demanded, emerald eyes glittering.

Sophie almost choked on her coffee. Placing the cup back on its saucer, she smoothed her hand down her jeans and sat back in her chair in astonishment. 'To be frank with you, Dominic, I thought this must be a one-off. Well...I mean, I know it happened once before, but I realise that you're a very busy man, and that you wouldn't normally be seeing someone like me. Anyway... I thought... That is, I didn't—'

'Let me be clear about this Sophie,' Dominic interjected firmly. 'I don't think I'm being conceited when I say I know when a woman receives pleasure from my touch. I also don't think that I imagined your soft moans and sighs in my arms last night. That being the case, I believe you wouldn't exactly be against seeing me again. Am I right?'

Sophie sensed that he was probably completely unused to anyone turning him down when he wanted something. Most people in his life probably wouldn't *dare* turn him down. But, as much as Sophie disliked the idea that Dominic could have anything he wanted just by snapping his fingers, she couldn't deny her own heartfelt need to be with him again. And that need far outweighed her personal feelings about the power and authority he was used to. After all, in bed he was just a man. A man with the same passionate needs and desires as any man who had far less materially.

'I honestly can't make Wednesday or Thursday. How about next Friday?'

Some of the incredible tension that had gathered in Dominic's shoulders eased slowly out of his muscles. Relieved, he ran his hand round the back of his neck. 'Friday I'm presenting a business award at the Guildhall in London.'

'Oh.'

'It's black tie, so you will need an evening dress. Is that a problem?'

Knowing intimately the rather scant contents of her wardrobe, Sophie guessed the sudden panic in her eyes must be self-evident to Dominic. 'I might have to borrow something from a friend,' she confessed, embarrassed.

'I'll phone my friend Emily and ask her to take you shopping for a suitable dress. Give me your phone number before we part, and I'll get her to ring you to arrange a suitable time.'

'Dominic, I don't have time to go shopping! Much less money to splash out on an expensive dress. I'm sorry, but it's not the kind of item that a primary school teacher's pay will easily stretch to.' There...she'd said it. And now her embarrassment at such a confession to a man for whom money clearly *was* no object just grew ten times worse.

He smiled. 'Let me buy you the dress, Sophie. It would give me immense pleasure to do so.' His hypnotic gaze lingered on her mouth as he said this, then moved slowly and deliberately down to her breasts, outlined by her close-fitting sweater.

Sophie found it impossible to breathe for a moment.

'I told you, I don't make a habit of accepting expensive gifts from men.'

'I'm not just any man, Sophie. We both know that I am your *lover*.'

On Monday, on her return to school, the gossip and speculation in the staff-room proved to be even worse than Sophie had feared. Barbara Budd had not wasted any time in telling anyone who'd cared to listen that Sophie had been picked up on Friday by a chauffeur-driven Rolls Royce, and they all inevitably wanted to know why.

Insisting on her privacy, Sophie endured the seemingly unending curiosity until home-time, and then on her way out she bumped into Victor Edwards, the headmaster.

'I take it I can expect your resignation any day now?' he started, adjusting his dark-rimmed glasses on his nose as he glanced down at her from his more superior height.

Hardly able to believe her ears, Sophie almost stumbled on the last concrete step in the hallway that led to the exit. 'I'm sorry?'

'Well, Sophie, it's not every day that teachers go home in Rolls Royces. We are either paying you far too much—which is extremely unlikely, as we all know— or you are moving in the kind of illustrious circles that are sadly closed to the rest of us mere mortals.'

Sophie had a lot of respect for their strict headmaster, even if he could sometimes be what the other staff referred to as a 'stick-in-the-mud'. She'd always found him to be very fair, and not likely to make impulsive judgements when it came to any kind of trying or difficult situation. Now, as she tried to gauge whether he was serious or not, she breathed a sigh of relief as she saw a smile break around his rather austere lips.

'I am, of course, only joking about your resignation. You're one of the best infant-class teachers at the school, and I would be very sorry to lose you should you ever decide to leave us—even though I know you are eager for your career to progress. I'm sure you've been driven round the bend today, with all the silly gossip that's been going around. My advice is just to ignore it, Sophie. Tomorrow they'll all find a new topic to gossip about, and that will be an end to it.'

'Thanks for that, Victor. I must admit it's been quite trying, to say the least.'

'How are preparations going for Easter?'

'Great! The children have all been making Easter bonnets today and I've been up to my eyes in crêpe paper and glue!' Her big blue eyes shining, Sophie glanced back at Victor with unconstrained delight. A slight flush stained the man's otherwise pale cheeks at her enthusiastic response, and Sophie experienced a twinge of surprise at this uncharacteristic indication of emotion.

'You certainly have a way with the little ones,' he commented kindly. 'I suppose there must come a day when you'll decide to have a brood of your own?'

'Maybe…I don't know.'

Suddenly more discomfited by the thought than she cared to confess, because for an outrageous, impossible moment she'd allowed herself to imagine Dominic as the father of that 'brood', Sophie self-consciously tucked a curl of dark hair behind her ear.

'Not for a long time yet, though.'

'Good.' Victor proclaimed, nudging his glasses further up his nose and adjusting his briefcase under his arm. 'That seems a sensible decision, if you don't mind my saying so. Keep up the good work, and don't ever hesitate to come and talk to me should anything at school get you down.'

'Thanks.'

'Well, I'll see you tomorrow, then.' Without a backward glance, Victor preceded Sophie to the twin doors of the exit and marched out of the building.

Shaking her head at this unexpectedly warm exchange, Sophie couldn't help but smile as she made her way out of school to the bus stop a few streets away.

Wrapping a huge yellow bathsheet around her, and hurrying out of the bathroom to the ringing telephone in the living room, Sophie snatched up the receiver, her stomach muscles clenched tight in anticipation that the caller might be Dominic.

It wasn't. But it *was* someone connected with him. Emily Cathcart—the woman he'd promised would ring to arrange to take Sophie shopping for a dress for an occasion that frankly filled her with dread. It was one thing sharing a night of passion in an anonymous hotel with him. It was quite another going out in public as his escort—and to such a clearly important event.

Before she'd taken her bath Sophie had spent a good hour or more looking at every reference to Dominic Van Straten on the Internet. There were literally *pages* of stuff about him. He was a busy man. A much-sought-after and admired entrepreneur, and a property developer *bar none*. Not only was he in demand to *give* awards, if the information that Sophie had read was correct, he had been on the *receiving* end of plenty, too.

'Emily Cathcart, here. Am I speaking to Sophie Dalton?'

'Yes, you are.' Sinking down into a nearby armchair, Sophie adjusted the towel more securely around her chest and tried to ignore the disconcerting bump of her heart against her ribcage.

'Dominic asked me to contact you, Sophie,' the woman explained cheerfully, immediately taking charge. 'Now, when can we meet to go shopping? I'm free tomorrow lunchtime—would that suit?'

How would Emily Cathcart receive the news that Sophie had changed her mind about the whole thing? she wondered. *It wasn't Emily's reaction she had to worry about.* Dominic was the one who would probably go ballistic. Besides, it was far too short notice to tell him that she wasn't going to go with him now. He'd more than likely have made arrangements for dinner, and that kind of thing.

'I can't do tomorrow; Wednesday lunchtime would suit me better. It will give me a chance to make arrangements at school. I could probably get another member of staff to cover for me for a couple of hours.'

'Wednesday lunchtime it is, then. I'll come and pick you up if you tell me where you are.'

'You don't happen to drive a Rolls Royce, do you?' Sophie asked light-heartedly, grimacing at the very thought. At the other end of the phone Emily guffawed loudly, and Sophie immediately found herself warming to the woman she hadn't even met, yet.

'Good grief, no, darling! I drive a common or garden Range Rover, if you want to know. Comes in awfully handy when you live in the country, like me. Bit intimidating, was it? Dom turning up in his Rolls Royce outside school?'

Smiling at the memory, Sophie relaxed back into the chair. 'You could say that. If you knew the part of London where my school is, you'd know that Rolls Royces are just about as rare as hen's teeth!'

'Dominic told me you were a primary school teacher, and Marcus described you as a pretty little thing. My husband met you at Dominic's the other night, when you had to leave early. Shouldn't be too difficult to kit you out in something special for the do on Friday. Give me your address, and I'll see you there on Wednesday at one. How's that sound?'

'It's very good of you…Emily. Thank you.'

'Not a bit of it! Dominic and I are old, old friends. I'd do anything for him, and that's the truth, so it's really no hardship at all, my dear.'

CHAPTER SEVEN

SHE was late, and Dominic felt as jumpy as a man on Death Row as he glanced over the heads of the two guests who were monopolising him towards the entrance of the historical, chandelier-lit anteroom.

He'd wanted Sophie to accompany him in the Rolls, but she had insisted she would get a taxi and meet him at the Guildhall because she'd had to go to an unexpected staff meeting after school and didn't want to risk keeping him waiting should she be late.

Impatiently Dominic glanced at his watch. *Why hadn't she told them she couldn't make the staff meeting tonight of all nights?* Did *his* needs count for nothing? Biting back his irritation, because it was almost time to go in to the main dining room for dinner, he sipped uninterestedly at his glass of chilled white wine and endeavoured to focus his attention on the conversation that continued around him.

Just when he'd resigned himself to the totally unpalatable but quite likely possibility that she'd decided to stand him up at the last minute, he saw her. Emily had assured him that the dress she'd helped Sophie pick was *exquisite.* Now, as Dominic's starved gaze crossed the distance of the marble floor that separated them, he saw with satisfaction that his friend had been quite right.

Sophie was standing next to a liveried steward, her lovely face in profile, the black full-length silk halter dress clung devotedly to her slender curves, showcasing her creamy shoulders and revealing quite the most tantalising glimpse of cleavage that he could imagine. Dominic's wasn't the only admiring glance that was drawn Sophie's way.

Even as he politely excused himself from the company he'd been with he sensed his blood infused with a building and eager excitement as he approached her, quietly stunned by the most intense reaction to a woman he'd experienced in a very long time. It merely illustrated to Dominic how much he'd anticipated seeing her again, and how impatient he'd grown in the interim, when he couldn't see her. Normally having no trouble whatsoever sleeping at night, no matter what had gone on during the day, for the past five nights, since he'd dropped Sophie home on Saturday, he had barely been able to sleep at all. Thoughts of the girl he'd spent two extremely passionate nights with had tortured him mercilessly, leaving his body aching and hungry, as though he were under the spell of some erotic love potion. He needed her in his bed *tonight*. There'd be no nonsense about her having to go home. He simply wouldn't hear of it.

'Mr Van Straten,' the steward said formally, 'I was just about to bring Miss Dalton over to you.'

'Thank you.'

Waiting until the man had left their side, Dominic delved deep into Sophie's startled cornflower-blue eyes with restless need, trying to gratify all the longing of the past five days in her absence.

'I'm sorry I'm late…staff meeting ran on a bit, and I couldn't get away. Start of the new financial year and all…that.' Her words petered out as she realised she was babbling, and that Dominic's lips remained worryingly unsmiling.

Was he furious with her for being late? Sophie fretted,

glancing round at the other impeccably attired guests. There hadn't been a lot she could do when she'd received the note at the end of class yesterday afternoon, advising her of the meeting. 'All staff are expected to attend', it had stated clearly, and Sophie hadn't wanted to say she was going to an important function and then have to explain why. The gossip regarding her lift on Friday had died down a little, but not as much as Sophie would have liked.

Now, as her gaze swung nervously back to Dominic's, her heart nearly stalled when she saw the way his blazing emerald eyes were devouring her. Inside her lovely silk dress her body tightened and tingled in helpless response. The crowd in the room melted away, because only one person demanded all her focus and attention…Dominic. She'd been secretly longing to see him again, but the awesome reality of the man's physical presence was almost too much to bear. His hard, fit body did things for that expensive tuxedo that would make the tailor who'd designed it weep for joy.

'You are here now, and that is all that matters.'

Still unsmiling, he put his hand beneath Sophie's elbow and was just about to lead her back into the glittering anteroom when the master of ceremonies announced that dinner was about to be served—could all guests please make their way into the dining room?

Half an hour later, seated at the top table with her handsome escort, dinner under way, Sophie glanced around at the sea of dignitaries and their partners, then back to Dominic. His profile, with its crown of bright hair, reminded her beguilingly of a beautiful Greek god—the kind paid homage to in sculptures. A little stab of pleasure jolted through her stomach.

Everybody wanted to talk to him, it seemed. And, although Sophie secretly yearned to have him to herself, she knew that in this glittering arena of worthies and VIPs Dominic Van Straten was 'king' and she was a mere admirer—along with all the other eager admirers who waited their turn to be noticed by him.

Reaching for her glass, Sophie took a too-hurried sip of wine and promptly spilled some down the front of her dress—the wildly expensive designer gown that Emily Cathcart had insisted that Dominic was only too delighted to pay for.

As she tried in vain to brush the spreading stain away, Dominic glanced down at her side and touched his hand to her thigh. For a long moment the press of his hand against her flesh—albeit beneath the sensuous silk of her gown—felt as if it had scorched Sophie, and she caught the hot flare of desire in his gaze and barely knew how to breathe.

'I'd better go and find a bathroom.' Already pushing back her chair, and feeling overwhelmingly self-conscious as several interested pairs of eyes at their table turned her way, she was astonished to see Dominic rise to his feet, too.

'Excuse us,' he announced to no one in particular, 'but I think my companion is in need of a little help.'

'You don't have to—'

'I very much *do* have to,' Dominic assured her in a vehement whisper as he deliberately guided her away from the tables and out of the palatial dining room.

Without a word, Sophie quickened her pace to keep up with his commanding stride, following him down thickly carpeted silent corridors to a door marked 'Powder Room'. As she turned to thank him for his help, Sophie's blue eyes grew round with shock when he opened the door behind her, gave her a gentle shove inside, then promptly joined her. Inside the scented room, with its gleaming mirrors and padded chairs, the purely naked lust reflected in Dominic's mesmerising gaze backed Sophie nervously up against a wall. Feeling her heart beat so fast she was certain that at any moment now she would fall to the ground in a faint, she saw his hand reach out to slide around her neck, and she moved inexorably towards him as though in a dream she had absolutely no control over.

'You—you really shouldn't be in here, you know. This is the— This is the—' But her words were drowningly cut off by Dominic's hard, hot mouth on hers, capturing her breath with a soul-shattering kiss and smashing every last bit of resistance Sophie might own to dust. Her body yielded like a rag doll's as he hauled her desperately against his own implacable contours of finely honed muscle and bone. And she had no thought to stop him when his hand slid down and deliberately palmed her breast beneath her silk gown, his thumb and finger coaxing the already aroused tip into pure burning sensation.

'Did I tell you how amazing you look in that dress?' Dominic breathed against the side of her bare neck, his heat skimming across her flesh like naked blue flame.

Before Sophie could even think to form an answer, he stole another voracious kiss, leaving her lips swollen and tingling and her head swimming, then stepped away and raked his fingers agitatedly through his precision-cut blond hair.

Dominic was in no doubt she was temptation personified. In that sexy, yet undoubtedly classy black silk dress, so perfectly chosen by his friend, Sophie Dalton was a *siren*, a mythical creature of dreams and wild imagination come to life to taunt him. The more he saw her, the *more* Dominic wanted her. He might have spent most of the evening so far talking to all and sundry apart from Sophie, but the mere fact that she'd been sitting just a few inches away from him had made his blood sing and his thoughts race. So much so that he was certain any comments he'd been making had hardly made any sense at all.

The idea that had formed and started to take shape back at the hotel in Suffolk was slowly but surely becoming more real—not to mention more *urgent*. It was playing on his mind like a symphony, the sound of which refused to leave him morning, noon or night. And Dominic fully intended to make it into the reality he desired.

'I want you to come back home with me this evening. I have something I want to discuss with you.'

Furrowing her brow, Sophie stepped away from the wall and smoothed her hands down the front of her dress. The damp stain from the spilled wine was not to be seen. It wouldn't have surprised her if the heat from their bodies—hers and Dominic's—had all but scorched it dry.

'What do you want to talk to me about?' She tried to scan her mind for reasons, but her teeming brain wouldn't readily yield anything very much. She was still feeling dazed from the passionate little scene she had been an unexpected player in just now.

'Now is not the time or the place,' he said in a clipped voice, his hand straightening his jacket sleeve as he assumed his previous cloak of formality.

How did he do that? Sophie wondered in awe. How could he be full of fire and passion one minute, then in the next appear so cool and remote—as though he couldn't possibly be acquainted with something so primeval as lust, at all? It made her want to go over to him, strip his jacket and shirt from his back and ruffle him up a little, with the provocation of her body.

'It will be late when we leave here, won't it? I want to get up early in the morning, to go for a swim, so I'll probably just go straight home afterwards, if you don't mind.'

Dominic could hardly believe she was turning down yet another invitation of his. Good God! What was this woman trying to do to him? Never before in the whole of his romantic history with women had Dominic been made to wait for *anything*. Let alone a stubborn slip of a girl who resisted every single request he put her way! He was seriously beginning to wonder if his own hardly insignificant attractions were no longer to be relied upon. Yet he knew he hadn't imagined her fierce response to his lovemaking, and so he calculated without conceit that any resistance in other departments must be purely to whet his appetite—to make his desire all the keener. *He could have told her that she already had him driven so crazy with lust that she needn't bother trying to whet his appetite with game-playing.* But first he had to persuade her to come home with him.

'I have a swimming pool in my house, as well as a selection of costumes available for my guests. You can swim there to your heart's content and you will not be disturbed by other members of the public.'

He turned towards the door, as though the matter were at an end, and Sophie took immediate umbrage at the way he so casually assumed she would do what *he* wanted her to do. When she'd been with Stuart, Sophie had regularly and idiotically relinquished some of her own needs in deference to meeting the needs of her boyfriend. *Look how he'd repaid her.* She had no intention of behaving in such a submissive way again...with *anyone*.

'I don't want to swim at your house, Dominic! I want to go home and go to my own sports centre, like I usually do on a Saturday morning!'

At her unexpected outburst he turned to regard her, with a frosty look in his green-eyed stare.

'You are such a creature of habit that you can't break an insignificant arrangement to be with me?'

'It may appear ''insignificant'' to you, but it's not to me! I am sure you would not break an appointment that meant a lot to you in preference to being with me, would you?'

Her chest heaving in indignation, Sophie felt her annoyance quickly replaced by something far more disconcerting to her peace of mind when one corner of Dominic's mouth quirked upwards into a provocative little half-smile.

'Haven't I already demonstrated how much I want to be with you, Sophie? I *could* go home after this, and work. I'm flying to Geneva on Sunday for five days. The deal I'm hoping to close there will mean employment for several hundred nationals. I hope to win it over a rival who would greedily cost-cut efficiency and good labour in order to make more money. Negotiations will be complex and difficult. The more preparation I do the better. That is something ''important'' to me—yet I would rather spend the time with you. I really do not know how else I may convince you of my sincerity in this wish.'

Put like that, how *could* Sophie refuse? She felt slightly shame-faced. It wasn't as though it was *really* any contest—swimming at the sports centre pool or going home with Dominic. It was just that the more time she spent with this man, the harder she knew it was going to be when they had to part. Dominic wasn't *serious* about her. She'd be a fool to believe that for even a second. Sooner or later this…this hot sexual thing they had going on between them would fizzle out, and he would go on to the next obliging pretty female who would gladly try and fulfil his every whim.

A soft, resigned sigh escaped her. 'If it's that important to you, I'll come home with you, Dominic. But I don't have any spare clothes with me for tomorrow. Could we drop off at my place on the way home to get some?'

'No problem.'

He had assumed the veneer of formality again, and Sophie experienced a sudden fervent wish that they could go home together right now, instead of returning to that 'stiff' formal gathering in the dining room. Anything to see the compelling light of attraction dancing in his eyes again when he looked at her.

'Oh, and…Dominic?'

'What is it?'

'Thank you for the beautiful dress.'

'It is my pleasure, Sophie…believe me.'

Sophie hadn't thought about the Press being at the banquet, but soon after Dominic had presented the award to a smiling recipient, and had his picture taken with the man, a gaggle of photographers descended on their table, snapping away at Dominic as though he were some kind of movie star.

When he insisted on pulling her to his side, whispering provocatively against her ear, for her hearing alone,

'Smile as though you are crazy about me,' Sophie found the smile frozen on her face.

She wished she were anywhere but where she was. She had always hated being the centre of attention. Which was another reason why weddings and the thought of being a bride filled her with horror. She didn't stop hyperventilating until they were finally in the car alone, with Louis driving.

After grabbing some clothes for tomorrow from her maisonette, and having been driven back to Dominic's lovely house in Mayfair, Sophie suddenly felt as if she could drop with tiredness. It had been a hectic, demanding day, and it wasn't over yet.

Settling herself in one of the sumptuous white couches that dotted the room, Sophie picked up a stunning velvet cushion and hugged it defensively to her middle. Dominic had told her again on the way home that he had something important to discuss with her, and right now her heart was all but leaping out of her chest at the thought of what it could be.

'Brandy?' he asked over his shoulder as he crossed the room to the walnut display case.

'Not for me, thanks. I'm so tired that if I drink any more alcohol you're going to have to carry me up to bed.'

Her lips froze as the words left her mouth. She couldn't believe she'd said such an unguarded thing!

Dominic turned to glance at her with a highly speculative and amused gleam in his unsettling gaze.

'Whether you have a drink or not, Sophie, the idea holds undoubted appeal for me as I am sure you are only too aware!'

Mutely, she pursed her lips. When he joined her just moments later on the couch, removing his exquisite jacket, throwing off his tie and loosening his shirt collar, the blood in Sophie's veins started to thrum with help-less desire. *Want* curled deep into her vitals, almost mak-ing her whimper out loud, and the sensual foray of his inviting cologne mingling with the intoxicating heat from his body merely helped exacerbate that desire.

'What was it you wanted to talk to me about?' she forced herself to ask through suddenly dry lips.

'I have had an idea.'

'Oh?'

Clutching the cushion to her middle even tighter, Sophie realised she was holding herself so stiffly that a pain had started between her shoulderblades. With a huge effort, she willed herself to try and relax.

'What do you mean, exactly?'

Dominic took a sip of his brandy before continuing, his expression serious. It drew Sophie's powerless gaze to the hard, clean lines of his implacable jaw, and a little frisson of awareness ran down her spine.

'A man in my position has many responsibilities, Sophie. Great wealth brings with it great responsibility. Contrary to what many people might think, I cannot just simply sit back and let the people who work for me take care of everything. I am actively involved in most of the decision-making that goes on around me. No doubt you think that makes me quite the control freak, but it is an action that is born out of great desire to do things well. I cannot stand mediocrity in any way. Whatever one does in life, one should do it to the very best of their ability. Don't you agree?'

Knowing the monumental desire she had herself, to be an inspiring and enthusiastic teacher and never to rest on her laurels as far as her pupils were concerned, Sophie gave a little nod.

'Lately, I have come to the conclusion that my particular path in life should not always be travelled alone. I am fast coming round to the idea that it would be much assisted by having someone in my life to share it with me. That is where *you* come in, Sophie.'

'Me?' Her throat was as parched as gravel. *Where was this leading?* she speculated in fright.

'Yes, you.'

Putting down his brandy glass on the coffee-table in front of him, Dominic adjusted his body so that he was facing her. As his compelling green eyes briefly skimmed the low-cut front of Sophie's dress, she barely knew where to look, she was so undone.

'I am tired of the short, unsatisfactory associations that have lately been my experience. I'm asking you to come and live with me, Sophie, and be my mistress.'

Momentarily struck dumb, Sophie stared. *Were live-in lovers still called 'mistresses' these days?* Her racing mind tried to assimilate her feelings on the matter. Never in a million years could she have contemplated someone like Dominic asking her such a thing! Did he really think that she would seriously consider such a position in his life?

'You mean be like a…a kept woman?'

Dominic threw her an impatient look. 'Is it so impossible for you to visualise yourself being looked after by me?'

'I don't want to be looked after by any man! I have a career I love, a home of my own. Why would I give that up?'

She is impossible! Dominic thought furiously. She had pricked his ego a thousand times since they had met, and short of begging her to take the role he so longed for her to take— His thoughts broke off, because for a moment they slammed against a brick wall.

'Have you not considered the fact that I am offering you the kind of opportunity a lot of young women your age would jump at? Think about it, Sophie. You would not want for anything. We could travel together. You would see parts of the world you have never seen before, and everywhere we go we would travel and stay in luxury and style. Does that sound like something abhorrent to you?'

He really didn't get her at all, Sophie realised disconsolately. *He thought she could be bought with his money and his billion-dollar lifestyle.* The so-called opportunity he was offering was a million miles away from what her secret heart truly longed for.

Then she was stricken by another, even more disconsolate thought.

'Is this some kind of a joke, Dominic?' Hurt at the idea of being strung along by him for some kind of sick amusement, she felt heartfelt pain wend through her bloodstream. It *had* to be a joke. Billionaires didn't proposition ordinary little primary-school teachers every day. The blood seemed to drain from his face.

'It is most definitely *not* a joke, Sophie. I have thought very carefully about this and I am perfectly serious.'

'It would be impossible!'

Rising to her feet, Sophie let the velvet cushion fall unheeded back onto the couch as she moved away from it, clasping her arms protectively across her chest as she turned back to face Dominic.

'Why?' His expression was stony, and hardly inspired confidence.

'Because you can't have thought about it carefully enough! We are poles apart, Dominic, can't you see that? What use would someone like me be to you? Take this evening. I was like a fish out of water in that imposing place! I was tongue-tied and self-conscious, and I absolutely hated having my picture taken by the Press! I'm a very private person…not someone who remotely seeks attention. The last thing I need is to be ''mistress'' to someone who is the total opposite of that!'

'I do not seek attention!'

'No, but because of who you are, your wealth and your business acumen, you can't help but command it. Be honest, Dominic. You don't really need someone like me as a mistress. Besides, I'm sure you know a lot more suitable candidates.'

She didn't say that if he had included a little more emotion or *feeling* in his proposition it would have perhaps been more palatable—even if she still wouldn't seriously have considered it. But Sophie wasn't a fool, and she didn't suspect for even a second that Dominic would have any feelings of affection for her at all. The only thing the two of them had going between them was a sexual passion so sizzling that they could start a fire just by gazing at each other. It would hardly make up for all the other glaring opposites in their relationship. And, besides all that, Sophie didn't *want* to be any man's mistress. Her independence was important.

She didn't want to entertain the fact that it was perhaps fear, as well as her belief that independence gave her more security than any man could, that stopped her from even considering the possibility of living with someone.

'I'm not considering other ''candidates'' for the position. Think about it, Sophie. You need never work or *want* for anything as long as you are with me. All I ask in return is that you be there for me when I need you. Is that really so reprehensible to you?'

No doubt any other woman faced with the same extraordinary dilemma would be jumping for joy round about now—not feeling overwhelmingly sad that Dominic seemed to imagine that his vast wealth was the main inducement for Sophie agreeing to become his mistress. That thought *did* cause her grief. *Did the man never stop to think that a woman should love him for himself—for the man he was—before all else?*

'I did not say your proposal was reprehensible.'

When he said that all he'd ask in return would be for Sophie to 'be there for him whenever he needed her', she guessed he meant sexually, and also physically, if it was an occasion like the one at the Guildhall tonight, where a partner would come in handy. He clearly wasn't talking about her being there for him *emotionally*.

Feeling suddenly cold, Sophie walked back to the couch and sat down again. She picked up the cushion she had discarded and clutched it to her middle once more.

'I suppose I should be flattered that you considered asking me, but I don't want to be your mistress, Dominic. And I certainly don't want to give up work. I love my job. It may not provide all the amazing material benefits that your career does for you, but I love it just the same, and wouldn't swap it for the world.'

Once again Dominic was struck by her integrity. He could hardly believe that a woman so highly principled as Sophie existed. Her adamant insistence that she wanted to keep her job, no matter what inducements he might put her way, frankly stunned him. *But what to do about it?*

'What if I said you could keep your job and still live with me? If we could somehow work it so that you could make yourself available when I needed you, and not nec-

essarily interfere with the demands of your career…would that induce you to consider my proposal?'

Gazing back into his indomitably handsome face,
Sophie felt her heart constrict. She couldn't understand
why he wanted her to live with him. She really couldn't.
There must be dozens of women who'd jump at the
chance to be the mistress of Dominic Van Straten—and
women with far more suitable credentials than her own.
But, beneath her undoubtedly strong desire to be close
to this remote, enigmatic man, Sophie also knew a deep
desire to be loved. She'd barely expressed it, even to
herself, and especially not after her abortive attempt at
a relationship with the man who had betrayed her, yet
still she couldn't deny her profound longing for it. If she
moved in with Dominic it was highly doubtful that he
would ever love her. She might fulfil any number of
needs he had, but beyond that—not the one she craved
herself.

'Let's just go to bed, Dominic.'

Linking her hand in his, Sophie tugged a little. Just
because she couldn't agree to become his mistress, it
didn't mean that she had to deny her physical need to
be close to him.

When Dominic saw the strong evidence of that need
in her direct blue gaze, he was riveted by it. Never before had a woman had the power to unravel him so.

'Sophie…I fully intend to keep you preoccupied in
my bed for most of the night, but before we go upstairs
I must have your answer. Will you agree to come and
live with me?'

Her eyes never leaving his face, and feeling the threatening and surprising sting of tears behind her lids,
Sophie dropped her shoulders and sighed.

'I'm sorry, Dominic…but my answer has to be no.'

CHAPTER EIGHT

SOPHIE heard his deeply in-drawn breath with profound unease. Freeing his hand from hers with a cold glance that did not bode well for further conversation of any kind—let alone intimacy—he stood up, went to the door, and called for Andrews.

Convinced that he was calling for his manservant to fetch her coat, Sophie anxiously got to her feet and followed him to the door.

'It's late,' he said, his tone deliberately aloof. 'You can stay in one of the guest rooms for tonight, then in the morning you can enjoy your swim, as promised. Andrews will tell you where the pool is.'

So... He no longer wanted to spend the night with her because clearly her company had suddenly become repugnant to him.

'Don't be like this Dominic... Please.'

Swallowing hard over the pain that was cramping her throat, she tried to reach him with a smile. Even now, when he was clearly angry with her, she didn't know what to do with all the treacherous yearning for him that was pulsating through her. It consumed her like a fever and made every inch of her skin pine and ache for his touch. Her need was so powerful and relentless that it was like standing alone in a hurricane, knowing full well that she could be swept away any moment now—possibly into oblivion. Yet she didn't care.

'You want me to make love to you, yes? Yet you will not consent to being my mistress!'

Silently elated at the longing that was evident in her beautiful eyes, yet at the same time enraged that she had dismissed his proposal so easily, Dominic felt his pride silently warring with his staggering need to have her in his arms once again.

If he relented, he would no doubt spend another unforgettable night of breathless passion with her, and it would go some way to easing the incessant ache he had inside him for her touch. It was almost unbelievable to Dominic how great his desire for this woman was. But, as much as his body cried out for such vehement fulfilment, he would not relent to his need until Sophie consented to what he wanted. As a man who dealt ruthlessly with facts, he would use the very fact that Sophie was as passionately drawn to him as he was to her to gain the advantage he so desperately coveted.

And when he had gained that advantage, he would manipulate it to its natural conclusion...

'Go to bed, and when you cannot sleep because of the ache in your body that will not go away I want you to think about my offer, Sophie. Perhaps in the morning, in the new light of day, you may see all the advantages of such a union between us...and less of the disadvantages. Hmm?'

Knowing that his arrogance would normally infuriate her—even possibly make her walk out of his house and never come back—at that moment, gazing back into his deeply compelling eyes, Sophie could not make herself move. With her blood scorching so hotly through her veins that she could hardly think at all—never mind plan—she could not propel herself to do the thing that would probably serve her best.

'Dominic, I—'

'We will not discuss the matter any further tonight. There you are, Andrews,'

'Yes, sir?'

'I want you to show Miss Dalton to a guest room, and also give her directions to the pool for the morning. Goodnight, Sophie. Sleep well, won't you?'

And before Sophie could say anything else she was forced to bite back her words as Andrews politely indicated that she should follow him upstairs. As she reached the first landing, and glanced back down into the hall, Dominic was standing there: hands down by his sides, staring up at her with a provoking little smile that made her want to run to him and beg him to take her to bed. Aghast at how weak-willed she was around this man, Sophie glanced quickly away and followed Andrews down the plushly carpeted corridor.

It was a miracle that she'd slept at all, in light of the way she and Dominic had parted. But now, as she did her laps in the gorgeous, ornate pool with its Romanesque friezes and blue and white mosaic tiles, the morning sun beaming in at her through the glass-domed ceiling, Sophie sensed the ache easing out of her body and an upsurge of energy replacing it.

She couldn't deny that the opportunity to swim totally uninterrupted like this was sheer joy. There were definitely some advantages about living in the lap of luxury she concluded, allowing herself a very wry smile.

Yet would she *seriously* entertain the idea of becoming Dominic's mistress and all that that entailed? She could converse with people on all types of subjects, yes—her teacher training had helped her enormously with that—and she could even make polite chit-chat, at a push—as long as it didn't go on too long. Yet she was no social hostess who could host fabulous dinner parties with ease, or spend her time going to haute couture fashion shows so that she would appear appropriately and fashionably dressed as the consort of a rich and important man.

She could just imagine what her parents would have to say about the whole thing! Her father, in his typically brusque no-nonsense manner, would immediately dismiss Dominic as 'no good'—else why wouldn't he ask Sophie to marry him and not just live with him?—and her mother would fret and worry that her daughter was going to get hurt.

As she reached the end of her lap Sophie paused in the deep end, treading water as she tried to marshal her thoughts. Now wasn't the time to be thinking about how other people would react should she relent to Dominic's proposition and move in with him. The question was, how did *she* feel about the whole idea?

Running her fingers across the smooth tiles, which surrounded the pool, Sophie briefly shut her eyes as a surge of powerful longing throbbed through her body. *She couldn't deny she wanted him.* But was sex a good enough reason to agree to what he desired? And if she did move in with him, became his mistress, wouldn't she be cheating herself out of the possibility of having someone really fall in love with her? *Yet how could she let someone else fall in love with her when her heart was already under threat of being stolen?*

'Good morning, Sophie.'

Her eyes flew open again at the sound of Dominic's voice. In shirtsleeves and suit trousers he walked alongside the pool towards her, his tall, commanding figure causing disconcerting butterflies to take up immediate residence in her stomach. Self-consciously she smoothed back her damp short hair.

'Morning.'

'I trust you slept well?'

There was no denying the barely veiled taunt in his voice, and heat spread between Sophie's thighs and travelled inexorably up to her breasts, the powerful extent of her passionate attraction to Dominic shocking her once again.

'It was a lovely comfortable bed, and, yes… I *did* sleep well.' Her answer was typically defiant…if unconvincing.

Unable to take his eyes off her, with her beautiful shoulders gleaming with wetness in the plain black costume she wore, and her gaze a sea of startling seductive blue, Dominic sensed a dizzying river of carnal longing rage forcefully through his veins. He had *not* slept so well…in spite of the comfort of his bed. It had not helped his case, either, when, driven to get up in the middle of the night, he'd taken a freezing cold shower to help ease his ardour. It had merely left him wide awake and aching with need. *Extremely* in need as he'd thought about Sophie, sleeping just a few doors down from his, in her room in the same corridor. *Had she given his proposal further and proper consideration?* he'd wondered?

Dominic absolutely despised the fact that she was keeping him on tenterhooks. He had never allowed himself to become this on edge about going into any potentially tricky negotiation or meeting. He had always had full confidence that his immaculate planning and consummate business acumen would win the day. He couldn't deny that he had taken his lead from his father and it had served him well.

'Never allow emotion to cloud your thinking,' he had

advised. 'Keep your head, don't be attached to the outcome and the desired result will flow to you with ease.'

But Dominic *was* attached to the outcome. He wanted Sophie to be his mistress. It would be true to say that he had become *obsessed* with the idea. Going out to dinner with his pick of beautiful women was no longer enough. He wanted just *one* beautiful woman in particular to be his companion. He was tired of empty sexual encounters just to fulfil a basic need. Sophie was an enchanting, engaging and *educated* woman. Someone he could converse with, discuss plans and ideas with, someone he could spend time with and not be bored out of his mind in her company. Dominic wanted a longer-term companion to share the amazing fruits of his success. And the woman he wanted, the woman he *had* to have, was Sophie.

'So…' he said, crouching down beside her. 'You are ready to come out now and have some breakfast?'

At the answering growl in her stomach, Sophie silently acknowledged she was starving. She had hardly touched the food at the banquet last night, and after her vigorous swim she was even hungrier. Yet she was acutely self-conscious at the idea of climbing out of the pool and revealing herself in her costume. Even though it was plain black, its high cut on the legs and deep neckline barely left much to the imagination.

'I will get your towel.'

Without further preamble Dominic went to the nearby cane lounger where Sophie had left her towel and brought it to her. Standing at the edge of the tiled steps, he waited for her to come out.

Smoothing back her saturated hair with a nervous hand, Sophie started to walk up the steps towards him. Dominic stared, making no secret of the fact that he was enjoying the privilege, and Sophie's skin burned to have him look at her, because his glance was as potent and powerful as his very touch. When she got close, so close that she was intimately acquainted with the pupils of his eyes, Sophie held her breath, convinced that he was going to kiss her. When he didn't, but instead merely draped the towel around her shoulders and started to walk away, she bit back her bitter disappointment and shivered violently beneath the towel.

'We will breakfast in the conservatory,' he told her over his shoulder. 'Walk to the end of the corridor, turn left, then right, and you will find it. I'll wait for you there.'

Dressed in jeans and a plain white cotton shirt, her body still glowing warmly from her swim, Sophie found her way to the conservatory.. and the sight of Dominic lounging back in his chair reading a newspaper. Around him bustled a small olive-skinned woman dressed in a black dress and white apron—presumably his house-keeper—busily laying breakfast things on the table in front of him.

'Sophie...come and sit down. Maria will bring you some tea or coffee. What do you prefer?'

'Tea, please,' Sophie replied, taken aback when Dominic stood up and pulled out a chair for her, then waited until she was seated before resuming his own seat.

'And to eat? Do you like the "full English breakfast," or are you one of those abstemious women who either don't eat at all or eat only fruit in the morning?'

Surprised at his light banter, Sophie couldn't help but grin. 'I *definitely* couldn't survive the morning on just fruit, so I would very much like the full English, if that's all right? The only time I ever get a cooked breakfast is if I go home to my mum's, so it will be a treat.'

Having grown up with a mother who had spent her days fundraising and social climbing, Dominic had *never* experienced anything so homely as having a breakfast cooked by his own mother. A brief flare of envy surfaced as he regarded Sophie's pretty, animated face, and he caught himself wondering if she would do the same for her own children. His envy was quickly replaced by a moment of deep and profound reflection on the topic. Then, realising that Maria hovered at his side waiting for his instruction, he asked his housekeeper for two cooked breakfasts and a large pot of tea. As she bustled away, he levelled his interested gaze back to Sophie.

'Do you see your parents often?' he asked conversationally.

'About two or three times a month, at most. I'm afraid I *do* tend to get rather caught up in my work. When I'm not at school, teaching, I'm either studying or attending courses to try and improve myself. It doesn't leave much time for visiting anyone. My parents understand, though. They sacrificed a lot to send me to university.'

They sounded like good people. Dominic's interest deepened. 'What does your father do?' he asked her.

'He's a builder. He works too hard, though, and he's getting on a bit. I do worry that he overreaches himself a bit too much physically. Only last month he hurt his back and was off for two weeks.' The memory jolted Sophie into a regretful reverie. Her dad was back at work now, but she should go and see him soon—make sure for herself that he was doing all right. Realising that Dominic was studying her intently, Sophie reached for the perfectly folded white linen napkin in front of her, shook it out and laid it carefully on her lap.

'What does *your* father do?' she asked quietly.

'He's a businessman. Officially retired, but still with his fingers in a lot of different pies.' Dominic's smile was rueful, and a little twinge of pleasure flared in Sophie's stomach.

'And what about your mother?' she ventured.

He shrugged, and a veil seemed to come down over his eyes. 'She keeps herself busy travelling and doing a lot of things for charity.'

'And do you get to see her very much?'

The last time had been almost a year ago, and that had been only briefly when she had made a flying visit to his office in London. 'No. Not really.'

'Oh.'

Sophie didn't know what else to say. Whether his comment signalled that he regretted that fact, or simply didn't care one way or the other, she couldn't have said. But the absent look on his face tugged at her heartstrings somehow.

'I'm sure it's a very tough job being a parent. I take my hat off to those hardy individuals brave enough to try. When I think of the energy and demands of my class of five year-olds, I can almost feel my hair turning grey at the thought!'

'But eventually...you would like children of your own?'

Dominic's question hung poised in the air, as threatening to Sophie's sense of safety as if she stood with her toes out over the edge of a cliff. She shifted uncomfortably.

'Not for ages yet. I'd have to be married first, and I haven't found anyone who—' She turned crimson as the words spilled out, and suddenly stopped as she realised what she was saying.

Beneath his light tan, Dominic's skin appeared momentarily flushed, and she knew the topic of becoming his mistress, as he had proposed, had been bubbling all the while beneath the surface of their ordinary conversation, and was about to come up again.

'I have come up with an idea that I would like you to consider.'

Frowning at this new development, Sophie linked her hands together in her lap and sat waiting.

'What idea is that?'

'A trial period of six months' duration. We will live together for six months, and if at the end of that period you find that the arrangement is not to your liking, for whatever reason, you can move out again and I will not pressurise you into staying. Does that idea perhaps hold more appeal than tying yourself to me indefinitely?'

Her heart thudding heavily in her chest, Sophie stared. 'Why do you want me to live with you at all? Why can't we just see each other like other couples do?'

Because with his schedule and her schedule Dominic thought they would barely get to see each other at all. At least if Sophie lived with him, there would be times when he could press her into travelling abroad with him on meetings and spur-of-the moment trips, etc. He was certain that once she got a taste of the kind of world-class travel that was the norm for Dominic she wouldn't object too loudly about travelling with him. And he might be able to persuade her that her career perhaps wasn't as important as she thought it was after all.

'Because that's not what I want. I want you to move in, or I will hardly get to see you at all. I have this big beautiful house and lots of room. It shouldn't be too much of a hardship for you.'

'So you have this idea that you're somehow rescuing

me from my lowly lifestyle? You think perhaps that I should be very grateful that you're making me this once-in-a-lifetime offer?'

For a moment Sophie was furious at his implication that what he was offering was such a fabulous inducement that she should immediately forget everything she'd worked so hard to achieve for herself and simply just move in with him and let herself be kept! Okay, she relented silently. It *was* a fabulous inducement, and plenty of other women might have jumped at the chance to be the live-in lover of a gorgeous rich billionaire like Dominic, but Sophie *wasn't* one of those women. As much as her feelings for him had grown, she would not relinquish her life totally for him.

'I do not understand why you are being so stubborn. Anyone would think I was offering you something despicable!'

'You don't understand because you don't really know me at all, Dominic! I love my work—I even love my little house—even though it could probably fit into your place ten times over! They both mean a lot to me.'

Sighing with undisguised exasperation, Dominic pushed his fingers through his hair. 'What if we agree that you could keep your little house, and your job, and still move in with me? What would you say to that, Sophie?'

'And if I agreed?' Her mouth going dry at the very idea of moving in with Dominic and sharing his fabulous lifestyle, Sophie nervously skimmed her tongue over her top lip. 'What…what would you expect of me, Dominic?'

He answered without flinching, direct and to the point. 'I would expect you to be my companion and my lover…of course. What else did you think I would expect, Sophie?'

Feeling hot at his undoubted implication that being his lover would be the most important part of all, Sophie felt her thoughts scatter wildly, like leaves swept up in a gust then blown away again.

'If I were to…to consider this new proposal…I want it to be understood that I won't give up my career. I'll live with you, and assume the role you want me to, but only if it is understood that I come and go as I please. I'm used to my independence and I won't consider anything less. I *couldn't.*'

Feeling hugely relieved and quietly elated, Dominic allowed his deceptively calm expression to give very little away as Sophie sat there looking back at him. He would give way on her desire to keep her job, he was thinking, but he would not want her to be too independent. When she realised that he was willing to give her everything her heart desired, she would soon come to accept that in effect Dominic was the boss, and that naturally *his* needs were the ones that would take precedence. Besides, if she were going to be his mistress he would want her beside him on his travels round the globe. Sometimes he was gone for weeks at a time, and there was no way that he would be leaving Sophie once she'd agreed to live with him—otherwise what would be the point of going through with the arrangement at all?

'We have an agreement, then?'

Reaching for her hand, he twined it in his own, his smooth fingers weaving through hers with a definitely possessive air.

Telling herself that she had well and truly taken complete and utter leave of her senses for even considering

Dominic's proposal—especially in light of the fact she hadn't exactly even been considering another relationship for a long, long time—Sophie could barely articulate a reply.

'I—I would like some time to take all this in before I move in. Do you agree?'

'How much time?'

'A week…maybe two?' She shrugged, indecision temporarily freezing her brain.

'I will give you seven days, then this time next week I will arrange for your things to be moved here.'

'And what about your family and friends, Dominic? Will you tell them about me?'

He avoided answering by turning the question around. 'Will you tell *your* parents?'

'There wouldn't be any point. Not when—not when it's not even a proper relationship.' Her expression was pained, and Dominic squeezed her fingers hard with his own.

'You are wrong! Of course it will be a proper relationship. Your parents will have no cause for concern. How could they, when I will look after you and you will want for nothing? I am merely suggesting the six months' trial period so that you do not feel as though I have trapped you into this arrangement. You can tell whoever you choose about it.'

'So you will tell your parents, too?' Sophie asked him, wide-eyed.

Yes, he would tell them. But he didn't expect them to jump for joy. Not when his mother found out that his new paramour was a simple primary school teacher, with working-class parents, and not the daughter of wealthy or even professional people. His mother expected her son to have relationships, of course, but she was very much a snob at heart, when all was said and done, and only expected the best for her one and only son. His father might frown and ask him if he could not have done better, but he would not disturb him half as much as his mother. Especially when she *met* Sophie. She was unlike any other girl Dominic had ever dated, neither a social climber nor a gold digger, and that, of course— apart from the hot sexual attraction that sizzled between them—was another reason for her appeal.

'Of course.'

Sophie didn't dare speculate if Dominic's parents would like her, should they ever meet. She had enough trouble focusing on the fact that she had agreed to become Dominic's mistress and—even more pertinent— what living with Dominic Van Straten was going to be like!

Back at work on Monday, it really only hit Sophie then—what she was proposing to go through with and the effect it would no doubt have on her life.

She'd been fully expecting to receive a phone call from Dominic in Geneva, where he had flown yesterday, to tell her he had thought over the matter some more and he was sorry but he'd made a terrible mistake. When she'd received no such communication Sophie had gone about the rest of her weekend in a complete daze, nervously reminding herself that she needed to pack some things ready for moving in with him in only a few short days' time. She'd also had a postcard from Diana in Cyprus, where she was on honeymoon, and the sight of her friend's familiar handwriting had made Sophie's stomach seesaw, as if she'd just polished off a glass of neat vodka before breakfast.

Diana would hardly be able to believe it! Away for

just a fortnight, only to return and find out that her best friend was moving in with her boss! And after they had clearly disliked each other intensely on sight!

'Good weekend, Sophie?' Barbara Budd asked slyly as she poured herself a coffee from the machine in the book-laden staffroom.

Pretending to concentrate on the staff bulletin she was reading on the board, Sophie shrugged lightly. 'Okay. How about you?'

'Nothing too exciting. Seen anything of your rich boy-friend lately?'

Feeling dizzying heat pulse through her body at the question, Sophie spun round. 'What are you talking about?' Studying the other woman uneasily, she felt a keen stab of dislike at the unconstrained curiosity in her eyes.

'You know very well what I'm talking about, Sophie. The one who owns the Rolls Royce. I wouldn't let him go in a hurry, if I were you. I'd jump at the chance to say goodbye to this place!'

It was well known by the other members of staff that Barbara hadn't chosen teaching as a vocation. She hadn't got the grades she'd wanted to study as a lawyer, so teaching was a poor second-best in her eyes. Sophie couldn't help but feel sorry for the class of eight-year-olds she taught.

'I'd really prefer it if you just minded your own business, Barbara, if you want to know the truth! My private life is nothing to do with you.'

'Pardon me for breathing, I'm sure.'

Tossing her head, the other woman picked up her vo-luminous handbag and marched out of the room as though she were the Queen of Sheba herself making an exit. Feeling her shoulders droop with a mixture of relief and defeat, Sophie collected her things together and made her way slowly to her classroom. At least that was one arena where she didn't feel so mixed up and afraid.

CHAPTER NINE

DOMINIC had rung Sophie to ask that she come with Louis to the airport to meet him. Almost a whole week had gone by since he'd left for Geneva, and every day that passed Sophie had surprisingly found herself missing him more. Stunned by such a heartfelt reaction, she barely knew what to do with all the tumultuous feelings that were racing around inside her. She carried his absence around with her as though she were bereaved, and even doing the simplest of tasks seemed to require an almost monumental effort of concentration. All she could think about was Dominic.

Not liking the idea that she'd become obsessed with the man, she'd irritably tried to shake off her morose mood. She'd even gone out a couple of evenings in succession for a drink with friends, determined to demonstrate to herself that she was definitely not one of those silly women who could only survive if they had a man in their life. It hadn't worked. All she could do when she got home again was play some unashamedly romantic CD and moon around the house as though some mysterious sickness had descended upon her.

Now, as she paced the VIP lounge at Heathrow, too restless to even pick up a magazine and read it, Sophie glanced nervously down at the lovely coat that Dominic had insisted she keep. It made her secretly marvel at how one thing could lead to another and take you down a very different path from the one you'd been intent on travelling. From a girl who'd wondered if she'd ever

have a relationship again because she'd become so commitment shy to contemplating moving in with a man
she'd only just met was a pretty big detour in a person's
life. She'd even taken particular care with her make-up
this evening, because she wanted to look especially nice
for Dominic, and Louis had kindly commented on how
well she looked when he'd come to pick her up.

'Sophie.'

A little bolt of heat shot through her at the unexpected
sound of that voice. Slowly she turned, her heart leaping
with unconstrained joy at the sight of him with a stylish
raincoat thrown over his dark suit, his blond hair a little
mussed and a suggestion of darkness beneath his amazing eyes that immediately concerned her. All it took was
just one little glance to make Sophie lose her centre of
gravity. Suddenly finding herself completely at a loss for
words, she willed her feet to move forward, but remained where she stood as Dominic disconcertingly
smiled and travelled towards her instead.

The long meeting-filled days of the past week had
somehow taken more out of him than Dominic liked.
He'd had to fight for his position long and hard, coming
up against stiff opposition from his rivals and having to
revise plans, assessments and financial projections deep
into the night every night he was there, to come up with
a viable and realistic package that would win him the
deal. His main desire that several Swiss nationals would
win gainful employment through his efforts had overri-
den his usual number-one need to make a substantial
profit. *The deal had been won.*

Elated, but weary, Dominic had flown home with only
one aim in mind to ease the tension and fatigue that had
accumulated over the past few days. *Sophie.* He was
desperate to see her, to make certain that she knew he

fully intended her to keep to their arrangement and move in with him either the following day or the day after that. He'd allowed her her seven days to take it all in, and he didn't want to wait any longer.

He'd made up his mind that he would make her remember how good they were together tonight in bed. The thought of that had sustained him throughout the flight, and now it was all he could think about. As his gaze settled on her small, slender figure, Dominic was gratified to see that she was wearing the coat he'd bought her, and he couldn't suppress a rush of excitement that chased his previous tiredness away and made him feel amazingly and insatiably *alive*.

'How are you?' he asked her, unable to prevent the definite traces of need and emotion straining his voice.

'I'm fine.' Smiling up at him, Sophie kept her hands down by her sides, nervous and unsure how to greet him even though instinct dictated that she fling her arms around him and kiss him.

But he looked almost too untouchable for her to concede to such unconstrained emotion in public. Dominic was exactly what he appeared: a perfectly groomed and handsome businessman, successful and wealthy beyond measure, from the tips of his shoes to the top of his gilded head. He wasn't just Sophie's boyfriend, returning home from a trip abroad. When this man said 'jump' people automatically responded with 'How high?' That put the matter of his homecoming into an entirely different perspective for Sophie.

For a long moment she was struck by how sheer outrageous fortune had manoeuvred her into the same amazing sphere as this man. *How could a relationship between two people from such diametrically opposite circumstances possibly work?* she thought soberingly. It was about time she woke up out of the dream she'd been in and started to get real.

'Don't I get a welcome-home kiss?' Dominic goaded softly, his honeyed voice commanding her attention.

Her stomach churning with nerves, knowing she would have to talk to him about this forthcoming arrangement of theirs again, Sophie stood on tiptoe and planted a deliberately informal kiss on his cheek. A mere peck.

Straight away, Dominic scowled. 'If that kiss was any true indication of how much you've missed me, then I am sorry indeed.'

'You look tired,' Sophie replied, latching on to the first excuse she could think of to explain her behaviour.

'But not so tired that I do not have the strength to show my woman that I have been thinking of her while I have been away…hmm?'

His lips descended on hers before Sophie could turn her head away. They were hungry and warm and sent fire rippling through her veins like the after-effects of cognac. Because she simply couldn't help it, she opened her mouth and drank the taste of him in, her heart pounding so hard inside her chest that she needed to hold onto Dominic until the dizziness that had overtaken her passed.

When he lifted his head to look down at her, he stroked her chin with the pad of his thumb and smiled. 'Perhaps you *did* miss me a little…huh?'

'How—how did your work go?' Standing back from him a little, Sophie smoothed her slightly trembling hand down her coat.

'Very satisfactory, since you ask. But I don't want to discuss work with you now, Sophie. All I want to do is go home, have a drink with you and go to bed. You will stay tonight, yes?'

He made it sound like such an easy and simple decision, and yet for Sophie it was as though she had to negotiate a path littered with landmines. The more she allowed herself to be intimate with Dominic, the harder it was going to be to walk away. Whether that would be six months down the road, at the end of their trial arrangement, or whether it would be tonight if Sophie confessed to him her doubts about their relationship—it made no difference. She'd missed him like crazy the whole time he'd been away, but maybe that was all the more reason for her to maintain a little sensible breathing distance between them? At least until she was certain she was doing the right thing.

'I'm sure you'd much rather just rest. It would probably be best if I just went home. I could come back tomorrow and see you, if you like?'

The distance she seemed to be trying to enforce between them both alarmed and infuriated Dominic. Had she been talking to someone about him while he was away? A friend, perhaps, who'd advised Sophie that moving in with him was a bad idea? If that was the case, then the sooner she moved in the better! Sophie would come to learn that people often had very preconceived ideas about wealthy and powerful men like him, and even friends would not necessarily always have her best interests at heart. Dominic wouldn't be surprised if some element of jealousy or envy had come into play during any 'friendly advice' she'd been given.

'Nonsense! I have waited all week to see you again, and now you tell me you want to go home tonight and will come back tomorrow? I won't hear of it. Of course you will stay with me tonight!'

His authoritarian stand immediately engendered resentment in Sophie. As much as she truly desired to be with him, she wouldn't be *ordered* to spend the night with him—as though she were some sort of powerless serf to his arrogant Lord of the Manor!

'Dominic… It might be second nature to you just to demand whatever you want and get it, and you might speak to other women that way, but in my book you ask first. This is the twenty-first century, remember? I come and I go at my own free will. I'm not your chattel!'

He sighed heavily and dragged his fingers impatiently through his hair, as though he found her indignation completely tedious.

'I cannot believe we are having an argument in the first few minutes of seeing each other! All right. I will concede that perhaps I should have asked you if you would like to spend the night. Well, I am asking you now, Sophie. Will you?'

All of a sudden Dominic was too weary to disguise the naked longing in his eyes. His guard down, all pretence fled in the wake of that powerful need. And on the receiving end of that revealing and earth-shattering look, Sophie sensed all her resistance rapidly melt away, like flotsam and jetsam carried off by the tide.

'If you're sure you're not too tired?'

'I am not an invalid, Sophie. I have only flown home from a business trip.' His gaze signalling his amusement at the very notion of being tired, Dominic took the liberty of tucking one of Sophie's tantalising curls gently behind her ear. 'I am quite happy to demonstrate my vigour to you as soon as we get home.'

Unable to do anything very much except blush scarlet, Sophie allowed him to take her hand and lead her out into the busy concourse that was Heathrow airport.

*   *   *

His bedroom was vast and stylish, the centrepiece a magnificently sumptuous draped four-poster bed. Sophie immediately felt lost inside such an imposing room, confronted as she was by the colossal differences in her own circumstances and Dominic's and wondering how not to feel intimidated.

But she soon had another challenge to contend with, when Dominic pulled off his tie, fixed her with a devastatingly possessive and sexy grin and then walked towards her with an altogether inflammatory glance that told her it wasn't their differences he was interested in right now. It was the one thing that they *definitely* had in common: their mutual *desire*.

'What are you doing?' she asked nervously, as Dominic's hands settled on her waist and with a forthright little pull brought her right up against his chest.

'What do you think I'm doing?' he asked, his hands caressing her back, then sliding down past the waistband of her jeans into her panties. 'I'm getting to know you all over again, Sophie Dalton.'

Even his voice, honey-rich and sensual, had the power to make Sophie lose all sense of reason. There was already such a primitive ache pulsating inside her that her very bones were restless with it. She forgot all about his status and wealth, and the fact that he lived in a house fit for royalty. When Sophie's guileless blue eyes met the glinting emerald of his, all they saw reflected back at her was a man—a very *human* and warm man who needed her touch just as much as she coveted his.

Raising her hand, she traced the outline of his near-perfect lips with her finger. A muscle throbbed in his cheek and he captured her hand, turned the palm towards him and kissed it. Just as Sophie went weak at his touch his mouth took ruthless possession of her lips and made her mindless with longing. Dominic Van Straten wasn't just a powerful and successful businessman. He was a man who knew how to kiss with the most devastating results. All his passion, all his *hunger* for intimacy and warmth, was contained in that all-consuming contact, and Sophie sensed a need in him that she hadn't been acquainted with before. An *emotional* need.

So he wasn't a remote 'island' after all? She seemed to have made the totally surprising discovery that his need to be loved was just as prevalent as any other human being's…just as prevalent as *her own*. Sophie kissed him back, barely conscious of the fact that they were moving in unison towards the bed, eagerly tearing at each other's clothes as though they couldn't wait for skin-to-skin contact.

In the lamplight Dominic's body exuded muscular strength in abundance, and he appeared like some mythical warrior of old—all golden hair and smooth, rippling biceps. He lay down and urged Sophie to straddle him. Persuasion was hardly necessary, because the primal need in her was swelling like a tide, and she couldn't wait so much as one minute more before joining her body with Dominic's. His length filled her with one smooth upward thrust and made her cry out with the pleasure of it.

Then suddenly he stilled, his hands resting on her thighs, as realisation stole into his hot gaze. 'Sophie, we need to use some protection. We can't take the risk of you falling pregnant.'

Even articulating the words, Dominic experienced the strongest and most surprising desire to make a baby with this woman. The awareness all but rocked his world off its axis. But even as he allowed himself the fantasy

Sophie was smiling down at him with her enchantingly shaped lips, her fingers sliding up his biceps and stroking them.

'You don't have to worry. I'm on the Pill. I take it for…because I have painful periods.'

Even though they were actually in the throes of making love, Sophie's cheeks heated with embarrassment at having to explain such an intimate reason for being on the Pill to Dominic. But this man was making her push at every emotional boundary she'd ever erected for herself, and she wasn't going to let embarrassment steal away the joy of being with him like this.

Hardly knowing whether to feel reassured or disappointed at the news, Dominic soon forgot his fantasy about making babies as Sophie slowly but very effectively rocked her slender hips against his, causing waves of volcanic pleasure to erupt inside him as his thrusts became deeper and more demanding. His hands covering her breasts, he stroked and played with the nipples that had hardened into dusky pink pebbles, enjoying her pleasure as much as his own. She started to exhale in breathy little gasps, calling out his name as he rocked into her with one more relentless thrust, and they both came apart in each other's arms. Sophie fell against him with her lips pressed into his chest, savouring every erotic musky scent that their entwined bodies exuded.

'Now, *that* is more like the homecoming I had in mind.' Chuckling softly, Dominic tangled his fingers into the short, silky strands of her hair, then slid both hands down the side of her face and lifted her head to make her look at him.

'We are not so different, you and I,' he told her, as he examined her flushed, aroused features. 'We are both passionate and fiery. A good combination, don't you think?'

'And you like passionate women? I mean, I'm sure you've known quite a few in your time, Dominic?' Feeling undeniably jealous at the thought, Sophie did not smile.

'A few…but never anyone like you, Sophie.'

'I've only had one proper boyfriend before you. Can you guess?'

'If you are asking me do I think your lack of experience shows, then, no. You are quite the femme fatale. Your sexy little body is enough to drive a sane man out of his wits with desire. Does that reassure you?'

Women would always look at Dominic and desire him. Sophie knew that. Whether she could handle it or not was another thing entirely. Until Stuart had betrayed her Sophie had never experienced the kind of jealousy that cut through a person's soul like a knife. For a while she'd despised the girl Stuart had spent the night with. But after a while she'd forced herself to let the hurt diminish and get on with her life. Nevertheless, she didn't particularly want to experience such pain again, if she could help it. *If she allowed herself to fall for Dominic unreservedly wasn't that the kind of pain she was signing up for? Only probably ten times worse…* A man as dynamic and charismatic as he was would always have many admirers. Sophie didn't doubt that a lot of them would be women.

'I wasn't fishing for compliments..really.'

She moved to lie by his side, staring up at the peach silk canopy that draped the sumptuous bed, feeling curiously vulnerable and afraid.

'I think the sooner we are together the better,' Dominic announced. He was a man of the world, but he did not particularly want to hear about Sophie's ex-boyfriend or wonder if she had been as easily aroused by him as she was with Dominic. 'You might like to spend some time thinking about where you would like me to take you for our first trip away,' he said, his fingers trailing gently down her cheek. 'I want us to go soon, so that we can spend a little time getting to know each other.'

Talking about trips away made Sophie's thoughts naturally gravitate to Diana. Her friend would be back at work for Dominic on Monday. Would she be surprised and pleased for her? Or would she be shocked that Sophie had taken such a U-turn and was contemplating a live-in relationship with Dominic when she'd so vehemently declared herself to be a man-free zone?

'Sophie?' Dominic coaxed softly, his glance concerned as she continued to stare up at the canopy without speaking.

'Soon, you say? Well, I just hope I can get time off school. If it coincides with the Easter break, then it will be fine. Otherwise, I might not be able to go.'

Unable to conceive that the school she worked for might make it difficult for Sophie to have time off, Dominic couldn't help but feel frustrated. If he had his way then Sophie would be handing in her notice, not pleading for permission to go on holiday!

'That is ridiculous!' He voiced his vexation out loud.

'No, Dominic,' Turning her head to study him, Sophie felt her heart leap helplessly at the sight of his fiercely handsome face. 'That's life. Even supply teachers are thin on the ground these days. And if I'm honest, I don't particularly want another teacher standing in for me while I'm away, anyway. The little ones get very attached to their teacher, and it takes them quite a while to adjust to someone new. I wouldn't want them to be upset in my absence.'

'Do you never take time off?' Dominic demanded, scowling.

'Of course! I get the school holidays off, like everyone else. But other than that I try and avoid it if I can. Like I said, the children—'

'Have you always been so stubbornly dedicated?'

Even as he posed the question Dominic knew he could hardly fault Sophie for a quality he meticulously adhered to himself, but part of him couldn't help feeling ridiculously jealous that she would put her class of five-year-olds before him.

'I've always wanted to teach. It was my dream career even as a little girl. Why wouldn't I be dedicated?'

'Did you never think that one day you might want a family of your own?'

Startled by the question, Sophie stared. 'I'm not saying that it's never crossed my mind, but there's still so much I want to do before—before that happens.'

Now it was his turn to glance up at the ceiling. Putting his arm behind his head, he sighed. 'I too have thought about having a family of my own one day. My work has really been my life, you know? But of course one must think of the future.'

Uncomfortable with the way the conversation was going, because it was clear to Sophie that when Dominic spoke of his desire for a family of his own he didn't mean with her, she bit back her hurt and forced a smile.

'Right now I would rather focus on the present…wouldn't you?'

'You echo my thoughts precisely. Clever girl!'

Before Sophie realised his intention he had moved, positioning himself above her, his strong thighs imprisoning her hips, and gazing down at her with a sexy little gleam in his eye that sent wild tingles of excitement racing up and down her body.

'Dominic…what are you doing?'

'I'm demonstrating my vigour, darling Sophie. Just like I promised you I would.'

Covering her surprised gasp with his mouth, coaxing her lips into a long, leisurely, extremely sexy kiss that felt like a dream she never wanted to wake up from, he commanded her full and devoted attention with exhilarating ease.

'I need to sit down.'

Finding one of Sophie's padded but threadbare armchairs close by, Diana sank down into it, her shocked face turning pale beneath her newly acquired Mediterranean tan.

'Let me get this straight. You're telling me that while I was away Dominic and you got it together and now he's asked you to move in with him? What the hell happened to make all this come about? The last impression I got from you before I left was that you couldn't *stand* him!'

Leaving the two steaming mugs of coffee she had made for them on the table, Sophie fingered a softly curling tendril at her ear and attempted a smile. 'I can hardly explain it myself, Diana, if you want to know the truth. It was just one of those crazy things that happen sometimes… Although I never thought it would happen to me.'

'He must be up to something.'

Her long scarlet nails curling into the faded material on the chair-arm, Diana appeared flustered and distracted. Sophie's heart thumped at her words, all her instincts immediately on alert.

'What do you mean, he must be up to something?'

'Be realistic, Soph! Here you are, an underpaid, over-worked, passably attractive primary school teacher, and there's Dominic—a mega-rich, mega-successful, drop-dead gorgeous hunk who reads the financial pages for relaxation and lives in just one of the most prestigious addresses in London! I mean, wake up and smell the coffee, Sophie! Yes, you're pretty, and I love you to bits, but you're no Catherine Zeta-Jones, darling!'

Her friend's words lambasted her like an unforgiving forest fire, treacherously flattening Sophie's self-esteem and pride. *Diana could be crass sometimes—but insensitive and cruel?* Right now, Sophie could have been looking at a stranger.

'Speak your mind, why don't you?' she said, hurt.

'For goodness' sake, Sophie! All he probably wants to do is sleep with you! He's obviously just teasing you with this ''moving in'' idea, to try and sweeten you up a little. He's found out you're not the kind of girl who sleeps around, and you can't be bought, so he's doing his damnedest to seduce you, that's all. As soon as he's got what he wants he'll drop you like a hot brick and move on to somebody else!'

'I've already slept with him, for your information.'

Feeling her throat tighten with pain at the realisation that Diana was clearly not the friend she'd thought she was, Sophie crossed her arms in front of her chest, her blue eyes glittering. 'And, as a matter of fact, he asked me to move in with him *after* we slept together!'

'I don't believe you!'

Pushing to her feet, Diana's gaze locked onto Sophie's with undisguised disdain.

'Why would he want to be with someone like you when he could have his pick of beautiful women? Do you know how many women ring him during a period of one week? You're just asking for trouble if you go through with this ridiculous arrangement, Sophie! He'll never be faithful to you! What reason would he have?'

CHAPTER TEN

HE'LL never be faithful to you…what reason would he have? The question caused her insurmountable pain, especially since she had allowed herself to start believing after last night in bed that Dominic might really care for her—that perhaps his attraction was more than just fascination.

Sophie sensed her heart twist with grief. Unwittingly she'd started to let down a few barriers and open her heart to Dominic, and now there was nothing she could do but admit to herself that she loved him. But the devastating words that Diana had expressed would wound anyone who cared deeply about someone else, and Sophie *was* hurt, without a doubt.

'You believe that Dominic can't possibly care about someone like me?' she asked quietly, her heart trying to fend off the sting.

'I don't want to hurt you, Sophie. That's the whole point. But you don't move in the same world as he does. You don't see what I see. Isn't it better you find out the truth about Dominic's character now, rather than later when your heart is in tatters?'

Was that why Dominic had suggested the six-month trial period? Sophie thought frantically now. Was it because he knew that he couldn't possibly stay faithful to someone like her for long? He might desire her above any other woman right now, because he'd become infatuated with her, but he was an intelligent, experienced man—he surely knew that his obsession for Sophie would not last.

'So what are you telling me? That he's a man who can't be trusted where women are concerned?'

'What do *you* think? I'm not trying to cast aspersions on his character, but with Dominic's good looks and immense personal fortune what reason would he have to settle down with any one woman? He's still young—he has plenty of time yet to play the field.'

'And yet despite all of that he *does* want a relationship with me! I never thought I'd find someone I really cared about, Diana...you know that. But I do have *feelings* for Dominic. Can't you just wish me well, like I did you and Freddie, and be happy for me?'

Diana said nothing for several moments. Then finally, throwing Sophie a disparaging glance, the blonde let her true thoughts be known.

'Who do you think you are, believing you can just walk right in and have someone like Dominic at the drop of a hat? To go from near poverty to unimaginable luxury in the blink of an eyelid just like that! Freddie and I have had to work hard for everything we've got...it hasn't just been handed to us on a plate!'

Hardly able to believe what she was hearing, Sophie tried desperately to gather her thoughts. It was just plain laughable if Diana truly believed that good fortune had been handed to Sophie on a plate. She'd worked hard too, and her parents had worked harder still to help her pay her way through college and university, making all kinds of sacrifices along the way. Diana, in contrast, came from a professional background—her parents were doctors. One practised in Harley Street and the other in a private clinic in Chelsea. If she'd had to struggle for the things she wanted at all, it was perhaps because

Freddie spent most of their money trying to fund a life-style that was obviously beyond their means. Finances had been the cause of most of the rows and breakups the two had had.

It was painfully clear to Sophie that her friend was extremely jealous of the idea of Sophie moving 'out of her class' and being with someone like Dominic. The realisation that her friend scorned her humble beginnings was like a brutal slap in the face.

'I'm sorry you've reacted the way you have, Diana. Now that I know what your true feelings are about me there's no sense in you staying, is there? Perhaps you'd better just leave.'

'And when I see Dominic I'll tell him exactly what I think of this whole pathetic fiasco, too!'

As Diana swept from the room out into the hallway, and practically slammed the front door off its hinges, Sophie very much doubted she would tell Dominic any such thing. Diana had always made it known that she was paid a very good salary for being PA to the Dutch billionaire. She doubted if her former friend would jeopardise that salary by telling Dominic exactly what she thought—no matter how vehemently she thought it.

'So, you're moving your pretty little Sophie in with you, are you? I suppose I should take my hat off to her. She's managed what no other girl has managed since I've known you! Are you certain this is what you want, Dominic?'

Smiling her typically wise smile, Emily Cathcart considered her very handsome lunch date with undisguised affection. It wouldn't have been an exaggeration to say that she'd been shocked to her very shoes to hear from Dominic's own lips that he intended to move his new lover in with him, and soon. And it had come as even more of a surprise to learn that the lucky girl was Sophie Dalton—the pretty primary school teacher that Emily had gladly helped kit out with a posh frock for Dominic's presentation at the Guildhall.

She wondered now if Dominic had any idea how this shocking news would send tremors of disbelief vibrating through the circles they both moved in? Dominic Van Straten had been quite the catch for several years now. There wasn't a single ambitious mother in Emily's entire acquaintance, with daughters of marriageable age, who hadn't hoped and dreamed that one day he would make them the most delighted of mothers-in-law.

Lord, but they were going to be greviously disappointed when they found out he'd moved his new lover in with him!

'I am not in the habit of making snap decisions, as you well know, Emily. Yes. I *am* quite certain that this is what I want. And, contrary to what people might believe, I have actually had a hell of a time trying to persuade Sophie that it is a good idea!' Dominic's mouth twisted wryly.

'You mean she resisted the idea of living with you?'

'It seems so.'

'I have to ask, seeing as it seems pertinent—are you in love with the girl, Dominic?'

Seeing no other reason that made sense for him to move the beguiling primary school teacher in with him, Emily satisfied herself that her supposition must be true—even though it was still hard to believe.

In love? Dominic didn't know about that. What did 'in love' mean, exactly? His father had schooled him so thoroughly in the art of containing emotion and not giving any credence to it that it was hard to know. He *did* know that Sophie was the most exciting and sensual creature who had come his way in a very long time: she was bright and without artifice, she hadn't set her cap at him for his fortune, and in bed they aroused each other to fever-pitch.

Dominic had no doubt he was *infatuated* with her. He'd met her at a time in his life when he no longer wanted to be alone—a time when he felt the need to share his life with someone, at long last. And Sophie perfectly fitted the bill. Yes…he had plenty of very persuasive reasons for making his little spitfire his mistress. Even just the thought of her could engender a tug of longing inside his chest. *But 'in love'?*

'You seem to be taking an inordinately long time answering the question, Dominic.'

Frowning, Emily reached for her wine and took a sip, her pale blue eyes considering her companion over the rim of her glass with concern.

'Of course I *care* for her, Emily. She is delightful, if you want to know the truth. You met her, so you must know that. She doesn't bore me, and she will no doubt keep me on my toes for a very long time. I think we will do very well together.'

'And how do you think a girl with no knowledge or experience of the kind of world you move in will cope with all the demands that that world throws at her?'

'I will teach her to cope. I told you she is very bright. I'm sure it will not be a problem.'

'And what about her own career?' Emily persisted, sadly seeing nothing but potholes ahead for the pair of them, because she knew the demanding nature of the man seated in front of her. 'She told me she loves her job. Do you think she'd be willing to give it up to put your needs first, Dominic?'

Dominic's hand tightened briefly round the stem of his wine glass, the question discomfiting him perhaps more than it should. 'She will have to,' he said, his green eyes slowly turning to resolute steel.

As she waited in the drawing room for Dominic to join her after his long-distance phone call, Sophie was still trying to shake off the horrible things that Diana had said to her and, worse, hating the fact that her doubts about being with Dominic had escalated. She was living in la-la land if she imagined this impending arrangement of theirs could possibly work.

Could she, in all honesty, envisage travelling to the primary school where she taught from this palatial house in Mayfair and trying to keep up the semblance of a normal life? And what would her colleagues think when they found out? She didn't have to be a brain surgeon to know that not everyone would be glad for her. If someone she'd considered a very good friend had not been able to wish her well, then what hope for people who knew her less well?

Twisting her hands together, Sophie walked around the room, her gaze alighting with interest and awe on some of the beautiful *objets d'art* on display in the walnut cabinets. There were pieces from all around the globe, which told her that Dominic must have been practically everywhere. What would he say if she told him that she'd only ever been abroad once? And that had been on a camping trip to France!

Her gaze lifted to study some of the stunning art that covered the walls. Feeling increasingly on edge, she let her glance settle on a lone birthday card in the middle of the mantelpiece. She moved towards it, her expression curious. Glancing behind her, to check that Dominic hadn't returned to the room, Sophie picked up the card, opened it, and read the words inside.

To Dominic on your thirty-sixth birthday. Best wishes from your parents.

He'd said nothing to Sophie about it being his birthday. He'd just invited her round for dinner, which his housekeeper was currently preparing. But, even more than feeling surprised because it was his birthday and he hadn't mentioned it, Sophie was stunned that he should receive such a curt, lukewarm greeting on his special day from his own mother and father. *Were they usually this formal with their own son? This cold?* Her heart constricting, she shivered and returned the card to its lonely place on the mantel.

Just as she did so, Dominic returned to the room. Sophie's gaze gravitated to him immediately. How could it not? Tonight he appeared to be even more handsome than ever, dressed casually in informal jeans and sweater, his shoulders filling out the deep blue cashmere with maximum heart-stopping impact.

'I didn't know it was your birthday,' Her smile was tentative as his expression seemed briefly to darken.

'I don't really celebrate birthdays, so it is not so big a deal.'

'Why not?' Immediately concerned, Sophie narrowed her blue eyes.

Shrugging, Dominic just stared back at her for a long moment, trying to garner his feelings on the matter and experiencing a very odd sense of embarrassment about being confronted with it.

'Why not? Because I choose not to. That's why not.'

He knew he sounded testy, and he disliked himself for it.

'That's no reason. I should think getting another year older and finding yourself in good health and in good circumstances is very much worth celebrating. I *always* celebrate my birthdays. It's the one day in the year that I make a point of having the day off work, if it falls on a weekday. And my mum always makes me a cake.'

'Lucky you.'

His sarcasm caused a spasm of pain to jolt inside Sophie's chest. Swallowing hard, she tried to rise above it. 'If you'd told me it was your birthday *I* would have made you a cake myself.'

'By all means make me a cake, if it makes you happy.'

He strode across the room to the drinks cabinet and poured a generous measure of Scotch into a tumbler. Watching him, Sophie wished she didn't feel like crying, but suddenly everything seemed so futile. She'd endured enough unpleasantness for one day and really didn't want to endure any more—least of all Dominic's hostility.

'Does it not appeal to you, my making you a cake?' she asked softly, trying to will him back into a more amenable mood.

Rounding on her, his green eyes cool as a glacier, Dominic put the tumbler of whisky to his lips and drank some before speaking. 'Why should it, when I can order myself a cake from the best bakery in the country if I wish? Or even from France?'

'*That's* not the same thing at all!'

Stung, Sophie stared at him as if she couldn't believe what she was hearing. 'Are you so far above everyone else that you can't see that something made with love is worth far more than something you can easily purchase with money?'

'Who said anything about love?'

His expression didn't warm one iota. If anything it became even colder. Shocked by his apparent disdain for her opinion, and his blatant disregard for her feelings, Sophie felt her feet were rooted to the floor.

'I didn't mean—that is to say I—' Struggling as the misery inside her escalated with the realisation that Dominic scorned the mere idea that she could love him, Sophie blinked hard to keep back her tears.

Leaving aside his drink, he stalked over to her and clasped her gently on either side of her arms. 'Make me a cake by all means—I'm sure it would be wonderful.'

But even as he spoke Dominic sensed that his placatory remarks might have come too late. Seeing tears shimmering in her lovely eyes, he wished he hadn't let his irritable mood taint their time together.

Sophie's mention of love had been a mere slip of the tongue, he was sure—her naïve way of trying to make him feel better. Added to that, he'd just heard from Geneva that there were problems already arising concerning the deal he'd struck, and it didn't exactly make him feel like dancing for joy. Now he was probably going to have to make a return trip to Switzerland to sort things out.

'It doesn't matter.' Sophie sighed. 'I'm hardly going to inflict my humble offering on you when you can easily buy some fabulous creation from Paris or somewhere! Let me go, Dominic. I want to go home.'

Immediately Dominic dropped his hands to his sides. 'I invited you to dinner,' he said through terse lips, irritated that she would not be so easily won round after his attempt at making the peace. 'And we have to talk about your moving in.'

'Well, I've changed my mind about staying. Clearly you'd prefer to dine alone on your birthday. Judging by the mood you're in, I'd say it was probably for the best anyway.'

'Don't leave. I might have to return to Geneva tomorrow. I don't know how long I'll be gone, and we might have to delay your moving in until I get back.' His brow creasing in frustration, Dominic found it hard to find a smile to coax Sophie into staying. Then an idea came to him—one that made increasing sense as it grew inside him.

'Come *with* me. Meetings will take up most of the day, but I always have a car at my disposal so you can do some sightseeing. Then in the evenings we can be together.'

Seeing the leap of hope in his eyes, Sophie nonetheless knew it was impossible. Plus, she didn't exactly feel eager to forgive him after the rebuff she'd received over her suggestion of making him a cake.

'I can't. Tomorrow the children are putting on a special Easter play for the parents. We've been rehearsing. Then the next day they're performing it for the rest of the school. It's a busy time for me.'

Biting her lip, she turned away, walking over to the couch where she had left her handbag.

'Have you forgotten about our arrangement? Surely I deserve more consideration than that? Or will your job always take precedence over the needs of our relationship?'

Hurt that he could believe she would be so intransigent, Sophie frowned. 'As part of a couple, of course I would always strive to compromise when things like this come up. Unfortunately the Easter celebrations are pretty much set in stone, Dominic. Performing in the play means a lot to the children. They've been rehearsing for weeks, and as their teacher I'm the only one who knows what's to be done. I couldn't possibly take time off during such a crucial time.'

She *hated* the fact that he was going away again when he had only just returned, but she was wary about expressing her true feelings when Dominic seemed to be setting the standard for the way their relationship would progress. He wasn't interested in her love. He desired her, and he wanted her to be with him because he was used to getting whatever he wanted *when* he wanted it, but so far he had not expressed any spirit of compromise whatsoever. The more she realised it, the more Sophie sensed their union could bring nothing but disaster for them both.

Her chest felt as if it had a huge rock inside it as Dominic's frosty gaze swept over her.

'So you won't come with me to Geneva?'

'I told you—I can't!'

'Then so be it. But when I return you and I are going to have to have a very serious talk.'

Did he mean that he was going to call off their plans? That he never wanted to see her again? Sophie knew she couldn't wait for however long Dominic was away in Geneva to hear the truth. The waiting and the nervous expectation of hearing the worst would likely *kill* her.

'Why don't we have that talk right now, rather than wait until you get back from Geneva?' Clutching her leather handbag stiffly between her fingers, Sophie stood her ground, feeling as if a chill factor of below zero had just swept in from the Arctic.

Used to calling the shots, Dominic would not be

moved. Even though he'd witnessed the treacherous wobble of her vulnerable bottom lip as she stood facing him, clearly expecting the worst. It hit him then that she must imagine he was going to suggest they part. The fact that Dominic intended no such thing, but merely wanted to lay down some important ground rules for their future relationship, caused relief and adrenaline suddenly to flood through his system. But it surely wouldn't hurt to play her along a little bit? It might after all make her think twice about putting the demands of her job over their relationship.

'No. We will wait until I return. Now, are you going to stay for dinner or not?'

Walking to the door, her head held determinedly high even though her heart was breaking, Sophie turned briefly to regard Dominic as he stood by the fireplace, beside that ominous lone birthday card that resided on the mantel.

'I'm not. Have a safe trip, won't you?'

CHAPTER ELEVEN

IT ATE at Sophie's soul that Dominic would be spending his birthday eating dinner alone. There he was, a man with more advantages and material assets than most people could dream of, and yet tonight he was all on his own in that big glamorous house in Mayfair, with just one abstemious birthday card from his parents on the mantel.

Did his friends not think Dominic's birthday was worth celebrating? Or perhaps he didn't *tell* them when his birthday was?

'It's not so big a deal,' he had explained, almost disdainfully. *But what if he hadn't meant that at all?* Sophie considered thoughtfully. What if secretly he would *enjoy* being made a fuss of on his birthday? If his parents were so reserved with their good wishes, perhaps he'd grown up taking their lead, and believing that birthdays weren't a big deal? But that didn't stop him from minding that they weren't celebrated.

Sophie's thoughts feverishly ran on. And if people around him perceived him as the man who had everything, how would they believe that he *needed* anything? Like simple good wishes and fun on his birthday? It was Sophie's opinion that when she'd left him Dominic had not looked like a man who had everything at all. She'd been left with the impression of something quite different.

The ridiculous feeling that she'd somehow abandoned him on his birthday wouldn't leave her alone for the rest of the evening. Finally, unable to bear her incessant fretting, Sophie ran herself a hot bath to distract herself. But as she lay back in the fragrant lapping water, trying hard to will the tensions of the day away, an even more worrying thought wormed its way into her thinking.

What if Dominic hadn't stayed alone when she'd left? What if he'd rung some *glamorous* female friend of his who was more than willing to come over and keep him company? Diana had more or less intimated that he was inundated by phone calls from women throughout any one week. What did that signify? That he could take his pick of women whenever he wanted? Surely they couldn't all just be 'friends'? Sophie groaned out loud in dismay. Unable to enjoy even the apparently uncomplicated simple pleasure of a long hot soak, she got out of the bath and with a heavy heart dried herself, then dressed in her night things and deliberately went to bed.

Returning the telephone receiver to its rest, Dominic rubbed ruefully at his throbbing ear. Having just spent the entire morning on a call to Geneva, trying to circumvent the need to fly out there at least for the next few days, he had achieved his object with not a small amount of difficulty.

The decision to postpone his trip had been reached last night, after barely doing justice to the beautiful dinner Maria had cooked for him. *A dinner he'd hoped to share with Sophie.* After he'd eaten Dominic had spent the rest of the evening in morose contemplation, finally picking up the birthday card he'd received from his parents, tearing it up and throwing the pieces in the bin.

He'd wanted to go round to Sophie's place there and then, to tell her that he'd rather spend the evening of his birthday with her than anybody else and apologise for being such a boor. But stubborn pride had stopped him. He wasn't used to admitting he might have been at fault, and he certainly wasn't used to apologising. And his antipathy to publicly owning to either of those two traits was so strong that he'd made himself spend the entire evening wallowing in misery rather than doing what his heart really desired.

However, *today* was a different matter. Having postponed the need to go to Geneva, Dominic vowed to do something about this intended agreement of theirs—and do it *now*. He picked up the telephone receiver once more and dialled out.

On playground duty, Sophie did up another button on her coat and crossed her arms in front of her chest to keep warm. The day—though bright—was particularly cold, and she envied the children tearing around—having fun, keeping warm, and paying no mind to the inclement temperature as only children could.

'Please, Miss… That man over there is waving to you.'

'Ashley!' Smiling down at the pretty five-year-old with her blonde curls, Sophie strained to hear the soft, sweet voice. 'What did you say?'

Crouching down to give her full attention to the child, she felt her heart start to beat wildly when she saw the little girl point to Dominic, standing outside the gates of the playground gazing in at her. The collar of his mackintosh was turned up, and his expression was hard to detect at the distance that separated them.

She couldn't believe he'd turned up at the school. *Wasn't he supposed to be flying out to Geneva today?* Fearful of what had brought him, and wondering what he was going to say, Sophie thanked the child and made her way towards him, self-consciously trying to pat down her wind-blown hair as she approached.

'Dominic! What are you doing here? I thought you were going to Geneva?'

'I postponed my trip. I rang the school office to speak to you, and they told me you were on playground duty. I wanted to meet you after school. I thought we could go and have coffee somewhere and talk?'

Even though they'd parted on uneasy terms, and she was still feeling sore, Sophie couldn't think of a single excuse to deny him just then. In truth, she was too happy that he *hadn't* left on his trip.

'Okay,' she agreed. 'School finishes in about an hour. I'll see you then.'

'Good.'

With an unexpected smile he briefly inclined his head, glancing over her shoulder at the children playing. 'Looks like you've got your hands full,' he commented wryly.

Something about that smile—the wary, almost cautious nature of it—as if he fully expected his conversational stance to be rebuffed—tore at Sophie's heart and caused her own enforced wariness to relent. Her lips parted in one of her brightest, sunniest grins.

'You don't know the half of it! But at least they're keeping warm tearing around, while I'm standing out here doing a good impression of an icicle!'

'I'll have to think of something to warm you up when I see you, in that case.' Dominic's emerald eyes briefly darkened, with palpable need and a flare of heat inside Sophie suddenly chased away the cold and made her tremble with longing.

'I'd better go. I daren't take my eyes off of this lot for a second!' She started to withdraw.

'After school then… Bye.'

He turned and walked away. Sophie watched him as he quickened his pace to cross the road: a tall, impressive figure with a bright crown of golden hair that would catch the eye of even the most short-sighted woman in the world and make her heart beat faster at the mere sight of him.

Louis opened the door of the Rolls and was ready at the kerbside waiting to help Sophie as she stepped out, closely followed by Dominic. Curious, she glanced around the busy London thoroughfare with its impressive array of up-market shops—mostly selling the kind of expensive items that she couldn't dream of buying on a teacher's pay—and wondered where Dominic was going to take her for coffee.

When he lightly touched the small of her back to direct her towards a nearby jeweller's, Sophie's shock was palpable. Especially when she read the inscription 'Jewellers to Her Majesty the Queen'.

Deliberately slowing on the pavement beside him, Sophie knew her blue eyes were clearly troubled as she commanded his attention. 'Where are you taking me, Dominic? I thought you said we were going somewhere for coffee?'

'I want to buy you some jewellery, Sophie—something to seal our agreement. Is that all right with you? I have made an appointment and we are expected.'

Sophie had truly believed that he was going to call the whole thing off, and instead he was professing to buy her yet another expensive gift—to 'seal' their agreement. She seriously needed a few moments to acclimatise herself to the idea. Last night Dominic had been morose and withdrawn, and what else should she have thought other than that he wanted to rescind his proposition? Indeed, Sophie had been mentally gearing herself up to hear him say the words that would no doubt herald the worst misery she had ever experienced.

But now, as she glanced at his usually guarded expression, she saw an intention blazing in his arresting gaze that couldn't help but make her hopes soar. 'After last night... I thought you might be having reservations about me coming to live with you,' she confessed, her eyes sliding away from his.

Because he had experienced the same doubt about Sophie's feelings towards him, Dominic experienced a strong upsurge of fierce satisfaction that she was still willing to go through with their agreement. *Especially* when he had behaved like such a jerk towards her last night. If she *had* changed her mind about their living together he would not have known what to do, he realised. For once in his life he would have been at a complete loss.

When he'd seen her in the playground of the school this afternoon, with the children running around her and her lovely face never wavering far from a smile, something hard inside him had melted. Like a large chunk of ice succumbing to spring sunshine. For a long moment the feeling had left him breathless. That unfamiliar *warmth* inside of him when he gazed at Sophie had illustrated with impact that her rejection would have been untenable. It would have seriously pained Dominic to let her go.

He had *never* felt such an attachment to anyone before—including his parents. It made him even more determined to have her by his side and introduce her to the privileged world he inhabited. No matter how cynical or shocked by his choice of lover his friends or family might be when they heard the news.

'We had an agreement, yes? I have no intention of reneging on it. It is what I *want*.'

It was not the answer that Sophie's heart ached for. Admirable though it undoubtedly was that Dominic was a man of integrity and honour, they were *not* the qualities she needed him to demonstrate right then. When he urged her onwards to their destination Sophie held back, hurt and doubt clouding her beautiful blue eyes as she continued to study him.

'Wait a minute, Dominic. We shouldn't just rush into this. More important than you buying me another gift is the fact that we need to talk about *us*.'

Surprise flitted across his handsome face. 'How much talking do we need to do, Sophie? We both know what we feel towards each other, don't we? I want you to move in with me, and the sooner we organise that the better.'

'That's what I mean, Dominic! You're making a lot of assumptions without even consulting me! It's just not practical for me to live in Mayfair—don't you realise that? Where I live right now, my school is only a bus ride away. It would take me twice as long to get there every day from your house!'

'Why are you worrying about bus rides? You can easily drive to school from where I live.'

It had seriously started to alarm Dominic that Sophie would even *think* of remaining in her own small house when they had already made what he considered to be a firm agreement that she would move in with him. She simply seemed set on creating difficulties where as far as he could see there *weren't* any.

'I can't drive anywhere Dominic...I don't have a car!

And, besides that, the West End traffic is too horrendous to make that feasible even if I *did* have one.'

'You're deliberately making a problem where there isn't one!' he concluded impatiently, drawing her away to the relative shelter of a shopfront awning, out of the jostling of hurrying passers-by. 'I'll happily buy you a car of your choice. And if you choose not to drive yourself to work I'll get Louis to drive you.'

Dominic didn't reveal to Sophie that he fully intended for her eventually to give up working as a teacher…quite *soon* after she moved in with him in, fact. So the thorny issue about how she would get there every day would no longer be a problem. He had months of business travel ahead, and he wanted Sophie with him. He had no intention of enjoying a relationship with her only to leave her behind when he went to work. Not when he wanted to experience more of this bewitching warmth he was feeling around her.

Sophie just about stopped herself from laughing out loud. The very idea that she would be dropped off each day at the school where she worked by Louis, driving the Rolls, was so ludicrous that it was like some unbelievable scenario in a comedy programme! But, staring dumbfounded into Dominic's completely serious face, she realised that the anomaly had not even struck him. He *was* just as she'd suspected that first day they had met, when she'd been splashed by that muddy puddle and Louis had pulled over. Protected by vast wealth and a lifestyle so far removed from the everyday concerns of most folk, he had no *idea* of the problems such a showy display of wealth might bring.

She would have happily been able to overlook the odd eccentricity on his part if he had loved her. But no amount of wishing and hoping would persuade Sophie now that there was even a possibility of such an event. Dominic wanted what he wanted, and right now, for some inexplicable reason, he wanted Sophie.

She had to ask herself would she be happy just being another acquisition for him, like some of those beautiful objets d'art in his walnut cabinets? She knew the answer straight away. Women like Diana might be open to entertaining such a situation, in return for experiencing wealth beyond their wildest dreams, but Sophie *wasn't*.

'Dominic, I really don't want to think about buying jewellery right now. Can you ask Louis to just drop me home…please? If that's not possible, I'll catch the tube.'

Sensing her determined withdrawal, Dominic felt shock and fury lace his gut in an angry cocktail. 'I cannot believe you are doing this! We had an agreement!'

A little vein in his forehead throbbed, and a wave of sadness rolled over Sophie at the realisation that he was probably just disappointed by not having his wishes fulfilled. If he had told her he needed her—or cared for her, even—she might have relented to this 'six-month' arrangement he'd been proposing. She might even have allowed herself to believe that Dominic *might* grow to love her eventually, and that they could make their union a happy and long-lasting one. But all she saw on his beguiling, handsome face right then was the petulant displeasure of a man who was not accustomed to being thwarted in any way.

'Some agreements *must* be open to renegotiation, Dominic. And this is one of them. You and I are too different to have a hope of making a relationship work. I think you really know that in your heart. You seem to see a relationship as something purely pragmatic, to fulfil a need, and I don't. As much as I've been hurt in the past, I don't want to give up on the idea of falling in love and spending the rest of my days with that person…rich or *poor*. I'm sure you'll think that's very naïve of me, and you're entitled to your opinion, but that's what *I* want. From what Diana has intimated you won't be without female company for long. Don't worry about giving me a lift. I'd rather catch the tube.'

And before Dominic could gather his wits and try and reason with her Sophie had joined the throng of passers-by travelling in the opposite direction. She was hurrying away from him, her expression determined, as if she couldn't escape quickly enough.

What had Sophie meant when she'd suggested that he wouldn't be without female company for long?

Pacing the large, some would say intimidating room that was his personal office, Dominic glanced out at the teeming rain that fell past his window and strove hard to will his misery away.

He'd been dissecting every part of their last conversation. From her accusation that he thought of a relationship between them as 'purely pragmatic,' to fulfil a need, to her confession that, in spite of being hurt in the past, she'd never given up hope of falling in love and spending the rest of her life with someone. *Rich or poor*.

He'd had sleepless nights because of that last part. Dominic wanted Sophie to fall in love with nobody but *him*. That desire had also come as a revelation. To realise that what he'd actually been craving all along was Sophie's love. He'd never wanted that from any woman before. He hadn't even believed in it. 'Emotions are notoriously unreliable,' his father had always taught him, and so Dominic had steered clear of emotional involvement ever since. Now he saw what *bad* advice he'd been given. He was tired of being alone. He *wanted* emotional involvement. He wanted it with Sophie.

Sighing, he remembered that Sophie had actually said that *Diana* had intimated that he wouldn't be without female company for long. If that was the case, then his assistant must have been discussing him with Sophie— and not in a good way, either.

Before he gave himself time to consider the thought further, he pulled open the adjoining door that separated his own office from his personal assistant's and marched straight over to her desk. In the middle of a phone call, Diana mimed, *Just a minute*, as Dominic leant over her, and was completely taken aback when he grabbed the receiver from her hand and slammed it down on its rest.

'What have you been saying to Sophie?' he demanded, his eyes glittering hard. At the sight of the swift colour that invaded the blonde's otherwise pale cheeks Dominic instinctively knew she had not been painting him in the best of lights to her friend.

'I don't know what you mean, Dominic.'

Her hazel eyes slightly panicked, Diana strove hard to retain her usually famous composure. Dominic blew hot and cold, she knew that. He could lose his temper with her one minute, then buy her a gift or treat her to lunch the next, in gratitude for all her hard work.

'Did you suggest to her that I might be seeing other women?' He came straight to the point, his chest constricted with fury that his own PA might have soured things for him with the woman he wanted to be with.

Dominic knew he'd played his part in driving Sophie away. He was quite aware that he'd tried to steamroller her into moving in with him, scarcely taking her wants and needs into consideration at all. But two days had gone by since she'd left him standing outside the jeweller's in Grafton Street, and he'd had plenty of time for reflection about what had happened, since. *He hadn't liked what he'd discovered about himself, that much was certain. But he didn't like being lied about either.*

It was true he had many female friends, but he certainly wasn't having sexual relations with any of them. Other than the odd one-night stand, to meet the most basic of functions, he'd steered clear of personal involvement until he'd met Sophie!

'I said that sometimes other women rang you at work,' Diana admitted, reddening even more. 'But when I said that I wasn't trying to suggest that you were having relationships with those women, Dominic.'

'And if you were in Sophie's shoes, and a friend said that to you, what would *you* think she meant?'

Before she could answer his question, Dominic swung away from the desk and paced to the other side of the room and back. 'I have a feeling that you have been saying other things to Sophie, Diana…perhaps not very complimentary things about me? Is that right?'

Feeling herself pushed into a corner, Diana sighed in exasperation. 'What you must understand about Sophie, Dominic, is that although she's a teacher, she's actually quite naïve in many respects. Sadly, she has some ridiculous idea that you want her to move in with you! Naturally I had to help her come to her senses.'

'Naturally.'

Dominic didn't know how he held onto his temper as he stared at the ice-cool blonde whose secretarial and organisational abilities had, up until now, always impressed him. 'If Sophie told you that that was what I wanted, why didn't you believe her? Is your friend accustomed to telling you lies?'

Seeing Diana flinch at that, Dominic was even more

furious with the woman for letting Sophie down than himself. Knowing the kind of warm, generous person Sophie was, he concluded that she deserved far *better* friends than Diana.

'Anyway, she told me she didn't want to get involved with another man for a long time! Her previous boyfriend went to bed with his best friend's girlfriend, and Sophie was devastated. She's totally cynical about relationships. I even had to practically blackmail her into coming to my wedding, she disapproves of them so much! And then she turned up covered in mud, looking like she'd been on an assault course with the army!'

Out of pure frustration and annoyance with Sophie, for putting her in such an awkward position with her boss, Diana was resorting to plain vindictiveness to protect herself. It made Dominic see his personal assistant in an entirely different light from the one he'd seen her in before, and he didn't *like* what he saw. No matter how busy or in demand he was, he'd always prided himself in choosing good staff. He liked to think that he had reasonably good intuition, as well as first-class interviewing skills when it came to the selection process. Now he realised that he might have made a mistake where Diana was concerned.

In Dominic's opinion, although he didn't ever particularly strive to be liked by anyone, he viewed loyalty to one's friends as paramount—unless it was proved in some way that that loyalty was misplaced. Diana had more than demonstrated that she felt no loyalty towards Sophie whatsoever. If she had badmouthed Dominic in any way to her, then clearly she did *not* have Sophie's interests at heart. Yes, Dominic had female friends that he occasionally liked to wine and dine, but true to his word he had mostly avoided more intimate associations because all they did was leave him feeling soulless. *Until Sophie…*

'I think you owe your friend Sophie an apology.' His voice was level, but his blazing green eyes nonetheless spoke volumes as he settled them on Diana. 'Knowing the kind of person she is, no doubt she will accept it. But I truly hope, for her sake, that she has nothing whatsoever to do with you again after that. In light of the current situation, we need to have a very serious talk Mrs Carmichael. Ten o'clock tomorrow morning in my office. Don't be late.'

Before Diana could even blink in astonishment, Dominic had stalked back into his office and slammed the door.

CHAPTER TWELVE

'SOPHIE...might I have a word?'

Victor Edwards's calm tones cut through the fog that had descended on her mind, and Sophie glanced up from the text on childcare she'd been only half reading. Still in a daze, she pushed to her feet.

'Of course.'

Following him out of the staffroom and along the echoing tiled corridor to the headmaster's office, Sophie was glad that Victor was mainly silent, because she really didn't feel like talking much. In his office he offered her a chair and a cup of coffee, and while he attended to the pouring of the coffee she tried hard to will her expression into one of composure. Unfortunately she knew that right now her emotions were precariously poised on a cliff-edge, and she hoped that whatever he had to say wasn't going to open the floodgates and tip her over.

It had been a week since she'd left Dominic standing outside the jeweller's and walked away. *A whole week and since then...nothing. No letter or phone call. Not even to acknowledge that what they had had between them was over. And each day that passed seemed like a lifetime...*

'There you are. White, one sugar—just as you like it.'

Beaming at her like some kind of fond uncle, Victor carefully placed the cup and saucer on the desk between them. Retrieving his own drink, he sat in the somewhat tired-looking leather chair that had been an integral part of his office for years, and linked his hands together in front of him.

'How long have you been with us, Sophie? I think it's three years now, isn't it?'

Where was this leading? Looking across at him, her attention suddenly switching to full alertness, Sophie blinked. 'I can hardly believe it myself but, yes…it is three years.'

'And you have enjoyed your time with us?'

Shifting uncomfortably in her seat, Sophie's spine prickled in anxiety at what might be coming next.

'I've enjoyed it very much. Is there something wrong, Headmaster? Is it something to do with my work?'

She really hoped not. No matter how she was feeling—good or bad—Sophie always strove to give of her best once she was in the classroom with the children. They might come from all kinds of family backgrounds, each with their own attendant problems, but the kids wouldn't ever receive negative vibes from her.

'There's nothing wrong, Sophie, and especially not concerning your work. No, my dear, I am sorry if I've alarmed you unwittingly. It's just that I know how dedicated you are, and how eager you are to progress, and a post has come up in another school that I think you might well be interested in. As much as I would hate to lose you, I thought it was only right to bring it to your attention.'

Victor paused for a moment to glean Sophie's reaction. Momentarily mesmerised by the startling cornflower-blue of her pretty eyes, he quickly glanced away to rifle through some papers on the desk in front of him. Then, regaining his composure, he gave Sophie a brief smile. 'Now, the position won't actually be available for another six months, but in the meantime they are interviewing prospective candidates, and if you are interested I would be very happy to arrange an interview on your behalf.'

Her interest definitely captured, Sophie leaned forward in her seat, her gloom put determinedly aside as she listened to Victor outline the very appealing benefits of this new post in another school...

Immersed in stripping wallpaper off the walls in the living room, in a bid to spring-clean her life, Sophie cursed beneath her breath when someone rang on the doorbell. She hated being interrupted when she had the bit between her teeth, but she wiped her wet hands down the front of her faded jeans and baggy overshirt and went to see who'd had the audacity to disturb her.

'Diana!'

All kinds of emotions clamoured inside Sophie at the sight of her friend, but the one most prevalent was sadness. They'd been friends for about four years now, since Sophie had temped as a secretary in the summer holidays leading up to her final exams. They were very different people, but somehow they had hit it off. Diana had introduced Sophie to lots of new and exciting experiences, and the two women had had fun together. Now, Sophie was shocked to find her at her door, a not-so-confident smile on her attractive face, and holding out a bouquet of spring flowers.

Sophie kept her hands deliberately down by her sides. 'What can I do for you?'

'I've been a bitch. I know it. I've come round to apologise and to tell you that I would like to be your friend again. Any chance?' Grimacing, Diana held out the flowers again.

Sophie accepted them...albeit reluctantly. It didn't

mean, however, that she was going to run full-tilt back into a full-on friendship with Diana again. Diana had said some dreadful things, that had really hurt, and Sophie realised that though she was willing to forgive, it wouldn't be so easy to forget. Pushing her fringe out of her eyes, she briefly sniffed the perfume emanating from the flowers and tried to get a handle on her emotions. Since she'd broken up with Dominic she'd turned into a real water fountain—crying at the drop of a hat at the slightest thing. Even though she'd told herself it was pathetic, she couldn't seem to help herself.

'I need some time to think about that, Diana,' she said quietly.

The blonde frowned. 'Can't I come in for just a minute? I can't talk to you properly out here on the doorstep.'

'I'm decorating, and everywhere is in a mess.'

'I don't care. It's you I've come to see, not your house!'

'Just for a minute, then. I really need to get on.'

Her chest feeling hollow, Sophie turned and walked back down the corridor, then turned off into the kitchen. She put the flowers in the sink and ran some water into the basin around the stems. Hearing Diana come in behind her, she turned slowly and folded her arms across her chest. Diana appeared as immaculate as usual—her make-up perfect, looking slim and elegant in an understated black trouser suit with a cream camisole. In comparison, dressed in her old jeans and shirt, with vestiges of dust in her hair, Sophie knew she must look a fright.

'What did you want to talk about?'

'Apart from telling you again that I'm truly sorry for the abominable way I behaved? *Dominic.*'

'What about Dominic?' Striving to keep her voice

level, not to let the other woman see how his name alone could unravel her, Sophie stared.

'He loves you.'

'What did you say?'

'I said he loves you! All those things I said to you, I said because I was jealous. You're pretty as a peach, you've got a great figure, and a career you love—and then someone like Dominic comes along and snaps you up! Not *that* many women ring him up at work, Sophie, and the ones who do are only friends. I promise. I've been his PA for three and a bit years now. If he was having a relationship with any of them don't you think I'd know?'

All Sophie had really heard was what Diana had said first. *Why was she taunting her with such lies? Hadn't she done enough damage already? Of course Dominic didn't love her!* As far as Sophie was able to conclude, he was *incapable* of loving anyone. Such a tender and strong emotion was just not part of the man's make-up. Whatever he'd learned as a child, it wasn't how to love…

'I don't want to hear any more, Diana. Please, just go, will you? I need to pop out to the hardware shop before it closes, and I don't have time to stand around and chat!'

Striding to the door, Sophie was totally taken aback when Diana caught her by the arm and pulled her back into the room.

'What do you think you're doing?' Shaking her arm free, she felt her cheeks go pink with indignation.

'You idiot!'

'What did you call me?' Hands on her hips, Sophie stared at the other woman as if she'd gone quite mad.

'You're not listening to me, Sophie! Dominic loves you! Doesn't that mean anything to you?'

A week ago it would have meant the whole world...*if it were true*. But, wherever Diana had got her information from, Sophie knew it was clearly a lie. The man hadn't even phoned her to see if she was all right. Was that an example of someone who *loved* her?

'And how do you come to such a blatantly untrue conclusion?'

'Because I've seen how he's been during the past week since you walked away and left him! He's not the most even-tempered guy at the best of times, but in the past week he's been hell on wheels! Do you know I've just about held onto my job by the skin of my teeth?'

Diana shook her head from side to side, remembering the scalding interview she'd had with Dominic where he'd read her the Riot Act and warned her that if she ever interfered in his personal business again she would be looking for another job. He'd told her the only reason he was keeping her on at all was because of her past exemplary record—but one step out of line and that would be it.

'He was furious with me for telling you about other women ringing him up at the office. Since then not a day has passed without him asking me if I've heard from you. Go and see him, Sophie. Put the both of you out of your misery!'

Could what Diana was saying be true? Sophie hardly dared hope. But *if it were true* she still couldn't understand why Dominic had not contacted her first. Then a stunning thought came to her. *Was stubborn pride getting in his way?*

Nobody liked being rejected, and Sophie had walked out on him when he'd been intent on buying her something nice—a piece of jewellery to cement their decision about living together. Even if her reasons had been sound ones, her actions *must* have caused him hurt. She remembered the lone birthday card from his parents on the mantel, the curt, minimalist greeting which was no loving greeting at all, and her heart just about turned over inside her chest with dismay.

'I—I can't just drop in on him unannounced. He might be busy. He might have visitors. He might—'

'Sophie?' Diana grabbed her by the wrists and smiled. 'Stop looking for excuses. Go and change out of those old clothes, put some lippy on and I'll run you over to his place. I'm meeting Freddie for a picnic in Hyde Park, so it's on my way. Now, go!'

'I need to stop off somewhere first. Do you mind?'

Diana gave her a little shove. 'Not if you hurry up!'

'Miss Dalton. What a pleasant surprise.'

Andrews answered the door, an unreserved smile on his lined face as he surveyed a nervous Sophie, standing on the step carrying a large white box.

'Hello, there. I was wondering if Dominic was at home?'

Now she'd come this far Sophie knew she would feel entirely foolish were he *not* at home. She didn't know whether she would be able to pluck up the courage to make a second attempt at a later date. Already adrenaline was shooting through her veins, making her light-headed as she considered the very real possibility that she might have made a terrible mistake.

What if he didn't love her at all? What if all Diana's convincing summations about the state of his feelings towards Sophie were wrong?

'Yes, miss. Mr Van Straten is in the drawing room,'

Andrews replied, holding the door wide for Sophie to come in.

'Is he alone?' She bit her lip, anxious that if he had company she wouldn't get the opportunity to say what she'd come to say.

'Yes, miss. Quite alone.'

Andrews discreetly left her at the drawing room doors with a smile, and told her to go on inside. Waiting until his footsteps had receded down the hall, Sophie took a deep, bolstering breath and, still carrying the white box, opened the door and walked in.

Dominic was seated in an armchair, a newspaper spread out on his knees and his eyes closed. From discreetly placed speakers drifted the languorous sounds of some gentle piano music. As quietly as she could Sophie managed to close the twin doors behind her. As the catch made a soft 'snick' Dominic's eyes flew open, and he stared at Sophie as though she were some ghostly figment of his imagination.

'Sophie.'

He neither smiled nor rose from his chair.

Feeling suddenly unsure about her own temerity, Sophie started to walk towards him. 'I took a chance that you'd be in,' she told him, her voice a little throaty because of nerves. 'I—I hope you didn't mind?'

'Mind?' He swept aside his newspaper and drove his fingers through his hair—as a person would when they were disturbed unexpectedly and were conscious of feeling momentarily vulnerable. But his unfathomable emerald eyes locked unsettlingly onto Sophie's and made her heart jump. 'No. Of course I don't mind.'

For a disturbing moment Dominic felt as if he couldn't breathe. He'd been dreaming about her, and waking to find her there in the flesh had been a shock...*if a wonderful one.* She looked sexy and pretty, in tight blue jeans, white shirt and a pale blue tweed jacket, her dark hair naturally settling softly around her lovely face. *If she is part of my dream still, then please let me dream it a little longer,* he thought with feeling.

'I've brought you something.'

Smiling, she put the box onto his knees and stood back while he lifted the lid to reveal a large iced cake.

'What's this all about?' His voice unwittingly husky, Dominic frowned.

'It's a birthday cake,' Sophie explained, her cheeks turning rose. 'You didn't have one for your birthday, and I thought you should. I'm only sorry that I didn't make it personally. But then again you might well have been sorry if I had. I'm not exactly the world's greatest cook. If my baking does turn out all right, it's more by luck than judgement, I have to say—'

'Sophie?'

'Yes, Dominic?' She stared as he put the box down beside the chair and rose to his full intimidating height. Her pulse started to race.

'Did you come and see me only to bring a cake?'

'No.' Her feet rooted to the floor, Sophie searched her mind desperately for the right words. 'I came to tell you I was sorry I just left you standing there like that. I know you meant well when you said you wanted to buy me something. It's just that everything happened so quickly, and I got scared when I realised what we were contemplating... Especially when you didn't—when you—'

'I love you, Sophie. In fact I'm quite crazy about you. I should have told you when I took you to the jeweller's, but I was scared too.'

'You were?'

'Love makes you vulnerable. I've never been vulnerable in my life, as far as I know. To love someone and to have them love you back—that is an awful risk, Sophie. One I was admittedly too scared to contemplate.'

'Life is a risk, Dominic,' Sophie replied tenderly. 'And as far as I can tell you've embraced that with both hands, or you wouldn't be as successful as you are. I *do* love you. So now I'm taking a risk too. We're in this together, Dominic.'

Sophie stared at him hard, barely daring to believe that this amazing man had just confessed that he loved her and that it scared him.

Stepping towards her, with a gentle brush of his fingers Dominic touched her cheek. 'I never believed in falling in love until I met you,' he admitted, smiling. 'You made me hot, yes. But love? It has quite taken me by surprise. My family are in for quite a shock, I think.'

'They don't believe that you could fall in love either?'

'My parents are pragmatists, Sophie. They never leave anything to chance. But when they meet you and get to know you I hope that they will grow to love you too.'

'Even if they don't, Dominic, it doesn't matter. I'll be quite content just to have your love.' Her voice falling to all but a whisper, Sophie stood up on tiptoes and kissed Dominic gently on the lips.

The touch of her mouth, damp and soft, made him groan and pull her hard into his chest. In just a few explosive seconds, he was on fire for her, his body primed to seduce her, needing the release of hot loving that only she could provide.

But before he could persuade her that making love would be good for both of them—and hopefully she wouldn't need *that* much persuasion—he had to know why Sophie had come back to him. Especially when he'd been certain that all hope of seeing her again was lost.

'How did you know?' he asked, briefly holding her away from him to study the expression in her eyes. 'How did you know that I must be in love with you?'

'Diana came to see me. She more or less told me that she thought you were missing me and had concluded that you must be in love with me.'

Dominic wasn't surprised that Sophie had entertained her friend's company once again. He'd never known a more generous-hearted woman than her. The warmth that he'd grown to feel around her seemed to expand inside his chest. 'Ah.'

'Yes, and I've got something else to tell you too.'

Needing to touch him more intimately, Sophie slid her hand down his shirt, her palm feeling the tremendous heat he exuded with a little thrill inside her. 'I've applied for a new teaching job.'

'Oh?' Knowing that this might be a bone of contention between them, even though they'd agreed they were in love, Dominic studied her animated face with silent reservation. He had several weeks' business travel ahead of him, and he was not looking forward to leaving Sophie behind for even a single day—let alone weeks at a time.

'It's at a progressive new school in Westminster, and if I get the post I'll start in six months' time.'

'Six months?' Dominic grabbed her hand where it was sliding up and down his chest, provoking him into a near spin, and deliberately stilled it. 'What does that mean, Sophie? Does it mean you can take some time off to go on honeymoon?'

'Honeymoon?' Sophie felt faint.

'Of course. I want you to be my wife, Sophie. Not my mistress.'

Sophie felt her heart race, her lip quivering helplessly with joy. 'Are you sure, Dominic?'

His serious loving gaze left her in no doubt. 'I am not accustomed to saying things I'm not sure of Sophie. Surely you know *that* much about me by now? Will you marry me?'

This was one time when Sophie didn't have the slightest doubt about the answer she would give him. 'Yes, Dominic. I would love to marry you!'

It was hard to keep his elation hidden—and for once in his life Dominic didn't even try to hold back his emotions. 'Thank God for that! You know you would have destroyed me if you'd said no?'

At the mere idea that she could hurt the man she loved and cause him untold pain Sophie felt quite ill. 'I would never do that to you, Dominic. Not in a million years! Although, would it be possible—I mean, would you mind—if we only had a very small wedding?'

She almost held her breath while she waited for his response. To her relief, he chuckled. 'Knowing your aversion to weddings, my love, I would not have expected your request to be any different. Of course... Whatever you want Sophie. Now, tell me what this new job of yours means.'

'It means that—if you wanted me to—I could give up my current post and take a few months off so that we can be together. And if I get the job in Westminster in six months' time—and it's been hinted at that I stand a very good chance—I could practically walk to work!'

As he let out a long slow breath, the crease between Dominic's dark blond brows disappeared. 'So...it was meant to be.'

'What was meant to be?' Allowing him to steer her firmly into his arms, Sophie smiled up at the contemplative expression on his handsome face.

'You and me. The fates have conspired to help us be together, so it seems.'

'You believe that?' Her big blue eyes awed, Sophie sucked in her breath.

'I am beginning to believe many outlandish things since I have met you, Sophie darling!'

And before she could say another word to delay the thing that he most wanted to do, Dominic brought his lips down onto hers and kissed her soundly…

PUBLIC WIFE, PRIVATE MISTRESS

BY
SARAH MORGAN

Sarah Morgan trained as a nurse and has since worked in a variety of health-related jobs. Married to a gorgeous businessman, who still makes her knees knock, she spends most of her time trying to keep up with their two little boys, but manages to sneak off occasionally to indulge her passion for writing romance. Sarah loves outdoor life and is an enthusiastic skier and walker. Whatever she is doing, her head is full of new characters and she is addicted to happy endings.

Sarah Morgan pulled up and ran past the stone parked in a cavity of roughly... land plus. Above... on... When she saw... who still cares... for... As soon as she came across of her inner... in her grip with their own... blur... too much... It must be... as well... and... persuade... looking... to... looking blue... she say that... in the... infinite... She said is the... such... is the... despair... to her... who... want... for... room... the woman that it... rather herself... from them... an immersive care... obvious to that primary cares of... past... looking... the others I know... to woman... ... Woman ally

CHAPTER ONE

SHE was *not* going to die.

Rico Crisanti, billionaire President of the Crisanti Corporation, stared grimly through the window that separated the relatives' room from the intensive care unit, oblivious to the dreamy stares of the nurses working on the unit. He was used to women staring. Women always stared. Sometimes he noticed. Sometimes he didn't.

Today he didn't.

His gaze was fixed on the still body of the girl who lay on the bed, surrounded by doctors and high-tech machinery.

The jacket of his designer suit had long since been removed, tossed with careless disregard for its future appearance over the back of a standard issue hospital chair, and he now stood in a state of rigid tension, silk shirtsleeves rolled back to reveal bronzed forearms, his firm jaw grazed by a dark stubble that made him more bandit than businessman.

For a man as driven as Rico, a man accustomed to controlling and directing, *a man accustomed to action*, the waiting was proving to be the worst kind of torture.

Waiting for anything was *not* his strong point.

He wanted the problem fixed now. But for the first time in his life he'd discovered that there was something that he couldn't control. Something that money couldn't buy.

The life of his teenage sister.

Rico swore softly under his breath, fighting the temptation to punch his fist through the glass.

He'd been at the hospital for the best part of two weeks and *never* had he felt so helpless. Never had he felt so ill-equipped to solve a problem that confronted him.

Blocking out the muted sobs of his mother, grandmother, aunt and two cousins, he stared in brooding, frustrated silence at the still figure, as if the very force of his personality might be sufficient to rouse her from her unconscious state.

There must be something more he could do. He was the man with a solution for everything and he *refused* to give up.

He sucked in a breath and tried to think clearly, but he'd recently discovered that lack of sleep, grief and worry were not a combination designed to focus the mind. Fear had induced a mind-numbing paralysis that was becoming harder to shake with each passing hour.

Trying to clear his head, he inhaled deeply and ran a hand over the back of his neck, clenching his jaw as his mother gave another poorly disguised sob of distress. The sound cut like a blade through his heart. The expectation of his family weighed on him heavily and for the first time in his life he knew what it felt like to be truly helpless.

He'd flown in a top neurosurgeon who had operated to relieve the pressure on Chiara's brain caused by the bleed. She was breathing on her own but still hadn't recovered consciousness. Her life hung in the balance and no one could predict the outcome. No one could answer the question.

Life or death.

And if it were life, would it be life with disability,

or life as Chiara had known it before the horse had thrown her?

He swore softly and raked strong fingers through his hair. To Rico, that was the hardest aspect to cope with. The exquisite, drawn out mental torture of waiting. He'd seen his mother worn down by it, had watched the black shadows grow under her eyes as she lived under the cruel shadow of uncertainty on a daily basis. *Had watched her wither slightly as she was forced to ask herself whether this would be the day when she lost her only daughter—*

Suddenly his own powerlessness mocked him and had he not been too drained for laughter, then he would have laughed at his own arrogance.

Had he really thought that he could control destiny?

The vow he'd made to his father, the vow he'd made to look after the family, seemed suddenly empty and worthless. What did it matter that he'd created an empire from nothing but dust using only fierce determination? What did it matter that his success in building that empire had been nothing short of staggering? Somewhere along the way he'd started to believe that there was nothing he couldn't control. Nothing he couldn't do if he set his mind to it. And it had taken this accident to remind him that no amount of riches could protect a man from the hand of fate.

Driven by the monumental frustration of doing nothing, he loosened another button on his silk shirt with impatient fingers and paced the room, his long strides and the confined space combining to provide little in the way of relief. Emotion, as unwelcome as it was unfamiliar, clogged his throat and for the first time since he was a small child he felt the hot sting of tears threaten his usually icy composure.

Cursing his own weakness, he closed his eyes and rubbed long fingers along the bridge of his nose as if he could physically hold back the building pressure of grief.

It would help no one if he crumbled.

The whole family was on the edge, grasping on to fragile threads of hope extended by grim-faced doctors. His was the strength that they used. The rock that they leaned on. If he caved in, gave in to the desire to howl like a baby, then the morale of the whole family would disintegrate. The game they were playing—the game of hope—would be ended.

So instead he stared in brooding silence at the bruised, immobile body of his sister, willing her to wake up, and he was still staring when the door opened again, this time to admit the doctor who was in charge of his sister's case together with several more junior doctors.

Ignoring the minions and the immediate response of his own security team to this latest intrusion, Rico's attention zeroed in on the man in charge, sensing from his manner that he had news to impart. Suddenly he was almost afraid to ask the question that needed to be asked.

'Any change?' His voice was hoarse with strain, lack of sleep and something much worse. The fear of prompting bad news. 'Has there been any change?'

'Some.' The doctor cleared his throat, clearly more than a little intimidated by the formidable status of the man standing in front of him. 'Her vital signs have improved slightly and she regained consciousness briefly,' he announced quietly. 'She spoke.'

'She spoke?' Relief flooded through him and for the first time in days he felt lighter. 'She said something?'

The doctor nodded. 'She was very difficult to under-

stand, but one of the nurses thinks that it was a name.'
He hesitated and looked at them questioningly. 'Stasia?
It sounded like Stasia. Could that be right?'

Stasia?

Rico froze, momentarily stunned into shocked silence, while behind him his mother gave a strangled
gasp of horror and his grandmother gave another wail.

Rico gritted his teeth and tried to shut out the sound.
He would have done anything to banish his well-
meaning family to the privacy of his estate but he knew
that, for the time being, that option was out of the question. They needed to be here with Chiara. It was just
unfortunate that their hysterical display of emotion was
making his job harder, not easier.

And now that Stasia had been mentioned the situation
was about to deteriorate rapidly.

The mere sound of her name was enough to detonate
an explosion within his family.

And as for his own feelings—

He closed his eyes briefly and rubbed long fingers
over his bronzed forehead. With his sister fighting for
her life, he didn't need to be thinking about Stasia. It
seemed that fate was determined to make further efforts
to crush him.

The doctor cleared his throat. 'Well, whoever she
is—could she be brought to the hospital?'

Ignoring his mother's moan of denial, Rico forced
himself to focus on the main issue. His sister's recovery.
Somehow he voiced the words. 'Would it make a difference?'

'It might.' The doctor shrugged. 'Difficult to say, but
anything is worth a try. Can she be contacted?'

Not without considerable emotional sacrifice.

His mother rose to her feet, her face contorting with anger and pain. 'No! I won't have her here! She—'

'Enough!' Rico felt the ripple of curiosity spread through the medical team and silenced his mother with one cool, quelling flash of his unusually expressive black eyes.

It was bad enough that the world's press was camped on their doorstep, tracking every moment of their darkest hour, without supplying them with further fodder for gossip.

Stasia.

How ironic that this should happen now, he reflected, when the connection between them was about to be severed permanently. He had thought that there was no circumstance that would ever require him to lay eyes on his wife again. For the past few months he'd had a team of lawyers working overtime to draw up a divorce settlement that he thought was fair. Enough to buy her out of his life and leave him with a clear conscience to marry again. This time to a gentle, compliant Italian girl who understood what it meant to be the wife of a traditional Italian male.

Not a fiery English redhead who was all heat and spark and knew *nothing* about compliance.

He sucked in a breath as a clear vision of Stasia— *wild, beautiful Stasia*—flared in his mind and he felt the immediate throb of raw sexual heat pulse through his body. It had been a year since their final, blistering encounter and despite the distasteful circumstances of their parting, his body still craved her with almost indecent desperation. *And he didn't trust himself to see her again.* She affected his judgement in ways that he didn't want to admit, even to himself.

Despite everything she'd done, Stasia was as addictive as any drug and seeing her again was *not* a sensible move. In the past year he'd learned to hate her, had learned to see her for what she was.

A mistake.

Rico paced back to the window and studied his sister in brooding silence, an ominous expression on his handsome face as he reviewed his options. They were depressingly limited. Reaching the unpalatable conclusion that his own needs and wishes had to be secondary to the issue of his sister's recovery, he forced himself to accept that he was going to have to see Stasia again.

He'd fully intended to end the entire fiasco of their marriage through lawyers and there was no reason why this couldn't still happen, he assured himself swiftly. This was just a temporary stasis in proceedings. He could fly her out and she could do whatever needed to be done and then he could have her flown home again.

It was entirely possible that they could avoid all but the briefest of conversations. Which would suit him perfectly. He had no desire whatsoever to indulge in any reminiscence of the past. *And even less desire to spend time with the woman.*

He gave a grim smile, knowing that the irony of the situation wouldn't be lost on Stasia. Dazzling, unconventional Stasia. The woman who had never conformed to his family's perceptions of the perfect Sicilian wife.

Or his.

He'd given her *everything*. Had done everything a husband should do. And still, apparently, it had not been enough.

The doctor cleared his throat discreetly and Rico stirred, making the only decision that he was in a position to make.

'I will send for her.' He turned to Gio, his head of

security. 'Contact her and make arrangements for her to be flown out immediately.'

He caught the startled glance of the man who'd known him from childhood, heard the shocked gasp of his mother and gritted his teeth as he battled to come to terms with the fact that he was going to have to do the one thing he'd promised himself that he'd never have to do again. Come face to face with Stasia.

One day soon he was going to put her behind him, he vowed. One day soon he'd be able to think of her without feeling an instantaneous reaction in every male part of himself. And the sooner that day came the better.

Anastasia put the finishing touches to the painting, stepped back with her eyes narrowed and gave a nod of satisfaction.

Finally. Finally it was ready.

Mark would be pleased.

With a final glance at the canvas, she cleaned her brush and then wandered out of her studio into the kitchen, flicking on the kettle and reaching for a pile of post that had been accumulating over the past two weeks while she'd been concentrating on her painting.

Still leafing through her post, she reached across to switch on her mobile and it rang immediately.

Knowing that it would be her mother, she answered the phone with a smile. 'How's business?'

'Business is booming.' Her mother sounded excited. And confident. Miles removed from the terrified, mouse-like woman she'd been, after Stasia's father had walked out with a blonde half his age, six years earlier.

Stasia gritted her teeth, trying not to remember that awful time. She'd been in her first year at university and if ever she'd needed evidence that depending on a man, any man, was not a good idea, she'd been given it in spades. Her mother had relied on her father for everything, and when he left she'd been totally unable to cope. Had lost all belief in herself.

It had been Stasia who had pointed out that her mother knew a great deal about antiques. Stasia who had helped her put that knowledge to commercial use by opening a small antiques business. Gradually the word had spread and soon her mother wasn't just selling antiques, she was advising clients on furnishing entire houses. And six months ago, thanks to a generous business loan, they'd expanded their premises and business was booming.

'We're going to have to employ more help, Stasia,' her mother was saying briskly. 'I need to go on a buying trip and I've been invited to a stately home in Yorkshire to advise on restoring some of their antiques and obviously I can't just close the shop. People travel from all over the country to visit. It wouldn't be fair on them if we closed. And you're too busy painting to help.'

Stasia smiled. It was wonderful to hear her mother so animated. 'You're running the show, Mum,' she said lightly, throwing a pile of junk mail into the bin. 'Employ away. The painting is finished, by the way. Mark can collect it whenever he likes.'

'Marvellous. I'll tell him, if I see him before you do. And how are you, darling? Are you eating?'

'Yes.' It was a lie. She hadn't done much eating at all in the last year. Since leaving Italy, her emotions had been so disrupted that eating no longer seemed important. But she didn't want her mother to worry. 'I'm fine, Mum. Truly.'

Her mother sighed. 'Which means you're still pining after that Sicilian.' Her voice took on a hard edge. 'Take it from me, Stasia, men like him never change. I should know. I lived with your father for all those years and he was exactly the same. I was just a possession and when he got bored with me he purchased something new.'

Stasia heard a car negotiating the potholes in the lane outside the cottage and snatched at the excuse to end the conversation. 'I can't talk now, Mum—I've got a visitor. It's probably Mark about the painting. I'll call you later.'

Without giving her mother time to protest, she hung up and switched off the phone, releasing a long breath. She adored her mother but that was one conversation she wasn't prepared to have with anyone.

The car came to a halt and Stasia pulled a face. She didn't really want to see Mark. He made no secret of the fact that he wanted more from her than her paintings and she wasn't ready for that. Maybe she never would be.

Glancing down at her paint-spattered jeans, she gave a rueful smile. She looked a mess. But if Mark insisted on dropping in without phoning first, what could he expect?

Anticipating the knock before it came, she opened her front door and froze in shock as she saw who stood there.

Rico Crisanti.

Billionaire and bastard.

The last person in the world she'd expected to see.

Her heart lurched, the whole world tilted, and for a wild, ecstatic minute she thought he'd finally come after her. And then reality struck and she remembered that it had been a year and that he was in the process of divorcing her. Which could only mean that he was here for an entirely different reason. And, whatever it was, she wasn't interested.

'No!' Her immediate impulse to slam the door in his face was thwarted by swift action on his part. Clearly he'd anticipated her response to his arrival and in a powerful movement he slammed a hand in the centre of the door, resisting her attempts to close it.

'You don't answer your mail and you don't have a phone,' he launched savagely, dark eyes connecting with hers with the lethal force of a missile, 'and you bury yourself in a place so remote that it is almost impossible to find you.'

'And it didn't occur to you that maybe I didn't *want* you to find me? If I'd wanted you to find me then I would have left a forwarding address.' She glared at him, previous hostilities rising to the surface with such frightening force and speed that for a moment she struggled to breathe, swept away on a tide of emotion. 'And if I'd thought there was *any* chance at all that you'd even look for me then I would have buried myself even deeper,' she shot back hoarsely, suddenly wishing she'd done just that.

But it had never entered her head that he'd come after her. Not after those first miserable months where she'd done nothing but stare out of the window, desperately hoping to see one of his flashy sports cars pull up outside wherever she was living. Gradually she'd grown accustomed to the knowledge that he wasn't coming after her.

That it was well and truly over. Ended with an explosion of bitter emotion every bit as intense as the fiery relationship that had gone before. She'd walked out. He hadn't followed. And that had said everything there was to say about their short, fragile marriage. To him it hadn't been worth saving. It had been an unmitigated disaster and she'd already promised herself that if she *ever* fell in love again it would be with a safe, mild-mannered, modern Englishman, *not* a blisteringly ruthless, own-the-world Sicilian whose attitude to women was firmly embedded in the Stone Age. Who thought that the answer to everything was money.

She stared at him furiously, her gaze drawn by the power of his broad shoulders, the arrogant tilt of his handsome head and the dangerous glint in his cold, hard eyes. It was wrong for one man to be so indecently sexy, she thought numbly, trying valiantly to ignore the kick of her heart and the sudden quickening of her pulse. She didn't want to respond like this. It was this response that had involved her with him in the first place.

Against her better judgement.

But Rico Crisanti was not a man that women ignored. He was indecently good-looking and the aura of power that he wore with the ease of a designer suit attracted women like sharks to blood-infested water.

And she'd proved as vulnerable to his particular brand of macho Sicilian sex appeal as all the others.

Suddenly aware that he was staring over her shoulder into her cottage, she saw the flicker of surprise cross his handsome face and had a wild and totally inappropriate impulse to laugh. Rico Crisanti, Italian billionaire and business tycoon, owned six homes around the world and had probably never been anywhere remotely like her tiny cottage. At another time she would have teased him about it, but they were way beyond teasing.

The differences in their attitudes and approach to life were so far apart that nothing could bridge them. He believed that a woman's place was at home, waiting for her man, whereas she wanted to get out of the home, grab life by the throat and rattle it hard.

He was frowning, night-black eyes glittering with a mixture of incredulity and amazement. 'What *is* this place?'

The desire to laugh vanished. 'My *home*, Rico,' she said stiffly. 'And you're not welcome in it.' She didn't need the reminder that he'd never even seen the cottage that she loved so much. *That despite their marriage he knew so little about her. Knew so little about the things that mattered to her—*

She made another futile attempt to close the door, knowing that it was a waste of time. In a battle of strength she would be the loser. Rico Crisanti was six foot three and powerfully built. Even without looking, she knew that somewhere close by would be a car full of bodyguards. Their constant presence had always amused her because no one with reasonable vision could ever doubt that Rico could handle himself physically if required to do so. He was an expert in martial arts, supremely fit, with the body and the stamina of an Olympic athlete. But the billionaire President of one of the most successful companies in the Western world was a prime target for corporate kidnapping and extortion and he had no intention of making access to him easy.

Stasia subdued a hysterical laugh.

If he was kidnapped then it would mean taking a day off work, and that would be more challenging for Rico Crisanti than any form of torture.

The man was driven.

He couldn't function without work and she'd loved to tease him about that fact. On one occasion she'd even hidden his mobile phone and he'd gone ballistic—until he'd discovered exactly *where* she'd hidden it.

She lifted her chin, trying not to remember those early ecstatic days of their relationship. Before reality had set in. Before they'd discovered that they had absolutely nothing in common. 'So how *did* you find me?'

'With considerable difficulty and much personal inconvenience,' he bit out harshly. 'And already I have wasted too much time. My pilot is refuelling as we speak. We need to be back in the air within the hour.'

Stasia gaped at him with the same blank astonishment with which he'd assessed her cottage. His pilot was refuelling? They needed to be in the air within an hour? What exactly was he saying?

'We?' She shook her head and gave a humourless laugh. 'I presume you're using the royal "we." You can't possibly mean you and me.'

They hadn't even spoken for a year. *Not since that night—*

He'd accused her. Matching his temper, burn for burn, she'd walked out without even bothering to defend herself, so angry with him that she hadn't trusted herself to speak. Hadn't trusted herself not to do him physical damage.

If she'd needed further evidence that they just couldn't live together, that they were just too different, then she'd had it that night. And if a small part of her had secretly hoped he'd come after her—*fight for their relationship*—then that part of her had soon been disappointed.

They hadn't seen each other since. He'd seen and he'd judged. End of story.

'In my vocabulary "we" means you and I,' he snapped impatiently, 'and, despite your constant digs about my lifestyle, I have *never* had delusions of grandeur.'

That may probably be true, she conceded, and yet in Sicily and Italy he was treated like royalty.

It had been another one of their shared jokes—Cinderella and the Prince.

But neither of them was joking now.

Why would he possibly want her to go anywhere with him?

They both knew that she wasn't what he wanted in a wife.

And yet here he was, standing in her doorway, his broad shoulders almost obliterating the light. And it wouldn't have surprised her to discover that Rico could control night and day. He had control over almost everything else. He was a man who led while others followed.

And something had led him to her door.

'I can't imagine what possessed you to come here when you know full well that I'd never agree to go anywhere with you again. I gave up being a groupie a year ago.'

Had given up being a slave to sex, because that had been the only level on which they had truly connected. Whatever else had gone wrong between them, the sex had always been amazing.

Instead of the incisive retort she'd been expecting, a tense silence followed her declaration. Anticipating the usual verbal sparring, Stasia braced herself and then registered the tension in his broad shoulders and the signs of strain stamped on his flawless features. With a sudden feeling of unease, she realized that he looked tired. And Rico Crisanti was never tired. He had more stamina than anyone she'd ever met. He'd frequently kept her awake all night only to leap out of bed at dawn to attend a business meeting, leaving her to sleep off the sex-induced exhaustion brought on by a night of continual love-making.

Something was very wrong.

She glanced behind him and noticed his driver and two bodyguards that she didn't recognize.

She frowned. 'Where's Gio?'

During the brief period of their marriage, she'd grown fond of Rico's head of security and she knew that he was much more than an employee to Rico. A fellow Sicilian who had known Rico from birth, Gio was frank and straightforward and was rarely far from Rico's side. He'd made Rico's protection and privacy his personal crusade.

'He is at the hospital.' Rico's tone was terse. 'He's the only person I trust to keep the mob at bay.'

His words sank in slowly. 'Hospital?' She frowned. 'Why is he at the hospital? What's happened?'

'Chiara had an accident. She came off her horse.' He delivered that piece of news in clipped tones, his voice displaying not a flicker of emotion. 'She is in a coma. I assumed you would have seen the papers. The story has been everywhere.'

Chiara was in a coma?

'I don't read newspapers any more.' She'd had enough of featuring in newspapers when they had been together and she had every reason to loathe the press. Since they'd parted, she'd stopped reading newspapers of any sort. Stasia stared at him. 'Is she badly injured?'

'*Si.*' He seemed to sag in front of her and she felt a flicker of concern.

She'd never seen Rico like this before. He looked grey. Exhausted. Like a man at the very limit of his reserves. Instinctively she stepped to one side. 'You'd better come in.'

He followed her into the cottage, stooping slightly to avoid banging his head on the door, a frown drawing his ebony brows together as he glanced around him. 'Why are you living like this?' He glanced round him, distaste evident in every angle of his handsome face as he surveyed her tiny sitting room with the one ancient sofa. 'Are you short of money?'

Temporarily forgetting her concern, she felt the anger bubble inside her. With him, everything came down to money. It never occurred to him that she might choose to live in this cottage because she liked it.

'My life is none of your business.' How could she *ever* have fallen in love with a man who was so emotionally stunted? 'You didn't show any interest in it before, so I don't see why you would now.'

'You do *not* need to live like this. You are my wife—'

The ultimate status.

If the pain hadn't been so great she would have laughed. 'I like living like this. And I was *never* your wife, Rico,' she said shakily, brushing aside the fiery red curls that threatened to obscure her vision.

The gesture caught his attention and his shimmering black gaze fixed on her wild mane of hair with almost primal fascination. The tension in the room suddenly increased. For a moment both of them had forgotten Chiara, too absorbed in each other to make room for the pressures of the outside world.

'I married you.'

Clearly he thought it was the biggest honour he could have bestowed on her and she suppressed a bitter laugh.

How could she have forgotten his unshakeable arrogance?

'An impulse that we have both lived to regret.' Stasia wished he'd stop staring at her hair. She recognized that look in his eyes and it was all she could do not to groan out loud. She knew he was seconds away from sliding a possessive hand into her tangled curls and exposing her throat to the heat of his mouth. The seductive stroke of his fingers in her hair had always been a prelude to the most incredible mind-blowing sex. Her breathing quickened. She did *not* want to think about that now! 'It wasn't a marriage in the proper sense. Marriages are about sharing and we never shared anything except sex.'

Incredible, blisteringly exciting sex, the memory of which still deprived her of sleep.

His gaze shifted reluctantly from her hair and settled on her pale face and she knew that his thoughts were running in the same direction as hers. 'I am *not* here to relive every painful moment of our disastrous marriage. But, like it or not, until the divorce is final you are still my wife,' he delivered, his slightly thickened tones betraying his physical response to her. 'As my wife I need you back in Italy. Don't misunderstand me—I have no intention of resurrecting our relationship in any shape or form. This visit isn't personal.'

Pain shafted through her.

Not personal.

She had known that, of course. So why did hearing him state the truth feel so brutal? Why did it hurt so much?

'Of course it isn't personal. Why would I even think that it might be?' Five minutes he'd been in her house. Five minutes and she was ready to scratch and claw until she drew blood. He just made her so *angry*. 'Our marriage was never personal. That was the problem. What we had was legalized sex.'

She heard his sharp intake of breath, saw the streaks of colour appear high on his cheekbones. She could almost taste his own anger. And yet he didn't deny it. How could he when they both knew it was the truth? The sex had been amazing but their relationship had never been any deeper than that. At least, not for him. For her it had been everything.

He was the love of her life.

Which made the whole situation so much more depressing.

'I'm not here to discuss our marriage.' His tone was a cold warning to change the subject and if she hadn't been so miserable and so furious with him she would have laughed at his complete inability to tackle anything emotional.

'Of course you're not. You'd prefer to divorce me without discussion,' she threw back angrily. 'You prefer to communicate through lawyers in sharp suits.'

His anger matched hers. 'You were the one who walked out on our marriage.'

'Because we didn't have a marriage! You didn't trust me! You didn't share with me! Every decision that had to be made, you made it without so much as a flicker of consideration for *my* opinion. And I hardly ever saw you! Which makes it all the more incredible that you're here now when you could have sent one of your minions. It must have been incredibly difficult for you to bring yourself to see me in person.'

His jaw was set hard. 'I'm not afraid of difficult.'

'Then why have you been communicating through lawyers, Rico?'

'*Dio*, this is *not* the time for this discussion!' He

looked at her with blinding hostility, his body language blatantly antagonistic. 'And I'm not asking you to come back to Italy for me. I'm asking you for Chiara.'

The burning anger was rapidly replaced by shame.

She'd forgotten Chiara. How could she have done that? How could being with Rico drive everything else from her mind?

'Naturally I'm sorry she's been injured,' she muttered stiffly, 'but I can't see why you want me in Italy.'

'You are part of the family.'

Astonishment diluted her anger and her mouth fell open. 'You're *seriously* pretending that you want me by your sister's bedside? What is this? A sudden show of family solidarity?' She gave a disbelieving laugh. 'It's a little late for that, Rico.'

She'd *never* been part of his family.

They'd made it clear from the first that they considered her to be a gold-digger, an accusation that should have been utterly laughable given her complete lack of interest in material things. But it hadn't been laughable. It had been tragic. Wrapped up in their own prejudices, they hadn't bothered to get to know her well enough to understand the things that mattered to her. Instead they'd gone out of their way to exclude her. To make her feel like a complete outsider. He'd married her without consulting them—without even inviting them to the wedding—and they'd blamed her for that. To them it had been further proof that she'd married him in a hurry, just to get her hands on his money. She wasn't what they had wanted for Rico and they hadn't been afraid to show it.

He gave a growl like a goaded tiger and his eyes flashed dangerously. '*Madre de Dio.* My sister's life is hanging in the balance and still you malign my family?'

She stilled, shocked by the news that Chiara was so seriously injured. 'She might *die*?' Her voice was a croak and she swallowed hard, suddenly understanding the reason for all the signs of extreme stress that he was displaying. He adored his little sister. 'She is that seriously injured?'

His eyes closed briefly and he let out a breath. 'They told us yesterday that they think she will live, but with what measure of brain damage—' he gave a fatalistic shrug '—they will not know until she wakes up properly. So far she has only uttered a few words.' His expression hardened. 'So you see that your criticism of my family is badly timed.'

'I said nothing bad about your family,' she said tonelessly, quelling her natural desire to defend herself against his accusation. He truly had *no* idea of the true situation. When it came to his family he was utterly blinkered. 'Only about my relationship with them. And I had no idea that Chiara's life was hanging in the balance.'

'She has been in a coma for more than two weeks. She has had brain surgery—'

Genuinely disturbed by that news, Stasia extended a hand in an instinctive gesture of sympathy only to let it fall again as she met those hard, cold eyes.

His look spoke volumes.

Don't touch.

Hands off.

She no longer had the right to deliver comfort of any sort.

Not that Rico Crisanti was a man who expected another's sympathy. He didn't let anyone that close.

Not even his wife.

She withdrew, both physically and mentally, her will

to fight shrivelled by his total indifference to her presence.

Once he hadn't been indifferent. Once he hadn't been able to keep his hands off her. He'd thirsted for her, *starved for her* and his obsession with her had been the biggest aphrodisiac going.

But she wasn't going to think about that now. Thinking about her relationship with Rico would be a fast route to self-destruction. And she really shouldn't care any more. She really *didn't* care.

She lifted her chin and exercised some of the self-control she'd been forced to learn while she had been living with his family. 'I'm truly sorry to hear about Chiara,' she said quietly, 'and of course I'll help in any way I can, but I really can't see why you would want me there.'

Chiara had made it perfectly clear that Stasia wasn't a welcome member of the family.

Rico ran a hand over the back of his neck and drew in a deep breath, as if he were forcing himself to deliver his next statement.

'She has been asking for you—'

Stasia stared at him, her green eyes wide with shock. Of all the things she'd expected him to say, the fact that Chiara had been asking for her had not been among them. 'Chiara *asked* for me? You have to be joking!'

It was the wrong thing to say.

'*Dio*. You, who always accused me of taking life too seriously. *Do I look as though I'm joking?*' His eyes blazed in his handsome face and she took an involuntary step backwards, startled by the violence of his response.

Clearly he wasn't joking. And if she needed confirmation of the degree of stress that he was under, then she had it now. It was so unlike Rico to reveal anything of his feelings, to display the slightest loss of control, that for a moment she couldn't respond.

'It's just that I find it hard to believe she asked for me—'

His outraged reaction to her mumbled statement was instantaneous. 'I thought we agreed that we are *not* raking over old wounds here,' he bit out harshly, pacing across the room and narrowly avoiding knocking his head on a beam. He lifted a hand to the offending beam and for a moment she thought he was going to try and rip it out of the ceiling with his bare hands. Instead he glanced upwards with a look of incredulity, as if he couldn't quite believe that anyone could have designed a house like this one. 'This cottage is a death trap.'

'It probably wasn't designed for someone of your build,' she muttered, wishing that he'd just leave. He dominated her small sitting room with the width of his shoulders and the force of his powerful personality and everything she'd spent months trying to forget came flying back into her mind.

Like the way it felt to kiss the bronzed skin at the base of his throat. And the fact that if she did that he'd instantly retaliate by sliding a hand down her spine and taking her mouth. And Rico had turned kissing into an art form.

Memories crowded her mind and suddenly she needed him to leave with almost fevered desperation. Before she forgot that this was the man who had broken her dreams into tiny pieces. *Before she forgot that she felt absolutely nothing for him any more.*

But he showed no sign of leaving. Instead he stood with his legs planted firmly apart, determined to defy the beams and her ill-concealed hostility. 'Since her accident two weeks ago she has emerged from an unconscious state only once and your name was the only word she uttered. *Your name.*' That fact clearly offended him and he made no attempt whatsoever to hide his contempt and distaste for the situation in which he now found himself. 'And, whatever you may think to the contrary, Chiara was very fond of you.'

Stasia stared at him in fascinated silence, wondering how a man so ferociously intelligent could be so blind when it came to his family.

She might have told him that Chiara was anything but fond of her. She might have repeated the many painful conversations she'd had with his sister when he'd been locked away running his fantastically successful global business empire leaving her to the mercies of his family.

Chiara *hated* her.

The teenager had resented her almost from the moment Rico had married her and she'd played a large part in the final destruction of their doomed marriage.

But Rico adored his sister. And Stasia had decided that it wasn't her place to tell him the truth; that she didn't want to be responsible for creating a rift in that famed Sicilian institution: 'the family.'

Deep in thought, she contemplated what could possibly have driven Chiara to ask for her. She knew nothing about the workings of the unconscious mind.

Guilt?

A subconscious desire to apologize? A sudden realization that she'd been in the wrong?

There was a discreet cough from the doorway and Rico turned impatiently, visibly irritated by the intrusion.

'Enzo is on the phone, sir.' The bodyguard looked apologetic. 'The plane is ready for take-off.'

Rico sucked in a breath and turned back to her, his body language purposeful and impatient. 'We need to go now. I have to be back at the hospital. Already I have wasted too much time coming here in person.'

A fact he clearly regretted. He had the look of a man who would rather be anywhere else but standing in this cramped front room with a woman he despised, and Stasia was in no doubt whatsoever that had he believed that someone else could have persuaded her to board his plane then he would have immediately delegated the task. But he'd known that she would try and refuse. And he'd been forced to deal with the situation himself.

He really expected her to go with him.

After everything that had happened, he really expected her to go with him.

Suddenly she regretted not answering the phone. At least then she would have had some warning of his impending arrival. She would have been able to prepare herself mentally for the shock and pain of seeing him again.

If she'd known what was coming she could have gone into hiding.

Or would she?

If Chiara was truly asking for her—if she was as badly injured as Rico was implying—how could she refuse to go?

How could she deny the girl the opportunity to apologize if that was what she needed?

She licked dry lips, knowing that she would never be able to live with herself if something happened to Chiara and she had refused to visit. The girl had been unbelievably cruel but Stasia was more than ready to forgive her. She'd always hoped that one day Chiara would find the courage to tell the truth.

But how could she go back there? *Back to where it had all happened.* And to face his family, who hated her so much, who'd thought she was so unsuitable for Rico.

She closed her eyes briefly and accepted the inevitable. Facing the enemy seemed less daunting than facing her own conscience should the unthinkable happen to the injured girl and she'd failed to visit. 'Give me five minutes to pack a bag.'

Rico let out a breath and some of the tension left his broad shoulders and it was only then that she realized that he'd been expecting to fight a battle. She suppressed a cynical smile. He obviously didn't realize that her taste for battles was long gone.

'You don't need to pack. You took nothing when you left.'

'I left everything because there was nothing I needed.' She met his gaze full on, the message clear in her eyes. *I was never interested in your money and I can't believe you don't know that.*

The only thing she'd ever needed was *him*, she thought sadly, and that had been the one thing he'd failed to understand. Clearly accustomed to women who craved access to his bottomless bank account, he'd been totally bemused by her indifference to his staggering wealth.

For a man driven by money and power, something as simple as love was as difficult to understand as a foreign language. And the more jewels and extravagant presents he'd given her, the less she'd felt like a wife and the more she'd felt like a mistress. It had been as if he was *paying* her for sex.

Reminding herself that all that was in the past, she

glanced down at her paint-stained jeans. 'At least let me change.'

She was past caring what his family thought of her but even she drew the line at entering a hospital covered in more paint than her easel.

'You can change on the plane,' he stated immediately, already striding towards her door, very much in control as usual. A man used to commanding those around him.

And she was going along with it. *But only for Chiara.*

She shook her head, exasperated with herself. She was independent in every sense of the word. And yet when Rico snapped his fingers she jumped. Every time. *And usually into his bed.*

But not this time.

Never again.

She closed her eyes briefly, suddenly overwhelmed by the enormity of what she was about to do. Did an alcoholic take a job in a brewery? Did a drug addict surround himself with illegal substances? And yet here she was about to walk off with the one man who made her forget the very person she was.

She must be mad.

Mad to put herself through the torture of being close to Rico for a teenage girl who had never shown her the slightest degree of warmth or friendship.

Aware that Rico was still watching her, impatience stamped all over his handsome features, she walked towards the door, her palms suddenly clammy and her heart thudding uncomfortably in her chest.

'All right. But this is going to be a short visit,' she muttered, her green eyes fixed on his, not allowing him to evade the issue. 'I see Chiara, I talk to her, I leave.

And you have your fancy plane waiting to bring me home.'

In normal circumstances she would have preferred to walk barefoot from Italy than avail herself of one of the trappings of his incredible wealth but these were not normal circumstances and she wanted to spend as little time as possible in the company of his family.

His lips curled. 'You can rest assured that I have no intention of prolonging your visit any longer than necessary.'

Of course he hadn't. Anger and misery mingled inside her. This had to be as difficult for him as it was for her. He'd made no secret of the fact that he'd made an enormous mistake in marrying her. That she wasn't the type of woman he wanted to have a permanent place by his side. *Just in his bed. Or any other available flat surface.*

She tried to ignore the intense shaft of pain that stabbed through her body, and reached for her keys and her bag. For a brief moment her eyes flickered to those wide shoulders, displayed in all their glory by the fabric of his perfectly cut designer suit. He had a fantastic body and from the first glimpse she'd been addicted. Dressed, the man was spectacular enough, but *undressed*—

The sudden memory of sleek, bronzed skin, of powerful muscle and dark, masculine body hair exploded into her brain and she shook her head slightly, trying to free herself from the seductive image imprinted on her mind.

As if sensing her sudden shift in thought pattern, he turned and their eyes locked with a fierce, mutual awareness that simply intensified the images in her brain.

Fire and flame surged between them and she felt herself take a step towards him in an instinctive response to the wild attraction that still existed.

For a brief moment something burned in his dark eyes and then it was extinguished and all that was left was ice.

She stopped dead, rendered immobile by the contempt she read in that cold gaze, remembering too late the two lessons that her marriage to Rico Crisanti had taught her.

That attraction, however powerful, was a shaky and precarious basis for a relationship.

And that loving someone with every beat of her heart didn't mean happy ever after.

CHAPTER TWO

'FEEL free to use the bathroom. You know where it is.'
Rico was sprawled on the cream leather seat, his laptop
computer open next to him, papers covered in figures
spread across the desk. As usual, his ear had been stuck
to the phone since the moment they'd become airborne
and he'd barely glanced in her direction since she'd sat
down and fastened her seat belt.

Nothing changed.

Stasia closed her eyes, flayed by his indifference and
furious with herself for caring. She didn't care. She really didn't. It was just the shock of seeing him.

And of course she knew where the bathroom was. It
was next to the bedroom. The same bedroom where
he'd once carried her, laughing and crazily in love with
him. *The same bedroom where he'd once made love to
her for an entire flight.*

Her eyes opened and her gaze settled on the door at
the back of his sumptuous private jet.

She'd spent twelve painful months trying to put it all
behind her. Trying to free herself of the agonizing wanting and needing that tore into her at unexpected moments. Was walking through that door going to undo
the little progress she'd made?

Oh, hell. It was just a bedroom, she reasoned, rising
to her feet in a determined movement and pacing to the
back of the plane, feeling the thick cream carpet give
under her feet. And anyway, she didn't have to go near
the bedroom. She'd just wash off the paint and make

herself decent enough to face his disapproving, dependent family.

Rico was talking on the phone again and her hand stilled on the handle of the bedroom suite as she listened.

When she'd first met him she'd loved to hear him speaking Italian.

It didn't matter what he was saying. He could have been reading the financial pages of a newspaper and still the sound of his voice would have made her stomach turn over and her body tremble. He'd teased her about it but she hadn't cared.

Rico speaking Italian was verbal seduction.

Not wanting to relive those early days of their relationship, days that had been dominated by the most unbelievable sexual excitement, she opened the door to the bedroom suite and locked herself in the stylish bathroom.

She didn't want to think about the beginning of their relationship.

The only way she was going to survive the next few days was to remember the reasons why it had ended.

She stared in the mirror, noticed the splodge of paint above her right eyebrow and gave a wry smile.

She looked nothing like the wife of one of the world's most successful businessmen.

Which was probably why they were currently in the throes of a divorce, she thought numbly, turning on the taps and splashing her face with cool water in an attempt to remove the paint and tone down the colour in her flushed cheeks.

She was completely wrong for him.

But wasn't that what had first attracted Rico to her?

The fact that she was different from his usual diet of models and actresses?

He'd been attracted to her because she was different, but ultimately it had been those very differences that had driven them apart.

Reaching for a towel, she dried her face and studied her reflection. What had Rico seen in her, that day in Rome? What was it about her that had driven him to approach her? Despite her resolve not to think about it, her mind wandered.

She'd been balanced on scaffolding, working on the mural she'd been commissioned to paint on one wall of the foyer. As usual when she drew or painted, she'd been totally absorbed in her art and it was only after she'd completed the intricate task she'd set herself that she'd suddenly been aware that she was under scrutiny.

She glanced down and almost lost her balance.

In a country that appeared to be populated by gorgeous men, he was the most staggeringly sexy man she'd ever seen. Unmistakably Italian, breathtakingly good-looking and staring at *her*, those scorching dark eyes raking every inch of her with blatant male appreciation.

'Is everything OK?' Her Italian was embarrassingly bad so she used English, hoping that he would understand her.

Since she'd started painting the mural on one wall of the foyer of the international headquarters of the Crisanti Corporation, a steady stream of people had stopped and watched her but she'd never felt remotely uncomfortable. In fact she'd hardly noticed them. But no woman could fail to notice this man. He was unreasonably handsome and she had to stop herself from drooling as her artist's eye roved over his perfect bone structure and the strong, symmetrical planes of his face. Her fingers twitched and if she'd had a pencil handy she would have sketched him instantly. Which would have been a frustrating exercise, she acknowledged dreamily. No two-dimensional drawing would ever be able to reflect the strength and power of the man in front of her.

He stood like a god, confident and all-powerful, and there was something about his cool, steady gaze that made her uncharacteristically nervous.

Noticing that the foyer seemed unusually full of people for the time of day, she glanced at his companions, noted their build and the respectful distance they kept, and finally realized just exactly who was scrutinizing her so closely.

She hastily descended the ladder and wiped the palm of her hand down her jeans before extending it. 'I'm Anastasia Silver. I'm a commercial artist. I was awarded the contract for painting your mural.'

Your mural—

She cringed as she heard herself speak. As if someone in Rico Crisanti's position was going to know or care who was decorating his office building. He undoubtedly left decisions like that to lesser mortals and concentrated his legendary brain power on amassing further millions to add to his already staggering fortune.

His hand closed over hers and she almost gasped at the strength and power of that grip. Aware that his gaze had shifted to the wall that she'd been painting, she followed his gaze, suddenly seeing it through his eyes and feeling a lurch of horror. Ideally she liked to work on a project in private until it was completed, but in this case it hadn't been possible.

'You're probably thinking that it looks terrible but it

always does at this stage. It's hard to imagine what it will look like when it's finished. In many ways the preparation is as important as the final painting. I—your architect approved my drawings and colour sketches,' she tailed off lamely, aware that his attention was now fixed firmly on her face.

'Are you always this tense? If so then I'm amazed you can wield a brush,' he murmured, bestowing her with an unexpected smile. 'Relax, Miss Silver. I like what you're doing to my wall.'

His wall.

He made it sound intimate. Personal. As if the wall was part of him.

Flayed by the seductive charm of that smile, Stasia felt her knees wobble and the colour rise in her cheeks.

Utterly self-conscious and not liking the feeling one little bit, she bit her lip and took a few steps backwards, suddenly realizing what a mess she must look.

'I'm covered in paint.' She lifted a hand to her burning cheeks, just hating herself for being so gauche when she should have been cool. 'I must look a total mess.'

His smile was the smile of a male well aware that if a woman was worrying about her appearance then he was home and dry.

'*Not* a mess. And I love your hair,' he assured her smoothly, registering her extreme discomfort with no small degree of amusement. 'So many shades of gold and copper blended together. It reminds me of England in the autumn.' His dark eyes scanned her hair in minute detail as if he were determined to memorize every strand. 'Apart from the white spotted bits.'

Feeling a deadly warmth spread through her body, Stasia fingered her wild curls. 'It will wash out.'

One dark eyebrow swooped upwards. 'The autumn gold? I hope not.'

'The white spots,' she muttered, glancing around her and wondering what the rest of his entourage was making of this ridiculous conversation. 'The first thing I do in the evening is get rid of the paint.'

He nodded, his gaze suddenly thoughtful. 'I should very much like to see you without the paint, Miss Silver. You will have dinner with me tonight.'

His arrogant assurance that she'd say yes outraged her intellect but her body was already trembling with anticipation. 'I might be busy.'

He smiled. The smile of a man totally confident in his own appeal. 'Eight o'clock. And you won't be busy.'

Still unable to believe that Rico Crisanti had asked her out, Stasia had to remind herself to breathe. 'Sure of yourself, aren't you?' She lifted an eyebrow in mockery. 'Is that a legacy from your Roman ancestors? Do you have the same fundamental need to conquer, pillage and plunder, I wonder?'

'That depends on the prize.' Dark eyes rested on her mouth with masculine fascination. 'And I'm not Roman, Miss Silver. I'm Sicilian. And we have a very different way of doing things.'

Without waiting for her to reply, he finally lifted his gaze from her mouth and strolled across the foyer towards the lift, followed at a respectful distance by his minions.

Stasia stared after him, stunned into a silence driven by disbelief. Not Roman. *Sicilian.*

Rico Crisanti, one of the richest and most powerful men in the world, wanted to have dinner with her.

For a wild, impulsive moment her heart leaped and her imagination followed.

And then reality interceded.

What would a man like Rico Crisanti want with her?

Compared to his usual diet of sleek, rich women she was a mongrel.

Her slim shoulders tensed and her mouth fell open at his arrogance. He'd just *assumed* that she'd want to spend an evening with him.

But then what woman would ever say no to him?

Confronted by temptation in its purest form, Stasia reminded herself that he hadn't even asked where she was staying so it was highly unlikely that he'd turn up at eight. And if he did—

She climbed back up the scaffolding and tried to continue with the design on the wall, ignoring the fact that her concentration was broken and her hand wasn't quite steady.

If he did, then she'd just have to tell him that she didn't have dinner with strangers.

Dragging her mind back to the present, Stasia showered and quickly plaited her heavy mane of copper hair so that it fell in a neat tube between her narrow shoulder blades.

Then she turned her attention to the wardrobe.

There were numerous designer outfits, all quite formal and not to her taste but towards the back of the rail she found a simple linen dress in a soft shade of peach. Simple in all but cost, she thought wryly as she caught a glimpse of the label. It was miles away from her usually colourful, casual style but it was that or paint-spattered jeans so she slipped it on anyway. One critical glance in the mirror told her that it suited her.

She looked elegant and classy.

Like a fortune hunter?

She bit her lip and then dismissed the thought. It was too late to start worrying again about what his family thought of her. Far too late.

She left the luxurious bathroom, chin held high, and settled herself back in the cream leather seat.

Rico was still on the phone and she gritted her teeth, remembering how many times she'd threatened to throw his phone away when they'd been together. She stared blankly out of the window, feeling steadily sicker as she contemplated the meeting ahead of her.

She actually hadn't seen Chiara since that fatal evening a year previously—

It was a moment or two before she realized that Rico had finally stopped talking and had transferred his lean, muscular length to the seat next to her.

'I'm sorry to just abandon you like that,' he said in cool tones, stretching out a hand for the drink that the uniformed hostess had prepared for him. 'There were calls I needed to make. That dress suits you.'

The unexpected compliment startled her and when his broad shoulder brushed against hers she had to stop herself from jumping back in her seat. She felt the tension spread through her body, felt the exaggerated beat of her heart against her chest as her body responded to his nearness. She breathed in his tantalizing male scent and suddenly all her senses throbbed and hummed. He was her power source. One touch and her entire body sizzled with sexual energy.

Angry with herself, she shifted in her seat.

What was the matter with her?

How could she still want him, knowing what sort of

man he was? Knowing that he didn't want her anywhere other than the bedroom?

Not once in their relationship had he actually said he loved her. So how had she managed to fool herself, even for a short time, that he might?

Because of the way he held her and touched her, she acknowledged miserably. For a short, blissful time she'd confused the touch of a man in love with that of a man who was a skilled lover. *Not* the same thing, as she'd eventually discovered to her cost.

Discreetly moving so that their arms were no longer touching, she glanced at him, attempting to match the indifference he was displaying. 'We both know this isn't a social visit,' she replied, her tone every bit as cool as his. 'I don't expect to be entertained and I certainly don't expect to interrupt your business. I never did when we were married. I finally accepted that you were, in fact, already married to your mobile phone. Why would I expect anything different now?'

For Rico, business came first.

'Don't bait me, Stasia.' He shot her a cold look. 'I'm not in the mood and since we can no longer end our rows in bed there seems little point in having them.'

The mere mention of bed made her tummy tumble and, against her will, her eyes dropped to his beautifully sculpted mouth. He'd kissed her into silence on more occasions than she cared to remember. When they'd both been devoured by the flames of anger it had been sex which had quenched that anger and left them both spent.

It was the only level on which they had communicated. Only even then they'd been saying different things. She'd been saying *I love you* while he'd been saying *I want you.*

Her eyes lifted to his. 'I'm not baiting you.'

'Yes, you are. With every flash of your green eyes and every word you don't speak.' His eyes narrowed and something shifted in his dark gaze. 'And it wasn't business. For your information, my first call was to a neurosurgeon who specializes in traumatic brain injury. I wanted to seek his opinion on the possibility of brain damage and make sure that there are no procedures that have been overlooked that could help Chiara. My second call was to the friend who she was staying with at the time of the accident and the third was to the hospital in Sicily. Having now been away from her side for most of the day, naturally I was keen for an update.'

'Sicily?' She stared at him, aghast, diverted from uncomfortable thoughts by the sheer shock of hearing his last statement. 'We're going to *Sicily*?'

He frowned. '*Si*, where did you think?'

'Rome.' She lifted a hand to her throat, feeling her pulse beating rapidly under her fingers. 'I assumed we were going to Rome.'

He had offices all over the globe but the headquarters of the Crisanti Corporation were in Rome. It was where he spent a large proportion of his time.

He shrugged dismissively, as if her misunderstanding were of no consequence. 'You assumed wrongly. Chiara was in Sicily at the time of her accident. That is where we are going.'

Back to the birthplace of her dreams. Back to the scene of perfect happiness. It would be the cruellest taunt he could have devised and for a moment she wondered whether he'd planned it. Did he hate her so much that he'd knowingly cause her that much pain?

'I don't want to go to Sicily!' The words left her mouth before she could prevent them and she closed her eyes, cursing her own lack of control and that impetuous streak in her nature that always caused her to reveal too much. If he'd intended to hurt her then she'd just given him the satisfaction of knowing he'd succeeded.

'Why? Why don't you want to go to Sicily?' His tone was harsh and if he was feeling smug then he was certainly displaying no outward signs of the fact. 'Conscience pricking you, Stasia? Remembering the beginning of our relationship? All those things you said and didn't mean? All those empty words of love?'

Empty?

She turned her head away from him, wondering how a man of his intelligence could be so blind.

The weeks they'd spent together in Sicily on their honeymoon had been the happiest time of their relationship and she'd trusted Rico completely. Had opened her heart without holding back. Had given everything.

Only now could she see how foolish she'd been.

How naïve and trusting.

Rico had never wanted what she'd wanted. Hadn't been capable of giving what she'd wanted him to give.

'Perhaps I should have kept you trapped on Sicily,' he said acidly. 'That way you wouldn't have had the opportunity to pursue your seemingly endless desire for variety.'

With a gasp of pain she turned towards him, her eyes flashing with contempt. 'I was *never* unfaithful to you.'

He flared up with such speed that she recoiled with shock. 'I find you with a naked man in your room and you expect me to believe that it was innocent?' He leaned towards her, his voice a primitive male growl, streaks of colour highlighting the arresting angle of his cheekbones. 'You were my *wife*. And you didn't even hang around to defend yourself. What does that make you, if not guilty?'

Anger smothered her ability to breathe normally. 'I saw the look in your eyes, Rico. You were beyond rational conversation. But you should have known me well enough to know that I would *never* have betrayed you. You should not have believed it of me, Rico!'

He turned on her like a beast in pain. '*Dio*, I saw him kiss you. *You were mine and I saw him kiss you.*'

One glance and he'd assumed he had all the facts. He was so primitive and possessive that it hadn't occurred to him that there might be another explanation for the scene in front of him.

At the time she'd been so shocked and appalled herself that she'd found herself without the means for defence. And part of her had felt that the innocent shouldn't need defence. She'd waited and waited for Chiara to tell the truth but the teenager had just given a small smile and slipped back to her room, leaving Stasia with an impossible decision to make.

Did she tell him the truth about his sister?

Confused, hurt and angry, in the end she'd just left, deciding that they both needed time to calm down. She'd walked out in the middle of the night, taking nothing with her but her passport.

But, instead of seeing her departure as a cooling off period, he'd seen her exit as further confirmation of her guilt.

And when she'd cooled down enough to swallow her pride and call him, he'd blocked her calls.

And that had been that. In one bleak moment she'd been damned.

He hadn't been able to believe in her and she hadn't been able to forgive him for that; she had known she couldn't live with a man like him. It had been the final straw in a marriage that had already been under strain. The next communication she'd had with him had been through his lawyers.

Stasia reached for the seat belt, her hands shaking as she fumbled with the buckle.

He frowned sharply as he watched her. 'What the hell are you doing?'

'Getting away from you. I was wrong to come. I can't see how my presence can possibly help Chiara. I'm sure that the last thing she needs is tension and that's all she'll get if you and I are by her bed together.'

'You're not going anywhere.' Long, strong fingers closed over hers, preventing her attempts to free herself. 'We are landing shortly. Keep the belt *on*.'

'I want to go home. And until I can go home I intend to stay in the bathroom. I don't want to breathe the same air as you.' She tried to free her hands from his but he held her easily, his strength so much greater than hers that it was laughable.

'*Dio*, sit *still*!'

'I want you to tell your pilot to turn this fancy toy of yours round and fly me home.' She still struggled but without any conviction that she could free herself. 'I'm not going *anywhere* with you.'

'You've already agreed to go to the hospital,' he reminded her curtly and she rounded on him, hurt and pain making her voice shake.

She hated him so much. She really, really hated him for being so cold and unfeeling. For not believing in her. *For not loving her.*

'To visit your sister, yes, but *not* to be insulted by you. I never agreed to that. I've been attacked enough by your family.'

He drew in a breath sharply and she knew from the dangerous flash of his eyes that he was struggling with his temper. That temper which he prided himself on having totally under control. *Except with her.* With her he shot fire and flame. No holding back. It was like watching a long dormant volcano suddenly come to life in a terrifying eruption. But his temper had never frightened her. In fact for some strange reason it had comforted her to know that Rico was capable of displaying emotion, even if it was anger. At least *something* threatened his cool.

'To deal with your first point—obviously we are going to Sicily, since that is where Chiara is.' He looked at her with ill-disguised impatience. 'Despite your worst assessment of my character I do, in fact, care about my family.'

Stasia froze. It was his obsession with family, so much a part of his Sicilian heritage, that had blinded him to the truth. And it had been that same deep love for his family that had prevented her from telling him the truth about his sister. How could she shatter his illusions?

'I've never doubted your love for your family,' she muttered, wondering why on earth they were discussing all this now, when it was all much, much too late. 'You said that you rang the hospital. Has there been any change?'

His glance was as contemptuous as it was chilly. 'Why ask, when we both know that you don't really care?'

Stasia gave a soft gasp of shock. She cared. Just as she'd cared when it had first become apparent that his family thought he'd made a mistake in marrying her. The first few barbed comments about her supposed obsession with his money had upset her badly. And those same comments had taken away any pleasure that she might have felt when Rico had showered her with gifts. In the end she'd stopped wearing the jewels that he was continually giving her, unable to cope with the knowing looks of his mother and sister. In case, by wearing them, she gave some credence to their unsavoury assumptions about her.

'I care, Rico.' Suddenly it seemed important to say it. To set the record straight on that, at least. 'If you truly believe that then it shows how little you know me,' she said stiffly and those glittering dark eyes clashed with hers.

'I established how little I know you some time ago,' he said, his voice cold and unforgiving. 'But, unfortunately for me, not before I'd married you. Had I known your true nature I never would have invited you into my home. And you would never have had the opportunity to corrupt my sister. You took her to nightclubs when you knew I had expressly forbidden her to frequent those places and goodness knows what else you encouraged.'

Stasia froze.

His accusation was so unjust—so far from the real truth of the situation—that for a moment she just stared at him.

How could he have been so intimate with her and still believe—?

'You're so wrong, Rico.' She'd promised herself that she wasn't going to waste any more energy in trying to defend herself but her sense of fair play was so strong that she couldn't stay silent. 'And one day you are going to go down on one knee and beg my forgiveness.'

'Save it,' he said harshly, his darkened jaw set at an

aggressive angle. 'You were caught out, my beautiful wife. Admit that you were in the wrong and perhaps we can move on.'

Move on?

Where to?

Hot tears suddenly pricked her eyes and she turned her head towards the window, desperate to compose herself before he noticed her distress. She refused to give him the satisfaction of knowing that he'd upset her.

And she was honest enough to acknowledge that the demise of their relationship couldn't be blamed entirely on the manipulative ways of his sister. Had they truly been a couple—*had there been more to their relationship than sex*—then he never would have believed those things of her. Never would have believed her capable of the things of which she was accused. Forced to acknowledge that their relationship had been doomed from the beginning, she sank back into her seat and he immediately released her hands.

'We will be landing in ten minutes,' he informed her curtly, 'and we'll go straight to the hospital.'

Stasia took a deep breath, telling herself that there was no benefit in raking up the past. She just needed to get through the present—this visit—and then she could go home. Away from him. To try and calm herself, she kept the conversation in the present.

'How did the accident happen?'

'She was staying on a friend's estate.' Rico rested his head against the seat and closed his eyes, as if doing so made it easier to recount the awful details. 'They went riding. Something frightened her horse and it bolted on to the road. Chiara came off and she wasn't wearing a hat.'

Stasia winced as a mental vision of the accident filled

her mind and for a moment she stared at him, at the thick dark lashes touching his bronzed skin, at the firm mouth and the perfect lines of his face. With his eyes closed he seemed less the ruthless businessman and more human. Less intimidating and more vulnerable.

More the man she'd fallen in love with.

As if feeling her gaze, he opened his eyes and Stasia looked away quickly, reminding herself that there was nothing vulnerable about Rico Crisanti.

He was everything tough.

She turned back to him, needing to speak. Needing to say something. Unlike him, she couldn't keep her emotions locked away. 'Whatever happened between us, I want you to know that I'm sorry about Chiara. Truly I am. This must all be so hard for you. The not knowing, the waiting—' She glanced at him cautiously and for a moment she thought she saw a wry smile touch his mouth.

'*Not* my strong point, as you well know,' he drawled, glancing at his watch as the plane taxied to a halt. 'We've arrived. I should warn you that my entire family presently inhabits the hospital. Tensions are running high and the atmosphere is already more emotional than is desirable. Needless to say your arrival is hardly going to be greeted with enthusiasm.'

The reminder that his family hated her was like a cold shower, quenching her tentative attempt to build bridges.

'You asked me to come,' she reminded him stiffly and he gave a sigh and stabbed long fingers through his sleek, glossy hair.

'*Si*, I was given no choice in the matter. Chiara asked for you. That was enough for me.' Stormy black eyes clashed with hers in blatant warning. 'But not all my family share my opinion. I would ask you to keep your outspoken views to yourself on this occasion.'

In other words she wasn't allowed to step out of line. And suddenly she realized just how hard this must be for him. Not just because of Chiara, but because of *her*. He'd cut her out of his life. To him she'd ceased to exist except as a name on various legal papers. And now circumstances had forced him to invite her back into his life. And he clearly *hated* that fact.

'Your family may not approve of me but that is their problem, not mine,' she said with quiet dignity. 'You've asked me to come here. You can't expect me to change my personality as well.'

He swore fluently. 'I am not asking you to change your personality! Just to show some sensitivity to the situation. They are understandably stressed by Chiara's condition. They do not need further pressure.'

This was not going to be a happy meeting. And, with that grim thought, she unfastened her seat belt and followed him to the front of the plane.

CHAPTER THREE

THEY drove from the airport to the hospital without exchanging another word.

Again Rico was attached to his mobile phone, his lean hands moving in silent emphasis as he spoke in rapid Italian. In the front, his driver and a bodyguard sat in watchful silence.

Stasia knew without looking that another car with bodyguards would be travelling immediately behind them. Rico's high profile status as a billionaire tycoon made such precautions mandatory and she'd grown accustomed to having company during their whirlwind courtship and the six months of their marriage. She'd even had fun behaving outrageously, knowing that they were being watched almost all the time.

To Stasia's surprise, they avoided the entrance of the huge modern hospital and instead Rico's driver steered the car down a series of side streets before pulling up outside an alleyway. There was a fire escape at the end and at the top of the fire escape, a door.

'Why are we going this way?'

'Because all the conventional entrances to the hospital are teeming with paparazzi,' Rico explained, his handsome face grim as he led her quickly down the narrow passage. 'This route leads into a corridor near the intensive care unit. So far the press don't seem to have discovered it.'

Safely inside the hospital, he strode purposefully along the corridor and paused outside the unit, anxiety stamped on every line of his bronzed features.

'Wait here.'

Stasia stood outside the entrance to the intensive care unit, her heart thudding against her chest. The prospect of meeting his family again made her gasp for air and when he reappeared by her side and announced that he was taking her straight to Chiara, she felt a flicker of relief that the inevitable confrontation with his family would be postponed.

The teenage girl lay still, her face as pale as the hospital sheets that covered her. A bruise cast a bluish haze over one side of her face and, next to her, frighteningly high-tech machines bleeped and hummed as they monitored every aspect of her condition. Confronted by the brutal evidence of medical technology, Stasia felt a sickness build in her stomach. Rico's brief, almost sparse, description of his sister's injuries hadn't prepared her for the horrifying reality of seeing someone so seriously injured.

Suddenly she realized just how strong he really was. He was living in a nightmare and yet he was still managing to function. To run a company, to prop up his family, to come and fetch her even though it must be the last thing he wanted—

She felt hot tears prick her eyes. Even now, he was only able to show his emotions in peripheral ways. He looked tired. He looked tense. But he still couldn't talk about how he felt. And that had been one of the fundamental differences between them.

How many times during their all too brief relationship had she wished he would really *talk* to her?

How many times had she waited to hear him say that he loved her?

But he'd never spoken those words.

And she knew now that it was because he never had

loved her. For a while he'd wanted her but not any more. Now he despised her.

The bleak reality of the situation swamped her. The tears spilled over and her legs started to shake. She didn't think she'd made a sound but she must have done because she heard him mutter something and the next moment he was by her side, a strong hand on her shoulder, a frown bringing his dark brows together.

'You are incredibly pale. Are you feeling unwell? It is very hot in here and the atmosphere is oppressive. I should have warned you.'

She struggled with the tears, wondering how there could still be tears left inside her. Surely during the past year she'd cried herself out? Mourning the death of their relationship, of her dreams. Missing him so much that the pain was almost a physical torment.

She really, *really* shouldn't be thinking about this now but there was something about the sterile, cold atmosphere of the hospital that made her feel more isolated and alone than ever before. *More aware of just how fleeting and fragile life really was.*

She felt the taste of salt on her lips and brushed away the tears with the back of her hand. 'I'm sorry—'

'Don't be.' His voice was rough and loaded with self-recrimination. 'Hospitals are not nice places at the best of times and in these circumstances—' He broke off and pushed her gently towards the nearest chair.

She sank on to it gratefully and looked helplessly at Chiara. The girl lay still, oblivious to anything going on around her.

Rico gave a driven sigh and took the chair next to her. 'Our lives do not always turn out the way we expect, do they?' His gruff tone betrayed a depth of emotion that she'd given up ever hearing him express and the strain was etched in his own dark features as he lifted his sister's limp hand.

For a moment he was silent, as if rallying himself, and then he sucked in a breath and fastened his gaze on his sister's face. 'Stasia is here—' The control was back, the emotion gone, and for a moment she wondered whether she'd imagined it. More comfortable in his own language, he switched to Italian, talking swiftly and gently, all the time holding Chiara's hand as if hoping to transfer some of his vital strength to the injured girl.

Stasia sat in frozen stillness, the tears now blocked somewhere deep inside her, staring at the girl who had made no secret of hating her. It was almost impossible to believe that she was the same person.

In her unconscious state, Chiara had lost all her defiance.

Instead she looked like a very young, very vulnerable teenager and Stasia felt her resentment melt away.

Rico lifted his head and looked at her, the strain making his eyes seem even darker than usual. 'The doctors thought it might help if she were to hear your voice— if you could say something. Talk to her.'

Stasia looked at him helplessly. This was *so* hard. She wanted to help, but what on earth was she supposed to talk about? The past? Hardly—when almost all their conversations had been hostile. Certainly on Chiara's part. Almost since the day Stasia had married Rico, Chiara had treated her as the enemy.

Aware that Rico was watching her expectantly, Stasia leaned closer to the bed, feeling more self-conscious than she ever had in her life before. If she said the wrong thing now—

'Hi, Chiara—' She broke off and cleared her throat. 'It's Stasia.'

She paused for a moment, half-expecting Chiara to leap from her bed and slap her around the face.

But the girl didn't move. Didn't respond in any way.

Suddenly she wished Rico would go for a walk. Leave them alone. But there was no chance of that, of course. He thought she was a corrupting influence and there was no way he'd leave her alone with his much younger sister. 'What have you done to yourself? Why weren't you wearing a hat? Maybe some gorgeous boy was watching and you didn't want to hide your hair—'

She caught Rico's sharp frown but ignored him. If she was going to talk to Chiara then she was going to talk about things that might make sense to the girl. Something that reflected the person she was. It would have been typical of Chiara to ignore the hat if someone was watching.

Stasia hesitated for a moment and then gently touched Chiara's shoulder.

'Everyone's pretty worried about you. Your brother's even taken a day off work—that should tell you how bad it is. Can't remember him ever taking a day off before now, can you? So if you don't want the Crisanti Corporation to collapse then you'd better start thinking about waking up—' She continued to talk, keeping it lighthearted, chatting about everything and nothing until finally Rico stood up in a sudden movement, almost as if he couldn't stand it any longer.

'That's enough for now.' His voice was rough and he seemed almost unbearably tense as he raked long fingers through his hair. 'It's getting late. You need some rest.'

'I'd rather stay.' She didn't want to leave the injured girl's bedside if there was a chance her presence could make a difference.

'You look worn out.' The words were dragged from

him, as if he was afraid she might misinterpret his concern as something sweeter.

But there was no chance of that. She knew exactly what he thought of her and knew that the fact that she was here was a measure of his love for his sister. Not an indication of any feeling for her. He had none. Or at least, nothing positive and she was miserably aware that nothing but desperation on his part would have induced him to make contact with someone he held in such contempt.

The knowledge choked her. 'It's been a stressful day.' Her voice was strangely flat and suddenly she realized that he was right. She *was* exhausted. She'd been painting non stop, throwing herself into her work, trying to forget—

'You haven't changed.' His voice was heavily accented and suddenly he sounded very, very Sicilian. 'You're still obsessed with your work. Do you realize you talked about virtually nothing else?'

Because there was nothing else in her life to talk about.

She managed an ironic smile, because that was undoubtedly what he would have expected from her. 'And this coming from you?' Her tone was dry but he didn't return the smile.

'And you still talk too much.'

Stasia's own smile faded at that bittersweet reminder of their past. He'd always teased her about that. The fact that she chatted all the time. 'I thought you wanted me to talk.'

He paced to the end of the bed as if he needed to distance himself from something. 'I did. But it's enough for one night. Enough for both of you. Today has been difficult for all of us.' His eyes met hers, his dark gaze conveying just *how* difficult. 'I'll arrange for you to be taken home.'

Home?

She swallowed, wondering if he even realized what he'd said. 'Don't get cosy with me, Rico. This isn't my home any more. We both know that.'

And she didn't want to be here a moment longer than necessary. Being this close to him tore her apart, inside and out.

She wanted to hurl herself on his broad chest and claw at him until he begged forgiveness for throwing away what they'd shared without trying harder to protect it. *Until he explained why he hadn't come after her. Why he'd let her leave.*

For a fierce, stormy moment his eyes clashed with hers and then he muttered something in Italian and his hands curled into fists.

'For the final time, we are still married.'

If ever she needed a reminder that their views on that particular institution were vastly different, that was it.

'I want to go to a hotel.'

'No hotel.'

'Rico—'

'Until she wakes up I want you at the villa, so that I know where you are. After that—' he gave a dismissive shrug '—you are free to go.'

She struggled with the familiar frustration. As usual he dictated. There was no question of him even *considering* her opinion. He was used to commanding and being obeyed.

She tossed her head back, her hair tumbling like fire down her slender back. 'I can make my own decisions, Rico,' she informed him in a hoarse voice. 'I'm not one of your employees.'

'No. You're my wife.' His voice was cold. 'And you would do well to remember it.'

She gasped. 'This is not the time for your macho Sicilian possessive streak—' She broke off, silenced by the warning look from his glittering black eyes.

And suddenly she knew. Knew that he was feeling the same pressures that she was.

He still wanted her. And that knowledge must be killing him.

If she hadn't been so angry, so wrenched apart by misery, she would have smiled. After the accusations he'd flung at her, the things he'd been willing to believe about her, to still want her must offend his sensibilities. For a man who had to control everything, not being able to control his physical response to her must be galling in the extreme.

But she didn't feel like smiling. She felt like screaming, like sobbing, like hitting him.

The hopelessness of it all, *the waste*, just flayed her. It didn't have to be like this. It could have been so different.

'Rico—'

Immediately he withdrew from her, both physically and emotionally, his dark eyes shuttered, displaying the self-discipline that was so much a part of the man he was. 'If you have business obligations, then make calls,' he said coldly. 'Do what you have to do. But you will stay at the villa.'

She no longer had the energy to argue with him. Arguing with Rico required a set of fully charged batteries and at the moment hers were distinctly flat.

As if assuring himself that she no longer intended to fight, he stared at her face for endless moments and then gave an almost imperceptible nod. 'I'll have you driven to the villa.'

The villa where they'd spent so much time together. Where they'd been so happy. She couldn't really believe he intended her to stay there. Surely it would increase the torture for both of them?

Or maybe he just didn't care that much.

She straightened her shoulders. 'What about you? You need sleep, too.'

She didn't question why, after everything that had happened, she was worrying about him. Rico Crisanti wasn't a man who needed or wanted the sympathy of others. He preferred to be seen as invulnerable.

His gaze was shuttered, forbidding any access to his emotions. 'I have some calls to make. I prefer to stay at the hospital.'

Part of her withered and died as the implications of his harsh statement penetrated her sluggish brain.

So that was why he was sending her to the villa. He had no intention of being there himself. Of sharing any part of himself with her. The knowledge made her ache and she looked away, giving up all hope of connecting with him. He didn't want her concern. Didn't want to acknowledge his own emotions.

Why the hell had he sent her to the villa?

Four hours later Rico was slumped in an unbelievably uncomfortable chair in the relatives' room that he had come to hate over the past few weeks. He'd finally decided that the peace of his villa held more attraction than this waiting room filled with his well-meaning but exhausting relatives. There had been no change in Chiara's condition, his mother and grandmother were insisting on staying at the hospital and the press were still baying like wolves, desperate for a story.

So why, when it was the only place that offered any sort of sanctuary from the unremitting strain of his current situation, had he sent her to the villa? What madness had possessed him?

And why, when he despised her from the very depth of his being, couldn't he get her out of his mind? His thoughts should have been filled with nothing but his sister, but he couldn't stop thinking about the one woman who had almost destroyed his sanity.

He clenched his fists and, without questioning himself too closely, glanced at the security guard in the doorway and instructed him to arrange for the car to take him to the villa.

Slumped in the back of the car, eyes gritty from lack of sleep, he acknowledged that the reason he'd sent her to the villa was because he didn't trust her not to leave if she went to a hotel. It was quite obvious that she didn't want to be here and she'd already proved that she was more than happy to run when the going got tough. And the going had got extremely tough, thanks to her taste for boys barely out of their teens. Jealousy shot through him and he grimaced as the pain flared, bright and agonizing as ever. Perhaps she'd been right to run. At the time he'd wanted to wring her neck with his bare hands, so running away had actually been a wise move on her part, although it had merely confirmed her guilt as far as he was concerned.

He strode into the villa with every muscle of his powerful body tensed in readiness, prepared for battle, but there was no sign of Stasia and he assumed she was already asleep. She'd certainly looked pale and exhausted when he'd finally sent her away from the hospital. Was it the strain of seeing Chiara, he wondered grimly, or the strain of seeing him? Was her conscience finally troubling her?

Dismissing the staff, he poured himself a drink and gave a grim smile, acknowledging the weakness of man.

Even knowing her tricks, knowing what she was capable of, he still wanted her. He'd taught himself to hate her and yet he still wanted her with a primitive desperation that drove almost everything else from his mind. Which just went to prove that their relationship had nothing to do with the mind and everything to do with the body, he reflected, taking his drink on to the terrace and standing for a moment with his face towards the sea.

Like it or not, Stasia was in his blood. And divorcing her wasn't going to change that fact. So the sooner he learned to live with it, the better for both of them.

It was just a reaction to his current situation, he assured himself. Seeking physical release was a natural male response to stress and tension and the tension in his life at the moment was reaching snapping point.

His thoughts turned to his sister and his shoulders sagged and his expression grew bleak. The strain of keeping it together for the rest of the family was starting to tell and he stared at the large swimming pool that lay just beyond the terrace, wondering whether a different form of exercise might relieve some of the pressure.

Later, he decided, pacing back inside and settling himself down on one of the long white sofas positioned to give an undisturbed view of the pool and the sea beyond.

The doctors had promised to call if there was any change and in the meantime he had some important calls to make. He was only too aware that his staff were making valiant attempts not to hound him but equally aware that his complex business empire didn't run itself.

He finished his drink, poured another one and then put in a call to his Finance Director, who was currently troubleshooting at the New York office.

An hour later he ended the call and picked at the plate

of cold meats that the maid had discreetly placed in front of him at some point earlier.

He ate without noticing the food, his head buried in a pile of papers that his assistant had sent over from the office. Occasionally he paused to scribble a note in the margin or make another phone call and it was after midnight when he finally tossed the papers on to the table and leaned back with his eyes closed.

The idea of a swim grew steadily more appealing and he rose to his feet in a fluid movement, stripping off his clothes as he walked towards the pool. The water shone blue, illuminated by a row of tiny lights that ran the length of the pool and he dived naked into the cool water, surfaced and swam to the other side with a powerful front crawl. He powered through the water with steady, even strokes, the physical demands he placed on himself sufficient to momentarily drive the present from his mind.

He felt her before he saw her.

Felt her presence on the poolside.

Something in the atmosphere changed. Something so subtle that to anyone else it would have been undetectable.

But not to him.

Their hyper-awareness of each other had always been part of their amazing physical relationship. Even in a crowded room he'd been able to sense her presence and he knew it was the same for her.

He surfaced, cleared the water from his eyes with a sweep of his bronzed hand, and saw her standing on the edge of the pool watching him, as slender and fragile as a young deer, her stunning fiery hair trailing loose over a white silk shirt.

His shirt.

'Stealing my clothes, Stasia?' Without thinking, he

spoke in Italian and he saw her quick indrawn breath, saw the shiver of response.

'I wasn't expecting to stay.' She replied in Italian, her voice smoky and slightly hesitant because she'd never been that confident in his language. 'I didn't pack anything.'

And usually she slept naked. While they'd been together, he'd never allowed her to do anything else. Had never wanted anything to hide her incredible body.

He switched to English. 'You always stole my shirts.'

And, with her innate sense of style, she'd managed to turn them into a fashion statement. She had a flair for making the ordinary extraordinary. A scarf tied in a certain way. Colours that no one else would dare to put together. Her artist's eye for design was visible in everything she touched.

And then there was her hair. A sinfully sexy mass of fire and flame that reflected the tempestuous nature of the woman. *It was enough to make a man lose his mind.*

She gave a tiny, almost imperceptible, shrug. 'You have good taste in shirts. I didn't think you were coming home. I heard someone in the pool—' Her voice still had the husky quality of the half-awake and even in the cool water he felt his body throb in response to her sleepy tones. How often had he woken her in the night to claim her body yet again, how often had she laughed softly and teased him in just such a tone as that?

He lifted himself out of the pool in an easy movement, seeing her eyes darken in response to his nakedness. His own eyes slid down, catching the movement of her slender throat as she swallowed, reading the unmistakable hunger in her glance before she concealed it with one sweep of her long, curling eyelashes.

His response to her involuntary glance was instantaneous and he reached for a towel that one of his staff had thoughtfully placed on a lounger, cursing his inability to remain indifferent to this woman. It was as if his body was out of his control. Which it was, of course. From the moment they'd met, he'd been under her spell. Made vulnerable by man's original temptation. Woman. *Only in his case just the one woman.*

Stasia.

'I had calls to make.' He wrapped the towel firmly round his waist, depriving her of the view. Perhaps if she stopped looking he'd stop reacting. 'Work to do. I needed a break from the hospital.'

And most of all from his relatives, he reflected wearily. He wasn't going to admit that to her but it was clear that she knew what he was thinking.

He could tell by the look in her eyes. Those all knowing, all seeing green eyes that took hold of a man and made him burn with wanting.

The silence around them throbbed and crackled with a tension that only the two of them felt and suddenly he was grateful for the towel. At least it hid the laughably predictable workings of his body. For a brief moment he wished he'd done as she'd requested and sent her to a hotel. Anywhere, as long as it was away from him.

Seeing her like this, half naked in his shirt, *in his home*, suggested an intimacy that no longer existed between them.

He had to remind himself that she was no longer his. That he no longer held the right to feel the primitive and possessive thoughts that had such an iron grip on his normally logical brain.

It didn't help that she wanted him too. He could tell by the way her soft mouth was slightly parted, the way it always had when she anticipated his kiss, by the way her fabulous green eyes darkened, drawing him in. The signs were subtle, but they were there and he recognized them as clearly as if someone had painted words on a wall.

He chose to dismiss them.

'Stop looking at me like that.' His voice was harsh. Harsher than he'd intended. 'Stop looking as if you want me, when we both know that you'll go after any convenient male body. I happen to prefer my relationships to be exclusive.'

Her beautiful face lost most of its colour. 'How can you say that to me?'

Innocent. Wronged. All those words came to mind as he looked at her and yet he knew none of them applied to her.

There had been nothing innocent about her when he'd caught her naked in their bed with another man.

'Because it's the truth.' Rico gritted his teeth. She managed to make him feel guilty even though he knew that he had nothing to feel guilty about.

Hadn't he caught her red-handed? Filling her days with the pleasures of the flesh when he was working? Spending her evenings in unsavoury nightclubs and taking his young, impressionable sister with her.

'You're looking at me, too. So what does that make you?' Her voice was a choke and he frowned slightly, unsure what to make of her uncharacteristic response. He'd seen the tears in the hospital and had been surprised by how much the sight had bothered him. He knew how tough she was, knew that Stasia wasn't a woman to dissolve into tears.

It must be the awkwardness of their current situation, he decided. Being forced to face him, after the ultimate betrayal. *The tears of a guilty conscience?*

'If I'm looking at you then it's because I can't quite believe I was ever foolish enough to marry you,' he said cruelly, watching her flinch and wondering why it felt so necessary to hurt her when it was supposedly all in the past. When his relationships had gone wrong in the past he'd always been content to walk away. Partings had usually been amicable, invariably smoothed by elaborate gifts on his part, selected to soothe the guilt of not caring enough. But never had he felt this driven, burning need to strike out and inflict pain as he did with Stasia.

'I *hate* you.' She spoke the words on a soft gasp and for a moment he thought he'd misheard and it took him a moment to respond.

'Maybe. But like it or not, you also want me and that's something you're finding it difficult to live with.' He saw her take a step backwards and suddenly he wished she'd worn something, anything, other than his shirt. It was as if she was mocking him. Those glorious legs bared to mid-thigh, the buttons undone to reveal the darkened hollow between her full breasts. She had a body designed to drive a man wild.

And he should know.

She'd driven him out of his mind.

He looked at her expectantly, feeling the charged atmosphere, waiting for her to fight back. Wasn't that what they'd always done? Fought and argued? He was used to women who fawned and agreed with him and Stasia had never done either. She'd challenged him. Had driven him crazy. Had infuriated him as much as she'd excited him.

But tonight it was as if the fight had been sucked out of her.

She stood by his pool, wearing his shirt, looking very young and very lost. 'I didn't come to fight with you.' She raked a hand through her gorgeous, fiery mane in a gesture he knew painfully well. She sounded tired and more uncertain than he could ever remember her sounding before. 'I heard a noise and I wanted to check who it was. And when I saw it was you I wanted to ask you about Chiara. You said you'd be staying at the hospital.' Her voice sounded dull. Strangely devoid of emotion. 'Has there been any change?'

'No change.'

And he realized that since Stasia had appeared on the terrace he hadn't given his sister a thought.

What sort of a man did that make him? he asked himself bitterly.

Disgusted with himself, he turned away from her and strode into the spacious villa, suddenly overwhelmed by the ever-building tension of the past two weeks. He hadn't had a full night's sleep in all that time and his normally sharp brain was definitely seeing the world out of focus.

He sprawled on to the nearest sofa and closed his eyes, feeling less in control than ever in his life before and deciding that it was *not* a feeling he relished.

'Rico—'

He felt the sofa dip next to him, felt the tentative touch of her fingers against the hard muscle of his shoulder.

This was a different Stasia.

A soft, gentle Stasia and this new side of her slid under his skin and increased the torment, like grains of sand in a raw wound.

Her light, subtle perfume teased his senses and he turned to face her, intending to dismiss her concern, to send her back to bed with a few cold words.

But something in her incredible green eyes held him silent.

'This must be terrible for you,' she said quietly, 'and maybe it's time to admit that you have feelings too.

Everyone leans on you. What they forget is that you need someone to lean on, too.'

He wished she'd move her hand from his shoulder. The gentle touch of her fingers seemed to connect to every male part of himself and he suddenly realized just how much he'd missed her touch.

He suppressed a groan and tried to drag his wayward libido back under control. 'I'm just tired. I've been at the hospital for over two weeks—'

'Being strong for everyone. Making decisions for everyone. You need to think about yourself, Rico. About your own needs.'

It was the wrong thing to say. At the moment only one need filled his mind and as he lifted his eyes to hers he remembered just how much this woman knew about his needs.

Mutual desire, dangerous and destructive, flared hot between them and he fought the urge to bury his face in her neck and taste her soft skin. She was all female. All temptation to the male in him, and suddenly he wanted her so badly it was like a fire inside him.

It wasn't clear who made the first move. Wasn't clear when her gentle grip on his arm turned from comfort to something else entirely. Something sexual. Either way, one moment they were apart, locked together in a visual intimacy which stirred all the senses, and the next his mouth was on hers—hot and demanding, taking, stealing, robbing her of breath and protest.

Or maybe there never was a protest. He felt her slender arms wind round his neck, responded to the scrape of her fingernails down his back with a violent shudder. It was primitive and basic, a primal expression of sexual desire that seized them both.

Needing to dominate, he pressed her back on the sofa, staking his claim, satisfying the clawing, greedy beast that had been devouring him since she'd opened the door of her cottage and glared at him with those daredevil don't-mess-with-me green eyes. He forgot the fact that he was torn with worry, that he was mentally and physically exhausted. He forgot everything except the thundering, driving force of his own libido and the fact that he was with the only woman he'd ever wanted to be with.

Without lifting his mouth from hers he swiftly dealt with the buttons of the shirt she was wearing. His shirt. Or was it her shirt now? His usually sharp mind was no longer working properly. Certainly it smelt of her. That subtle, floral, feminine scent that teased his nostrils and other more distant parts of him. That scent that was totally Stasia.

He stroked a possessive hand over the swell of her breasts, her gasp of pleasure sending another thud of answering desire straight to his groin. Then he dragged his mouth away from hers so that he could look, his eyes feasting on the pale softness of her skin that seemed even paler set against the bronze of his own flesh. He'd always been fascinated by the contrast between them. Fragility against strength. English pallor against Mediterranean dark. *Soft woman against hard male.*

Her dusky-pink nipples jutted upwards, tempting, begging, and he bent his dark head and answered her silent plea, sucking her into the moist heat of his mouth, flicking with his tongue until he felt her arch her hips and sink her fingers into his hair. Lost in a sensual feast, he refused to release her and he heard her sob his name and arch again as his tongue flicked with relentless skill and expertise, driving her higher and higher.

And he knew this woman so well.

Knew just how to touch and tempt to send her hurtling towards the edge.

For a moment he was the master, the one in control. And then he felt her fingers on the towel, felt the gentle tug as she unwrapped him, followed by the breath of cool air on his flesh. And he remembered that she knew him too. And she used that knowledge as she covered him with her hand and took the control right back.

Her touch drew a thickened groan from him, an involuntary acknowledgement of what this woman did to him. The way they connected. It would have gone all the way. The way it had from their very first date. Once they started there was no stopping, their mutual passion totally beyond control. But the time wasn't theirs and as usual it was his phone that came between them—that small, seemingly innocent gadget that always seemed to rip holes in their time together.

They froze, locked in intimacies that had come so naturally and which now seemed so shocking and inappropriate.

With a soft curse, Rico sprang to his feet and reached for the towel, securing it quickly before answering the phone with one impatient stab of his finger.

CHAPTER FOUR

'SHE's awake?' Stasia struggled to sit up, her tangled hair forming a curtain over her flushed, mortified face. How could she have done that? Her whole body hummed with sexual frustration and utter humiliation.

She hadn't even meant to follow him into the room, but then she'd seen him slumped on the sofa looking utterly done in and something had ached inside her. And that same something had made her cross the room and offer comfort. But she should have known that it wasn't safe.

One touch.

One touch and she'd lain down for him like the pathetic groupie she was never going to be. Did she have no pride? No will-power? *No sense of self-preservation?* The way to get over Riccardo Crisanti was *not* by allowing him unlimited access to her body.

But being back in the villa, where they'd been so blissfully happy, had made her vulnerable. Weepy. Weak and pathetic. And when she'd seen him, so gloriously naked, a man designed to tempt woman, she'd been unable to maintain the angry front.

'She recovered consciousness five minutes ago.' There was no missing the tension in his voice and she suspected that it wasn't all due to concern for his sister. She wasn't blind. She could see the proud jut of his arousal under the totally insubstantial towel. Knew that he was still throbbing with unfulfilled need.

As she was.

The sexual frustration was so agonizingly acute that she could have screamed with it.

He looked at her, his dark jaw set hard. 'We need to get back to the hospital.' His eyes slid to the swell of her creamy breasts, streaked red from the scrape of his stubble. He turned away as if he couldn't stand the reminder of his own weakness. 'Cover yourself.'

'Damn you, Rico!' Her voice was hoarse as she struggled to do up buttons with shaking fingers. 'I won't let you blame me for this!'

How dared he look at her like that when he'd been every bit as responsible as she for what had flared up between them?

'You came out here dressed only in a shirt.'

'You were naked!'

His gaze was hard. 'Perhaps you think that offering sex makes me more inclined towards forgiveness.'

Offering sex?

'I don't need your forgiveness, Rico—' her voice was hoarse '—but you may well need mine. Get out.'

They glared at each other, neither prepared to take responsibility for the fact that they had a complete inability to be together and not make love. Both refusing to acknowledge the fact that the sexual chemistry between them was such a powerful force that it was outside their control, the pull between them as natural as breathing.

'Willingly.' He stared at her for a moment longer, a tiny pulse beating in his hard jaw, his eyes dangerously dark as he punched a number into his phone and ordered the car to be brought round. 'Get dressed. We're leaving in five minutes.'

And with that he strode out of the room, giving her

a final view of his broad bronzed shoulders and long muscular legs.

For a moment Stasia just sat there staring after him, despising herself for wishing he'd turn round, come back to her and finish what he'd started.

She gave a groan and resisted the temptation to drum her heels into the sofa.

At that particular moment she didn't know who she hated more. Rico, for losing his ice-cool control whenever he came near her or herself, for wanting him every bit as much as he clearly wanted her.

Her only consolation was that Rico hated losing control almost as much as she did. And if she was suffering then there was no doubt that he was suffering too.

And at the moment she really, *truly*, wanted him to suffer. If he felt only one portion of the agony that she was feeling then that would go some way towards satisfying her sense of justice.

She wrapped the shirt around her and padded silently to the sanctuary of her bedroom where she stupidly risked a glance in the mirror. It was a mistake. Her reflection stared back, mocking her. She didn't see the woman she wanted to see. She wanted to see smooth and sleek. She wanted to see calm and control. Instead she saw wild and wanton. Her fiery hair fell around her face in soft tangles, hair that had very evidently been severely disturbed by a rampant male. Her pale, sensitive skin showed all the evidence of his uncompromising sexual demands. Demands that she'd met, bite for bite, lick for lick.

Oh, God.

She covered her swollen lips with shaking fingers.
She should never have come.
She was a strong, independent woman with a mind

of her own and a successful career, but Rico was like a dangerous drug. She couldn't be close to him and not want him and she despised herself for that weakness.

They were as far apart in their attitudes as North was from South but still it seemed she couldn't resist him.

She'd never get over him unless she could put distance between them.

And now that Chiara was awake she was going to do just that.

She was going to make the required visit to the teenager's sickbed, make the right noises and then vanish back to England and find a cottage with such low ceilings that Rico wouldn't be able to gain access without risking extreme physical damage.

As the car sped towards the hospital Rico sat in brooding silence, his mind and body throbbing with an unrelieved sexual tension that did absolutely nothing for his temper.

He couldn't bring himself to look at her.

Couldn't bring himself to focus on the visible signs of his earlier lack of will-power. When he'd dragged her beneath him in a state of sexual desperation, he'd given no thought to the immediate future. To the fact that her delicate skin always displayed the evidence of his attentions for several hours after they'd touched.

The fact that her pale skin was so sensitive had always been a point of fascination for a man whose own skin simply turned a deeper shade of bronze on exposure to the sun. By contrast, the slightest touch of the sun and her skin turned pink and her freckles increased. Worshipping her creamy pallor, he'd made it his mission to protect her, buying her a selection of hats designed to permanently shade her from the powerful Italian sun.

But tonight he'd thought about nothing but his own satisfaction. And now, he reflected grimly, he was about to pay the price for that display of reckless masculine self-indulgence.

In less than ten minutes they'd be meeting his family and he'd be on the receiving end of horrified, questioning glances from his mother.

Questions that he didn't want to answer.

Questions that he *couldn't* answer.

He had absolutely no idea why he behaved with such total lack of control with Stasia. In all other matters he considered himself to be a strictly disciplined man. He'd learned the benefits of self-control at an early age. But with Stasia he reverted to hormone-laden, sex-driven teenager. Unfortunately mind over matter didn't come into it. In his case it was libido over brain.

It was just the stress, he assured himself. A purely physical release from the relentless pressure of the past few days. It didn't mean anything. He was human, after all, and she'd offered comfort.

Was it his fault if the sort of comfort he preferred involved being horizontal?

He stared out of the window and gritted his teeth, aware of her sitting only inches away from him, her bubbling curls pinned in a haphazard style on the back of her head, her curvaceous body once more concealed by the peach linen dress.

But it didn't matter whether she was dressed or naked.

The sexual pull between them was stronger than both of them and the sooner he sent her back to England and delegated communication to his lawyers, the safer for both of them.

He'd give her time to visit his sister, just in case her presence would in any way speed Chiara's recovery, and then he'd have her taken straight to his plane.

And he'd make sure that the engines were already running.

The whole family was standing by Chiara's bedside and Stasia felt her heart plummet. After her steamy, heated encounter with Rico she felt more vulnerable than ever and was well aware that, despite her best efforts with make-up, she was displaying signs of his attentions for all who looked.

She wanted to sink through the floor with humiliation.

Even more so when she met Rico's mother's shocked gaze.

'So—you have come back.' His mother's voice was stiff and her eyes scanned Stasia's heightened colour, rested on her bruised mouth and then shifted to her son with a look of undisguised horror and disbelief.

Eternally indifferent to the opinion of others, Rico met his mother's reproachful gaze with admirable cool and took Stasia's hand, openly defying anyone to challenge him. Then he stepped towards the bed, leaving no one in any doubt about who was in charge.

Pathetically grateful to him for his gesture of protection, even though she knew that it meant nothing, Stasia held his hand as though it were a lifeline.

His mother stepped back respectfully but the glance she gave Stasia was so pained that the younger woman felt a lump building in her throat. What had she ever done to deserve that look? Nothing. Except marry a billionaire. Apparently that had been enough to earn her the label of 'gold-digger.'

'Chiara—' Rico's voice was roughened with concern as he bent to kiss his sister.

Her eyes fluttered open and for a moment she stared at her brother blankly. Then a smile touched her mouth.

'Rico.' Her voice was little more than a whisper but the entire family released a collective sigh of relief. Rico's mother stepped forward and embraced her daughter, and Chiara's grandmother sank into a chair by the bed and took her hand, tears pouring down her wrinkled cheeks.

'She's come back to us—'

Which sounded like Stasia's cue to leave.

Without even realizing that she was doing so, she freed her hand from Rico's and backed towards the door.

She wasn't needed here. She wasn't part of their family and never had been. Chiara had regained consciousness. It was time to go home.

But Chiara was saying something else, her voice so hushed that Rico had to bend his dark head closer in order to hear her.

He straightened and his gaze arrowed in on Stasia who by now was by the door, preparing to leave. 'Wait.' His voice was roughened by emotion. 'She's wondering where you are. She wants to speak to you.'

Stasia froze. For a moment she thought she must have misheard him. Why on earth would Chiara want to speak to her now that she had fully regained consciousness? Uttering her name in a semi-comatose state was one thing but this was something quite different.

Aware that the whole family was looking at her,

Stasia swallowed and released her hold on the door handle.

After all, what could Chiara say that she hadn't already said? What could she do to hurt her that she hadn't already done?

Feeling the increased beat of her heart, she walked towards the bed, every step a supreme effort of will.

Rico stood to one side as she approached and she stared down at Chiara, noticing that the bruise on her forehead seemed even more livid.

'Hello, Chiara.' Her voice was little more than a croak. 'I'm so glad you're awake. We've all been worried.'

'Stasia.' Chiara gave a soft smile and her eyes drifted shut. 'Beautiful Stasia. When I'm better, can we go shopping? You always look so fabulous. I want you to teach me how to dress like you.'

There was a shocked, disbelieving silence from all those gathered around the bed.

Stasia stood rigid, unsure how to respond. She and Rico had lived apart for the whole of the past year. Why would Chiara say a thing like that, unless she was trying to drive the knife in the moment she regained consciousness? She searched Chiara's face, looking for signs of the mockery she knew so well, the defiance and sarcasm that had been so much a part of the girl when she'd known her, but they were missing.

Chiara's eyes opened and she glanced around her, trying to interpret the silence. She looked wary. Puzzled. As if she sensed that something was wrong.

'What's the matter? Wh—what have I said?'

'Nothing, *mia piccola*,' Rico was quick to reassure her, his hand covering hers. 'How are you feeling?'

Chiara winced slightly. 'I have a headache. And I don't understand why you're all here. What happened?'

'I told you about the accident.' Rico's dark brows locked in a frown. 'You don't remember the accident?'

Chiara thought for a moment and then shook her head slightly. 'Nothing. I just remember that you're on your honeymoon.' She gave her brother a wobbly smile. 'And you were really mad at me for turning up unannounced and disturbing your romantic twosome. Are you still mad at me or am I forgiven?'

Rico looked as though he'd been turned to stone, his powerful body motionless. Standing close to him, Stasia felt his tension and heard his mother's murmur of concern from the other side of the bed. She did a swift mental calculation and worked out that the incident that Chiara was referring to had occurred almost a year and a half ago. At the beginning of their honeymoon.

Before they'd had time to recognize their insurmountable differences.

So what did that mean? Was Chiara playing yet more games?

Chiara's smile faltered and she glanced between them, sensing something in the atmosphere. 'Rico? Are you still angry with me?'

'No, *piccola*, I'm not angry.' Rico's eyes flickered over his sister's face, as if searching for clues. 'But is that the last thing you remember? Arriving when Stasia and I were on our honeymoon?'

Chiara nodded. 'Why?'

Rico smiled. 'No reason.' His deep voice was strong and reassuring and betrayed none of the worry that he was clearly feeling. 'I need to talk to the doctors again. Try and rest. Don't worry about anything.'

The doctors gathered round the bed at Rico's bidding

and the family retreated to the relatives' room for yet another tense wait.

They didn't wait long. Within minutes Rico was called back to the bedside and he returned to the waiting room moments later, looking more stressed than Stasia could ever remember seeing him before.

'The doctors say that she has amnesia. Memory loss.' His eyes slid to his mother as he spoke, checking her reaction to the news. 'Apparently it's common. She can remember nothing since that day when she turned up at the villa when Stasia and I—' he broke off and then continued with what appeared to be considerable effort '—Stasia and I were on our honeymoon.'

Stasia felt her colour rise as everyone turned to look at her.

She remembered that day so well.

They'd been on the beach, swimming and making love endlessly. When they'd finally dragged themselves back to the villa, still locked in each other's arms, Chiara had been in the pool.

Rico had been furious with his sister and Stasia had gently intervened, although she too had been disappointed to find that suddenly they had company.

In the end Rico had heeded Stasia's pleas and allowed Chiara to stay for the weekend and had then dispatched her back to school with a severe lecture about concentrating on her studies.

Stasia let out a breath, realizing that if this was the last thing that Chiara could remember then she was missing a substantial chunk of her life.

Shocked by the news of this new complication, his mother sank into the nearest chair, a look of horror on her face. 'Is it permanent?'

Rico gave a shrug that made him seem more Sicilian

than ever. 'They cannot say. There's every probability that her memory will return but no one knows when. In the immediate term the priority is her physical recovery. They are extremely pleased with her progress. All being well she should be able to come home to us in a few days, which is nothing short of a miracle.'

His mother smiled with relief, her hands clasped in her lap. 'You will take her to your villa?'

Rico gave a nod. 'She needs peace and a restful atmosphere. The villa is the obvious place. I'll make arrangements to work from Sicily for the time being so that I can keep an eye on her.'

'I will come and stay also and take care of her,' his mother said immediately but Rico shook his head.

'There's no need. She needs to be kept as quiet as possible. It would be far better if you stayed in your home and visited from time to time.'

His mother gave a reluctant nod. 'If you think it's best.'

As usual she deferred to Rico, as did the entire family.

When Stasia had first met them their total dependence on him for every decision had astonished her and then later it had driven her crazy. Weren't any of the women in his family capable of thinking and acting for themselves, without his permission?

Stasia glanced at her watch and realized that it would be dawn soon. 'Well, it's clear that I'm no longer needed,' she said quietly, her eyes sliding to Rico, trying to subdue the desire to throw herself at him. *Trying not to think that this was probably the last time she'd ever see him.* From now on it would be back to the lawyers.

The reality of that fact left her feeling profoundly depressed.

'I'm afraid it isn't that simple.' Rico's expression was grim, as if he were dealing with an issue that he found distinctly unpalatable. 'Unfortunately, Chiara's memory is locked at that point eighteen months ago when we were on our honeymoon. She thinks we're happily married.'

Stasia took a long, slow breath. That fact hadn't escaped her. 'Then, I suppose, at some point you'll just have to tell her that we've been living apart for the past year.' But not the reason why. Only she and Chiara knew the truth and Chiara no longer had a memory. 'You'll have to tell her the truth.'

What choice did they have? At some point Chiara would presumably seek an explanation as to why they were no longer living together.

'In this case the truth is not an option.' The words were dragged out of him and he looked like a man who was well and truly stuck between a rock and a hard place. 'The doctors are insistent that she should have no shocks. That everything around her should be as calm as possible. She shouldn't be subjected to any stress.'

So what exactly was he suggesting?

Stasia gave a short laugh that held not a trace of humour. 'And we both know that Chiara was hardly devastated by the failure of our marriage, Rico. Let's not play games here. She was delighted when our relationship failed. Being reminded of the truth is hardly going to send her into a decline.'

Rico's mother made a sound of protest but neither Stasia or Rico spared her a glance.

It was as if they were the only two people in the

room, their eyes locked together as the conflict built between them.

'Unfortunately for us, Chiara is living at a different point of our relationship,' Rico growled, everything about his body language suggesting that he was finding this whole situation as difficult as she was. 'And we are *not* going over old ground again now. *Dio*, do you think we don't have enough stress at the moment without dredging up bad feeling from the past?'

Her heart started to beat more rapidly. 'So what are you suggesting?' Fuelled by nerves that she didn't understand, Stasia couldn't keep the sarcasm out of her tone. 'You want to play happy families? You want to put that wedding ring back on my finger?'

There was a long pulsing silence and then Rico released a long breath. 'If that's what it takes, then yes.'

CHAPTER FIVE

STASIA stared at him in shocked silence. That was the one response that she had *not* expected. Finally she found her voice. 'You *can't* be serious.'

'*Dio*, would I joke about such a thing? My lawyers have virtually completed the paperwork necessary for the divorce. Do you think I want to prolong it?'

If he'd intended to hurt her then he succeeded admirably.

Even his mother looked slightly startled by his lack of tact.

To give him his due, Rico swore softly and ran a hand over the back of his neck, fighting for control. 'That was uncalled for and I apologize,' he muttered and Stasia tossed her head back, her hair gleaming like a beacon under the bright hospital lights.

'For what, Rico? Being yourself?' She would have died rather than let him see the effect he had on her still. Died rather than let him see that he had the ability to wound her deeply. 'But I think your reaction more than proves that your suggestion is utterly ridiculous. You can put the ring back on my finger but we'll never act like two people who love each other. It's a totally ridiculous proposition.'

With a grim expression on his handsome face, Rico turned his gaze on his family. 'Chiara would like some company.'

He didn't order them to leave but his meaning was

perfectly clear. He wanted to talk to Stasia without an audience.

They left like lambs, no one daring to question him. They never questioned him.

Stasia watched them leave in incredulous disbelief and then turned to him, eyes blazing. 'Do you know your problem?'

'No—' Rico caught her gaze with burning black eyes every bit as mocking as her own '—but I feel sure that you're about to tell me.'

She ignored the warning in his silky tone. Ignored the signs that indicated the slow build of his temper. 'No one has ever said "no" to you. You stride through life, always the one in control, always the one making decisions, crashing through obstacles like a bull. Well, I've got news for you—' she drew several short breaths, trying to get air into her starving lungs '—I am *not* one of your pathetic groupies who hang around with their tongues hanging out, just waiting to be given a morsel of attention from your illustrious self. I'm not one of those irritating, perfectly groomed women who say "yes" to you all the time.'

He stepped towards her so quickly that she didn't see it coming. 'We both know that I can make you say "yes" any time I please, *cara mia*.'

'Don't call me that.'

Conscious of his superior height and every inch of his throbbing masculinity, her heart pounded and she took a step backwards, then wished she hadn't when she caught the sardonic lift of his black brows.

'Afraid of me, Stasia?' He stepped closer, the movement deliberate and designed to provoke. 'Or are you moving away because you don't trust yourself to resist me?'

He was just *so* arrogant. So maddeningly sure of himself.

'I'm not afraid—I just don't approve of men who use their size to intimidate women. It's a low trick.'

He threw back his head and laughed in genuine amusement, a rich, dark sound that coiled around her insides and cranked the tension even higher. 'You expect me to believe that I intimidate you? You, with your sharp tongue and those flashing eyes that dare me all the time? Tell me one thing that you're afraid of. Just one thing!'

Stasia swallowed. *Her own feelings.*

She was afraid of her own feelings for him. They were totally at odds with the person she was. Or the person she believed herself to be. She wasn't a clingy person. She despised clingy people. Unfortunately, since meeting Rico, she'd made the painful discovery that there were parts of her that she'd never known existed. *Sensual depths that he'd plundered like a master.* And with him she wanted to cling. Cling and never let go.

'This is getting us nowhere.' She licked dry lips and then regretted the gesture instantly as his gaze dropped to her mouth and his eyes gleamed gold. That look was as familiar to her as the insidious melting sensation in the pit of her stomach that followed. She rejected the feeling instantly. 'But it has proved that we can't remain in the same room and not want to kill each other. Unless Chiara has lost her intuition as well as her memory then there is no way we'll convince her that our relationship is genuine. I'll say goodbye to her and then I'm leaving.'

'You're not going anywhere,' he said silkily, 'and if

you're worried that we can't convince Chiara that we're in love, then let me help you out on that one.'

She should have seen it coming. Should have sensed his intention before he acted. But her brain was foggy and thinking suddenly seemed impossibly hard work. Even more so when his hand snaked round her waist and his mouth came down on hers with the assurance of a man totally confident in his own sexuality and her response to him.

As kisses went it was as skilled as it was brief. He controlled and led, coaxing her lips apart with a teasing flick of his tongue, delving inside in a lazy exploration that promised so much more than it delivered. And, just as he'd intended, he set her on fire.

He drove her higher, to the point where she forgot everything. She forgot where they were. Forgot that they were standing in an impersonal waiting room illuminated by harsh lighting with his sister seriously ill nearby. Forgot their differences, the fact that they seemed to have absolutely no common ground except between the sheets.

All she was aware of was *him*. The scrape of masculine stubble against her sensitive skin, the suggestive lick of his tongue and the bold thrust of his manhood pressed against the burning heat of her pelvis. Sexual tension throbbed and vibrated through her whole body and her arms crept around his neck, drawing him closer still.

And then he ended it.

With humiliating ease, he lifted his head and stepped back, his eyes cold and totally lacking in emotion. 'I think that's enough to prove that we can be fairly convincing when the time comes.'

She swayed dizzily, just *hating* him for being so controlled when she felt so completely out of control.

His dark eyes registered her dazed expression with something approaching insolence. 'You like to think you don't need me, Stasia, but we both know that you'll lie down for me whenever I like, so it's useless pretending otherwise.'

The sharp sound of her hand connecting with his cheek echoed round the small room.

'You are a smug, conceited bastard, Rico,' she said shakily, hugging her stinging hand to her chest, shocked by the unaccustomed violence which had erupted inside her at his callous taunt. Up until this moment she'd never struck another human being in her life but Rico was hurting her all over again. 'And I'm not staying here a moment longer. Please instruct your pilot to make whatever preparations he needs to make to fly me home.'

'You're not going home.' His lean cheek displayed the livid mark made by her hand and his black eyes glittered dangerously.

'You asked me to come when Chiara was in a coma. Well, now she's awake so you don't need me any more.'

His jaw tightened. 'I've already explained why I need you.'

'To be your convenient slut?' Her eyes blazed into his. 'I don't think so, Rico. There are millions of women out there just gagging to fill that role. Go and grab one of them instead.'

'I want you to be my wife for however long it takes for Chiara to regain her memory,' he growled, digging his hands in his pockets, as if he were afraid of what he might do with them if they were allowed continued freedom. 'But being my wife is not something you ever excelled at, was it, Stasia? I gave you everything. You had a lifestyle beyond your wildest dreams, but when I returned home from a long working day, expecting to find my wife waiting for me, I found her gone!'

'Twice! Twice I was away. I had a business to run too!'

'For what purpose?' His careless shrug betrayed his complete lack of insight into her character. 'You didn't need the money. You had access to unlimited funds. You had everything a woman could possibly need.'

Except love.

She spread her hands in a gesture of exasperation. 'Money, money, money! Life isn't always about money, Rico. There are other things that matter, like independence and self-belief. I like my work. I need to know that I'm good at something. Making a contribution that matters.'

'You were good in my bed,' he said softly, his eyes fixed on hers, 'and that was what mattered to me.'

Her cheeks flamed and she dragged her eyes away from his with an exclamation of disgust. 'You are totally primitive, Rico! You didn't want a wife. You wanted a mistress.'

'I already had two mistresses before I married you,' he said icily, his tone bored and his dark eyes never shifting from hers. 'Why would I have wanted a third?'

Her face lost the rest of its colour at that stark reminder of the man she'd taken on. Had lost her heart to. She'd been crazy to think that what she felt for him would ever be returned. Rico didn't know what love was. He wasn't capable of connecting with a woman emotionally. Only physically. He had an almost insatiable sex drive. She'd heard rumours that he had a mistress both in Rome and in Paris but at the time she'd chosen to ignore those rumours. Rico was a drop-dead sexy guy and she didn't for one minute expect him to have lived like a monk.

'As usual, our conversations lead us nowhere,' she said flatly, picking her bag up from the chair and slinging it over her shoulder. 'I'm leaving, Rico, and there's nothing you can do to stop me. If you won't let me use your plane then I'll just get a commercial flight.'

Anything to get away from him.

At this point she was so desperate that she would have chartered her own plane if that were the only option remaining to guarantee her escape.

'The only place you're going is back to the villa to play happy families.'

'I'm not a member of your staff, nor am I any longer a member of your family,' she said tartly, 'so I don't follow orders.'

'You never did,' he said coldly, 'but you're still going to do as I say.'

'And by what means do you intend to coerce me?' She tilted her head to one side, her expression blatantly challenging. 'Thumb screws? The rack?'

'I don't have to resort to anything so crude,' he replied evenly. 'I merely have to instruct the bank to foreclose on the loan for your mother's antique shop. One phone call, Stasia. That's all it would take.'

There was a long silence, broken only by the sound of Stasia's rapid breathing. When she finally spoke her voice was far from steady. 'You can't do that. You shouldn't even know about that.' She shook her head slightly, denying the possibility that he was telling the truth. 'That loan is nothing to do with you.'

He looked bored. 'Now who is being naïve, Stasia?

Why do you think the bank agreed to the loan so easily?'

She stared at him. 'It *wasn't* easy. We presented sound business plans—'

'Which were ambitious,' Rico said smoothly, 'and the loan was granted because I agreed to act as guarantor.'

'That isn't true.' *Dear God, don't let it be true.* 'You're lying.'

His gaze didn't waver. 'Phone the bank.'

Her mind was racing through all the possibilities, examining the facts. 'But I applied for the loan in my mother's name. I didn't mention you.'

'You were my wife and I have a great deal of trouble remaining anonymous, as you should know by now,' he said dryly. 'Some hotshot at the bank recognized you from the papers. After that they were only too pleased to help you in any way they could.'

With dawning horror, Stasia remembered how the staff at the bank had gone from being condescending and downright obstructive to obsequious. At the time she'd confidently assumed it was because they'd given her business plan proper consideration. Now she cringed at her naïvety.

How could she have been so stupid? How could she not have suspected that her relationship with Rico was behind the sudden change in attitude? Hadn't she seen it before a million times? The way people fawned over Rico, doing anything to win his approval.

'No.' She closed her eyes, wanting it not to be true, but knowing that it was. Suddenly her legs felt ridiculously shaky and she felt physically sick. 'I never wanted that. I never wanted to take anything from you.'

Or she would have become exactly what his family had thought she was. *A gold-digger.*

The thought appalled her. She wanted to achieve things on her own merits. And she'd never been interested in Rico's money. Just in him. *The man himself.*

She stared at him, uncomprehending. 'Why?' Her voice cracked slightly. 'Why did you do that? We weren't even together—'

His handsome face was blank of expression. 'Call it compensation,' he drawled, 'payment for services rendered.'

She turned away so that he couldn't see the pain on her face. Payment. He saw everything in terms of money, including their relationship. And that attitude explained why, for the entire duration of their marriage, she'd felt like his mistress. Never his wife. He'd showered her with gifts and extravagant jewellery, as if money could compensate for the deficiencies in their relationship. It was the only form of currency that he understood.

'I mean it, Stasia,' he drawled with deadly emphasis. 'Either you stay and play the part of the loving wife until such time as I decide that Chiara is well enough or I close down your business. I can and will do it.'

She looked at him with loathing. 'I can't believe that even you could stoop so low.'

'Your opinion on the matter is totally irrelevant.' He was totally unmoved by her passionate declaration and she curled her fists into her palms to stop herself striking him again.

'If you do *anything* to hurt my mother—'

'The decision whether or not to hurt your mother lies in *your* hands,' he pointed out, his tone silky smooth. 'Agree to stay as my wife for as long as it takes Chiara to regain her memory and the loan is secure. When we finally divorce I shall make sure the business is yours.'

She swallowed hard, her gaze filled with contempt as she considered the position he was putting her in. He was leaving her with absolutely no choice and he knew it. 'You are utterly ruthless—'

'When I want something, then I go after it until I get it. If that's ruthless then yes, I'm ruthless.' He gave a dismissive shrug that showed how little the accusation troubled him and she turned away in disgust, knowing that he'd applied exactly that philosophy in his pursuit of her.

He'd wanted her and he'd been prepared to go to any lengths in order to have her.

'Why are you doing this?' Her voice was little more than a whisper. 'Our marriage was a disaster. We both know that. Why would you want me back?'

They'd had no contact for over a year.

Surely he couldn't be asking this of her.

His brief glance revealed the depth of his contempt for her. 'I don't want you back. But Chiara needs a stable environment. Until her memory recovers, she needs to be protected from shocks. And our marriage was *not* a disaster.' His eyes glittered dangerously in his handsome face. 'But you were too stubborn to allow it to work, too fiercely independent to accept that marriage is a partnership. And I won't have Chiara punished for your failings in that direction. I don't want her to know that our relationship is over.'

For a moment Stasia just stared at him blankly, astonished by his accusation. *He* was telling *her* that marriage was a partnership? That *she* was stubborn? When all the compromises had been hers—

She shook her head, uncomprehending. 'I can't believe you'd do this to me. To yourself.'

Because this had to be hurting him too.

She could read his distaste for the task in every angle of his sharp, masculine features, in the way he kept his powerful body at a safe distance from hers. As if to come too close might contaminate him.

Stasia gazed at him helplessly. No wonder he was such a successful businessman. Like the most dangerous predator, he looked for the weakness in his prey and then used that weakness to achieve his own ends. How could she have fallen in love with a man like him? How could she have been so blinded to the person he was? How could she have ever thought that this man might be capable of so gentle an emotion as love? 'It isn't a practical solution, Rico. I need to work—I have commissions—'

'You can work from the villa.' His black eyes slammed into hers. 'But no travelling. Anything that would take you out of Sicily will have to wait until Chiara's condition allows us to finally reveal the truth.'

She wanted to argue, but how could she when her mother's happiness depended on her compliance? He was leaving her absolutely no choice and he knew it. This wasn't about their relationship, it was about his need to control.

'All right.' She could barely frame the words. 'I'll do it. But don't expect me to like you for this.'

'How times change.' His gaze didn't shift from hers and the sarcasm in his hard tone bit into her flesh. 'I can remember a time when you used to call me on my mobile every hour to beg me to come home and make love to you.'

It was a cruel reminder of just how open she'd been

with him. How honest. She'd never been afraid to tell him how she felt, even though he'd never revealed anything of his own feelings in return.

With the benefit of hindsight she realized that it was because he hadn't shared her feelings. How could he express what he didn't feel?

She lifted her chin, trying to hang on to the last of her pride. 'I never begged.'

'Oh, you begged, Stasia, in that sexy, husky voice of yours—' his own voice was soft and tormenting '—and when I arrived you'd be naked in the bed. Waiting. Waiting for me. *Wanting me.*'

Stasia closed her eyes, just hating the picture he was painting. A picture of a clingy, dependent woman, something she'd always promised herself she'd never become. And that was part of the reason their marriage had failed, of course. She'd never been comfortable with the woman she became when she was with this man.

'I certainly remember the waiting,' she said coldly, making a supreme effort to hold herself together. 'I remember endless days and weeks spent waiting for you to come home from yet another business trip. Sitting there, bored and alone.'

'So boring that you took a lover?'

'That is *not* what happened.'

'Then how else do you explain a naked man in our bedroom? *Our bedroom*?'

A tense silence followed his outburst of raw emotion and her heart almost stopped.

They'd never even talked about what had happened. Incensed by the accusation in his eyes and frantic at the steady destruction of their relationship, she'd walked out, expecting him to follow and demand an explanation. He hadn't.

She lifted an eyebrow. 'You finally want to talk about this? A year after the event? Don't you think it's a bit late?'

He chose to ignore her sarcasm, but streaks of colour highlighted his incredible bone structure, always a warning of impending trouble. 'Did he know how wild you were in bed? How totally insatiable? There's no way a pathetic little guy like that ever would have been able to satisfy your appetite for sex.'

Stasia paled. *Only with him.* He was the only man who'd ever done that to her. The only man she'd ever been to bed with. But then he'd always credited her with more experience than she had. The night he'd discovered that she was a virgin he'd been so shocked that he'd almost been driven to apologize, which would have been a first for Rico Crisanti, a man not given to apologizing for anything.

'*Madre de Dio*, why are we even talking about this?' He raked a hand through his dark hair and snatched a jagged breath. 'I need to get some air or I will do something I regret.'

With a final dangerous glance in her direction that left her in no doubt as to the volatile state of his temper, he strode out of the room, slamming the door behind him.

CHAPTER SIX

CHIARA was allowed home a few days later on the understanding that she rested and was supervised.

Stasia knew that she should feel pleased that the teenager had recovered sufficiently to be discharged from the hospital, but instead her anxiety levels grew.

She and Chiara had spent a fair degree of time together when she had lived in Rome as Rico's wife and it had been a thoroughly stressful experience. She knew that Chiara hated Rico's villa in Sicily, finding it isolated and boring in the extreme. How would they get on, forced to endure what might be weeks in each other's company?

But Chiara, it seemed, was a changed person.

From the moment she arrived at the villa she was pathetically eager to please, determined not to be a nuisance and outwardly charmed by the view from the terrace.

'Do you think I might be able to swim in the sea,' she asked, staring longingly across the private beach to where the ocean sparkled in the summer sunshine.

'Try the pool first,' Rico advised, handing her a hat and gesturing to a sun lounger. 'Sit down and Maria will bring you a drink. And you should probably try and sleep. I need to make a few calls. If you need anything, ask Stasia. I'll see you at dinner.' He brushed his sister's head in an affectionate gesture and then strode off, leaving her staring after him.

'He's always been more of a father to me than a brother,' she murmured and Stasia looked at her warily, unsure how to respond. She knew that, in the past at least, Chiara had hated that fact. Had hated the fact that Rico was so strict with her.

Stasia kept her response neutral. 'He loves you very much.'

Fortunately Chiara fell asleep and the afternoon passed quickly. Stasia went for a wander through the fruit orchards that surrounded the villa, struggling with memories of the first time Rico had brought her here. She'd fallen in love with the island, with the blend of history and culture and the sheer beauty of the scenery. As excited as any tourist, she'd made Rico take her to all the most famous sights and together they'd visited magnificent Greek temples, Norman cathedrals and Baroque palaces until the heat and the sheer volume of people had driven them back to the cool privacy of his villa and more intimate pleasures. But those heady, happy days had given her some insight into what it meant to be Sicilian. And she knew that for Rico it was everything.

Deep in thought, Stasia walked under the trees, picked herself an orange and then returned to the cool, vine-covered terrace. Chiara still slept and Stasia curled up on a sun lounger and lost herself in her sketchbook, enjoying the faint breeze from the sea.

By the time Chiara woke it was time to dress for dinner.

Retiring to the sanctuary of the bedroom she'd been using while Chiara had been in the hospital, Stasia found it stripped bare of her belongings.

Immediately she went and found Rico's housekeeper.

'Your things have been moved to the master suite, *signora*,' the woman told her gravely and Stasia frowned.

Why would Rico have done that?

Feeling decidedly uneasy, Stasia marched to the master bedroom and walked in without bothering to knock just as Rico strolled out of the shower, his glorious bronzed body touched by specks of water, a small towel in his hand as he dried his sleek, dark hair.

Stasia stopped dead and ceased to breathe.

Her eyes feasted on him, taking in his broad shoulders and the powerful swell of his biceps. She bit back a whimper of need as her eyes drifted to his powerful chest. The shadow of dark body hair seemed to intensify his masculinity and guided the greedy female eye down over his board-flat stomach and lower still to his awesome manhood.

Suddenly feeling dizzy, she finally remembered to suck breath into her starving lungs, but she couldn't shift her eyes.

His response to her gaze was instantaneous and shockingly basic but he showed absolutely no embarrassment by his body's blatant arousal. Instead of using the hand towel to preserve his modesty, he threw it carelessly to one side, his eyes fixed on Stasia's face.

'Well, I think if my little sister could see us now, we wouldn't have any trouble convincing her that we're very much together,' he said with a sardonic lift of his black brows.

Stasia jerked as if he'd slapped her, appalled by her own response to him.

She'd stared. Oh, dear God, she'd stared and stared.

She turned away, totally flustered, but he gave a laugh that contained not the slightest trace of humour.

'I think it's a bit late for either of us to pretend indifference,' he drawled, strolling towards her, still gloriously naked. 'The fact that you still do this for me, even knowing what I know about you, says quite a lot about your appeal, *cara mia*.' There was an edge to his voice that suggested that he was far from pleased to discover that she still affected him.

She kept her eyes averted and clasped her hands behind her back so that he wouldn't see that they were shaking. 'Maria said that my things had been moved.' Her voice was husky and suddenly the room seemed airless. 'I wondered why.'

'Why do you think?' He strolled into his dressing room and reached for a T-shirt, pulling it over his head.

Stasia closed her eyes briefly, wishing desperately that he'd started by dressing his lower half.

But what difference did clothes make, anyway? she reasoned helplessly. Whoever said that 'clothes maketh the man' had never met Rico. In his case it was more a case of 'man maketh the clothes.' He turned the softest, most casual T-shirt into a fashion must-have but Stasia knew that he spent virtually no time considering his appearance. He bought the best and then he forgot about clothes. His sophisticated style was more a result of accident and physical perfection than design.

Mockery in his night-dark eyes, he reached for a pair of silk underpants and drew them on, his gaze holding hers, challenging her. 'I would have thought the reason is obvious.' Trousers came next and finally he was fully clothed. Stasia waited for the high frequency buzz of sexual excitement to die down but there seemed to be no relief. Her entire body was on fire for the man.

It was just because she hadn't had sex for a year, she told herself hastily, backing towards the door, trying to ignore the spread of heat low in her pelvis. 'I'll come back later.'

'Of course you will.' His voice was smooth. 'From now on you'll be sleeping in here. Sleeping, dressing— all the things that a normal married couple do in their bedroom.'

She froze. 'You're expecting me to share a room with you?'

'Absolutely.'

'Then you're delusional.' Her heart started to thud. 'There's no way I'm sleeping in here with you.'

He couldn't be serious.

He couldn't—

He walked across the room with a cool sense of purpose. 'Then I call the bank.' He lifted the receiver and she stopped dead.

'No!' Her tone was sharp and she lifted a hand to her forehead as she tried to think clearly. 'Don't do that. Put it down.'

Her heart slumped in her chest as she considered her options. Again he was leaving her no choice. But how was she supposed to share a room with him?

It was the very worst kind of torture.

He replaced the receiver, his eyes fixed on her face. 'From now on, this is your room. Chiara's room is just two doors away. If you don't sleep here, then she'll know.'

She forced herself to breathe. 'I'm *not* sleeping in the bed with you!'

He glanced at his watch, ignoring her passionate statement. 'Dinner is in ten minutes. Don't you need to change?'

She glared at him for a moment and then walked into the dressing room and slammed the door.

Stasia lingered over dinner, prolonging the moment when she would have to return to the bedroom.

Rico's bedroom.

'It will be so great to be at home with you both,' Chiara said happily, helping herself to more olives. 'But I do feel guilty, making you stay here. I know you must be itching to get back to Rome, Rico.'

Stasia jumped as Rico's hand covered hers. 'As it happens this is a perfect time for me to spend some time with Stasia.' Dark velvety eyes caressed hers. 'I have neglected her in the past while I've been working and I intend to rectify that.' He lifted her hand to his lips, his gaze loaded with sensual promise.

To her utter horror, Stasia felt a lump building in her throat. Those were the words he should have spoken when they were married and still together. Not now, when it was too late and just for the benefit of his sister.

Chiara just smiled, ignorant of the undercurrents in the room. 'Well, I promise that I won't get in the way this time. You can be as romantic as you like. You won't even know I'm here.'

Romantic?

Swamped by an excess of emotion, Stasia snatched her hand away from Rico's and dropped her fork. 'I'm sorry—I'm feeling a little tired. I think I'll have an early night.' She ignored Rico's warning glance and rose to her feet. 'I hope you have a good night. I'll see you at breakfast.'

With that she left the room and sought refuge in the bedroom. If there'd been a key she would have locked the door but there wasn't and she knew that it was only a matter of time before Rico joined her.

He strode into the room minutes later, a grim expression on his handsome face as his dark eyes swept over her pale cheeks. 'You'd better work harder on your performance or I'll be making that phone call.'

She sat on the edge of the bed, feeling slightly sick. 'Unlike you, I find it hard to live a lie. It's something I need to learn.'

'Then learn quickly,' he advised silkily, 'or the deal is off.'

'I'm trying.'

'You call sitting in silence throughout dinner trying?' Dark brows rose in question. 'You stared at your plate. What happened to the loving looks?'

'I'm working on them.'

'Then work harder and faster. And from now on I want you to talk as you normally do. Silence is *not* your trademark, as we both well know. And I want you to smile. And I want you to act as though you can't keep your hands off me, *cara mia*.'

'Does it count if I strangle you?' Her eyes flashed with some of her old fire and his eyes gleamed in appreciative response.

'Save that for the bedroom,' he suggested with a predatory smile that made him seem more dangerous than ever. 'In public I want you to touch me like a lover.'

She looked at him sickly. 'But I don't want to touch you like a lover.'

'That's a lie, and we both know it,' he said softly, reaching for the hem of his T-shirt in a slow, deliberate gesture designed to torment. He pulled the garment over his head to reveal a bronzed torso that would have made a Greek god groan in envy. 'We may both hate the fact, but the truth is that you and I have never been able to keep our hands off each other. Perhaps you need reminding of that fact.'

She tried to scoot off the bed but he moved with lightning speed, sliding an arm around her waist and preventing her escape.

'Let me go. This wasn't part of our agreement.' Her heart was thudding so hard she thought it would burst and she lifted both hands to his chest, intending to push him away. It was a mistake. The minute the sensitive tips of her fingers made contact with the hair on his chest and the sleek, bronzed skin beneath, she wanted to cling. Desperately she tried to summon up the will-power to free herself from his hold but he was too close. Too tempting. Suddenly she felt dizzy and light-headed.

It had been so long. So long since he'd held her. So long since she'd breathed in that male smell that she found so seductive.

They stayed like that for a moment, poised on the edge of sexual insanity. And then his mouth came down on hers.

It was pure possession. A statement of intent, his tongue immediately demanding access, probing the depths of her mouth with a skill and precision that left her shaking just as he'd known it would. He'd always known exactly how to drive the maximum response from her.

His hands slipped from her waist to her buttocks and he jerked her against him in a primitive male gesture, bringing her burning pelvis into contact with the hard ridge of his arousal. And he held her there. Male against female. Hard against soft. The muscles of his shoulders bunched under her fingers, his mouth plundered and stole and still he held her. Making her aware of what she did to him.

And finally she couldn't stand it any longer. The fire was so intense that she needed relief and he was the only one who could give it. Nothing else mattered.

She groaned into his mouth and he tipped her backwards on to the bed and came down on top of her, removing the rest of his clothes so swiftly that she wasn't even aware that he'd undressed until she felt the shockingly delicious feel of his naked body against hers.

His eyes fixed on hers, his expression one of grim purpose, he stripped her quickly and then spread her legs for his heated gaze.

She made an embarrassed protest but he ignored her,

sliding a warm, leisurely hand from the soft swell of her breast down to the cluster of bright curls that should have hidden her femininity. But he wasn't allowing her to hide. His eyes held hers, increasing the intimacy as his fingers explored her most sensitive flesh with erotic precision.

And it felt wickedly good.

So good that when he gave a low laugh of masculine triumph she didn't even hear him. And if she had heard she wouldn't have cared. She was totally focused on the moment and what he was doing to her body.

She closed her eyes and moved against his hand, past hearing, past reacting to anything except the sensations that he was creating throughout her totally responsive body.

And when she opened her eyes again he was looking at her, thick dark lashes shielding his expression as he witnessed her total unrestrained surrender to his masterly touch.

When it came, her climax was so intense that she dug her nails into his shoulders and cried out his name so sharply that he lowered his head and kissed her deeply, taking the sobs and gasps into his mouth, smothering the sound. It went on and on and his fingers stayed deep inside her, drawing every last ounce of response from her quivering body.

When the last pulses of her sexual peak died away he lifted his head, but still didn't move his hand, his eyes slightly mocking as he surveyed her hectically flushed cheeks and her parted lips.

'You always were the most sexually responsive woman I ever went to bed with,' he said thickly, not even bothering to conceal his own arousal. 'Perhaps it was no wonder you had an affair. You were always so desperate for it and I obviously left you alone for too long.'

It was a cruel comment, particularly as she wasn't mentally or physically equipped to respond. The intensity of her climax had left her slightly stunned and weakened, but still her body craved more and she dared not move because to move would have been to invite a further caress from his long, clever fingers.

'Did he do that for you?' His voice was hard and his fingers suddenly moved with a skill that made her gasp and arch her back. 'Did he know what turns you on? And were there others, or just him?'

She closed her eyes and shifted her hips, trying to move away from him, but he pinned her to the bed with his superior body weight, his power over her unquestionable.

'Rico, no!' Her own voice was little more than a groan. 'You don't mean this. You don't want this, and neither do I.'

'I think we've just proved what you want,' he said silkily, lowering his mouth to her breast and tormenting one nipple with a skilled flick of his tongue. 'Now it's time to clarify what *I* want. And that, my dear wife, is you.'

She tried to push him away, tried to argue, but his fingers were still deep inside her and the deliberate drag of his tongue over her breast sent shock waves pulsing right through her overexcited body.

Finally she managed to speak. 'You don't want me—'

'No?' His tone was ironic and he moved slightly so that she could feel the press of his erection against her leg. 'Irritating though it is, unfortunately the brain and the body don't always work together.'

'You think I've slept with other men—'

'As I said, brain and body don't always work together. Knowing you're a slut doesn't seem to cure my
problem.' His voice was rough and he stared down into
her dazed eyes with a grim sense of purpose. 'And at
the moment I don't really care about your past. I just
have to get past the fact that other guys have enjoyed
what used to be mine exclusively. I'm not that great at
sharing but I'm working on it.'

Wounded beyond belief, she shot the insult right
back. 'And if I'm a slut, what does that make you?'

'Desperate?' He rolled her beneath him with a thickened groan, his mouth coming down on hers with a
force that prevented further speech on either part.
Sexual excitement, held at boiling point for far too long,
erupted with a dangerous force, devouring both of them,
sweeping them along in its greedy path.

This time there was no slow build.

No gradual seduction.

The seduction had begun from the moment he'd arrived at her cottage and the time for slow had passed.

He didn't hesitate. Didn't give her time to prepare for
what he was about to do. He just slid a hand under her
bottom, tilted her to his satisfaction and took her with
a hard, almost brutal thrust that drew a cry of shock and
ecstasy from her parted lips. He was so big—*she'd forgotten how big*—and for a moment she had to force
herself to relax, reminding herself that her body could
accommodate this man. Had done so on many occasions.

He paused, a sheen of sweat on his bronzed skin, then
he muttered something in Italian and thrust deeper still,
fiercely, like a man driven by something other than simple lust. It was shockingly basic. Sex at its most prim-

itive. Totally overwhelmed by the physical reality of his possession, Stasia dug her nails into the muscles of his shoulders and wrapped her legs around him, welcoming the demands of his body.

'Whoever you have been with before, you are mine now.' He thrust again, as if staking his claim, and his voice held a triumphant, possessive note but she was past reacting to anything except the physical sensations consuming her body. She arched towards him, offering more, her movement the instinctive response of a female to a virile, potent male.

'Rico—' she breathed his name, lifted her mouth towards his in blatant invitation and he hesitated for just a flicker of time before lowering his head. And then he took. He took her mouth in a hot, drugging kiss from which there was no escape. He took her body on a breathtaking, sensual ride. But most of all he took her heart, so that when their shared climax finally exploded she held him close, drowning in the knowledge that she'd never stopped loving this man.

He could hurt her, he could infuriate and anger her more than any other person she knew, and yet still she couldn't stop loving him.

She closed her eyes and held him, feeling the thud of his heart, the slick heat of his skin and the warmth of his breath against the sensitive skin of her neck.

He didn't move.

His weight should have troubled her, but it didn't. Instead it was comforting. It was too long since she'd lain beneath him and she closed her eyes and held him, wondering how she was ever going to move forward in her life when this was the only place she ever wanted to be.

The only man she ever wanted to be with.

When he finally rolled away from her and covered his eyes with his forearm, she felt bereft.

She swallowed, risked a glance sideways and instantly regretted the impulse.

If ever a man was in torment then it was he.

If she'd been expecting soft words of love and the gentleness that so often followed on from such an explosive release of passion, then she was doomed to disappointment. There was no gentleness. No prolonging of the intimacy that they'd shared. Only an aura of self-recrimination that thickened the atmosphere until she could almost taste it. Clearly he felt he'd sullied himself by giving in to his own needs and touching her.

Without a word or a glance in her direction, he sprang to his feet and strolled into the bathroom, closing the door behind him.

And then she let the tears fall.

It was symbolic, that closed door. Symbolic of the barriers that Rico Crisanti always put between himself and the women in his life. And she was no different. He might have married her but he shared nothing but his body. She'd chosen to fall in love with a man who kept himself locked away and he didn't need to close a door to create a barrier between them. She'd been nothing more than a mistress with a ring on her finger. *Legalized sex.*

She heard the hiss of the shower running and imagined the stream of water cascading over his sleek black hair, washing the evidence of his torrid encounter from his body. The knowledge that he felt the need to do that cut her to the bone. And the knowledge that she would never be able to free herself of the feelings that she had for him made the pain almost unbearable.

Quickly she turned on her side, curling into a ball

and pulling the sheet over her in a protective gesture. She loved him with a force that would never be reciprocated. Somehow she was going to have to deal with that.

Dio, he had *not* intended that to happen.

Still aroused and despising himself for that weakness, Rico stood under the shower, allowing the freezing water to sluice over his heated flesh. His eyes were closed, his wide shoulders braced against the tiled wall as he attempted to wash away the guilt and shame.

He'd been rough.

No matter that she'd writhed and sobbed in ecstasy. The knowledge that he'd lost control did *not* make him feel good. In fact the realization that he had very probably hurt her appalled him. Whatever she'd done to him, no woman deserved that.

Realizing that no amount of cold water was going to assuage his guilt or the insistent throb of certain parts of his body, he cut the flow of water and reached for a towel.

Why had he behaved like that?

He cleared the water from his eyes and knotted the towel around his lean hips.

Perhaps it was a pride thing, he mused, pacing across to the mirror and registering the degree of dark stubble on his jaw with a frown. She'd left him, so he wanted to show her that he was more of a man than any of her lovers. *That no man understood her body as he did.*

At that thought his fingers clenched on the edge of the basin until his knuckles showed white.

It was nothing to do with pride. He just couldn't cope with the image of another man's hands on her.

On his woman.

Despite the cold shower, beads of sweat shone on his

brow and he cursed softly, recognizing the ravenous, tearing emotions inside him for what they were.

Jealousy. A primal male jealousy that had driven him to take possession of what was his.

But she wasn't his any more.

She'd left and he'd let her go, so consumed by his own emotions that he hadn't even considered a different option.

Was that why he'd been so quick to agree to the doctor's request that Stasia be brought to visit Chiara? Had he subconsciously wanted the chance to take a different route?

He breathed deeply and stared at his reflection in the mirror. From the moment Chiara had uttered Stasia's name he'd known this would happen. There had never been even the slightest chance that they'd be able to exist alongside each other without responding to the white-hot chemistry that had always connected them.

He remembered their first date. He'd taken her for dinner in his *palazzo* in Rome and she'd spent the evening telling him that she wouldn't be staying, pretending to both of them that she was going to be spending the night alone in her hotel room. But her protest had lacked conviction and both of them had known it. Their fate had been sealed from the first moment they'd locked eyes in the marbled foyer of the headquarters of the Crisanti Corporation. Sex between them had had a delicious inevitability that had simply fuelled the excitement and anticipation.

And from the moment he'd discovered that she was a virgin there had been no way that he was ever letting her escape. He'd wanted to keep her. And he did it by offering her the one thing he'd never offered another woman.

Marriage.

He'd given her everything she could possibly have wanted and yet apparently it hadn't been enough and the knowledge left a bitter taste in his mouth.

Until last night he'd believed that there was no going back. Now suddenly he wasn't so sure. He gave a cynical laugh. Which just went to show what a complete fool he was. Even knowing what she was, he was still totally hooked on her.

He splashed his face with cold water and stared into the mirror again, his expression suddenly cold. So why was he denying himself? Stasia was a beautiful woman and she was still his wife. The sex was unbelievably good and, despite her denials, it was still perfectly obvious that she wanted him with the same fevered desperation that he wanted her. So there was absolutely no logical reason why they couldn't still enjoy each other physically.

Wasn't that the best sort of relationship? No empty I love you's. No emotional baggage. Just amazing mindless sex between two people who understood each other.

And when Chiara finally regained her memory then he'd walk away from Stasia without a backward glance. For the final time.

Having managed to rearrange the facts in such a way that he could more than justify a repeat performance in the bedroom, he reached for a razor and started to shave.

CHAPTER SEVEN

WHEN Stasia awoke the next morning Rico's side of the bed was empty and it was obvious from the pristine plumpness of the pillow that she'd slept alone. The narrow sofa in the corner of the room bore all the signs of occupation, the white cushions slightly rumpled. She winced as she tried to imagine the degree of revulsion that must have driven Rico to choose what must have been a fiendishly uncomfortable night over the chance to sleep in his own bed.

Clearly he hadn't wanted to be anywhere near her and why that knowledge should fill her with such a profound depression, she didn't know.

What had she expected? To be woken by a loving kiss?

Hardly.

Loving wasn't what last night had been about.

Rico was a highly sexed guy and he wasn't likely to deprive himself of physical satisfaction just because he had the misfortune to be trapped in his villa with his soon-to-be ex-wife.

She swung her legs out of bed, registered the unfamiliar ache of her body with a wry smile and made for the shower. The long shower he'd taken the night before had obviously worked for him. Perhaps she'd try the same treatment.

Reluctant to face him and having no faith at all in her ability to project the loving front that he was demanding, she took her time dressing, hoping that by the time she finally made an appearance Rico might have finished breakfast and disappeared to his study to work.

She was unlucky.

He was lounging on the terrace looking disgustingly handsome and healthy; he looked like a man who had slept undisturbed a full ten hours rather than one who had snatched the minimum of sleep on a sofa that was most definitely *not* designed to deliver comfort to a person of his build.

She delayed the moment when she'd have to join them by strolling over to the nearest fruit tree. She stood for a moment, lost in memories as sweet as they were painful, and then reached up and picked an orange. It had always enchanted her—the notion that she could pick her breakfast straight from the tree. And Rico had teased her that she had such simple tastes.

She turned the orange in her hand, admiring its perfection. She *did* have simple tastes. But he'd never seemed to understand that. And neither had his family.

Reluctantly she strolled back to the terrace to join them.

Chiara was finishing a sweet pastry and chatting to her brother. She glanced up with a smile as Stasia sat down.

'You had a long lie-in. You must have been tired.' She handed Stasia some coffee and her eyes narrowed. 'Did you have too much sun yesterday? Your skin is quite red round your neck—'

Aware that Rico was looking at her, his long fingers toying idly with his coffee cup, Stasia reached for a plate and a knife. 'I have sensitive skin,' she said quietly and Chiara coloured as understanding dawned.

'Oh—I didn't—' thoroughly flustered, the teenager

stared out towards the sea. 'It's going to be a really hot day. I might go to the beach.'

'Well, take Gio with you,' Rico instructed immediately. 'You shouldn't be on your own. And don't stay there too long. You need to rest in the shade.'

Clearly anxious to escape from the scene of her *faux pas*, Chiara mumbled something, turned a deeper shade of pink and hurried off towards the villa.

Stasia watched her go, peeling her orange with smooth sweeps of the knife. 'Well, I think we can assume that your sister is now convinced that we're very much together,' she said tartly, dropping the peel on the plate and dividing the orange into segments. 'You must be delighted. It all worked out exactly as you'd planned.'

Rico drained his coffee. 'Not exactly. I have regrets about last night—'

'Oh, that's right—' She struggled to keep her voice steady. 'Touching me wasn't part of the plan, was it?'

He tensed. 'Stasia—'

'Do you really think I didn't know how you felt after we made love?' Despite her efforts, her voice shook. 'You hated yourself, Rico. Hated yourself for losing that control that you pride yourself on, hated yourself for touching someone like me.'

He inhaled sharply. 'That isn't true.'

Something in his voice made her look towards him. Their eyes clashed, her breath caught, and suddenly she was remembering every moment of the night before. The heat. The power of masculine thrust. *Raw sexual excitement.*

And he was remembering it too.

'Let's just both agree that it won't be happening again.' She dragged her eyes away from his and concentrated on her plate, wondering if she was ever going to feel like eating again. Even a fresh orange had lost its appeal. 'Unless you're intending to invite Chiara to share our bedroom, there's no point. So you can save your regrets.'

'I don't regret making love to you,' he said, his Sicilian accent suddenly unusually pronounced. 'And the point,' he drawled slowly, 'is that you and I can't be together and not rip each other's clothes off. And don't pretend you were a victim last night. You wanted it every bit as much as me.'

She wanted to deny it. She wanted to wipe the smug, self-satisfied look off his impossibly handsome face. But how could she? When she'd dug her nails into his sleek, muscular back and virtually begged him for more? She couldn't even convince herself so what chance was there of convincing him?

She took refuge in attack. 'You really think you're the ultimate lover, don't you?'

He didn't hesitate, his black eyes burning into hers. 'If your reaction last night was anything to go by, then yes.' He gave a casual lift of his broad shoulders and she licked dry lips, wondering if there was any way she could learn control over her body. Surely there must be something she could do to make her indifferent to this man? She lifted her chin.

'So what do you regret then?'

'Hurting you.' His voice was velvety smooth and as intimate as his gaze. 'I was rough and I'm sorry.'

He caught her by surprise and astonishment stifled the sharp remark she'd intended to make. She'd never heard him apologize for anything before. He had more self-confidence than anyone she knew, a trait that had guaranteed him unrivalled success in business. When negotiating deals he waited for others to lose their nerve—

Suddenly she felt incredibly self-conscious, which was utterly ridiculous considering the intimacies they'd shared the night before. 'You didn't hurt me.' Her voice was croaky and he gave a half smile.

'Good. But if I didn't then it was only because you were as desperate as I was.' The smile faded and suddenly his eyes were cold and assessing. 'So what's your excuse, my beautiful wife? Lover not been satisfying you lately?'

'Damn you, Rico.' She rose to her feet so swiftly that her chair scraped the terrace noisily and almost fell. Goaded and furious that he'd somehow turned what for her had been an act of love into something sordid and purely physical, she turned on him. 'You spent your entire time working. You only came home for sex and towards the end even that wasn't very often. You employ thousands of people. You need to learn to delegate.'

She took a step towards the villa but his hand closed over her wrist like a vice, preventing her escape. Her heart was suddenly pounding at a frightening pace and she met the fierce blaze of anger in his eyes with a sinking feeling. *She shouldn't have said that.*

'When I need a lesson on how to run my business, I'll ask you. And when I need a lesson on how to keep my wife satisfied, I'll ask for that too.' His voice was even but the tiny muscle flickering in his cheek betrayed his fury. 'Clearly I didn't keep you anywhere near busy enough in the bedroom. It's probably only fair to warn you that while we are at the villa you're going to be too exhausted to move, let alone look at another man, *cara mia.*'

'Rico—'

He ignored her shaky protest, his expression revealing a grim sense of purpose as he lifted her easily and carried her back to the bedroom.

'Rico—for goodness' sake—' She struggled for a few seconds but already her body was responding. He only had to glance in her direction and she was lost. She felt the familiar curl of desire low in her pelvis, her whole body achingly sensitive to his touch.

He deposited her on the bed and came over her, pinning her down when she would have rolled away from him.

'You wanted more of my attention—' his voice was muffled in her neck and she cried out as his tongue licked a sensuous path towards her ear '—and now you're going to get it.'

'Rico—this is just pretend—'

'*Not* pretend,' he murmured in thickened tones, stripping her with a skilled precision and spreading her legs for his seeking mouth.

She gasped in shock and then cried out as the skilled flick of his tongue sent shock waves of sensation scorching through her trembling body. He was merciless, exploring her with ruthless intimacy until she hovered on the edge of sexual ecstasy, her mind and body beyond her control.

When he finally penetrated her shivering, desperate body she gave a low moan and he paused, a sheen of sweat on his bronzed features, his own breathing decidedly unsteady. 'Does this feel like pretend?' Perhaps realizing that she was incapable of answering, he thrust deeper, his movements slow and deliberate. If the night before had been crazy and wild then this was slower and more controlled but it was no less devastating. *'Does this feel like pretend, Stasia?'*

He slid a hand under her buttocks and lifted her, thrusting deeper still and then almost withdrawing until she gave a sob of protest and clutched at him, urging him back. But this time he was totally in control. And he took her like a master, driving her to mindless, agonized ecstasy over and over again. And finally, when she'd peaked for the fourth time, he took his own pleasure, driving into her again and again until she felt his powerful body shudder and the spill of his seed deep inside her. He moaned her name, crushed her against him and unbelievably her own body exploded into orgasm once again, contracting, squeezing, drawing him in. He felt it. She felt it. He swore and thrust deep again and again, driven skyward by the pulsing of her muscles and the erotic violence of his own release.

An explosion so violent it had to be followed by calm.

Finally he rolled away from her, drawing his body away from hers and covering his eyes with his forearm. Lying in a state of sensual shock, Stasia risked a glance in his direction, wondering if he felt the same way. If she hadn't known better she would have thought he was lost for words.

But of course that wasn't the case.

As if intercepting her thoughts and determined to minimize what they'd just shared, he opened his eyes and yawned.

'You'd better get some rest,' he advised silkily, springing to his feet with the smug satisfaction of a jungle cat having made a kill, 'so that you are fully recovered for later.'

Later?

Feeling dazed and foggy, Stasia struggled to find her voice. 'We can't keep doing this, Rico—'

'We can.' He spoke with the same assurance that characterized his every move. 'We are, after all, still married. So why not?'

And that was that. To him, sex and marriage were synonymous.

It was truly that simple. The fact that there was a huge gulf between them emotionally just didn't enter into it. The fact that he believed her capable of the most distasteful episode of infidelity didn't enter into it either. He'd decided that he wanted to have sex with her, so that was fine. He was prepared to conveniently forget everything in order to satisfy his rampant desire for sex. It was as if their problems were irrelevant. And perhaps, to Rico, they were.

She was obviously good for sex, and that was all he wanted from her. Stasia stared up at the ceiling with blank incomprehension. Were men and women truly so different? Could he truly experience that degree of physical intimacy with her and feel nothing?

She covered her eyes with her arms so that she couldn't see his magnificent naked body. Her entire body was throbbing and exhausted and yet if he'd turned round and made love to her again she would have welcomed it. And she just hated herself for that. She wanted to be able to lie there and seem bored. She wanted her body to be still and unresponsive.

But it seemed that when it came to Rico, she was insatiable.

It took a few seconds for her to realize that he'd finished in the shower and was now dressed in a pair of shorts and a loose shirt undone at the throat to reveal a tantalizing glimpse of male chest hair.

He looked replete, handsome and extremely satisfied. 'We are joining Chiara on the beach. Can you walk or do you need me to carry you?'

As he'd no doubt intended, the question brought her to her feet with almost indecent haste. 'I need a shower.' She wanted to sound cool and indifferent but it was hard when he was watching her with that penetrating dark gaze that she had always found so disturbing and so erotic.

'Then be quick. I don't want her left on her own.'

'She's surrounded by bodyguards,' Stasia pointed out as she walked into the bathroom for the second time that morning. 'She's hardly on her own.'

'That's not the same thing,' Rico growled, following her and leaning broad shoulders against the doorway.

She shot him a pointed look. 'I'm not showering with you watching.'

'A little late for modesty, don't you think,' he mocked gently, his eyes flicking over her breasts and down her legs with blatant male appreciation, 'when already I know every inch of you?'

She stared at him. 'You don't know me at all, Rico.'

His eyes clashed with hers. 'I know exactly how to touch you to set you on fire,' he said silkily, 'exactly what tips you over the edge.'

She walked towards him and gave him a gentle push, just enough to make him take a step backwards so that she could close the door. 'That's physical stuff, Rico,' she said calmly. 'I'm talking about the emotional stuff. And emotionally you don't know me at all. I'll join Chiara on the beach in five minutes.'

And then she closed the door.

*   *   *

When she finally walked on to the sand she was surprised and more than a little unsettled to find Rico stretched out next to Chiara in a part of the beach that was still enjoying shade.

She hadn't realized that he intended to linger.

'Not working, Rico?' She sank down on the section of the large blanket that was furthest away from him. Unfortunately it was the only portion still in the sun and she saw him frown.

'*Idiota*—' His voice was rough and he reached out a hand and pulled her towards him. 'You know how easily you burn. Five minutes in this heat and your skin will be raw, *cara mia*. Stay in the shade.'

The concern in his tone and the warmth of his gaze were almost more than she could bear and she had to remind herself that this was all for his sister's benefit. Not hers. Consoling herself with the fact that he would undoubtedly be leaving to go and work in his study any minute, she reluctantly shuffled into the shade, even though that brought her closer to him.

She concentrated on Chiara. 'How are you feeling?'

'Pretty well. Just a bit of a headache.' The girl glanced up from the teenage magazine that she was devouring and gave a rueful smile. 'And I can't remember anything that's happened since your honeymoon, apparently. I'm relying on you to fill in the gaps.'

'Just live in the present,' Rico advised smoothly, reaching across for a tube of sun cream and squeezing some on to his hand. Then he smoothed the cream on to Stasia's back, massaging it into her skin with a gentle, seductive motion.

She couldn't help turning her head to look at him and instantly their eyes clashed, heat flaring between them as it always did when they touched. His hands knew her body so well. Where to stroke, how to draw the maximum response from her—

Stasia bit back a moan of frustration. It was less than an hour since he'd left her lying utterly sated on the bed. And still it seemed that her body hadn't had enough…

'Now I know why I lost my memory.' Chiara laughed, rolling on to her stomach and covering her eyes in mock horror. 'It must have been the sight of you two on your honeymoon. If this is how you are together after a year and a half, you must have been completely unbearable when you were first married. Did you ever get out of bed?'

'Chiara!' Rico's dark brows clashed in a disapproving frown and his tone was sharp. Suddenly he was very much the older brother. 'You will *not* speak like that.'

Chiara sighed. 'I'm hardly a child, Rico,' she pointed out mildly, 'and I do know the facts of life. If I didn't, you'd be worried.'

Stasia gaped in astonishment. It was the first time she had ever heard Chiara stand up to her brother.

'I'd be worried whatever you did,' Rico said roughly, reaching out a hand and touching his sister's sleek, dark hair in an affectionate gesture. 'It is a brother's role to worry. And I have always felt responsible for you, you know that.'

Chiara smiled. 'You have a wife to worry about now, Rico.' She yawned. 'And what I want to know is why haven't you two had children yet?'

For perhaps the first time in his life Rico looked totally shell-shocked. The silence stretched on and on and in the end it was Stasia who answered.

'That's probably my fault,' she said quietly, reaching across and taking Rico's hand in hers. If she was going to play the part then she might as well play it to the full. 'I had a career, you see. A career which I loved and which involved lots of travelling while I painted. I didn't want a child immediately. We decided to wait.'

It wasn't a lie, although it wasn't exactly the truth either. The truth was that they hadn't decided anything. They'd never talked about children. Just as they'd never discussed anything of importance. They'd just fallen into their marriage without looking left or right.

Some of the tension left Rico's shoulders and his hand tightened around hers in a gesture of approval and gratitude. Clearly he thought it was a good answer.

'I'm amazed he let you wait,' Chiara drawled, rolling on to her side and looking at them both with amusement in her eyes. 'I may have lost part of my memory but I do know that my brother is the original primitive male. He wants his wife to produce plenty of little miniatures of himself. If he's let you off the hook so far then don't be fooled. He's just biding his time. He'll get you pregnant any day now.'

Oh, dear God—

Stasia's face burned and Rico frowned.

'That's enough, Chiara.' His words were for his sister but his eyes were on Stasia, acutely watchful. 'You are too hot?'

'No.' She shook her head and managed a smile. She wasn't hot. She was panicking. Neither of them had thought of contraception…

Feeling slightly sick, she did a quick mental calculation and worked out that it was very unlikely that she could be pregnant. She'd have to be extremely unlucky. *Or lucky.* Somehow, despite everything that was happening between them, she couldn't bring herself to feel anything other than warm and excited at the prospect of having Rico's baby. *Despite the fact that their relationship had no future—*

And what sort of a fool did that make her?

Chiara was rubbing sun lotion into her arms. 'You said you didn't want children because you had a career? Don't you have one now?'

Stasia tried to drag herself from the image of possibly being pregnant. 'I no longer paint murals,' she murmured. 'Now I just paint pictures, almost always to commission, so I don't have to travel as much, and sometimes I—' She broke off just in time, realizing with a flash of horror that she'd been about to say that she helped her mother with the antique business. Realizing how close she'd come to revealing the truth that she and Rico were no longer together, Stasia bit her lip and quickly finished the sentence she'd left hanging. 'Sometimes I just like to potter around the house.'

Which wasn't far from the truth. Since she'd returned from Italy she'd been unable to summon up the energy to do anything much. Her little cottage had been her sanctuary.

'I wish I could paint,' Chiara said wistfully, dropping the bottle and lying back with her eyes closed. 'It sounds very restful.'

'It can be restful,' Stasia agreed, 'but sometimes it's frustrating. When a painting doesn't come quite right, it drives me mad.'

'I'd like to learn to paint. I'd like to learn about colour and things. Will you teach me?'

Stasia looked at the teenager in astonishment and Chiara opened her eyes.

'What's the matter? You look really surprised. Did I hate painting, or something?'

Aware that Rico was watching her through narrowed

eyes, Stasia pulled herself together. 'I don't know,' she said honestly. 'We never really talked about it.'

Chiara frowned and propped herself up on her elbows. 'So what *did* I like doing?'

Stasia stared at her helplessly, trying to formulate a suitable reply. The truth certainly wasn't appropriate. In the end she chose to be vague. 'You were a typical teenager,' she hedged. 'You liked clothes and your friends—'

'Friends.' Chiara frowned quizzically. 'Did I have a boyfriend?'

Rico sucked in a breath, his handsome face suddenly like a thundercloud. 'You did *not* have a boyfriend. I was very strict about that. Lots of your friends spent their time hanging around in nightclubs, drinking and picking up men. Fortunately for me, you never saw the attraction of spending your evenings that way.'

Stasia stared out to sea, careful to reveal nothing in her expression. The conversation had moved on to dangerous ground.

Chiara sat up and wrapped her arms round her knees, her eyes fixed on her brother's face. 'So how did I spend my evenings?'

Rico shrugged. 'Studying, mostly. Sometimes you would join the family for dinner.'

Stasia kept her eyes fixed firmly on the horizon. *And sometimes she had such a major teenage tantrum that she spent the evening locked in her room. And on the nights that her brother was away she'd slipped out to a nightclub or invited friends into the house. Unsuitable friends. Friends who Rico had banned his sister from seeing.*

His mobile phone rang and Rico sprang to his feet with a soft curse and cast an apologetic glance in their direction. 'This is one call that I *have* to take. I will be back in one moment.'

He strolled further down the sand and for the first time Stasia noticed the bodyguards positioned at different ends of the beach, intent on their mission to ensure that no overeager tourist or paparazzi intruded on private Crisanti land.

'So go on—' Chiara reached for a bottle of water. 'Now he's gone you can tell me the truth.'

Stasia's mouth dried. 'About what?'

'Well, I may have lost my memory but something about what Rico just said doesn't feel right,' Chiara muttered, rubbing her forehead with her fingers. 'I wish my head would stop aching. I wish this cloud in my mind would clear. It's as if the answers are all there but they're hidden away.'

'Perhaps we should go back to the villa,' Stasia suggested but Chiara shook her head.

'The headache stays wherever I am. I might as well be here.' She glanced at the sea and breathed in deeply. 'I like it.'

Stasia looked at her, unable to hide her surprise. 'Do you? I'm glad.'

'I didn't used to like it, did I?'

Stasia hesitated and then shook her head. 'You used to say that it was boring. But you are older now, and—'

'Less of a pain?' Chiara's tone was dry. 'I had boyfriends, didn't I—and he didn't know. I can tell by your face.'

Stasia froze. How was she supposed to respond to that? Was she supposed to tell Chiara the truth? That it had been one of *her* boyfriends that Rico had discovered that night? That Chiara had been the catalyst that had destroyed their already crumbling marriage?

No. Of course she couldn't say that. Chiara was supposed to be shielded from shocks and, anyway, what good would telling the truth serve now? It was too late for Stasia's relationship with Rico. That was long since over.

All that mattered now was facilitating Chiara's recovery so that Stasia could return home to England as soon as possible.

'I don't think the past is very relevant,' Stasia said finally, giving Chiara a warm smile. 'I think it's the present that matters. And you need to concentrate on getting well.'

Chiara stared at her for a moment and then shook her head with a groan and lay back down. 'I've got this fog around my brain. I know the answers are there somewhere but they're just not clear enough for me to grab hold of.'

What would happen when she finally regained her memory? Stasia wondered.

Rico returned at that moment and sprawled on the rug next to them.

'Why aren't you working in your office?' Chiara murmured and Rico's eyes held a sardonic gleam as they rested on Stasia.

'I am learning to delegate,' he drawled softly and she couldn't help smiling.

'Next thing I know, you'll be talking about how you feel.'

'Best to keep your expectations at reasonable levels, cara mia—' He leaned forward and dropped a lingering kiss on her parted lips. 'I'm still a man and men, Sicilian men in particular, do not know weakness.'

She knew he was a man. She didn't need any reminding. With his powerful shoulders, his muscular chest and the roughness of dark stubble on his jaw, Rico Crisanti couldn't be anything but a man. And an incredibly sexy man at that.

'You mean *you* can't show weakness,' she corrected, needing to lighten the atmosphere that was suddenly pulsing with a sexual tension so thick that she could almost taste it.

'That's probably our fault,' Chiara said with a yawn. 'Rico's been the man of the house since he was fifteen years old. We all lean on him and always have. We expect him to be strong and we expect him to always have the answer to everything. If I ever saw Rico looking vulnerable, I'd panic.'

Stasia sat in stunned silence, digesting Chiara's words. She'd never even given his situation any thought. Of course he'd mentioned that his father had died when he was young. And of course she'd observed that he was considered the head of the family. But she'd just assumed that they were a typical Sicilian family. Following Sicilian traditions. She'd never really considered what it must have meant to him to be given such responsibility at such a young age. How could grown women depend on a boy of fifteen?

She glanced at him, her gaze uncertain, suddenly wanting to ask him all sorts of questions that she'd never asked before. Like how it had felt to suddenly be a man when he was only a boy. And who had looked after him while he was looking after everyone else?

When they'd first met she'd accused him of being too serious. But was that surprising?

On impulse she sprang to her feet and shot him a challenging smile. 'Fancy a swim?'

Without waiting for an answer, she sprinted towards

the water and plunged into the glass-clear water without giving herself time to hesitate.

He was right behind her.

She gave a gasp and a squeal as the cold water closed over her shoulders and he laughed and grabbed her around the waist.

'Don't push me under,' she begged, clutching him and trying to keep her balance. 'It's so cold.'

In fact the water was deliciously cooling on her over-heated skin, but she hated the feeling of almost childlike panic that came from being ducked with no warning.

'It's early in the season,' he reminded her. 'The sea will warm up soon. And don't forget that it seems colder because the sun is so hot. If you stay under, you won't feel cold.' His eyes gleamed with wicked intent and she gave another squeal and tried to free herself, all too aware of what he had in mind.

But she was no match for his strength. With an easy movement, he lifted her and then held her suspended while she clutched at him and begged him not to drop her.

He did, of course, and she sank under the water, still kicking.

Spluttering to the surface, she gave a howl of outrage and hurled herself at him. He fell backwards, laughing, and soon she was laughing too.

'Ugh—I think I've swallowed half the ocean.' She struggled upright and smoothed a hand over her face to clear her vision. 'Enough!'

'You surrender?'

'Never.' Her eyes flashed at him but she was still laughing. 'I'm going to wait until you don't expect it and then creep up on you.'

'Is that right?' His Sicilian accent was suddenly very

pronounced and she felt her heart miss a beat as he moved towards her, the water clinging to the hairs of his broad chest.

'No! Rico, not again! I'll be sick if I swallow any more sea water—' She tried to back away from him but her limbs were heavy in the water and he caught her easily.

But this time he didn't try and duck her. Instead he pulled her against him and looked down at her, his thick, dark lashes shielding his expression.

She swallowed hard, her mind venturing back to a time she'd trained herself to forget.

He drew in a breath, reading her mind. 'This reminds me of our honeymoon.'

She closed her eyes. 'No, Rico—'

She didn't want to go there. This wasn't about revisiting the past. It was about healing Chiara and then moving on. And she had no doubt that this playful display was entirely for Chiara's benefit.

'It's a long time since I saw you laugh like that.' His voice was rough and he lifted a hand and stroked her fiery hair away from her damp forehead. 'When I first met you, you never stopped laughing. You were always laughing. Usually at entirely the wrong moment. You were irrepressible.'

Breathlessly conscious of the heat of his body against hers, of his fingers in her hair, Stasia struggled to breathe. 'When I first met you, you laughed too. On our honeymoon, you laughed.'

And no one had been watching.

His hands slid up to cup her face. 'So what happened?'

'Are you asking me when we stopped laughing?' She looked away from him, the pain so acute that it compromised her breathing. 'I suppose it was when we went back to Rome. You were working. I was working. We were both stressed—'

'If you hadn't insisted on working too then the stress would have been less—'

'Damn it, Rico!' She freed herself and glared at him. 'Don't let's start that again! I wanted to work. You knew that. Painting is part of who I am.'

'I never tried to stop you painting.'

'But you never encouraged me. You didn't want other people to enjoy my work. You didn't want me to have any sort of career.'

He frowned. 'You didn't need a career. As you yourself have just pointed out, our lives were very stressed. Your insistence on carrying on a full career merely added to that pressure.'

'So why did I have to make all the sacrifices? You were just thinking about yourself and what you needed. Well, what about what I needed? I needed a useful occupation. I'm no good at sitting around looking decorative just in case you happen to come home for sex.'

He stiffened. 'That is not how it was.'

'That is *exactly* how it was. You married *me*, Rico. You knew the person I was. And yet for some reason the moment we were married you expected me to become someone else. You expected me to fit the mould of the perfect Italian wife.'

'I did *not* expect you to fit a mould. I gave you everything you could possibly have wanted. I provided you with *everything* you needed. Your life should have been perfect.' He sucked in a breath. 'Our marriage should have been perfect.'

She stared at him with frustration. 'What I needed

wasn't material things but you were so self-centred that you couldn't even see it.'

He shot her a look of pure male incomprehension. 'What is the point of landing yourself a billionaire if you then go out to work?'

'For an exceptionally bright guy you can be impossibly dense, do you know that?' She clenched her hands into fists to prevent herself from hitting him. 'I don't just work for the money, as you would know if you'd bothered to talk to me occasionally instead of just stripping me naked on each occasion we met.'

He was staring at her as if she'd actually thumped him instead of just imagining it and for once he seemed at a loss for words.

She glanced around her and gave a humourless laugh. 'Do you realize how ridiculous this is? We've never even discussed this properly before, and suddenly we're tackling the subject in the middle of the sea when it's all too late.' She glanced across the sand and saw Chiara stand up. 'She'll know we're arguing if we're not careful. We should get back.'

Without waiting for his reply, she waded out of the sea and sprinted across the sand towards his sister.

She didn't want to talk about this any longer. What was the point? They both knew that their marriage was long since over. And once Chiara recovered her memory she and Rico would go their separate ways.

And if that thought just *tortured* her, well, she'd have to get used to it.

CHAPTER EIGHT

RICO paced the length of his study, wrestling with feelings that he didn't want to acknowledge.

It was happening again.

Just a few days and he was falling under her spell. It wasn't enough that he had her in his bed every night, he wanted her in every part of his life.

So what sort of a fool did that make him?

Blind to the spectacular view, Rico stared out of the window, remembering the conversation on the beach.

He was not a man given to introspection, not a man given to dwelling on the past. What was the point, when the past couldn't be changed? So why was it that since that conversation he hadn't been able to concentrate on anything?

How could she accuse him of being self-centred?

He worked punishing hours to provide security and a lavish lifestyle for his family. In what way did that make him self-centred? He'd given everything to the marriage. Had offered total commitment, and she'd thrown it back in his face.

Deciding that women were totally incomprehensible, he stared across the garden, forcing himself to review his marriage from a different angle.

Her angle.

Had he really been blind to her needs? His frown deepened. It was true that their relationship had changed once they had returned to Rome after their honeymoon.

He'd been aware of the change but he hadn't stopped to question that change. Until now.

He cast his mind back and shifted slightly, realizing for the first time that he *had* spent a large amount of time working and possibly neglecting his bride. But previous girlfriends had been all too happy to spend their days exercising his credit card and he'd assumed that Stasia would be the same. Instead he'd found her impatiently pacing the marbled floors of his *palazzo*, waiting for him to come home. And then she'd stopped waiting and had started working. And there had followed several occasions where he'd arrived home and she hadn't been there.

He gritted his teeth, acknowledging the fact that he had *not* reacted well to the fact that his wife had been pursuing her own business interests. But then he wasn't exactly a modern guy, was he?

What did she think? That he wasn't capable of looking after her? That he couldn't provide for his own family?

He rubbed a hand over the back of his neck with a soft curse, remembering that night when he'd come home unexpectedly and found her with a naked man in their bedroom.

Their bedroom.

Sweat broke out on his brow and Rico felt his muscles bunch in an instinctive territorial reaction. No, in some areas he most definitely wasn't a modern guy.

But in others—

He paused for a fraction of a second, looked round his study with narrowed eyes and then lifted the phone.

Chiara didn't join them for dinner.

'She has a headache,' Stasia explained as soon as

Rico strolled on to the terrace. He'd changed into a pair of casual trousers and an open-necked shirt and Stasia allowed herself one glimpse and then fixed her gaze firmly on the view across the terrace. Looking at Rico was a fast route to self-destruction because she knew only too well that looking was never enough. Looking led to touching and before she knew it all her senses were involved. Not just seeing and touching but taste, smell and hearing. Her enjoyment of him was all consuming.

She expected him to sit down opposite her, so when she felt the brush of his thigh against her bare leg she jumped.

'Wine?' Without waiting for her answer, he filled her glass and then his own, his hand strong and steady. 'Is Chiara ill? Do I need to call the doctor?'

Stasia shook her head and tried to inch her chair away slightly. *He was too close.* 'She just stayed up too long today, I think. She needs to have a siesta tomorrow.'

He nodded and helped himself to some olives, leaning back in his chair while one of his staff served the first course. 'She is starting to look a little better.'

Stasia found it hard to concentrate. She was just too aware of him. Did he have to sit so close? What was the purpose, when Chiara wasn't even here to see it?

Unable to stand the mounting tension, she rose to her feet, her breathing rapid, her pulse racing. 'I'm not that hungry—I think I'll just go and paint on the beach—'

Strong fingers closed around her wrist. 'Sit down.' His dark eyes swept her face. 'It's time we talked. And you should eat. This mozzarella is delicious. The best. It has a very delicate flavour. My cousin keeps one of the top herds of buffalo. The milk is too rich to drink but it makes the very best cheese. Try it.'

She didn't want to eat and she didn't want to talk but one look at his face told her that she was being given no choice so she sat down again and picked up her fork.

'What's the point of talking,' she muttered, 'when Chiara isn't here to listen?'

'This isn't for Chiara,' he said, releasing his grip on her wrist and reaching for his fork, 'it's for us. I want to talk about our marriage. Being here in Sicily has reminded me of how it was at the beginning.'

His voice was slightly roughened and she knew instinctively that his mind had been down all the same paths that hers had been down. And she knew that he had found it an equally painful experience.

She reached for her wine. 'We should have known that could never last.'

Dark eyes connected with hers. 'Why couldn't it last?'

'Because it wasn't real. When we first met we didn't share anything except our bodies.' Her cheeks heated slightly at the memory. 'We spent our entire time in bed.'

'Not always in bed, *cara mia*,' he teased softly, his eyes sweeping her flushed cheeks with visible amusement. 'Sometimes it was the floor. Sometimes the sofa. Sometimes the beach. Several times we—'

'All right, all right,' she interrupted him hastily, rejecting the images he was conjuring in her mind. 'You know what I mean. At the beginning, our relationship was all about sex. We didn't spend time getting to know each other. When we went back to Rome, suddenly we reverted to who we really were. We were strangers, Rico. And we never got to know each other. You were always away.'

He frowned. 'I reduced my foreign travel drastically.

I slept in my own home more during our marriage than in the ten years before.'

'That's sex, Rico,' she said flatly. 'You always made it home for sex, but rarely for dinner and conversation. Do you realize that there were days when we didn't talk at all?'

He inhaled sharply. 'I was working long days—I had a business to run.'

'Did you?' She toyed with her wine. 'Or were you afraid of intimacy?'

There was a long pulsing silence. 'We were intimate.'

'Sex again,' she muttered, taking a gulp of wine to give her courage. 'You never shared anything with me except your body and your bank account.'

'I gave you everything.'

'You gave me gifts. Money again. With you, everything comes down to money.'

'If it does then it's because I've seen what a lack of money can do to a family.' His voice was suddenly harsh and she looked at him, slightly startled by his tone.

'Money isn't everything, Rico.'

'Try telling that to a woman who has just lost her husband and her only means of feeding her two children,' he said hoarsely. 'Try telling that to a family on the brink of starvation, about to lose the roof from over their heads.'

It was so unlike Rico to be so verbally expressive that for a moment she fell silent, shocked by his sudden uncharacteristic display of passion.

Instinctively she knew he had to be talking about his mother. She was almost afraid to speak in case he backed off, retreated emotionally as he had always done in the past whenever she'd tried to tackle the subject of his childhood and his father's death. 'You supported her.'

He shot her an impatient look. 'I was fifteen. Not exactly in a position to provide the level of support she needed.' He reached for his wine and drank deeply before replacing the glass on the table. 'This is not something I talk about and after tonight I do not want the subject brought up again, but before you dismiss the importance of money so easily you should know something of what it is like to be without it.'

He looked cold, distant, and she sat totally still, afraid to speak in case she said the wrong thing.

'Every day my mother went without food so that I could eat, but my sister was barely weeks old and because my mother wasn't eating herself she couldn't feed the baby. Her milk dried up.' He rubbed long, strong fingers over the bridge of his nose and closed his eyes briefly as if the image he conjured was almost too ugly to confront. 'Every night my sister cried because she was so hungry and every night my mother cried along with her. I started refusing the food on my plate so that my mother could eat it with a clear conscience.'

Stasia swallowed. 'Rico—'

'Do you know?' His hand dropped to the table with a thump and his eyes were suddenly fierce. 'Do you know what it's like to be hungry? I mean really, *really* hungry?'

She shook her head, unable to answer, and he gave a humourless laugh.

'Well, I do, *cara mia*. And so does my mother.' He stared at the food on his plate, clearly remembering what it had been like to be denied even the most basic of human requirements. 'And in the end it was hunger that drove my desire to succeed.'

His expression was so bleak that she wanted to reach out and touch him, offer comfort in some way, but she sensed instinctively that to offer sympathy at this point would be an insult to his Sicilian pride.

'I went to my neighbour, Gio's father.' His tone was flat. 'I asked him for work. Any work. I just needed enough money to feed the family. He hardly had enough for his own family but he gave me what he could and in return I worked for him, although there was little enough to do. But he understood what it means to be Sicilian and to be a man of honour. He knew that I needed to do something for the money. And he knew that one day I would repay him.'

Stasia swallowed down the lump in her throat. The image of Rico as a young boy, fiercely determined to provide for his mother and baby sister, choked her. 'And Gio is still with you.'

Rico took another mouthful of wine. 'Ours is a bond that goes deeper than friendship. My family owes his family everything. Without his father's help, we would have starved.'

But it was Rico who had found the solution. Rico who had laboured to provide for his family. No wonder his mother was so protective of him. No wonder money was so important to them. They'd known what it was like to live without it, to face poverty and starvation.

Suddenly she was ashamed of herself. It was easy to dismiss money as unimportant when you'd always had enough.

'And you have repaid the debt to Gio's father.'

'Many times over, financially. And the loyalty between our families is unquestionable.'

Stasia was silent for a long moment, shaken by this unexpected insight into Rico's character and past. And she was touched by the loyalty he'd shown to his family. *And envious.* Why had she not been given that same unflinching loyalty?

'And your mother depended on you for everything. I see that now. To them you're some sort of god. But I didn't have the same background,' she said simply, her glance a little wistful because she knew that he wouldn't understand. 'The money wasn't what I wanted. What I wanted was *you*, Rico. I wanted to know every single corner of your mind. I wanted to know what made you tick. I wanted to know what made you laugh and what made you afraid. I wanted to know what drove you. And I wanted you to show the same interest in me.'

'I married you. I assumed that confirmed my interest,' he said dryly and she felt her heart flutter.

'Why?' She hardly dared voice the question. 'Why did you marry me?'

'Because once I made you mine there was no question of letting you go,' he replied immediately, his tone possessive and unmistakably male.

'But you did,' she said quietly. 'You *did* let me go, Rico.'

His fingers drummed on the tabletop. 'You walked out.'

'You didn't try and stop me. And you didn't come after me.'

He drained his wine. 'You betrayed me.'

'I was innocent.'

He thumped the glass down on the table. 'The innocent don't run.'

She rose to her feet, her legs shaking. 'But the angry do, and I was angry, Rico. Angry with you, angry with—' She broke off before she could voice his sister's name, reminding herself that there was no point to any of this. 'I can't believe we're even talking about this now.'

'Neither can I.' His voice was thickened and he ran a hand over the back of his neck like a man who was confronting demons that he didn't want to confront.

'You raised the subject.'

'My mistake. Let's drop it,' he growled, 'before I do or say something I regret.'

Stasia stared at the table. She already had so many regrets that it hardly seemed possible to add more. She regretted the fact that she'd allowed the distance to grow between them. She regretted the fact that she'd walked out that day. *That she hadn't stayed to fight for her man.*

She'd been very quick to fling accusations at him, but could she have changed things? If he'd told her all these things about his past sooner, could she have changed things?

Tears pricked the back of her eyes and she heard the sharp hiss of his breath as he registered the depth of her emotion.

'*Not* that.' His voice was rough and he curled a hand round the back of her neck and brought his mouth down on hers. 'You are the *only* woman who has never used tears on me.'

'I'm not crying.' She muttered the words against his seeking mouth. 'I never cry.'

'Tough to the last—' His tongue was seeking, tasting, and they both knew where this was leading.

'Not that tough—' She slid a hand round the back of his neck, drawing him closer, feeling his tension. 'I wish you'd told me all this before.'

'It is *not* something I talk about—'

She felt the warmth of his breath against her mouth

and suddenly her stomach dropped alarmingly. She needed to be with him. *Now.* And the future didn't matter.

It didn't matter that he still believed her capable of doing things that she could never have done.

All that mattered was that she wanted him. That she loved him. When they'd married she'd wanted every part of him. Now she was so desperate she'd take whatever she could get. For as long as it was available. No matter that she'd spent the whole of the past year learning to live without him. No matter that with one taste she'd fallen straight back into the habit, like the worst of addicts.

She wanted him and if the price to pay for that need was going to be high then she was still willing to pay it.

Without shifting his mouth from hers, he rose to his feet, taking her with him, and lifted her into his arms as if she weighed nothing.

'It's fortunate that our bedroom is close, *cara mia*,' he groaned as he negotiated the door and kicked it shut behind them. He lowered her on to the bed and came down on top of her, one hand locked in her hair, the other tracing a path up her thigh and taking her skirt with it. 'You feel like silk—'

'I want you—' She clawed at his back, tugged at his shirt. 'I want you so much.' The throbbing, pounding ache of desire built and built until she was almost begging. 'Rico—'

'I know—' his tone was teasing '—you want me—' Finishing her sentence before she could repeat the words yet again, he jerked her skirt higher still, exposing her trembling, excited flesh to his hungry gaze. 'You don't need to tell me that. You say I don't know you, but there are some things that I know very well.'

She gave a sob and writhed beneath him. 'I don't want to wait—not even for a moment.'

His hands undid the tiny buttons of her top and underneath she was braless. '*Dio*, you are enough to drive a sane man crazy—so beautiful—'

'Now—now—' She was clawing at his back, clutching, just *desperate*. Then she moved her hands to his trousers, trying to strip him but shaking too much to coordinate her movements. 'Rico, now—'

His mouth captured hers again in a hot, sexy kiss and his hands completed the job she'd been unable to perform.

Immediately her hand closed over him and her breath left her body in a rush. 'You're so big—'

'Because I am about to explode,' he muttered, trailing kisses down her neck and trying to move away from her seeking fingers. 'Give me a moment—'

'No—' The evidence that he wanted her so badly simply fuelled her desperation. 'Now. Now.'

'If you say "now" one more time I won't be responsible for my actions,' he groaned, lifting his mouth back to hers and silencing her in the most effective way he knew.

She fell into the darkness of his kiss, floated on the excitement and the promise and finally felt the throb of his arousal against her most intimate place.

Her level of need and desperation was so great that when he finally entered her with a primitive thrust she cried out his name and immediately exploded into an orgasm so intense that she couldn't catch her breath—

Her body pulsed around the thickness of his shaft,

drawing him in, her legs wrapped around him, locking him in place.

Her man.

He'd always been her man.

'Stasia—' His throaty acknowledgement of the violence of her response was followed by an increase in masculine thrust that intensified her never-ending orgasm.

It was as if her body was making up for the long, lonely months when she hadn't had this man. *And for the long, lonely months when she might not have him again.*

The excitement was so shockingly good that she wanted to scream, but he kept his mouth clamped on hers, deepening the intimacy and keeping her silent.

But he couldn't last.

It was all too intense. Too hot. *Too basic.*

Her uncontrolled, electrified response sent him over the edge and she felt his shudders, felt the power in his tight buttocks as he pumped harder, spilling his essence deep inside her.

And still her body held on to his. Even when he rolled on to his back and took her with him they remained joined, their bodies slick with sweat, their hearts thumping in unison.

Stasia kept her eyes tightly closed, shattered by what had happened.

Did she really think that she was ever going to find that with another man?

It happened with Rico because he was the one.

And if she really thought that she could walk away from him and forget him then her brain was soggier than she thought.

*　*　*

As usual he was gone when she awoke.

And it was probably just as well, Stasia reflected miserably as she pulled on a skirt and top and made her way to breakfast. Waking up next to a man that you'd begged was humiliating and undignified at the best of times. Even more so when that man didn't love you any more and probably never had.

She'd never felt less like food in her life, but reminding herself that she was still supposed to be playing a part for the benefit of Chiara, she forced herself to join them at the breakfast table.

As soon as she walked on to the terrace Rico stood and walked to meet her, dropping a gentle kiss on her forehead.

It would have been the perfect way to start a beautiful day if it hadn't been for the fact that Chiara was watching and Stasia knew that she was the reason for the unexpected display of affection.

'Good morning—' His tone was husky and sexy and she felt her stomach turn over.

Oh, not again—get a grip!

He'd made love to her for most of the night. Surely there couldn't be any more sexual energy left inside her? She stared at him helplessly, acknowledging the fact that he only had to walk into a room for her to reach meltdown.

He didn't even have to touch her.

Thoroughly depressed by the realization that she had absolutely no defences against this man, she sat down at the table and then her heart stumbled. In front of her place was a bowl of oranges, still with the leaves attached.

She looked at him and he gave a half smile that made her tummy leap in response.

'I thought I would save you a trip to the orchard this morning.' His smile grew wicked. 'I thought you might be tired.'

She blushed and reached for an orange, unbelievably touched by the gesture and wondering what it meant. 'Thank you.'

They ate breakfast and talked about nothing and Stasia managed two cups of coffee.

Rico was affectionate and attentive, passing her food and making sure that she was in the shade.

His gentleness towards her was all the more poignant because she knew it wasn't real. This was how she'd always wanted their relationship to be. How it had been for those few blissful weeks after they'd first met. She had to remind herself that this display of affection was all for the benefit of Chiara. That none of this was real.

But she wanted it to be real.

She wanted it to be real so badly that it was almost a physical pain.

'Talking of the shade, I'm avoiding the beach today,' Chiara said ruefully, lifting a hand to her head. 'I'm going to have a day indoors.'

'Then perhaps I can suggest something in the way of occupation,' Rico said smoothly, rising to his feet and indicating that they should follow him back into the villa.

Mystified, Stasia glanced towards Chiara but the other girl just gave a baffled shrug.

Rico opened the door to a room that Stasia had never been into before and she gave a gasp of amazement and delight as she glanced around her.

The room looked like an artist's shop. A wide range of different items were piled up on tables, still in the packaging with prices attached.

'Oh, Rico—'

'You say I don't think about you, *cara mia*.' His voice was rough and for possibly the first time in his life he looked uncertain, as if he were struggling to predict her reaction. 'Well, now I'm thinking about you. You wanted to be able to work. Now you can work. And you can teach Chiara to paint.'

Stasia glanced around her, unable to speak.

'I didn't unpack it,' Rico said stiffly, his gaze slightly wary as he glanced at her, trying to gauge her reaction. 'I thought you'd rather do it yourself.'

Stasia stepped forward and picked up a tube of paint. It was the first time he'd ever made concessions towards her painting. 'Where did you get all this? How?'

'I rang your mother,' Rico confessed, 'and then had it flown in. Are you pleased? This room has north light. I remember you saying that it would have made a perfect studio.'

And suddenly she recognized the room. 'This was your study—'

He lifted broad shoulders in a dismissive shrug. 'I preferred the view from one of the other rooms.' But there was a warmth in his eyes that held her captive.

For one wild, blissful moment she thought he'd done it for her. That last night had changed something for him.

And then she heard Chiara sigh and remembered that a change this big must have required some planning and that Rico never did anything that didn't serve a practical purpose.

And in this case the purpose was to convince Chiara that they were a happily married couple. That he was a thoughtful spouse.

The gilt of the moment was instantly tarnished. 'It's wonderful,' she said woodenly. 'Thank you so much.'

He frowned slightly, gave her a searching look and then glanced at his watch. 'I have an important call to make. I'll see you both later.'

Without warning, he pulled Stasia towards him and dropped a kiss on her parted lips but she couldn't respond. It was both a reminder of the night before and a promise of things to come but she couldn't respond.

How much would she have given for Rico to provide her with a studio when they were first married?

And how much would she have given for him to have done it now for her benefit, rather than for Chiara's benefit?

But if it weren't for Chiara she wouldn't even be here, she reminded herself. What with the lovemaking and all the extravagant gestures of 'love', she was having trouble remembering that none of this was real. That at any moment Chiara could regain her memory and all this would be over in a flash.

Rico was still looking at her and his cool expression left her in no doubt that he was affronted that she'd been less than effusive about his latest gesture.

Remembering that she was supposed to be playing a part, Stasia glanced round the room again and forced a smile. 'It's great, Rico,' she said stiffly. 'Really great. Thank you.'

His gaze rested on her for a moment longer, his dark eyes giving away nothing. 'I'll see you both later.' Unusually tense, Rico strode from the room without a backward glance and Stasia watched him go with a lump of lead where her heart should have been.

But Chiara didn't appear to have noticed anything amiss.

'Never thought I'd see my brother so crazy about anyone,' she drawled, strolling across the room and examining some paints. 'And I certainly never thought I'd see him give up his beloved office. This is the best room in the villa, do you know that?'

Stasia managed a smile. 'It's the best. Perfectly natural lighting.'

Chiara frowned and lifted a hand to her head. 'It isn't like my brother, is it? Taking all this time away from work—'

Stasia hesitated. 'Not really,' she said finally and Chiara pulled a face.

'I'm being a bother. Asking endless questions. Trying to complete a mental jigsaw puzzle.'

'No.' Stasia shook her head and on impulse leaned forward and gave the other girl a hug. 'I'm really enjoying spending time with you.'

It was true. The teenager was a changed person since her accident. Gone was the defiant, moody girl who had made Stasia's life so difficult and in her place was a thoughtful, sweet natured girl.

Chiara pulled away slightly, her expression puzzled. 'You make it sound as though we've never done this before. But I lived with you in Rome. Didn't we spend time together then?'

Stasia tensed, realizing that she'd inadvertently stimulated questions that she wasn't ready to answer. Wasn't able to answer. 'Of course we did,' she hedged, 'but we each had separate lives. Now, about this painting—how do you feel about making a start?'

Chiara smiled. 'Let's do that.'

Rico stared at the painting, recognizing the real talent displayed on the canvas.

It had been a week since Chiara had been discharged from the hospital and during that week the three of them had spent a considerable time relaxing by the pool. But he was aware that whenever the occasional business issue demanded his attention Stasia vanished to her studio. And curiosity had driven him to find out exactly how she was spending her time.

He uncovered another canvas and sucked in a breath, captivated by what he was seeing. It was amazing. With a flash of discomfort he realized that he'd never taken any notice of her art before. He'd been too busy looking at her to waste time looking at what she was painting.

He stepped closer, examining the bold brush strokes, the vivid colour. The painting was bright and eye-catching—like the woman herself.

Feeling like a voyeur, he walked over to the other canvases stacked neatly against one wall of the studio. One by one he went through them, his dark eyes narrowed in concentration as he examined each one in silence.

As a collector he knew instinctively that he was looking at something special. As an investor he knew that he was looking at something that would appreciate in value. But as a man he knew that he was looking at something that was part of the woman. *His woman.*

How could he ever have expected her to give this up? It was like asking her not to breathe.

A frown touching his dark brows, he settled the paintings back against the wall and strode broodingly back to the canvas that she was working on at the moment. How could he have thought that marriage to him would be enough to satisfy her?

The truth was that he'd been so obsessed with her physically that he'd given very little thought to her happiness. He'd been putting in long days at the office and he hadn't asked himself what she was doing with her time. He'd assumed that she'd lunched with his family, gone shopping...

But she'd never once used the credit card he'd given her.

When she'd flown back to England to talk to clients he'd been furious. What was the point of having a wife when you arrived home and the bed was empty?

Dealing with the uncomfortable truth that his own behaviour had done nothing to enhance their relationship, he stepped back from the canvas and rubbed a hand over the back of his neck.

It was true that he hadn't wanted her to work. That he'd wanted her to be home whenever he was. He'd hated coming home to the *palazzo* and finding her gone.

Which, roughly translated, meant that either he was an egotistical control freak or he just couldn't bear not to be with Stasia—and what did that say about him?

Acknowledging that he was in serious trouble, he strode from the room and closed the door firmly behind him.

The next few days passed in a haze of pleasure and Stasia was forced to remind herself at regular intervals that this wasn't real. That any minute now Chiara was going to regain her memory and her life with Rico would end again.

But for the time being it was perfect.

During the day she painted, lay on the beach or by the pool. And, even though she knew it was for Chiara's benefit, she loved the fact that Rico had become so attentive. All of a sudden it seemed that he couldn't discover enough about her. He wanted to know every minute detail of her life from the day of her first memory to the moment she'd met him. But if the days were for Chiara, the nights belonged to her and Rico.

Locked in their private world, they made love until they were so exhausted that they slept and when they awoke they did the whole thing again and it was just so *right*—

They were well into their second week on the island and Stasia was quietly sketching on the terrace when Chiara screwed up her face as if she was in pain. 'Oh—'

Stasia frowned. 'Are you all right?'

Chiara shook her head slightly. 'My head feels funny—I don't know why.'

'Have a lie down,' Stasia urged, taking her arm and leading her into the villa. 'The doctor said that you were going to need lots of rest. You probably haven't been getting enough sleep.'

Chiara walked with her without resisting and sank on to her bed with her eyes closed.

Genuinely concerned, Stasia removed her sandals and closed the blinds. 'There. That should help. Call me if you need anything. I'm only on the terrace.'

Then she tiptoed out of the room, acutely aware that her own happiness would last only as long as Chiara failed to remember the past.

Sooner or later Chiara was going to regain her memory and then the whole façade would fall apart.

She was right.

And it fell apart at midnight—

CHAPTER NINE

THE loud sobs woke both of them.

'*Dio*, that's Chiara—' Rico was out of bed in a flash, responding instantly to the sounds of his sister's distress. He paused only to pull on a robe and then sprinted out of the bedroom with Stasia right behind him.

Chiara's bed looked as though a tornado had struck. The sheets had been dragged from the bed and she was sitting in a heap on the floor, shivering, her face blotched with tears and her eyes wild. She looked utterly tormented and Rico gave an exclamation of concern and dropped to his haunches beside her. He spoke softly in Italian, his deep voice soothing and reassuring but his sister flinched away from him.

'Don't! Don't touch me!' She shrank away from him, her brief glance full of accusation before she once more covered her face with her hands. 'You lied to me! Both of you lied to me!'

Rico inhaled sharply. 'Chiara, you are upset, but—'

'Of course I'm upset!' Her hands dropped and her breath came in great jerking sobs. 'I had a terrible dream and when I woke up I remembered. Everything. *Everything, Rico!* Including the fact that you and Stasia haven't lived together for the last year.'

Rico closed his eyes briefly and swore fluently under his breath. 'You need to calm down, *piccola*. Everything will be all right.'

'No. You don't know. You don't know *anything*.' Chiara shook her head and the sobbing continued until

157

finally Rico leaned forward and scooped her into his arms. He settled himself on the bed, holding her in his arms while she sobbed against his bare chest.

Stasia watched in horror, feeling totally helpless. What had induced such a depth of emotion? Was it simply regaining her memory? Suddenly she wished she'd taken the time to find out more about amnesia.

'You have to stop this crying,' Rico said roughly, stroking his sister's dark hair away from her face with a gentle hand. 'You will make yourself ill again, *piccola*. Regaining your memory must be a shock, I know.'

'It's not regaining my memory that's the shock,' Chiara whispered, wiping her eyes with the back of her hand like a small child. 'It's what I remembered.'

Gulping back another sob, she lifted her head and looked at Stasia, her distress both genuine and moving.

Looking at her face, there was little doubt in Stasia's mind exactly which memory was causing the other girl so much anguish and suddenly she felt as though she'd been showered with cold water.

At the time she'd waited to see some evidence of remorse but there had been none. But the Chiara she'd known then wasn't the same person as the Chiara she'd come to know over the past few weeks. And she certainly didn't want her feeling guilty. It was far too late for that. It was time to move on.

Aware that Rico was looking at her with a puzzled expression on his face, Stasia pulled herself together.

'Whatever it is that you've remembered is in the past,' she said quietly and on impulse she leaned forward to touch the other girl on the cheek. 'I think it should remain there and that we should all just think about the present and the future.'

Chiara's eyes filled. 'But—'

'I think we need to get you something for that headache,' Stasia said firmly, straightening and lifting the sheets from the floor. 'And then we need to get you back to bed. Regaining your memory must be a terrible shock.'

Chiara glanced between them, still struggling with sobs. 'You were separated, but these last few days you've been behaving like lovers. Was that for my benefit?' There was a hope in her voice that only Stasia truly understood. She knew what Chiara wanted to hear. That Rico and Stasia were genuinely reconciled and then her actions in the past would no longer be relevant.

But she couldn't give her that reassurance.

Rico dragged a hand through his hair, looking totally out of his depth in the face of so much raw emotion. 'The doctors said that you weren't to have any shocks. When you woke up in the hospital you remembered joining us on our honeymoon. Nothing beyond that point. And you seemed pathetically pleased to see Stasia. To have told you that she was no longer a part of our lives would have been a nasty shock.'

Chiara seemed to shrink. 'I feel *so* bad—'

'That is to be expected,' Rico reassured her swiftly. 'You are still suffering from the effects of the head injury.'

Only Stasia suspected that Chiara wasn't talking about her physical condition.

She tried once more to put the girl's mind at rest. 'You have to stop worrying,' she said quietly. 'Nothing matters now except your recovery.'

'How can you say that?' Chiara was shivering now and Rico rose to his feet with a soft curse.

'I am calling the doctor.'

'I'll do it,' Stasia said immediately, making for the

door. It was obvious that her presence was making it worse for Chiara but, short of telling Rico the truth, she didn't see what else she could do. And what would be the point of telling the truth now? It was too late. Too late for all of them.

Feeling unutterably depressed, she called the doctor and then returned to their bedroom where less than an hour earlier they'd been wrapped around each other, their bodies closely entwined as they slept.

For the last time.

She closed her eyes briefly and then reached for a suitcase.

There was no point in staying. Her reason for being here no longer existed and Chiara obviously found her presence a distressing reminder of her own behaviour.

Not trusting her legs to hold her, she sank on to the edge of the bed and, for the first time in months, allowed her mind to wander back to that awful night.

Rico had been away for a week in New York. She'd been asleep but noises had woken her…

It was gone midnight and she'd already been asleep for two hours. Judging from the giggling in the corridor outside her bedroom, Chiara had sneaked a man into the house again. And Rico had strictly forbidden her to date.

Stasia gave a groan and covered her face with her hands, her brain still foggy from sleep. What was she supposed to do? Chiara already loathed her. If she marched into the corridor and suddenly came on all heavy-handed then their relationship would be damaged even further. On the other hand, she owed it to Rico to at least try and make the girl understand his point of view.

'You're fifteen, and I don't want you seeing boys,'

Rico had told her bluntly only the week before. 'You concentrate on your studies. There'll be plenty of time for boys when you are older.'

'You can't tell me what to do!'

'I can. And you will show respect when you are living in my house.' Rico's voice was lethally soft and even Chiara gave a shiver, knowing better than to cross her brother when he was in this mood. 'If I hear that you have been seeing men I'll send you back to Sicily.'

Chiara's face had blanched. She loved Rome, although Stasia herself yearned for the peace and beauty of Sicily.

Lying there remembering Rico's threat, Stasia glanced towards her bedroom door, trying to decide on the best course of action. She was still deciding when the door opened and Chiara's boyfriend slid into the room, stark naked.

Without uttering a word, he joined her in the bed, covering her mouth with his hand when she would have screamed.

'Sorry about this,' he murmured. 'On the other hand, you are rather beautiful so perhaps I'm not really that sorry. I can see why big brother married you.'

Smelling alcohol on his breath, Stasia struggled frantically to free herself and then suddenly the lights came on and Rico was standing in the doorway, incandescent with rage, Chiara hovering behind him, a smug expression on her face.

'Oh, Stasia—' Her voice held a convincing wobble. 'I tried to warn you—'

Rico's blazing eyes were fixed on the naked man. 'Get out of my house while you still can. You've got two minutes and then you'll be leaving in a body bag.' His voice was thickened and it was obvious to everyone watching that he was hanging on to his temper by a thread.

Chiara's boyfriend needed no encouragement to leave. With a nervous glance at Rico's furious features, he left the bed in a flash and raced down the corridor, still naked.

Rico's gaze was fixed on Stasia, who was lying in the bed shivering from shock.

How had that happened? One minute she'd been asleep and the next—

She never locked the door. Had never thought there was reason to. He must have wandered into her room by accident.

And then she remembered what he'd said about her being beautiful and realized that it had been no accident.

Her eyes slid to Chiara, who was standing behind her brother, and she knew exactly how it had happened.

Chiara knew that if Rico had discovered her with a man in the house she would have been banished to Sicily and that would have been a fate worse than death for the young teenager.

But surely even Chiara wouldn't stoop so low as to hide her boyfriend in another woman's bedroom?

Stasia struggled to sit upright, her eyes still on Chiara, waiting for her to tell the truth. To tell Rico what had really happened.

But she said nothing. And she even had the gall to put a sympathetic hand on her brother's shoulder. He shrugged it off with a growl of rage and left the bedroom with his sister following.

For a moment Stasia sat there, shivering and then her natural sense of justice reasserted itself. She had done nothing wrong! Nothing. And she refused to take the blame for his sister's wrongdoings.

She dressed quickly and found him downstairs in his study, a bottle of red wine half-empty beside him.

'If you've come to talk your way out of it then you're wasting your time.' He drained his glass and looked at her, his dark eyes glittering, although whether from drink or anger she couldn't be sure. 'I don't want to listen.'

'Not even to the truth?'

His long fingers tightened on the glass. 'The truth is that I found my wife naked in bed with another man. An explanation for that, other than the obvious, would need to be extremely creative in order to stand a chance of convincing me.'

Stasia stared at him helplessly.

She was tried and convicted and yet she was totally innocent.

'You don't trust me, do you? After all these months, everything we shared, you don't trust me.'

'I trust my eyes.'

'Use your brain, Rico.' She, who never pleaded with anyone, was pleading with him now. She understood that it looked bad and she knew that she was in an impossible situation. To tell the truth would have implicated his sister and would destroy their relationship for ever, but to leave the truth untold might destroy her marriage and she wasn't prepared to let that happen. 'You know how much I love you. I'm always telling you that.'

His eyes clashed with hers. 'You're also always telling me that you're lonely and bored while I'm away working. It would appear that you've found yourself a distraction, my beautiful wife.'

'That is *not* what's happened here.'

He made a sound that was something between a

growl and a roar, the sound of a possessive, jealous male.

'Get out,' he said thickly, 'while I decide what to do.'

His complete refusal to listen to her sent her own temper soaring. 'While *you* decide what to do? Well, let me save you the effort, Rico. I'm deciding for both of us. I'm leaving you and this sham of a relationship that we laughingly call a marriage. I'm fed up with spending my days just waiting for you to come home. You don't want a partner. You don't want equality in a relationship. You just want a live-in mistress and I'm not prepared to be that any more. I deserve more.'

Without waiting for his response, she turned sharply, wincing as she heard the sound of glass smashing against the door as she slammed it behind her.

Stasia's thoughts returned to the present and she realized that the time had come to be practical. Nothing could be changed now. Too much time had passed.

She'd leave quietly, without saying any awkward goodbyes. Without subjecting Chiara to any further trauma.

And it occurred to her suddenly that she didn't need the suitcase. Everything here belonged to a life that was no longer hers. She would leave the way she'd arrived—with nothing.

Not allowing herself to look at the rumpled bed, the scene of their earlier loving, she found her bag, checked that she had her passport, and rang Gio to ask for the use of the car. Hoping that there would be too much activity in the house with doctors coming and going for anyone to notice her departure, Stasia made her way to the front of the villa.

Although the sun had barely started to rise it was unbelievably warm and she glanced at the sky, thinking numbly that it was going to be another beautiful day.

A day that she would not be here to enjoy.

Gio gave her a searching look. 'You are leaving?'

'It's time.' She managed a brief smile. 'This wasn't for ever, Gio. We both know that.'

He frowned, clearly far from happy with the idea that she was leaving. 'Does the boss know? I think I ought to—'

No. That was the last thing she wanted. Painful good-byes were not on her list of favourite experiences. And for once she understood the reason for Gio's loyalty. Their families were bound by something far stronger than mere friendship. Each had contributed to the other's very survival.

'I need to get going, Gio,' she said quickly, 'and you needn't worry. Rico knows.'

She comforted herself with the fact that she wasn't telling a lie. Rico did know. He'd made it perfectly clear that this scenario would last as long as it took for Chiara to regain her memory.

Stasia slipped into the car, trying not to wish that Chiara had taken a little longer to achieve that state. The teenager was obviously now on the road to recovery and that was a very good thing.

She sat in silence as the car sped through the spectacular sunrise towards the airport, drinking in her last view of Sicily.

She knew that she would never be back.

'It's fantastic.' Mark stared at the painting in awe. 'A bit late, but worth the wait.'

'I had to go abroad unexpectedly,' Stasia said stiffly,

packing the painting carefully and helping him lift it and carry it out of her studio to the front door.

She'd been back for two weeks and she was operating on automatic. She woke up every day and went through the motions of living, but it wasn't living as she knew it. Since leaving Sicily life had lost its sparkle and so had she. She felt like a glass of champagne left to go flat at a wedding.

'Are you listening to a word I'm saying?' Mark frowned at her and she dragged herself back to the present.

'Sorry. I was miles away—'

'It's him again, isn't it?' Mark looked exasperated as they walked towards his car and Stasia gave a lopsided smile.

'I'm a lost cause.'

Mark sighed. 'Well, in that case you're going to be pleased by my next piece of news.'

'What's that?'

He looked over her shoulder. 'There's a shockingly expensive sports car losing its suspension on this track that you laughingly call a road.' He craned his neck. 'I think you're about to have company. Billionaire Sicilian company.'

Stasia felt her heart lurch. It had been two weeks. Two long, torturous weeks during which she'd agonized over what might have followed her departure. Had Chiara confessed? Did Rico finally know the truth? And, if he did, would he come after her?

It would seem so—

She'd spent every moment of every day in a state of heightened anticipation, just in case, and now she stood frozen to the spot as the car approached. Even as Rico uncurled his powerful frame from behind the wheel she still didn't move.

He should have looked ridiculous standing in her overgrown front garden but he didn't. He looked spectacular and it occurred to her that she'd never seen Rico look uncomfortable or out of place. He was a man totally at ease in any situation.

But he wasn't looking at her. He was staring at Mark with blatant hostility, the set of his broad shoulders unmistakably confrontational.

Mark had evidently spotted the same thing because he retreated towards his van, clearly intimidated. 'Right then—' He kept his eyes on Rico, as one might watch a lethal predator who had suddenly escaped from captivity. 'I'd better be off.'

'Good decision,' Rico said silkily, his black eyes flashing a warning that only a fool would miss.

Stasia stared at him in exasperation.

What was he playing at? It was far too late to play the jealous husband.

At any other time she would have invited Mark to stay just to make a point but there was a dangerous glint in Rico's eyes that she didn't trust. And she wasn't prepared to use Mark just to get at Rico. So she quickly ushered Mark into his van and helped him stow the painting safely.

'I hope they like it,' she said quietly. 'And thanks, Mark.'

'Any time. You can call me, you know—' He cast another wary look at Rico and Stasia closed the door hastily and stepped back to allow him to drive away.

'What were you thanking him for?' Rico's tone was icy-cold and Stasia gave a sigh.

She wasn't in the mood for confrontation and one

look at Rico's face told her that she was about to get it by the bucketload.

'For being a good friend,' she said wearily and then immediately knew she'd said the wrong thing.

'How good a friend?' Rico's mouth tightened and streaks of colour touched his incredible bone structure. The artist in her stared at him in fascination while the woman inside her just melted.

'This is utterly ridiculous,' she muttered, talking to herself as much as him. 'You're acting like a jealous husband and yet there's nothing between us any more.'

'You're still my wife.'

'Just a piece of paper.'

'*Not* a piece of paper.' He inhaled sharply and raked long fingers through his sleek blue-black hair. 'If you *ever* walk out on me again without so much as a conversation then I will not be responsible for my actions. That's twice you've done that. There won't be a third time.'

She stared at him in astonishment. Surely he'd *wanted* her to leave. 'I—'

'You are a woman,' he grated, looking like a man at the edge of his patience. 'You are supposed to storm at me and have tantrums. You are *supposed* to express your feelings. You're *not* supposed to just walk out.'

Her astonishment grew. This conversation was not going the way she'd expected. 'You don't express your feelings.'

'I'm a man,' he returned immediately, his tone dry. 'I'm not supposed to express my feelings.'

'So I'm supposed to tell you everything I feel and receive nothing from you in return. Is that it?'

'No.' He muttered something under his breath in Italian. 'That is *not* it. But I used to know everything you were thinking. It was one of the things I loved about you. You were so uncomplicated. You didn't play games. If you were happy you fizzed and bubbled and if you were angry you threw things. And you told me that you loved me all the time.'

And he'd never said it back. Never. Not once.

'This is a pointless conversation,' she muttered. 'I walked out because I honestly didn't think that we had anything left to say to each other. Chiara had her memory back. My role was over.'

'*Not* over,' he breathed, stepping towards her, his expression that of a man with only one mission in mind. 'You should probably know at this point that I have no intention of divorcing you. Ever.'

Her heart skipped a beat and then she remembered what was behind this.

Chiara.

Finally he knew the truth.

Stasia stared at him, feeling totally numb inside. She should have been overjoyed that he now knew she was innocent but instead she felt strangely flat. What did it change? Nothing.

'It isn't that simple, Rico,' she croaked. 'You didn't believe in me. And if Chiara hadn't suddenly decided to confess, then you still wouldn't believe in me. I can't be with someone like that. What happens next time Chiara decides to hide one of her boyfriends in my bedroom? Are you going to trust me then or do I have to rely on other people to confess? Because that hasn't proved to be a very reliable way of clearing my name.'

Rico stood still, not one single muscle moving as he stared at her. She looked at him with exasperation.

What was the matter with him now? Was he shocked because she'd actually brought the subject up? What had he expected? That this was going to be another one of those subjects that they just ignored? Didn't he realize that their problems went deeper than that one incident?

He opened his mouth and then closed it again, as if he was struggling to find the right words. 'Run that past me again—' His voice was strangely hoarse, as if he was struggling with his English.

Stasia frowned. Rico never struggled with his English. He was fluent. 'I was just saying that the fact that Chiara finally told you the truth about that night doesn't change anything,' she said flatly. 'You didn't trust me. And that says it all.'

'Is that so?' His bronzed skin had taken on a greyish tinge and she looked at him in total confusion, not understanding his reaction. All right, so it probably wasn't the most comfortable of subjects, but it was all in the past. Was it really this hard for him to talk about it?

'Rico, we both know that if she hadn't told you then you wouldn't be here now.'

He closed his eyes briefly and when he opened them again they were totally blank of expression. 'I want to hear in your words what happened that night. And I want to hear it right now.'

'And that's why you came here? To hear me tell it in my own words?' Not understanding why he wanted to go over it again when Chiara had already given him the details, Stasia looked at him warily. 'Why now? At the time you didn't ask.'

'I'm asking now.' His tension was unmistakable and she wondered why he wanted to spend more time on a subject that he was clearly finding it difficult to tackle.

'What's the point?'

'Indulge me.' His voice was slightly thickened and she gave a sigh and glanced around her.

'Here? Or do you want to come indoors?'

He glanced towards her cottage as if he'd forgotten it was there. Then he seemed to stir. 'I think we have endured enough head injuries in the family without me knocking myself unconscious in your ridiculous cottage. Let's walk.'

She hesitated and then gestured towards the lane. 'All right. We can walk down here.' She glanced towards him as he fell into step beside her. His broad shoulders were tense and there was something about the hard set of his jaw that made her uneasy. 'How is Chiara?'

'If you'd stayed then you would have no need to ask me that question.'

Stasia stopped dead and raked her copper hair away from her face. 'Rico, you cannot seriously be saying that to me!' She stared at him with a mixture of incredulity and confusion. 'You wanted me there until Chiara regained her memory. And it was perfectly obvious to me that once she *did* regain her memory my presence was making it worse. Clearly she remembered that she was the ultimate cause of our split.'

'Clearly. Now tell me everything. And leave nothing out.'

So she did.

And if she faltered slightly as she recounted the moment when a total stranger had climbed into her bed, then it was only because she saw the thunderous look in his black eyes. Suddenly anxious, she glanced at him searchingly. 'I hope you weren't angry with Chiara. She so obviously regretted it and at least she confessed in the end.'

He stopped dead and turned to look at her, not a trace

of emotion on his handsome face as his eyes clashed with hers. 'She has *not* confessed.'

Stasia stopped too. 'But you said—' She broke off, trying to remember exactly what he *had* said. 'You said that you were here because Chiara had told you the truth—'

'No. That was what *you* said,' he breathed, streaks of colour accentuating his amazing bone structure. 'I said nothing. You *assumed* she'd confessed. As it happens, you assumed incorrectly.'

Feeling as though she'd just jumped naked into a freezing river, Stasia stared at him in consternation. 'No—'

'Yes. Chiara has said nothing to me,' Rico stated with lethal emphasis, a hard glint of anger in his black eyes, and Stasia gave a groan of self-recrimination.

'I don't believe this—' She covered her mouth with her hand and shook her head. 'Are you seriously telling me that Chiara didn't—?' Her hand dropped to her side. 'Oh, what have I done—?'

'Something you should have done a year ago,' Rico said coldly, 'and something Chiara should have done a year ago. And what I don't understand is why she didn't tell me this herself.'

'I thought she had,' Stasia whispered, just *mortified* that she'd inadvertently told him. 'I never, *ever* intended to be the one to tell you—'

'Even though it might have meant saving our marriage?' He ran a hand over the back of his neck and swore fluently, first in English and then in his native Italian.

Trying to remember a time when she'd seen him so close to losing control, Stasia struggled to redeem the situation.

'Our marriage was already on the way out,' she said quietly, suddenly full of anguish but not knowing how to make the situation better. Of all the scenarios she'd imagined, this hadn't been one of them. 'The mere fact that you could even *consider* that I would have an affair showed that.'

'Did it?' He growled the words, his black eyes alight with anger. 'Think about it. You come home early, un-announced, and find me in bed with a stunning blonde. Naked. What do you think?'

She stared at him, speechless, the image he'd conjured so painful she could hardly bear to consider it.

He took a step towards her, his expression grim. 'Come on Stasia, *what do you think*?'

Suddenly her heart was thumping so hard she could hardly breathe. 'I—I don't—'

'You'd think I was having an affair,' he bit out harshly, turning away from her with an impatient sound, everything about his body language suggesting a man at the edge of his limits. 'We are both hot-blooded, passionate people. People like us don't react to a situation like that with cool intellect. You would have assumed what I assumed. You would have thought the same.'

Stasia swallowed. Was he right? Would she have assumed that? 'Straight away, then yes, maybe I would have thought the same. But later, given time for reflection—'

'Reflection?' His voice was a barely restrained growl of raw masculine frustration. 'When did you *ever* offer me the luxury of reflection, Stasia? When? You walked out. *You left.*'

'Because I was angry with you for not believing in me—'

He gave a humourless laugh. 'And I was angry with you for sleeping with another man in our bed. And then I was angry with you for leaving without even giving me the opportunity to vent my jealousy.'

Her face had lost every scrap of colour. 'But you assumed—'

'I *assumed* that you were sleeping with another man,' he interrupted harshly. 'A reasonable assumption in the circumstances, I think you'll agree. And then I *assumed* that the fact that you left me so precipitously meant that you no longer wanted to be with me. That you were guilty. Another reasonable assumption in the circumstances.'

Her pulse was thundering round her body. 'I tried to call you—'

'You left.'

'I was innocent.'

'*You left.*'

She closed her eyes and struggled to regulate her breathing. 'Because I was angry with you, *not* because I was guilty. I couldn't understand how you could think it of me after everything we'd shared.'

'In the heat of the moment,' he said, his tone raw, 'but now, when the situation has cooled, can you understand how I could have thought it? *Can you understand it now?*'

She looked at him, stared into the depths of his dark eyes and switched positions. If she'd found him in the same situation... 'It looked bad,' she agreed, her voice little more than a whisper.

'If you had stayed around then maybe, given time, I would have reached the right conclusion,' he said heavily. 'But as it was you left without further discussion and I was not given the luxury of reflection.

Emotion piled on emotion. My own and then my family's.'

Stasia's legs were shaking so badly she wondered if they would continue to hold her. 'But if you didn't know, why did you come here today?'

Rico gave a twisted smile. 'Because, once again, you left. And this time I decided to follow you. If I'd made that same decision a year ago then maybe we'd be in a different place now. *Dio*—' He glanced at her with a frown and then scooped her into his arms in a powerful movement. 'Your face has no colour at all. On second thoughts I'll risk the head injury. You need to sit down and I need a drink.'

'If I'm pale then it's because you're always covering me with a hat, and I *don't* need to sit down,' she muttered, trying to resist the temptation to bury her face in his neck. 'I'm not that pathetic—'

He ignored her and strode back up the lane with her in his arms. After a few strides Stasia gave up the fight and buried her face in his neck, feeling too shattered to resist. He hadn't known about Chiara. So why was he here? Why had he followed her?

'So if you being here has nothing to do with Chiara, then why did it take you two weeks to follow me?'

'Because for once my emotional reaction to your departure was followed by a period of calm reflection, undisturbed by my well-meaning but interfering family,' he said grimly, pushing open her front door and ducking his head to avoid knocking himself unconscious. 'And during that period of calm reflection I considered a great number of things.'

He sat her down on the kitchen table and planted an arm either side of her so that she couldn't escape.

His nearness sent her senses into overdrive. Suddenly

breathing seemed an effort. 'I thought you wanted a drink—'

His eyes dropped to her mouth and he took a deep breath and drew back. 'Good idea,' he breathed, glancing around him. 'What is there?'

'Wine.' She leaned across the table and reached for a bottle of wine that she'd opened the night before. 'This is the only alcohol in the house. Will it do?'

He gave a wry smile, taking the bottle from her. 'I don't know. That depends on your answers to my questions. I might need something considerably stronger.'

'What questions?'

'About Chiara.'

She bit her lip. 'Rico, I can't—'

'You can and you will,' he gritted, handing her a glass of wine and putting the bottle on the table. 'The time for tact and sensitivity is long past. What I want now is the truth. And I want it fast and undiluted, Stasia, starting with how often my sister invited her boyfriends into my house.'

Stasia took a gulp of wine. 'Quite often,' she mumbled and Rico released a breath with a hiss.

'And you didn't tell me—'

'I was in an impossible position.' She gave a helpless shrug. 'Your sister already resented me—how would I have developed a relationship with her if I went running to you every time she did something I knew you would have disapproved of?'

His mouth tightened. 'So you encouraged her—'

'No!' She interrupted him quickly, her eyes blazing with anger and hurt. 'That isn't fair! I didn't encourage her. I talked to her. I tried to teach her to do the right thing. And she just resented me even more.'

Rico closed his eyes, like a man bracing himself to

hear news that he was most definitely *not* going to like. 'Those nightclubs you went to with her—'

Stasia hesitated, still reluctant to reveal everything, but one warning glance from those fierce black eyes was sufficient to convince her that the time for discretion was long past.

'I didn't go with her,' she said finally. 'I followed her to try and persuade her to come home. If your spies had been doing their job correctly they would have told you that she arrived first and then I arrived after. We weren't together.'

'You should have said something—'

'When?' Stasia's tone was weary. 'When would I have said something? You were never there, Rico. I only ever saw you at night and even then only when the lights were out. We never even had a conversation about our own relationship, let alone anything else. We made love and fell asleep. End of story.'

He tensed, obviously struggling with the knowledge that his own behaviour had contributed to the situation. 'It was a particularly busy time for me at work—'

'Was it?' Stasia's voice was soft and she looked at him curiously. 'I had no idea. I assumed that was normal for you. I didn't know you well enough to know differently. I assumed that you really only wanted to spend your nights with me.'

He winced, visibly discomfitted by her accusation. '*Not* true.'

'But that was what we had, Rico,' she said sadly. 'And I didn't help, I can see that now. Chiara wasn't responsible for the death of our marriage. We did that all by ourselves. By not spending time with each other. My days were lonely and I filled them with work. And, as I saw less and less of you, I became more and more convinced that you thought that our marriage was a mistake.'

'So you worked because you thought you would need an income,' he said grimly. 'After what you revealed about your father when we were in Sicily, I finally understand your need to feel financially independent. But *you* need to understand that I would never have left you without money, whatever the state of our relationship.'

'But I didn't want your money,' she croaked with a helpless shrug. 'I understand now why the drive to provide for your family is so important to you but you have to understand that I never wanted your money. I didn't want it when I married you and I certainly didn't want it when we separated.'

He glanced round her cottage, a strange smile playing around his firm mouth. 'So I see.'

She stiffened defensively. 'I love it. I adore the English countryside.'

'My quarrel is not with the English countryside,' he drawled, a wry expression on his handsome face, 'but with the height of the ceilings in quaint cottages. This quaint cottage in particular. I would rather *not* have to walk round bent double. Which brings me to the other reason it has taken me two weeks to come after you.'

Her heart missed a beat. 'What other reason?'

He gave a frustrated sigh and muttered something under his breath. 'This meeting is not going at all the way I planned it.'

'How did you plan it?'

'I was going to come here, apologize, and you were going to forgive me. Then I was going to give you my present and we were going to live happily ever after.'

Happy ever after?

Another present. Hadn't he learned that it wasn't gifts that she wanted?

She stared at him in silence as she digested his words. She was still the same woman. And he was still the same man. *Or was he?* She frowned slightly. 'You were going to apologize? But you didn't know about Chiara—'

'I wasn't apologizing for that,' he muttered. 'I was apologizing for everything else. Now I don't know where to start. One apology obviously isn't going to cut it.'

She looked at him dubiously. 'Start with what you were going to say before I told you about Chiara.'

He looked at her for a moment and then let out a ragged breath. 'All right.' A muscle flickered in his bronzed cheek. 'But first you have to understand that you were just *so* different from all the women I'd ever met before.'

She bit her lip. 'I was *too* different—'

'Let me finish,' he growled, a muscle flickering in his lean jaw. 'Apologies are *not* my speciality and if I'm interrupted in mid flow I may get it wrong and I'm not sure I can do it twice.'

Despite the emotions churning inside her, she had to hide a smile. That was so like Rico. Always a perfectionist, even in the art of apology! 'Go on, then.'

'I loved the fact that you were different,' he confessed roughly, 'and I loved the fact that you were unconventional. But then we married and I expected you to fit into my very conventional life. And I can see now that I chased away the woman that you were. It was like picking a wild flower and expecting it to thrive indoors. It is not surprising that you were unhappy. I was having an exceptionally stressful time at work and coming home too exhausted to do anything but fall into bed.'

A smile flickered in her eyes. 'You had the energy for some things—'

He didn't return the smile. 'I know that, and I still remember the things you said to me in Sicily. You were right when you said I treated you like a mistress. I did and I'm very ashamed of that fact, *cara mia*. I see now how you could have believed that. But you have to understand that the women I'd known before you were perfectly happy to spend the day using my credit card and the evenings thanking me.' He gave a smile of self-mockery. 'I thought that you would be more than happy to be left to your own devices during the day.'

She smiled. 'Your credit card company must have loved me.'

'You spent nothing—'

She gave a self-conscious shrug. 'I've told you hundreds of times that it isn't your money that interests me. But I didn't know about your work. I didn't know you were so busy. And until that conversation we had in Sicily I never understood why it mattered to you so much.'

'No woman has ever shown the slightest interest in how I generate my capital,' he drawled, a wry expression on his handsome face, 'so naturally I assumed you would be the same.'

She bit her lip. 'We didn't spend long enough talking—'

'Evidently.' He nodded. 'As you rightly said, we shared our bodies but very little else. I learned more about you during these last few weeks in Sicily than for the whole of our marriage.'

'What did you learn?'

'That you are a warm, loving person and extremely forgiving.' He closed his eyes briefly. '*Extremely* forgiving. In spite of the wrong she did you, you came to the aid of my sister. That must have been very hard.'

'Not that hard. She was young—'

His eyes hardened. 'Don't make excuses for something which we both know cannot be excused. I will talk to Chiara at some point but that is not for you to worry about.'

'So that is why you came here?' She hardly dared ask the question. 'To apologize?'

He frowned. 'And to tell you that the divorce is off. I thought I'd made that clear.'

Her heart leaped but she held herself back. 'Nothing's really changed, Rico.'

'Everything has changed,' he announced with his usual self-confidence, grabbing her hand and sweeping her off the table. 'This time I *really* understand what you need and I'm about to prove it to you.'

Stasia swallowed. What she really needed was love. His love. But, as usual, love was the one thing he hadn't mentioned. 'Where are we going?'

'To show you the other reason that it took me two weeks to come and claim you. I was busy.' He looked smugly satisfied with himself and she followed him to the sports car, mystified.

They drove for a short distance and then he turned up a tree-lined road and drove half a mile up a drive to a private house.

He parked the car and they both walked a little way up the drive.

'You said that I didn't understand you, and this is the proof that I do.' He sounded amazingly pleased with himself. 'I know that you love the English countryside but I can't live in a house that is smaller than the average bathroom so this is my compromise.' He looked at her but she returned his gaze blankly.

'Sorry?' Her gaze slid from his to the beautiful Georgian mansion at the end of the drive. 'What has this house got to do with us?'

'We own it.' He made the announcement in the matter-of-fact tone of someone with a bottomless bank account and she gaped at the house and then back at him.

'We *own* it?'

'That's right.' He dealt her a brilliant smile, totally confident in himself and his decision. 'You like the country. I bought you this. *Now* tell me I don't understand you.'

As his words sank in she closed her fingers into her palms and closed her eyes. She could feel him looking at her. Feel the weight of his expectation.

'You are pleased.'

'No.' She spoke through gritted teeth, wondering if there ever was a man as infuriating as Rico Crisanti. Finally she opened her eyes and looked at him. 'If you *must* know, I'm trying to resist the temptation to throttle you.'

Dark, incredulous eyes swept over her. '*Cosa?* It is not to your taste?'

'Of course it's to my taste. It's beautiful. It would be to anyone's taste.'

He gave her a look of pure masculine frustration. 'Then *why* would you want to throttle me?'

'Because you've totally missed the point and, despite what you think, you clearly don't understand me at all—' Her voice was choked with emotion. 'It isn't about the house, Rico. It isn't about living in the country. It's about *sharing*. About making decisions together. About being equal. *That's* what I want. I don't want to be *given* a house, however stunning. I want to choose something together.'

He stiffened, growled something under his breath in Italian and strode off down the path towards the gardens, clearly a man at the limits of his patience.

Stasia sank on to the nearest piece of lawn and just sobbed. They were *so* different; it was no wonder that their relationship had never stood a chance. He just didn't understand the first thing about her.

She cried until there were no tears left and when she finally gave a gulp and opened her eyes he was standing there.

'I just can't get it right with you, can I? I create a studio for you in Sicily, expecting you to love it and you look so hurt that I have no idea what I have done wrong. And I chose the house because I thought you would like it,' he said flatly, spreading his hands in a supremely Italian gesture. 'You love England. You love the country. I thought this was perfect. I'm trying so hard to understand you that it's become an obsession. I am delegating so much at work that my own staff barely recognize me any more.'

She scrubbed her cheeks with the back of her hand. 'Rico—'

'Perhaps you need to understand something more about me. I'm not used to being around women who want to be part of the decision-making process. I'm used to women leaning on me. You didn't lean. Ever since my father died I have been making decisions for all the women in my family. They don't breathe without checking with me first. If I expected you to fit the same mould then it is just because I have had no experience at all of what you are describing. But I can learn.'

She gave another sniff. 'Why would you want to—'

'Because I *want* our marriage to work and I'm prepared to work very hard at understanding you, even if that will mean a steep learning curve. For both of us.'

'B—but I'm not what you want in a woman—' She was stammering now and she just hated herself for being so gauche when she should have been cool and sophisticated. But it was time they were honest with each other. Time to stop pretending and playing games.

He gave a wry smile. 'You are *exactly* what I want in a woman.'

She coloured. 'I'm not talking about the bed bit.'

'Neither am I. Believe it or not, I actually like the fact that I never know where I am with you. I like the fact that I can buy you a house and you metaphorically throw it back in my face.'

She bit her lip, suddenly contrite. 'It's a beautiful house—'

'I will sell it and we will choose one together.'

She glanced at the mansion and then back at him. 'I like this one. I choose this one.'

An exasperated look flashed across his handsome features and he reached out and grabbed her, dragging her to her feet. 'Have I ever told you that you are the most contrary, infuriating woman I have ever met?'

She stared at him, her heart suddenly racing in her chest. 'You instructed your lawyers—'

He ran a hand over the back of his neck. 'I think we could *both* do with being less volatile—that is another part of the learning curve.'

She swallowed. 'I looked hurt about the studio because I thought you did it for Chiara's benefit.'

'By that point I had ceased to think about my sister,' he confessed, tension visible in every angle of his powerful frame. 'I was thinking only of you. And me. And somehow getting back into your good books.'

Good books? Her eyes filled again and he swore under his breath.

'I have *never* seen you cry until recently and suddenly you are doing it all the time—'

'Because you're just trying so hard and it's all useless,' she muttered, wondering why she was suddenly turning into a watering can.

'What now? *Why* is it useless?' He stabbed long fingers through his dark hair, a man at the end of his tether. 'Tell me what I have to do to make this work.'

She gave a hiccough, looking every bit like a miserable child as she brushed the tears away. 'Love me. You have to love me.'

There was a throbbing silence and he looked at her with disbelief. 'I have to love you?'

'That's right.' Her voice shaking, she waved a hand towards the magnificent house. 'This is lovely, the studio is lovely, and I know you're trying *so* hard, but the truth is that I would live in a shack with you, Rico. The one thing I want is your love. And that's the one thing you've *never* understood. The one thing you've never been able to give.'

'Wait a minute—' He shook his head slightly as if he needed to clear it, as if he was afraid there might be a language problem. 'Are you saying that you think I don't love you?'

'I *know* you don't.'

One dark eyebrow swooped upwards and it took him a moment to respond. 'I spent an indecent sum of money on a house in a country with a dubious transport system and an outrageous quantity of rainfall,' he drawled. 'I give up my favourite room in the villa and allow it to be covered in paint, even though you seem less than pleased by the gesture. *Why* would you think I don't love you?'

'Because you've never said it?' Her voice was a whisper and he sucked in a breath.

'I gave you everything. That should have told you that I loved you.'

'Because your way of showing love is providing for your family,' she said softly, suddenly understanding him more than ever before. 'But I needed to hear it, Rico. I *need* to hear it.'

He pulled a face. 'I schooled myself for so long not to say it that it became a habit. I think I believed that if I said those words I'd suddenly be vulnerable. But *not* saying them didn't change the way I felt. I loved you. Right from the moment you challenged me in my foyer. I assumed you knew that.'

She stared at him, her heart thudding. 'I *didn't* know that—'

'Then why did you agree to marry me? If you didn't think I loved you?'

Knowing that she was making herself vulnerable, she hesitated briefly. 'Because I loved you enough for both of us.'

Rico sighed. 'I pursued you as I have never pursued a woman in my life,' he said dryly, 'and I *married* you. Never have I offered another woman marriage. If that didn't tell you how I felt, then—'

'I wanted you to *say* it.'

He tensed. 'I have never been demonstrative, verbally at least.'

She couldn't hide a smile. 'Then get on that learning curve,' she suggested, a note of invitation in her voice, 'because if this relationship is truly going to work then you need to learn to say how you feel.'

'Desperate? Frantic that I might lose you? Willing to do anything to win you back?' He caught the look in her eyes and smiled. 'I love you,' he said huskily. '*Ti amo, cara mia.*'

Stasia closed her eyes and experienced perfect happiness for the first time in her life. 'Say it again.'

He hauled her against him, locking her against his powerful body. 'English or Italian?'

'Italian,' she whispered huskily, her green eyes drifting open and clashing with dark. 'You know how I feel about Italian.'

'I also know what usually happens when I speak to you in Italian,' he teased gently, easing her towards the car. 'And, bearing that in mind, I think we'd better leave before we risk being arrested. That sort of publicity I can definitely do without.'

Stasia followed without question, her body already throbbing with desire for this man. 'Where are we going?'

'The nearest place where we can be assured of privacy.' He reversed the car and hit the accelerator. 'Which is probably your cottage.'

She slid a hand on to his hard thigh and felt his muscles tense under her fingers. 'I thought you hated my cottage.'

'I will be lying flat,' he said silkily, his glance loaded with sexual promise, 'so the height of the ceilings will cease to be a problem, at least in the short term.'

Her heart missed a beat. 'I love you, Rico.'

His hand covered hers. 'And I love you too, *cara mia*. For always.'

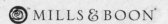

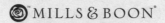

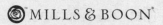

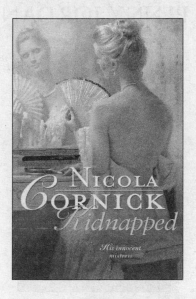

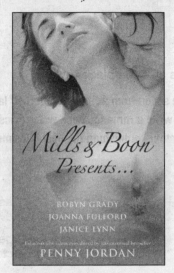

millsandboon.co.uk Community

Join Us!

The Community is the perfect place to meet and chat to kindred spirits who love books and reading as much as you do, but it's also the place to:

- **Get the inside scoop from authors about their latest books**
- **Learn how to write a romance book with advice from our editors**
- **Help us to continue publishing the best in women's fiction**
- **Share your thoughts on the books we publish**
- **Befriend other users**

Forums: Interact with each other as well as authors, editors and a whole host of other users worldwide.

Blogs: Every registered community member has their own blog to tell the world what they're up to and what's on their mind.

Book Challenge: We're aiming to read 5,000 books and have joined forces with The Reading Agency in our inaugural Book Challenge.

Profile Page: Showcase yourself and keep a record of your recent community activity.

Social Networking: We've added buttons at the end of every post to share via digg, Facebook, Google, Yahoo, technorati and de.licio.us.

www.millsandboon.co.uk

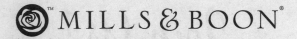